Songs for the Dead

STEPHEN PULESTON

ABOUT THE AUTHOR

Stephen Puleston was born and educated in Anglesey, North Wales. He graduated in theology before training as a lawyer. Brass in Pocket is his debut novel and the first in the Inspector Drake series

www.stephenpuleston.co.uk
Facebook:stephenpulestoncrimewriter

Inspector Drake Mysteries

Worse than Dead
Against the Tide
Dead on your Feet
A Time to Kill
Written in Blood
Nowhere to Hide
A Cold Dark Heart
Dead and Gone
Prequel Novella– Ebook only - Devil's Kitchen

Inspector Marco Novels

Speechless
Another Good Killing
Somebody Told Me
Times Like These
Dead of Night
Prequel Novella– Ebook only -Dead Smart

Copyright © Puleston Publishing Limited
All rights reserved.
ISBN: 9798879287318

Prologue

He watched them leave the police station and drive away. He inched the stolen car out of the lay-by and followed them. An hour into their shift he watched them stop and question a speeding motorist. He knew the driver would get booked, even if he were just over the speed limit.

Soon, they were on the move again.

He could set his watch by their routine. He knew where they would be heading halfway through their shift. They parked on the grass verge of a junction on a long, straight section of road, waiting. From his vantage point, he could make out the driver pointing the speed gun towards the oncoming traffic.

When they drove away, empty handed, he heard them joking with Area Control on his radio scanner. He followed them. When he got too close, he fell back. Sometimes he parked a safe distance from them, listening to the messages.

Later, they stopped for petrol. He parked in the shadows, out of sight of the CCTV cameras on the forecourt. From the car he saw them laughing and joking with a girl behind the counter. An open-topped sports car drew up and a tall woman wearing a short skirt stepped out. He watched as they eyed her filling the car. Then they pulled off the forecourt; an indicator light pulsed as they stopped at the kerb. He saw the driver scanning for traffic, before driving away.

He lingered a few moments before firing the engine into life. After the pubs closed, they drove on, past the boarded-up buildings and fish and chip shops, full of hungry customers, before parking and waiting for drunk drivers. He parked his car as near as he dared. He sat patiently, counting down the time to his first telephone call. He could feel his pulse increasing with anticipation.

He picked up one of the mobiles sitting by the MP3 player on the passenger seat. On the scanner he heard a voice relaying a message and moments later they pulled away. It was dark now as he followed them over the long causeway and, fearful they might notice him, he slowed and watched as the taillights of their car moved away from him. To his left, through the darkness, he saw the moon's reflection on the surface of the estuary and on his right the dark shadow of the causeway wall.

After a few miles they pulled into a lay-by. When he passed them, he listened to their crackled speech on the scanner, complaining about the hoax.

He pulled into a junction and made another call.

He heard them receive the message from the Area Control Room. He drove on to the Crimea Pass through the narrow streets of the deserted town. The road out was clear. He sensed the presence of the mountains towering either side of him as he accelerated towards the top of the pass.

He parked and got out of the car, opened the boot and reached for the long coat, carefully threading his arms through the sleeves. He leant down again and moved a blanket to one side, before closing his fingers round the cold metal.

Far down the valley, he saw the lights of their vehicle approaching. Soon, very soon, they would arrive. His mouth was dry; his heart pounded.

As they approached, he knelt by the rear tyre, out of sight.

Their car slowed, the hazard lights flashed, and they parked exactly where he knew they would. He walked to the front of his car and then towards them.

Perfect.

Chapter 1
Tuesday 1st June

After the fourth ring Ian Drake hauled himself out of the warm bed and picked up the phone. He rubbed the sleep from his eyes, the night air chilling his skin. It must be a domestic, he thought.

'Drake.'

'Inspector Drake?' He didn't recognise the voice.

'Area Control Room. We've got two officers down on the Crimea Pass.'

'*What* …?'

'Two officers have been killed. Responding to a routine call.'

He glanced at the clock on the bedside table. It was a little after two and he had slept for barely an hour. Beside him Sian was stirring.

'When did this happen?'

'Call just came in, sir, from the local station.'

'Who's the senior officer on duty?'

'Superintendent Price. He's on his way.'

'What are the details?'

'Sir, I was just asked to call you.'

'But you must have more details …'

The news curled a knot in his stomach, but he knew that Area Control staff just made the calls; he would have to talk to Price.

'There's a car on its way, sir.'

The phone went dead.

Drake scrambled about the bedroom, dragging on clothes discarded earlier. He mis-timed thrusting his leg into his trousers and fell to the floor. He sat on the side of the bed, struggling with his shoelaces.

'What's wrong?' Sian mumbled.

'I can't believe it …'

'What's happened?' Her hand dragged the duvet from

her face.

'Two officers have been killed on the Crimea Pass.'

'Policemen?'

Drake nodded.

His wife sat up, hair dishevelled, eyes wide. 'It can't be true.'

Before Drake could continue, the front doorbell rang, followed by a loud banging.

'That'll be the car,' Drake said, as he ran for the stairs.

The young officer standing outside the front door – head shaven, high-visibility vest – looked tense and alert, his eye contact direct. He turned and Drake followed him down the drive to the white BMW idling on the road. Opening the rear door, Drake mumbled an acknowledgment to the driver before closing the door behind him. He listened to the first officer radioing confirmation of their location and as the light in the cabin dimmed, Drake saw the flickering lights of the dashboard and noticed, with approval, the clean, sanitised smell. On the A55, the main trunk road that crossed North Wales, the driver accelerated hard. Drake checked his safety belt as they passed the occasional lorry and slowing car, pulling over to let them past. He fumbled through his jacket, knowing he had calls to make.

Detective Sergeant Caren Waits woke moments before the alarm clock went off and reached out to silence it before the noise disturbed Alun, sleeping by her side. He had been up three nights running and now it was her turn. Padding downstairs, she pulled on a pair of old boots and grabbed a torch before walking out over the fields. She drew the zip of her fleece up under her chin, thrust her hands into the warmth of the pockets and saw the outline of the shed against the moonlight. Then she saw the long necks of the alpacas moving slowly in front of her. The animals had not been well but were improving, and, once she had checked them, she would be back to the comfort of her bed. She ran her hand down each alpaca's warm, woolly back, the light from her torch reflecting in their eyes, before returning to the farmhouse, pleased that Alun could sleep on undisturbed.

Her mobile rang as she closed the back door. The screen said *DI Drake*.

'Morning, sir.' She made a point of sounding wide awake.

'Oh ...'

'I was awake.'

'Two officers are dead on the Crimea Pass.'

'What? Oh my God ... Who?'

'I've just left Colwyn Bay. Super Price is en route.'

'Are they Traffic?'

'No details. Get ready. We'll be through Llanrwst in fifteen minutes.'

It looked like being another long day – longer than usual: most days she slept until seven. After washing in lukewarm water, she drew a brush through her hair before waking Alun.

'I've got to go to work.'

His voice slurred underneath the bedding. 'What time is it?'

'Just after two.'

He pushed his head above the duvet, his hair a tangled mess. 'What?'

'Drake's just called.'

'And what did Mr.Personality want at this time of the morning?'

'Two officers have been killed.'

'What ... I mean where – who?'

She brushed her lips against his cheek, his stubble rough against her skin. 'I'll call you later.'

The car turned off the A55 onto the narrow, deserted

roads of the Conwy valley. The driver ignored the speed restrictions. Drake shifted uncomfortably in his seat.

'Do you lads know any details about what's happened?' he asked.

The officer in the passenger seat answered.

'Nothing yet, sir. Our orders were to get you there – fast.'

Drake sat back as the driver swept the car down the valley. He glimpsed the moonlight as it caught the surface of the river, casting long curves of light into the trees and hedges that lined the riverbank. The car slowed through the narrow streets of Llanrwst, eventually pulling to the kerb to collect Caren, standing on the pavement. The officers grunted an acknowledgment when she got into the car before the driver accelerated away.

'What are the details, sir?'

'Two officers responding to a routine call.'

'When did it happen?' Caren stared at Drake closely. 'Who are they? Are they Traffic or from the local station?'

'Area Control sounded shocked when they spoke to me.'

'Who would want to kill two cops? I can't believe it.'

Drake sat back, averting his eyes from the heads-up display as he gathered his thoughts.

The deaths of two police officers would make international news. He shuddered when he recalled the media attention the deaths of other police officers had received – but two officers killed together would mean certain and intense press activity.

Drake had driven over the Crimea Pass once before and he knew the bleakness of the windswept terrain and the landscape disfigured by generations of slate mining. It was isolated and inhospitable: not the place for a drive-by killing or opportunistic attack. The implications sent a shiver through Drake.

He knew they were making good time. He peered out at

the darkened houses and empty streets of the villages as they approached the Crimea. The radio message from the marked police car parked at the bottom of the pass was clear.

'No vehicles ahead. You're clear. Over.'

The driver threw a switch on the gear stick and the car accelerated hard. The heads-up display said one hundred and twenty miles an hour. Drake averted his eyes. The BMW's headlights pierced the darkness as it raced to the top of the pass. Drake leant forward and saw, in the distance, the stark, blinding lights of the generators.

Chapter 2
Tuesday 1st June

The seat belt cut into Drake's shoulder as the car braked hard, stopping a few yards from the Scientific Support Vehicle. The yellow tape marking the inner perimeter of the crime scene flickered in the artificial light. After leaving the car they passed an Armed Response Vehicle, its boot open, empty of weapons. Drake looked towards the white police Volvo, the tailgate and passenger door open, the lights blazing.

The scene was eerie, almost unreal. Beyond the open tailgate of the Volvo, traffic cones and warning triangles were set out in no apparent order. Superintendent Wyndham Price stood with Mike Foulds, the crime scene manager, who was busy fastening the buttons of a white one-piece suit as Drake and Caren joined them. Price looked at Drake, his eyes hard.

'Ian, this is a nightmare, unbelievable ...' Price said.

'Who are they?' Drake asked.

'Paul Mathews and Danny Farrell,' Price replied. 'From Traffic.'

Drake looked over at the car. 'Let's get started.'

They walked over to the patrol car and gazed in at the officer sitting in the driver's seat, head thrown back, his body twisted to one side. A dark stain had spread over the white fabric of his shirt from a jagged wound in the centre of his chest.

Caren gasped when she noticed the face of the dead officer. The left eye socket was a mass of mangled tissue and bone. Blood had saturated the head restraint, drenched the officer's shoulder and covered the rear seat. Drake guessed he had been trying to escape when he was shot.

They moved round to the passenger side. The second officer was sitting on the tarmac, his back resting against the rear door. His stab jacket was open, the plastic tie hanging loose from one side of his collar. His shirt was a sodden, blackened mass of cloth and the right eye stared out blankly – the other eye socket was unrecognisable, blood drying sticky down his cheek. Drake knelt, but he could sense the bile gathering in his throat, so he straightened up and faced Price.

'This is worse than I could imagine,' Price said.

'Who found the bodies?' Drake asked Foulds.

'Call from a passing motorist. Then a team from the local station responded.'

'Where are those officers?'

'In their car, over there.' He motioned past the yellow tape. 'Really cut up. One of them threw up all over the tarmac.'

A mobile rang and Price dug into the pocket of his jacket for his phone. He strode away, his voice loud. Drake looked down at the body on the tarmac, and then through into the car. It seemed like the car had been sprayed a deep crimson colour. The knot of anger returned. Two of their own.

Behind them two vans from the dog section drew to a halt. The handlers jumped out and hurried to the rear of their vehicles. Drake heard the yelping of the dogs as the doors opened and the animals bounded out onto the tarmac.

'Get everyone over here,' he said to Caren.

She passed the generators into the semi-darkness, emerging moments later with the two armed officers. Drake saw the light dancing off their shaven heads and they hefted their weapons, grimly scanning the darkness, although Drake knew that the killer had long since left. Perhaps they had passed him on their journey up the valley. He might have been parked, waiting for them to pass, before returning to the safety of his home. Drake considered his first move. Someone with a reason to kill two traffic officers would mean trawling through the lives of both men. The possibility of a terrorist attack couldn't be excluded, but this was a killing on an isolated mountain pass.

Soon a crowd had gathered around Drake: the armed response officers, the dog handlers, pulling at leashes, straining to keep the animals in check, and the two officers who had driven Drake and Caren to the scene. Foulds stood with the CSIs behind him – Price was still talking into his phone. Drake scanned the faces before him; there were twitching jaw muscles and tired eyes and wide-legged postures, but everyone listened intently. Drake raised his voice above the noise from the generators.

'Let's get the dogs onto this first.' Drake pointed over at the car.

'We'll need the torches from the vans,' one of the officers said.

Drake glanced at his watch. 'My guess is that daybreak will be in an hour.'

Caren fiddled with her mobile and stared down at the dim light on the screen.

'Quarter to five this time of the year, sir,' Caren said, raising her head and sounding pleased with herself.

Drake muttered an acknowledgment and continued. 'We need to secure the scene fully before the press can get anywhere near.' He turned to Foulds. 'How long until you get the tent finished?'

'Twenty minutes.'

'And the pathologist?'

'Due any time.'

Caren twisted the top off a bottle of water and drank a mouthful, before offering it to Drake. He put the plastic bottle to his lips and drank half of it without stopping. He heard a vehicle pulling up beyond the perimeter tape and recognised the duty pathologist leaving the patrol car. Dr Lee Kings, a small, thickset man with large glasses, marched over towards Drake.

'Inspector Drake,' he said formally. 'Terrible business.'

'I know, Lee. We need to get the results as soon as.'

'Of course.'

They walked over towards the car and watched as the CSIs hauled a tarpaulin over the frame covering the vehicle. The pathologist knelt by the driver's side as Caren and Drake looked on. They could still hear Price's voice booming into his phone as he approached.

'Could be terrorists, sir,' Caren said, making sure no one else could hear her.

Drake grimaced. This was worse than the worst-case scenarios they were taught at management training sessions. He knew the standard operating procedures for a terrorist incident would mean Special Branch and the Secret Intelligent Services getting involved. There would be reports to write, liaison officers to keep informed, and everything would be dragged into paperwork ten feet thick.

Drake felt the chill of the night air on his face and a cold apprehension – almost fear – filled his mind, as the realisation that the Wales Police Service had lost two of its own hit him again.

'Let's get the forensics finished before we jump to any conclusions.'

The pathologist worked silently, moving his hands over the body until he exposed the narrow wound, drilled into pink flesh speckled with grey hairs. He straightened up and moved away from the car, pushing the glasses back up his nose.

'Well, Lee?' asked Drake.

Price suddenly materialised at Drake's side. 'We need to know how this maniac shot these officers. Was it a pistol?'

'I ...' Lee Kings paused.

'Come on, we don't have time to waste,' Price pressed him.

'I'm not certain—'

'Of what?' Price said, a note of incredulity in his voice.

'Time of death?' Drake suggested.

The pathologist drew breath and stood up. 'No. Two hours maximum. And it wasn't a gun.'

'What do you mean?' Drake this time.

'It looks like a bolt of some sort ...'

Drake saw the intense expression on Kings's face.

'You must have some idea?' Price asked.

'Small piece of metal, like a dart. Never seen anything like it,' Kings said. 'The post mortem will give us a better idea.'

With the pathologist finished, the serious work could begin. Drake glanced at his watch. If Caren was right about the time of sunrise, then soon it would be first light and the generators could be turned off. The CSIs would have to search the car until every inch had been examined. He knew the painstaking fingertip search of the road would take hours. The first glimmer of morning sunshine climbed over the mountains as the silhouettes of the steep cliffs formed. A photographer adjusted the settings on his camera which was screwed down to the top of a tripod. Price finished his final call and came up to stand next to Drake and Caren.

'This is the most serious crime I have ever dealt with,' Price said, his voice matching the hard, cold surface of the tarmac. 'We'll commit everything we have,' he continued. 'Killing police officers is, well ...' He struggled for the right words.

And he looked Drake straight in the eye.

'It's an attack on society itself.'

Drake nodded. Caren stood quite still, hands thrust deep into her pockets, listening to Price.

They walked round the car, stepping over the kerb, avoiding getting too close.

'This is a desolate place. Why here?' Drake said, squinting into the darkness, noticing the tips of the mountains streaked orange.

Drake passed the CSI team photographing the vehicle from every angle, and he walked towards the cones and warning triangles set out for several metres behind the Volvo. The camber of the road banked from the centre and some of the cones had fallen over onto the tarmac.

The image of the dead officers wouldn't leave his mind. The bodies appeared staged. His mind tried to process the thought as it developed. He walked past the cones, down the hill before turning to look back at the car. Something was out of place, he knew it. He motioned to Caren.

'Who put these cones out?'

Caren looked blank.

He shouted to Foulds, who broke into a jog and joined Drake and Caren.

'Get a photographer here. Now.'

'The Traffic lads wouldn't have done this,' Caren said.

'That's what I'm thinking.'

Caren upended all the overturned cones as Drake directed the photographer. After a few seconds she stood back and called over to Drake.

'Something you ought to see,' she said, pointing at the surface of the tarmac.

Once all the cones and warning triangles were upright, the shape they formed was unmistakable.

The outline of the number four was clear.

Chapter 3
Tuesday, 1st June

The early morning sunshine reflected against the windows and rooftops as the car neared Northern Division Headquarters. The image of the number four had dominated Drake's thoughts – and his conversation with Caren – during the journey from the Crimea.

'What does it mean?' Caren said again.

Drake drew a hand over his face; it felt damp and sticky. He turned to look at Caren and he could see the unease in her eyes.

'Does it mean there are going to be more deaths?'

At that moment, all Drake could really focus on was the need to get clean and tidy. His shirt was dishevelled, his trousers had accumulated grime from the scene, and he was desperate for a shave and a shower.

'It could mean anything,' he said, without conviction.

'But the number four?' she persisted.

'A lucky number.' Drake shrugged. 'Part of a car registration.'

He was reminded of the sudoku riddles that had been the focus of his rituals lately. It was as if something inside him had to get a daily fix by defeating the puzzle. It was logic, after all, and that was his job – working things out, detective work. Caren was right to believe it had significance, but he put the possibility that it signalled more deaths to the back of his mind.

A little after half past seven Drake and Caren entered the Incident Room and the muttered conversations came to an abrupt end. Drake could feel the tension, sense the anger in the room.

Detective Constables David Howick and Gareth Winder turned to look at him. Howick managed a brief, stern nod and Winder clenched his jaw. Caren sat down at the nearest desk. Drake glanced along the board scattered with photographs of each of the dead officers. One other sheet of paper clung to the board – on it was the number four.

'You all know how much media attention this investigation is going to get,' he began. 'But that will be nothing compared to the attention we will give it.'

He paused; he had never sensed such concentration in an Incident Room before. He had their complete attention.

'It's our job to find the bastard who did this. We check everything twice, three times. And then we recheck it.'

He cleared his thoughts, watching the sharp alertness in the eyes of his team.

'I knew Danny Farrell, sir,' Howick said. 'I played badminton with him and his wife. She'll be devastated.'

Stillness fell on the room. This was more than the murder of colleagues – they were friends, too. Drake broke the tension by allocating tasks. Establishing what cases the dead officers had been working on was the top priority.

'But they were traffic cops ...' Howick began. 'There could be hundreds of motorists we might never be able to trace. Do we know how they were killed?'

Drake hesitated. 'It looks like they were shot in the chest and in the head through one eye.'

Winder pulled folded arms tight against his chest and Howick put a hand to his mouth; neither had been involved in a double murder before and the Wales Police Service had never lost two of its officers at the same time.

'Mathews was killed in the driver's seat and Farrell was lying outside the car. The pathologist thinks they were shot by some sort of dart or bolt. We will have to establish if they were moved. And I want to know everything about both men.'

Caren made her first contribution. 'How could one man have killed both of them?'

The room went quiet at the possibility of a vigilante-style killing. Drake drew a hand through his hair and adjusted his footing. 'Let's not get ahead of ourselves.' He tried to sound cautious, catching sight of the intense look on Howick's face.

Winder cleared his throat and raised his voice.

'Did the officers make a radio report?'

'That's your job.' Drake gave him a stern gaze.

'Yes, boss.'

Drake continued to allocate tasks to Winder. 'Find out where they'd been since they started their shift. And we need to know how long they had worked together.'

Caren added, 'And we'll need details of all the tickets they issued.'

Drake turned to Howick. 'Dave. Contact HR for the personnel files.'

The door swung open and crashed loudly against the wall. Price strode in, his right hand outstretched; the junior officers stood up and stiffened.

'This has just arrived.'

He slammed a plastic stationery pocket down on the nearest desk. There was a small Polaroid photograph in the bottom.

'It arrived by taxi. The driver's been called back.'

Drake picked up the envelope and caught his breath as he looked at the image on the photograph.

It was a close-up of one of the dead officers.

He passed it over to Howick, who squinted. 'What sort of sick bastard …'

Winder took the envelope from Howick's hand. He gave the image a long cold look. 'For fuck's sake …'

'There's more,' Price said. 'Words on the back.'

'Looks like a kid's poem,' Caren said, before handing the envelope back to Drake, who read the words, trying to block out the sound of the voices in the room. He had to concentrate. He read the message several times until he had the answer.

'It's a song lyric.'

The room went quiet.

Price turned to him. 'Do you know the song?'

Drake nodded. 'It's 'Brass in Pocket' by The Pretenders.'

'And what the fuck is that supposed to mean?'

Drake looked at the words and he heard the song in his head, with its clear opening chords and memorable hook line. Instinct told him the investigation was going to be difficult when this was all they had, no explanation: just the lyrics.

He turned to Winder. 'Gareth, I want to know who wrote the song.'

'Yes, sir.'

'I want to know when it was published. I want to know what album it was on. I want to know what the reviewers thought at the time. And I want to know if there are explanations out there for the song lyrics. You know, websites, blogs, etc. ...'

'Yes, sir.'

Price cleared his throat noisily. 'We need to catch this maniac. We can't have him taunting us with song lyrics from some pop band.' He curled a fist with both hands. 'He's killed two police officers. I want this madman caught.'

He brought both fists down onto the tabletop with a loud crash.

Rio Hawkins had a series of tattoos lining his neck and a set of stars on the knuckles of each hand. Drake guessed he was ex-forces.

'When did you get the job?'

Rio rubbed a hand over his chin and glanced at his watch.

'Are you expected somewhere?'

'I've got a hospital run in twenty minutes. Good money. Can't miss it.'

'Well?'

'Job came in an hour ago. Some man came into the office. I'd just started my shift.'

'Describe him.'

'Didn't see much. He talked to the boss on the desk. I was having a brew.'

'Did you see his face?'

Rio rolled his eyes. 'Sort of. He had a baseball cap. And long hair. Yeh, ponytail at the back and thick glasses.'

Drake, hiding his mounting irritation, thought about the photograph albums Rio could spend the next two hours thumbing through, and with an effort controlled himself.

'And?'

'He gave the boss the envelope. Told her to deliver it here. Gave her twenty quid.'

Drake moved forward and lowered his voice.

'Two police officers were killed this morning. The message was from the killer. So it's important you remember as much as you can.'

He watched the colour drain from Rio's face.

'That's all I saw. Honest.'

The self-important look had disappeared from the face of the taxi driver. Drake got up and snapped his notebook closed.

'We'll need your fingerprints.'

'I've done nothing wrong.'

'Just for us to eliminate you from the inquiry.'

After the interview with Rio, Drake stood in reception at headquarters. His skin felt greasy and he drew a hand across the stubble on his chin, reminding himself he had to clean up. He knew that if he couldn't wash, and wear clean clothes, the tension would gnaw away at his mind. Within ten minutes, Drake slammed the door of the duty sergeant's car and stepped into the drive of his home, searching for the front door key in his jacket.

He looked in the mirror before shaving; his eyes looked tired and his stubble was the colour of dirty snow. He set the temperature of the shower to high and let the hot water pour over his face. He towelled himself dry and reached for a navy suit and white shirt. He adjusted the knot on the silk tie with precision before he checked his hair in the mirror. The stubble was gone, his eyes looked healthier, but the bags were still there. He thought about food but his teeth were furry, so he cleaned them for a second time. Then he made a final small adjustment to the towel on the curved radiator – it had to be folded straight and neatly placed on the bottom rung. Sian always moved it and it drove him mad.

He drew the front door closed behind him and stepped onto the drive; the temperature was rising and a batch of white clouds drifted across the sky. On the journey back he stopped at a newsagent and bought a paper, turning at once to the sudoku. He hesitated, knowing he should be at his office, before deciding that he had to spend two minutes on the puzzle.

Price's office had large windows overlooking the parkland that surrounded the headquarters. He looked better than he had earlier that morning. His shirt was clean and crisply ironed, and Drake guessed from the faint smell of deodorant and aftershave that he had been using the executive bathroom.

'The Chief Constable's on his way from the airport,' Price said.

'I noticed some of the TV vans outside.'

'Fucking vultures. But the people from PR say we can't do anything about it. They've even had a call from a Japanese TV crew.'

Price hesitated, narrowed his eyes.

'This is an important case, Ian.'

Drake nodded.

'No stone is to be left unturned.'

'Yes, sir.'

'It will mean twenty-four seven. For the whole team.'

'Of course.' Drake knew everything else had to wait.

Before Price could continue, the telephone rang. The call was short.

'Chief Constable's arrived,' Price said.

The Chief Constable shook Price's outstretched hand. Price's secretary followed behind him with a tray, carefully laid out with a plate of sandwiches, a bottle of Ty Nant water and a bowl of fruit – the Chief Constable's insistence on a healthy diet was common knowledge. The appointment of Commander Riskin of the Metropolitan Police as the first Chief Constable of the Wales Police Service had been unexpected. He was in his late forties but his lean build made him look younger. He looked every inch the ambitious police officer. He probably ran every morning before breakfast, Drake thought, now regretting his own lack of exercise and expanding waistline.

'Detective Inspector Drake.' The Chief Constable emphasised each word.

The handshake was firm, the expression determined and clear. They sat round the conference table as Riskin continued.

'We met last year.'

'That's right, sir.'

Drake remembered the pride he had felt when he had been awarded the Chief Constable's Commendation Medal for an arrest of a prolific burglar.

'You did very well in that case.'

'Thank you, sir.'

'What's the Crimea like?' Riskin asked, before reaching for a sandwich.

'It's bleak, sir.'

'Must have been a difficult scene.'

'It was unreal. Looking at two dead police officers.'

Drake kept the description of the scene brief, summarising the pathologist's comments, Riskin nodding without averting his eye contact. Price poured some Ty Nant for Riskin.

'Press conference at midday,' Price said, which Drake took to mean the meeting was over. He left, disappointed that he hadn't been offered a sandwich, realising he was hungry.

Back at his office, Drake picked a wooden hanger from the coat stand and draped his jacket over it before smoothing out the shoulders carefully. He hated seeing jackets crumpled on the back of office chairs. His desk was a mass of Post-it notes and reminders and immediately he arranged them into neat columns, before adjusting the position of the telephone a few millimetres. Once he had finished, his attention fixed on the two thin files placed in the middle.

He picked up the file of Danny Farrell and skimmed the various sections, before deciding where to start. The officer's disciplinary record made for unhappy reading. There were allegations of violence, bullying and a harassment complaint by a woman police officer. It was clear once he picked up the second file that Mathews and Farrell were two of a kind: there were numerous complaints about both officers.

Drake searched unsuccessfully for the appraisals and detailed reports from the investigation, knowing that there should have been more paperwork. An uneasy feeling churned through his mind.

The sun filtered through the blinds on the window, warming Drake's shoulders. He moved the papers on his desk and fiddled with a biro as he thought about the families he would have to see later: the widow who had lost her husband, and children who wouldn't see their father again. He knew that family liaison was supporting Danny Farrell's wife and young children. Another set of officers were with the children and the former wife of Paul Mathews, but his girlfriend couldn't be found. An image of a family liaison officer in his own home came to him and he wondered how Sian would cope if it had been him. He glanced at his watch; Sian would be in the middle of another demanding surgery and the children busy at school. Until today, he had never thought that policing meant putting his life at risk and presumably had neither Mathews nor Farrell.

The telephone rang. Howick's voice interrupted his thoughts.

'I found something interesting about Mathews.'

Chapter 4
Tuesday, 1st June

Howick bowled into Drake's office, his face flushed with excitement.

His clean, straight parting reminded Drake of his grandfather and, at twenty-seven, Howick looked and acted older than his age. Howick's promotion to CID, after five years in uniform, had been the most important day of his life, he had said – more important than getting married.

'You've got to hear this.'

'Sit down.' Drake pointed to the chair.

Howick's white shirt looked new, the tie a sombre dark blue and Drake wondered whether he had resembled Howick at that age. Twenty-seven seemed a distant memory.

'You won't believe this.'

He moved forward in his seat, wide-eyed and unusually garrulous, barely stopping for breath. 'All the lads in Traffic are talking about it. Mathews tried to arrest a Stevie Dixon on the roadside three years ago but everything turned nasty. Dixon assaulted Mathews but he got the better of Dixon. He kicked the shit out of him.'

Howick fell over his words in his eagerness to tell Drake about the day of the trial. The prosecuting barrister had made clear his reservations before Mathews had given evidence, but the CPS solicitor had been determined to continue. Drake guessed that much of Howick's version was apocryphal, but he allowed him to finish – the arrest and trial had clearly become the stuff of legend in the Traffic Department.

'Guess who corroborated Mathews's version of events?' Howick said finally.

Drake had an uneasy feeling that he knew the answer. 'Don't tell me it was Farrell.'

Howick nodded, a frustrated look on his face. 'The other traffic officers thought Farrell and Mathews were lucky to get away with it. Everybody knew that Mathews had a violent temper. Dixon got sent down for four years and after that Mathews seemed to think he was invincible.'

Howick paused for effect. 'But that's not the end of it. Within a week, the death threats began.'

Drake's attention focused and the adrenaline pumped again, defeating his lingering tiredness. Howick began another detailed explanation.

'Highlights please, Dave,' Drake snapped.

'Anonymous letters. No DNA: all the usual checks were made. Neither of the officers took any of the death threats seriously.'

Drake focused his mind. All the letters would have to be re-checked. Forensics would have to convince him that they had done every test known to science.

'Any link to the court case?' Drake said.

'None that could be proved.'

'So why is this so important?'

'Stevie Dixon was released on parole a month ago. Quite the model prisoner. Glowing reports from the prison officers and probation. But his pre-cons read like a Who's Who of how to hate police officers.'

Howick sat on the edge of the chair, a serious and expectant look on his face. Drake shouted through the half-open door for Winder, who appeared in his office moments later.

'Gareth, you and Dave have to interview a possible suspect.'

As soon as Howick and Winder left, Drake reluctantly turned his attention to his emails. There was a press release from the PR department, in advance of the press conference, which he scanned quickly, knowing the reporters would have questions that they couldn't answer because they had so little to go on.

Glancing at his watch, he knew he had some time to spare. His hands felt greasy, his neck sweaty. He fished around in the drawers of his desk and found a toothbrush and toothpaste. In the nearest bathroom, he removed his tie and rolled up his sleeves, and he stared into the mirror. He knew he should be at his desk, moving the investigation forward, motivating his officers, leading the team, but he had to be clean, had to feel fresh. He thought about Sian and her latest comments about his compulsive behaviour. He knew he washed his hands too often, but it helped and he had to be presentable. He leant forward, staring at his reflection.

He worried about the Post-it notes on his desk. He would have to bring order to his paperwork, file everything away, and make extra copies, just in case. He stared at the face in the mirror and pushed at the receding hairline at each temple. He pulled in his waist and straightened his shoulders. Then he washed his hands and face with hot, soapy water.

The effort was worth it; he felt invigorated and almost clean again. He re-knotted his tie, checked his teeth in the mirror and drew a comb through his hair. Now he was ready for the press conference.

Price was sitting at the end of the oval conference table with neat piles of papers in front of him. The Chief Constable sat next to him, both senior officers in full uniform, their caps in the middle of the table. Drake vaguely recognised the woman from public relations and managed to remember that her name was Lisa. He groaned when he saw that Andy Thorsen was the duty Crown prosecutor. The lawyer nodded at him without saying a word. Drake had worked on many cases with the prosecutor, who was a good lawyer but had all the personality of a dead fish.

Price took charge of the meeting and ran through the draft press release, inviting comments. He reminded everyone there wasn't a great deal they could tell the press. Lisa stressed how inundated her office had been with requests for details.

'And S4C will expect a Welsh language interview. DI Drake?' she asked.

Drake agreed. This was familiar territory and it wasn't the first time his ability to speak Welsh would get his face on the television news.

The Chief Constable reminded everyone, unnecessarily, that they were dealing with the deaths of two police officers. So no matter what reservations they had about the press, they had little choice but to involve them.

'At this stage we don't make any reference to how they were killed.' It was Drake's first contribution. 'Let's stick to the basic facts. Appeal for witnesses. And we don't mention the message.'

Price turned to Thorsen.

'Andy, any thoughts?'

The lawyer was restless in his seat, trying to find a comfortable position. He drew a breath, rolled his eyes and replied. 'That's an operational matter.'

Drake screwed his eyes at Thorsen; he could have contributed something more constructive. Typical bloody lawyer – always hedging his bets. He glanced at the Chief Constable and thought he saw a look of irritation in his eyes. Price and Riskin scooped up their caps and led the others downstairs.

Drake glanced through a glass door and saw the expectant faces of the press sitting in rows. He heard the chatter amongst the journalists and spotted some faces he knew from the television – he had never seen a press conference so well attended.

When they entered the room he heard the clicks and whirls of the television cameras, and the light bulbs fizzed into life, bathing the room in artificial light. There were folded cards with the names of each officer placed on the table and Drake found his seat at the far end. Drake shifted uncomfortably in his chair, aware of all the eyes on him. He kept his gaze fixed to the desk in front of him, as the expected questions from the journalists and the standard evasive answers from Price echoed round the room. He looked up when he heard his own name mentioned.

'Inspector Drake,' said a young reporter, 'Is it true that there's been a message from the killer?'

Drake thought about looking over at the Chief Constable but, hiding his surprise at the question, looked at his notes and composed a reply.

'We are pursuing several lines of inquiry, although it would be inappropriate to comment on specifics. What I can say is to underline what has been said already. We will do everything to catch the killer.'

The Chief Constable finished the press conference and as they left the room staff from the public relations department distributed copies of the press release. Price stormed through headquarters, flushed a scarlet colour, unable to contain his annoyance.

'How the fuck did he know about the message?'

Chapter 5
Tuesday, 1st June

Drake tried to control the anger welling up inside him, that somebody on his team had leaked information to the press. He couldn't think of a more serious breach of trust. Back in his office, he slammed the door and kicked a bin, sending it flying across the floor. He worried about the mess and looked at the rubbish strewn across the carpet tiles, before wondering what the price of a police officer's indiscretion was these days. No more than a few pints and a curry, probably.

He had to get his team together, right now.

He strode out of his office into the Incident Room and stood in the middle. Caren raised her head and Howick and Winder glanced at each other, seeing that something was on his mind. Drake folded his arms and drew breath slowly.

'I never want that to happen again. You don't talk to anybody about the case. Understood?'

Howick chewed his lips and Winder blinked rapidly, but Caren gave him a neutral gaze.

Drake raised his voice.

'We can't afford for anybody to talk to the press. Any leak, and I mean any leak, could damage this investigation. We've got two dead officers for Christ's sake!'

He unfolded his arms and walked back to his office but hesitated as he reached the door. He turned to face the room again. 'We've got work to do. So let's get on with it.'

The catharsis of venting his anger soon waned. Drake realised that the leak could have come from anywhere. They had to be ahead of the killer: he would make certain of it. He stared down at the crumpled notes and shreds of torn paper that littered the floor, and his pulse raced and his chest tightened. He knelt down and started to collect the discarded rubbish. Once he had finished, he slumped into his leather chair, trying to get a clear perspective. He moved the piles of unfinished reports, arranging them out of mind in the middle of a bookcase. He opened his notebook and set about the task of creating a to-do list, rearranging the priorities he had set various officers. The simple act of restructuring his records enabled him to clear his mind and refocus his attention.

A worry crossed his mind that perhaps it had been unwise to be so aggressive earlier. After all, he had no proof that anyone in his team had been responsible. He heard Caren's muffled voice on the telephone in the adjacent Incident Room. Drake guessed things weren't going well. He opened the door and heard her lecturing somebody about house-to-house inquiry techniques. There was an exasperated look on her face when Drake walked over to her desk. She finished the call and began a tirade about the ineffectual training of junior officers.

'Better bring me up to date,' Drake said.

'There's still a mass of TV crews outside,' Caren said as they walked into Drake's office.

Drake noticed her clothes – the jeans were too baggy and the blouse hung loosely around her hips, and the trainers were shabby and worn. At least her hair had been brushed into a knot behind her head, instead of a tangled mass falling over her shoulders. He liked to do things properly and working with Caren reminded him how sloppy the attitude of more junior officers had become.

'I don't know if the house-to-house inquiries will help,' Caren said.

'Any results yet?'

The furrows on her brow deepened and Drake sensed her irritation. Caren knew the inquiries were needed – essential even – but it still didn't stop her frustration.

'Look, Caren, I know how you feel. But we've got to do it. Tick all the boxes.'

'I know. But—'

'No buts about it. We've got to follow procedure.'

'It's pointless—'

Drake raised a hand and she stopped mid-breath.

'The politicians and the public expect us to do the house-to-house. Think about the reaction if we didn't.'

As a young recruit Drake had wanted to make a difference – to improve the lives of ordinary people, lock up the bad guys and help make society safer, but the more paperwork he had to complete the more he felt estranged from his idealism. He could see Caren was beginning to feel the same way.

Caren nodded slowly and he continued. 'I know it's a pain in the backside. Results so far?'

'Nothing yet, sir. I've got two teams working. One in Blaenau Ffestiniog itself and the other on the Dolwyddelan side of the pass. They could take days to finish the work. So many of the houses are isolated farms and smallholdings. Everybody was in bed at two o'clock in the morning.'

Drake had to concentrate but his eyes burnt with tiredness, and they still had to visit Danny Farrell's widow and Paul Mathews's ex-wife: something he was dreading.

'It's time to go and see the families,' Drake said. 'I'll meet you in the car park.'

The front gardens at Trem-y-Mor were neat but anonymous. Vertical blinds and net curtains hung at front windows and lazier occupants had left wheelie bins on their front drives. There were three cars parked in a row outside the house so Drake parked two doors away. Before they left the car, Caren cleared her throat.

'Do you think somebody in the team spoke to the journalist?'

Drake darted a glance at her but she avoided eye contact.

'He must have got his information from somewhere.'

Caren nodded slowly.

'I don't think it was either Dave or Gareth.'

'We have to be careful,' he said after a moment's hesitation, when he realised what she meant. 'And two officers. Well …' Drake found the words drying up. 'The pressure will be intense for a result here,' he continued.

'You can depend on the team, sir.'

He nodded but said nothing. They left the car and walked down to the bungalow, Drake mulling over Caren's comments. She was right and yet, while he blanked out his own worries, the horror of the crimes struck him afresh; he hoped that he could cope with the investigation and that the obsessions that drove his rituals would subside.

The paths around the house were dirty, the flags uneven and lush with weeds. Danny Farrell hadn't exactly been the domestic type.

One of the family liaison officers opened the door. Standing behind her was an older woman with an expectant, worried look on her face, her hair unkempt, and her face drawn and tired.

'Paula's in the lounge,' the officer said.

Drake and Caren followed her into a room where a woman in her late thirties sat on one of the sofas. Paula Farrell had deep shadows under her bloodshot eyes. Drake felt bad for disturbing her but knew that his presence couldn't make matters any worse. The older woman left the room when they sat down, announcing that she would make tea.

Drake looked around the lounge. At one corner a section of wallpaper was peeling away. A glass-fronted bookcase had photographs of a boy and a girl in school uniform – Drake remembered that Danny Farrell had children of school age. Underneath the television, a games console lay on top of a pile of DVD cases. Although it was June, the room felt cold.

Drake never found expressing condolences easy and despite having faced grieving partners, widows and widowers many times, he always stumbled to find the right words or the right emotion. With Paula Farrell it was doubly hard.

'Look, I know this is a bad time but I need to ask you a couple of questions.'

Paula Farrell nodded, her eyes dull.

'Tell me about Danny.'

'Danny was just an ordinary bloke,' she said. 'He loved being in the police. Always looked forward to going to work.'

'Did he enjoy working with Paul Mathews?'

Paula hesitated.

'Was there a problem with Mathews?'

'No problem for Danny. I just didn't like the man.'

'Any reason?'

Paula screwed up her eyes and gave Drake a sideways look.

'I knew he was trouble.' She shook her head before brushing away a tear. 'From the things Danny said about him. About the way he could be. And he tried to come on to me one night. It was at a party. I told Danny but he laughed it off. Told me I got it all wrong – must have drunk too much.'

Her energy to talk about Paul Mathews seemed to peter out.

'Do you remember a case about two years ago that went to court? An allegation that Mathews had assaulted a civilian?'

She nodded and looked down at the carpet. Drake paused.

'Did Danny talk about it?'

'Just that Paul was in the shit,' she said. 'I don't really remember the details, but Danny didn't go to court very often, so it stuck in my mind.'

Drake shifted to the edge of the sofa.

'Do you remember anything at all?'

'Just that Danny was worried.'

Paula's mother arrived with the tea.

'Thanks, Mam.' As her mother left the room, Paula added, 'I couldn't cope without her.'

Drake sipped the sweet tea, listening with increasing irritation to Caren slurping the hot liquid. Paula didn't seem to notice. Drake continued with his questions, but without uncovering any useful information. Danny was a good man, kind to the kids, took them to football and the scouts. Their marriage wasn't perfect of course, but what marriage is? And no, she had no idea if there was anybody that wanted him dead.

After an hour Paula had slumped back in her chair and raised a hand to her mouth, stifling a yawn.

Caren leant forward. 'You've got some lovely photos of your children,' she said. 'How old are they?'

Paula smiled wanly.

'Delyth's ten and Jack's thirteen.'

'How are they coping?'

Paula turned to look at her. 'I don't know what to say to them.'

Paula stood by the front door as they left the bungalow and in the evening light, her complexion appeared even paler. She pulled her arms round her body against an imaginary chill.

They drove down towards the A55 that skirted the edge of the village. The sea looked calm, the sky a crystal blue. Soon the tranquil scene gave way to the traffic rushing along the main road.

They travelled on, in silence, eventually finding a parking space outside the home of Paul Mathews's ex-wife. When Fiona Mathews opened the door she stood for a moment staring – then the faintest hint of a smile twitched her lips. Her clothes were expensive and the perfume sweet and cloying. It smelt too young for her – Drake guessed she was forty, maybe even forty-five.

'Inspector Drake,' he began. 'And this is Detective Sergeant Waits.'

Fiona stood to one side as though she had expected them. She motioned briefly with her head towards the inside of the house. The hallway was long and immaculately tidy – Drake noticed immediately that nothing felt out of place; there was no sense of grief or loss. Fiona's world seemed unaffected by the death of her former husband. She sat down on a sofa, piled with perfectly positioned scatter cushions, crossed her legs, drew back her thin blond hair from her face and gave Drake a formal smile.

'You've come about Paul.'

'Mrs Mathews, I know—'

'Trick, please.'

Drake hesitated.

'I've reverted to my maiden name. Trick.'

'Of course,' Drake sensed Caren staring at her.

It was clear that condolences weren't needed: no sympathetic body language required. He adjusted his position on the chair opposite Fiona.

'When did you last see Paul, Mrs – Ms – Trick?'

Fiona folded one hand inside another. 'We've been divorced for three years and frankly not a day goes by that I'm not deeply grateful about the divorce. I dreaded seeing the man.'

The conversation continued, with Fiona making it clearer with every word that she hated Mathews. Drake heard the floorboards groan upstairs, then the sound of a television, and a toilet flushing, and he remembered the family.

'How often did he see the children?'

'He couldn't be bothered.' Fiona's eyes hardened. 'He was more interested in his computer games and his young girlfriend.'

'Can you think of anyone who might have wanted him dead?'

She snorted.

'Did he mention a case a couple of years ago when he had to go to court?'

She shook her head.

Drake gave up the questioning, thanked her and left. They returned to the car and once Drake had fired the engine into life, headed for Mathews's flat. Talking to Fiona Trick had been a gloomy reminder of how emotions can change from love to hatred. It made Drake feel despondent that she would not be able to grieve with her children, if only for their sake.

Mathews lived in a self-contained flat in a small purpose-built block on the outskirts of Colwyn Bay. After fumbling for the right key, Caren opened the front door and, once inside, closed it quietly behind them. The laminate flooring and minimalist decoration made the flat feel clinical and antiseptic. An enormous flatscreen television dominated one corner of the lounge, speakers of the surround-sound theatre system standing in each corner. A large bookcase was stacked to the brim with DVDs and games for the computer. No book in sight, not even a Stieg Larsson.

'Typical bachelor pad,' Caren said.

An unfinished mug of coffee stood on the draining board alongside a half-empty packet of cereal, poignant reminders of Mathews's domestic routine.

Caren went into the bedroom. 'Has anyone spoken to the girlfriend yet?' she called out, as she looked at the women's clothes hanging in the main wardrobe.

Before Drake could reply, he heard the scratching sound of a key in the front door. He called out to Caren and they both stood in the narrow landing as the door opened.

'Who the fuck are you?' The young woman stood rigid by the door. 'I'm going to call the police.'

Strands of long auburn hair brushed her shoulders, her make-up millimetre-perfect. The high heels and narrow skirt made her look slimmer than she actually was. Drake and

Caren flashed their warrant cards.

'Anna, we've come about Paul,' he said.

'What's happened?' The colour drained from her cheeks.

They went into the kitchen and she sat on one of the chairs by the table.

'Paul was killed this morning. He was on duty with Danny Farrell. They were both killed in their patrol car on the top of the Crimea Pass. We've been trying to contact you all day.'

She began to cry, harsh tearing sobs. The tears scarred her make-up, the mascara mixing with blusher as they rolled down her cheeks. She explained, between gasps for breath, that she had been away on a training course. Caren fetched a glass of water and asked whether there was someone she could stay with for the night.

'My mother lives near Rhyl,' she said to Caren, in between sips.

Caren agreed to stay with Anna until her mother arrived. The girl seemed relieved at the offer of help. Drake left the flat and returned to headquarters.

The building was quiet and only the night staff remained. He could hear the vacuum cleaners in the corridors and the smell of cleaning fluids and he knew that he should be at home with his family. But when he thought about leaving, his mind kept telling him he had to stay, that he might miss something, a vital snippet of information, the clue that would crack the case wide open. Now his mind started replaying the song lyrics again, over and over, until he could think of nothing else.

Tomorrow he had to make progress. He had to know what the lyrics meant.

Sitting by his desk, he turned on the light. His arms felt wooden. He eyes burnt. He turned over in his mind the events of the day. He had to have time to think.

He wondered why he had returned to the office. Then

he remembered he had wanted to organise his papers again and check that the cleaners had emptied the bin and hoovered the floor. He looked down at the pristine carpet tiles and checked the bin once more, cursing himself for letting his obsessions get in the way.

He knew he would have to go home soon.

He reached to switch off the light when his mobile rang. It was Winder.

'Boss, Dave's been assaulted. He's in hospital.'

Chapter 6
Wednesday 2nd June

'Crucify the bastard who did this.' Chief Inspector Prewer clenched his jaw and gave every word a hard, steely edge. 'Are you in charge of the investigation, Ian?'

'Yes.'

Dealing with the Traffic Department would be difficult, so better to start with the right tone, Drake decided. He fidgeted with the files on his lap, gathering his thoughts. 'I need a complete picture of Mathews and Farrell.'

'They were effective officers,' Prewer replied.

Drake wanted the truth, not a justification of the dead officers, so he ignored the comment and moved on. 'I've read the files you sent over yesterday—'

'Good.'

'I don't seem to have the appraisals and all the reports I would have expected.'

'Everything you need to know is in there.'

'Are there more papers, sir?' Drake struck a balance between interrogation and polite request. 'I'll need all the papers. Everything.'

Prewer narrowed his eyes. 'The appraisals are part of the personnel file. These officers are dead. What possible use could they be?'

'I need to know everything about both men. The two aren't exactly model police officers, are they?'

Prewer stuck out his chin. 'Let's say they had some disciplinary issues.'

Issues. Drake wanted to remind Prewer that a dozen complaints against Farrell and more than that against Mathews was more than just *issues*.

'Did they always work together?'

'No. We tried to keep them apart,' Prewer said, 'but last week they were rostered on the same shift. We were short. Look, they got on well and they were good and effective traffic officers.'

Prewer moved his gaze away from Drake.

'What happened in the case of Stevie Dixon?'

He could see the shutters coming down in Prewer's mind. Through gritted teeth Prewer spat out a reply.

'Dixon is a toe-rag. The worst sort. Lies through his teeth. And anyway, he's in prison.'

'No. He was released last month.'

Drake could see the surprise mixed with a flash of apprehension on Prewer's face.

'I'll need all the files,' Drake said.

Prewer nodded slowly, 'Of course.'

Drake continued, 'There was a sexual harassment claim against Farrell. What happened?'

'It was withdrawn.'

'Any reason?'

'It was pointed out to the WPC at the time that her promotion prospects might be damaged if she allowed such a complaint to proceed.'

'What happened to her?'

'She left the force.'

Drake nodded. He didn't like it, but that was how things worked. The service would look after itself, protect its reputation, and avoid self-inflicted embarrassing headlines.

'Either up for promotion?'

Prewer had crossed his arms and self-consciously looked at his watch; Drake could see him preparing another unhelpful reply.

'No.'

'Sergeants' exams?' Drake suggested, offering Prewer the opportunity to fill out his reply.

'Mathews. Failed them.'

'I'm going to send over one of the DCs. We need to have access to everything about Mathews and Farrell, including all of the HR files.'

Prewer gave Drake a narrow smile. It wouldn't be easy,

another officer digging though the department's files, exposing any awkward cases to the harsh and unforgiving wisdom of hindsight. Drake would need Price's help to cut through any obstacles. He left Prewer pondering and threaded his way back to his office, exchanging greetings and the occasional disjointed conversation. He could sense that the raw tension of the day before had dissipated.

His office was unchanged from the night before; all the Post-it notes and papers were in the same neat order but the room smelt stale and musty. He pulled at the catch of the window until it gave way and he felt the cool air stream into the room. He stared out over the landscaped grounds. Why choose the Crimea? What was special about the pass? Why the message and what did the number four mean? He found neither satisfactory answers nor inspiration.

He heard a noise behind him and turned to see Winder standing by the door, an expectant look on his face. Drake motioned to the officer, who came into the room and sat down.

'What time did you get back last night?' Drake asked.

'Three in the morning.'

Despite only a few hours' sleep, Winder looked alert and Drake could see he wanted to share the details of the night before. The sergeant at the local police station had warned them about Dixon and insisted on sending two uniformed officers to accompany them.

'"*Just in case lads*". That's what he said, boss. Now I know what he meant'

Howick believed it was an open-and-shut case, and talked about nothing else on the journey to Merseyside, but things had turned nasty, right from the start.

'Dave was wound up, boss,' Winder explained. 'He was convinced Stevie Dixon was our man.'

Drake could imagine how Howick felt. He had seen the anger in the faces of the officers at their first meeting, shared their outrage at what had happened and wanted a result as much as they all did.

'Finding Dixon was easy enough,' Winder continued. 'First we went to his house. Only person there was his wife and she told us he was in the gym. But there was no sign of him. After asking around somebody told us he was at his girlfriend's house.'

'How old is this guy?'

'Mid-fifties, but very fit,' Winder said. 'He was outside, gardening. Dave got straight to the point. Asked him where he had been the night before last. Didn't give Dixon a chance to reply. You could see Dixon was getting defensive. Then he squared up to Dave.'

Winder leant forward and paused.

'Then Dave put his hand on Dixon's shoulder, told him he was being arrested. And bang, before I knew what was happening Dixon had head-butted him. Blood everywhere, boss. Dave was holding his nose, shouting and cursing. The whole thing went tits-up. It was a complete mess.'

Drake groaned. It was the last thing they needed.

'It took three of us to hold Dixon down.'

'Did Dave caution him?' Drake began to think of the legalities.

'It all happened so fast I can't remember.'

'Well you'd better try. It needs to be in your statement.'

'Yes, sir.'

'And where is Dixon now?'

'Birkenhead nick. I'm going to collect him with a couple of uniforms later. The custody sergeant insisted the bastard have eight hours' uninterrupted rest – regulations, sir.'

Drake nodded. He had once been a custody sergeant and knew the rules well enough. An interview with Dixon could start later that afternoon.

'Gareth, don't take any chances with this guy,' he said seriously. 'I want everything done by the book.'

Winder nodded and left.

Drake spent an hour scanning the numerous emails in his inbox. He relegated most to the bottom of his to-do list and prioritised those from Price and the press office. Drake had learnt that Price liked to impress his junior officers by sending emails wherever possible, and that he expected prompt replies. Price wanted a progress report on Howick. He composed a reply, suggesting a meeting later that morning. Before he had finished reading the email from the press office, Price had replied.

Meeting. My office. One hour.

Drake watched Winder pinning photocopies of the death threats to the board in the Incident Room. Caren was reading the pages of the printed versions circulated in plastic stationery pockets and Howick had his arms crossed severely.

Drake strode over to read the messages. All four had been assembled from newspaper cuttings but the sentences had the same poor grammar, threatening to dismember Mathews and Farrell.

'What did the SIO at the time think?'

'Laughed them off as far as I can tell,' Winder said.

Howick stared at the board. 'They look serious enough to me.'

Drake took a step back, in line with Caren. 'They must have thought it was a joke.'

'But Dixon had just been sent down. They must have thought it was related,' Caren said.

'Someone might have had a grudge against Mathews and used the aftermath of the court case as an excuse to send these messages,' Winder suggested.

Howick wasn't convinced. 'And what would that achieve?'

Winder persevered. 'He was getting off on the thrill. Knowing that Mathews and Farrell would be shit-scared.'

Drake was still staring at the messages. 'I want to see all the DNA tests done last time and then I want them all done again. We'll send them to a different lab. Tell them we want the results yesterday.'

Price moved an expensive chrome biro through his fingers as he listened to Drake. Through the open windows, Drake heard the clatter of a train slowing and detected the hint of salt in the air.

'I've been to see Paula Farrell and Mathews's ex-wife. Caren and I were at his flat when his girlfriend arrived. We broke the news to her.'

'Anything?'

'Paula Farrell looked like death but Mathews's ex-wife seemed almost pleased.'

Price looked surprised, 'What about the children?'

'We didn't see them, but family liaison are with both families.'

'Good,' he said, still tapping the biro on the desk.

'I'll be interviewing Stevie Dixon later this afternoon.'

'Have you made any sense of the message?'

'Not yet, sir. However, there has to be a link somewhere.' Drake tried to sound optimistic.

'There's a lot of pressure in this case, Ian,' said Price. 'We'll need to get a profiler in as soon as possible.'

'But the investigation's only just started,' Drake protested.

Price appeared torn; he opened his mouth before hesitating, trying to find the right words.

'Can't have the country turning into some sort of banana republic. We'll have to use all the resources at our disposal.'

Drake knew the Chief Constable and politicians in Cardiff would want a result soon.

'I gather you've been to see Prewer,' Price continued.

Drake looked at Price, trying to guess what Prewer might have said, 'Like it or not, we've got to dig into their past.'

Price stopped fiddling with the biro and raised his hand.

'I know, Ian. Just take it easy.'

Drake tightened his grip on the biro in his own hand. 'I don't want the investigation compromised to protect the reputation of the Traffic Department. Neither Mathews nor Farrell were paragons of virtue.'

'That may be, Inspector, but we're not having our dirty linen displayed in public. This is an important investigation. You must appreciate the sort of pressures we're under. Just look at the headlines. Imagine what the politicians are thinking.'

Drake didn't respond. Price continued.

'Until we get a clear motive we're going to have all this wild speculation from the press. We all need to work together, Ian. Whatever help you need, we'll make the resources available.'

'I want to get a result here as much as anybody.'

'Politics, Ian – politics.'

Drake left the meeting feeling annoyed. He knew Mathews and Farrell were a disgrace. Why couldn't Price see that too? He closed the door of his office, trying to isolate his irritation from his ability to think, separating himself from the conversations and activity in the Incident Room beyond his door.

He sat down as his mobile bleeped; Sian's text reminded him to call his mother, who had sounded subdued on the phone the day before. When he dialled, it rang out for far longer than normal before she answered.

'Ian.' She sounded relieved. 'I'm so glad you've called.'

Drake could tell she was worried about something. 'What's wrong?'

'It's your father. He's not well. He's very down these

days. Nothing I can do seems to help. Can you come and see him?'

'I'm right in the middle of this investigation.'

'Yes, I know. We both saw the news last night. You looked tired.'

'I'm fine, Mam.'

'Just call some time. Please, Ian.'

'Saturday. I'll call Saturday.'

Chapter 7
Wednesday 2nd June

Drake opened the chilled cabinet at the supermarket and pulled out a bacon, lettuce and tomato sandwich that he paired up with a packet of crisps and a Coke. He walked through the stationery section, scanning the aisle until he found a book of sudoku puzzles to add to his collection. Back in the car, he reached for the antiseptic wipes and cleaned his hands twice, before breaking open the sandwich. Then he turned to the paper and the sudoku he'd started that morning. He'd struggled with the first few numbers but he enjoyed the achievement of completing two squares.

He powered down the window, allowing the summer breeze to fill the car while he drove to the Area Operational Centre for the interview with Stevie Dixon.

Drake had been at the custody suite many times, but the CCTV cameras that watched and recorded every movement still caught his attention. The custody sergeant sat behind a heavy Perspex screen, a flickering computer monitor in front of him, talking to Caren. The air stank: a combination of cold chips, urine and vomit hung in the air. Drake remembered the stench from his days as a custody sergeant; it clung to the inside of his nostrils and even long showers couldn't eradicate the smell.

The sergeant smiled at him. 'Inspector Drake. Your man's brief has just arrived.'

'Thanks.'

'Better be careful. He's one of those fucking hot-shots from Liverpool. Thinks we're all plebs in the country.'

'Have you been looking after Stevie Dixon?'

'Oh yes. First-class treatment. Generous to a fault. We even took turns to gob in his coffee.'

Caren winced and Drake stifled a laugh.

Stevie Dixon and his solicitor were already waiting in the interview room. The windowless, soundproofed space had a small table pushed against a wall.

Drake made the necessary introductions, sat down and thought he noticed something floating on the surface of the cold coffee in one of the plastic cups standing at one end of the table. He scanned Dixon and his brief. The custody sergeant had been right about the solicitor. The suit was a designer label and the shirt an expensive cutaway-collar design with a knitted silk tie. Drake noticed the Liverpool accent through the cultured tone Marcus Frome adopted.

Stevie Dixon had no neck to speak of; his head protruded off massive shoulders, the short sleeves of his shirt bulging from the definition in his arms.

Dixon's stare was hard – Drake sensed this would be a difficult interview.

'Do you know why you've been arrested?' he began.

'Spare me that fucking do-you-know-why-you've-been-arrested bullshit. I know why I'm here. Some young snivelling policeman, who's just had his first wank, assaulted me without reason. I defended myself, as I am entitled to do.'

'I'm investigating the murder of two road traffic officers on the Crimea Pass the night before last.'

'What the fuck does that have to do with me?'

'One of the police officers was Constable Paul Mathews and the other Constable Danny Farrell. Do you remember them?'

Stevie Dixon pushed back the chair, balancing on the two rear legs, all the while staring at Drake.

'Is my client a formal suspect in these two murders?' Marcus Frome said.

'I was asking your client if he remembered the two officers.'

'And I was asking if my client is a formal suspect.'

Drake ignored the solicitor and turned to Dixon again.

'Did you know Constable Paul Mathews and Constable Danny Farrell?'

'They're the bastards that stitched me up.'

'Can you account for your whereabouts the night before last?'

'I was home, shagging the missus. Then out at a party.'

Caren was busy writing in a notebook. Drake continued with questions, asking about specific times, wanting Dixon to give a detailed account that could be double-checked. Dixon sounded casual and unconcerned, almost convincing. The solicitor gave up interrupting and satisfied himself by keeping detailed notes of the questions and answers.

'You were arrested yesterday on suspicion of assaulting a police officer.'

'It was self defence.'

Drake scanned the papers in front of him. 'The medical report states that Constable David Howick suffered a severe assault resulting in a broken nose and a black eye.'

He looked at Dixon and caught the end of a smile crossing his face.

'These injuries are serious.'

Dixon tried to sound authoritative. 'It was a legitimate act of self defence.'

Drake had satisfied himself before the interview that he had sufficient grounds to charge Stevie Dixon with assault, giving them enough time to check out his alibi. He could tell Dixon wanted to give his version of events; very few suspects said nothing – that was for television soaps.

'Tell me what happened yesterday.'

Dixon brought the front legs of the chair back to the floor, straightened up and cleared his throat. The solicitor looked uncomfortable but Dixon was enjoying the attention.

'I was acting in self defence. How many times do I have to say this?'

'The officer wanted to question you about a serious matter. You refused to cooperate.'

'That's fucking shit.'

'Once the officer told you were being arrested you

assaulted him without provocation.'

'He assaulted me. Doesn't the law say that I can act in self defence?'

'You failed to cooperate after you were cautioned and arrested.'

'He didn't caution me. If he says so, he's fucking lying.'

'Are you saying that three police officers are lying?'

Dixon folded his arms and said nothing further.

Once the interview had finished, Drake and Caren returned to the custody desk. 'Well, did he cough?' the sergeant asked.

Drake sat down on a hard plastic chair and let out a slow groan. The sergeant nodded as Drake told him the details.

'So you want me to deny him bail on the grounds that he might abscond, interfere with witnesses and because he's a fucking toe-rag.'

'That's about it.'

It took another hour to finish the formalities. Despite quoting a Court of Appeal decision Marcus Frome failed to intimidate the custody sergeant and settled on having his representations noted in writing. Once Dixon was back in a cell, Drake left.

He stepped into the warmth of the evening sunshine. He shook his jacket and brushed away some imaginary flecks of dirt before folding it over one arm. His hands felt dirty, his face grimy, but he was glad to be in the fresh air, out of the stifling atmosphere of the custody suite.

He loosened his tie, pointed the remote control at the Alfa, and then laid his jacket on the passenger seat before allowing the smell of the leather to invade his nostrils. It was time to go home.

Drake drove to headquarters instead.

The Incident Room was quiet, the offices tranquil and he slumped into the chair by his desk. Then he reordered all the papers on his desk and tidied the pens and biros in the pot by the telephone. Finally, he began on the bookcase, rearranging the files and folders into piles that made sense, that had order. When Price knocked on his door, Drake was on the floor, rummaging through papers.

'Jesus, Ian. What are you doing at this time of the night?'

Drake scrambled to his feet. 'Just tidying the papers.'

Price gave him a puzzled look. 'You've got a family. Go home.'

Once Price had left, Drake brushed the dirt from his trousers and sat back into his chair. An hour later he left, after he'd heard the approaching cleaners and realised the time.

.

Chapter 8
Thursday 3rd June

Caren woke a few minutes past six and stared at the alarm clock.

She abandoned trying to sleep and padded downstairs. From the kitchen window she saw Alun moving in the fields below the farmhouse, tending to the alpacas. She and Alun had been married for five years and on mornings like this, she didn't want to interview murderers, thieves or burglars for a living. She caught herself brooding about children, a prospect they had discussed although they had never come to a final decision. And she wasn't certain that she would be a good mother. She knew from colleagues that combining a career as a police officer and being a mother was stressful.

She busied herself making tea before tidying away the remnants of supper from the night before. She listened to the radio announcement about a special programme on the television that evening on the *horrific murder of two police officers in North Wales.* Instantly she imagined herself back at the top of the Crimea Pass, looking down at the bodies of Mathews and Farrell. Since the murders she'd slept fitfully, often waking thinking about the investigation. Normally she could forget about work at home but the murders had invaded her comfort zone and challenged the routine she took for granted.

She heard Alun grunting by the back door as he struggled to take off his boots. He smiled when he saw her. 'Couldn't sleep?'

She consigned the investigation to the corners of her mind, realising that his presence in the kitchen had brought her back down to the normalities of life.

'Tea?' she said.

He nodded.

After breakfast, she soaked in the bath, allowing her body to sink into the hot, clean water, and her mind turned to her interview with Anna later that morning.

It was another clear summer's day as she pulled the back door closed behind her. Approaching the car she heard a rustling sound in the narrow ditch – a field mouse, more afraid of her than she was of it. A buzzard clung to the air currents high above her head and the cloudless sky promised more high temperatures.

Driving east on the A55, her progress was slowed by the early morning traffic and she caught sight of the whirling blades of the wind farm far out to sea. The colourless estates of bungalows on the outskirts of Rhyl made Caren realise how much she valued her farmhouse. She passed the sprawling caravan parks and amusement arcades that disfigured the coastline and wondered how people could enjoy themselves in this environment. Where was the attraction in spending two weeks by a funfair?

The directions she had scribbled on a piece of paper were unclear and she became more and more frustrated as she turned into one cul-de-sac after another until she spotted Anna's car and parked behind it.

Anna opened the door as Caren raised her hand to ring the bell. She led Caren into a small sitting room at the front of the house. The room was airless and stuffy. A display cupboard in one corner was full of tea sets and various china trinkets.

'How are you this morning?' Caren said.

Gone was the heavy make-up of the night before. Gone were the high heels and the fashionable clothes. She wore an unflattering tracksuit. Her eyelids were swollen and red – the bags under her eyes suggested a night of little sleep.

Anna grunted a reply. 'Do you want tea or coffee or something?' she said, without conviction.

'No, nothing thanks. I need to ask you about Paul.'

Anna blinked heavily and Caren thought she saw a tear gather in the corner of one eye.

'I knew what he was like, you know.'

Caren ignored the remark. 'How did you meet?'

'He picked me up one night when I was at the Sports Club in town. He was with his friends.'

'Which club?'

'It was the Archery Club. He used to go there a lot. He could be a real charmer. He knew all the right things to say. One of my friends told me to be careful.'

'How long have you been going out with him?'

'Fifteen months.'

'Did he talk about work at all?'

'Sometimes he used to talk about Danny and some of the other lads.'

Anna could remember some names and she described some faces of the officers she knew had been friends with Paul, but she looked blank when Caren asked about any court cases involving Paul.

'What about the children? How often did he see them?'

'He saw them once a month, sometimes more often. It was the one constant thing in his life. He loved them.'

Caren moved to the edge of her chair, her attention focused – this was very different from Fiona Trick's account. 'Would you be with him?'

'Sometimes,' she said. 'Usually he saw them on his own. Sometimes he took them bowling and always to McDonald's.'

Caren nodded: it sounded typical. 'Did that get in the way of what you wanted to do?'

'I didn't want kids.' Anna averted her eye contact. 'And I knew Paul didn't want any more commitments. I knew what he was like.'

Anna looked away and then repeated her offer of tea. Caren hesitated and read her notes, sensing Anna's pain.

'Did he confide in you?'

'Yes, I suppose so. As much as he did to anybody.'

Caren continued. 'Do you think he had any enemies?'

'Anybody who might want to kill him you mean?' She

grimaced. 'The husbands of all the women he slept with?'

'Anyone in particular?'

'He didn't give me the names. But …'

Caren looked up. 'But what?'

'He caught chlamydia from someone. I only found out when I happened to find an empty packet of pills. He didn't tell me about it. He never knew about it for a long time.'

'Did he pass on to you?'

'No, we always took precautions.'

'Did he pass it on to anybody else?'

'Can't say.' Anna seemed to be tiring. Her head drooped and her concentration lapsed.

When Caren ended their conversation, the relief on Anna's face was obvious.

Feeling the sun on her face, Caren was pleased to be outside, and as she drove away, she raised her hand to Anna, still standing by the front door, still looking quite different from the night before.

Drake read the CSI report from start to finish, trying to fix the details in his mind. There were no samples, no footprints, no traces – he often wondered how the CSIs could enjoy fingertip searches of crime scenes, looking for the merest scrap of evidence. He ticked off each paragraph, the frustration that they had found nothing to help the investigation building. He found a piece of plain paper and in the middle drew a large circle in which he wrote the number four. He always found this exercise calming, directing his mind by the physical discipline of writing something down.

Through the closed door of his office he could hear the voices of the officers in his team. He thought about the sudoku in the newspaper that morning. Despite sitting in the car concentrating on the puzzle, pencil in hand, he hadn't managed one square and it was starting to rile him. He sipped from his mug of coffee. The packet had said finest Italian, but Drake regretted not sticking to his usual brand, as the coffee was weak and tasteless. He continued drawing arrows into the centre of the circle on the paper. At the beginning of each arrow he scribbled an explanation – house number, unlikely; clue to another song, maybe; connection with the Crimea Pass, tentative; counting down to more killings, frightening. He couldn't shake off an overwhelming feeling of foreboding.

He placed the report into one corner of the desk before leaving his office. In the middle of the Incident Room, Winder was sitting at his desk, staring at the computer.

'Something odd about these messages, boss.'

'Explain, please.'

'I put together a log of where the patrol car had been that night. Everything seemed to be normal until midnight. They did the usual sort of patrol. Up and down the A55 then stationary, waiting for speeders. They called in when they stopped for something to eat. Then they stopped to fill the car with petrol – we have the exact time from the petrol station. The first hoax call took them from Porthmadog over the causeway.'

'Have we traced the caller?'

'It was a mobile number and he left a message.'

'Haven't they got protocols about taking details?'

'Normally, they would get a date of birth and a contact telephone number. I've listened to the recording of the call. This guy didn't let them interrupt at all – he just kept talking. His voice sounds like a tape-recorded message.'

'And the second call?'

Winder looked grim. 'That was the one that took them to the Crimea. After the first call, they were the closest patrol car. Same as the first call – no details – just a message. Our man must have been following them.'

'He could have followed them all night,' Drake said slowly.

'Bastard.'

'Might be two, of course.'

'Fucking bastards.'

Drake ignored the anger in Winder's voice. 'Any CCTV pictures?'

'Nothing so far. I haven't been able to identify every single CCTV camera that they might have passed but—'

'If we can identify a car that was following them, we might get a lead?'

'Yes, boss.' Winder turned back to the computer screen.

Drake stared at the photofit likeness and he knew that, despite the artist sitting for two hours with Rio Hawkins and Mildred, the owner of the taxi firm who had delivered the original message, the image wasn't going to help.

Rio Hawkins was scratching the tattoos on his arms and Mildred had a wide-eyed look on her face that suggested she had no idea what was going on. Drake decided that Mildred was probably responsible for the smell of dirty clothes and unwashed bodies in the room.

He longed for a case where a photofit would be an exact representation of the culprit.

'Can we go now?' Mildred asked.

Drake ignored her. The artist gave a half-hearted cough but it didn't interrupt Drake's concentration as he willed himself to believe that somehow the exercise of creating this face would help.

'What was his accent like?' Drake asked.

'We get all sorts.' There was an irritated edge to her voice.

Drake looked at her. She was rotund and her cheeks had been coloured a damp-grey, probably from hours spent in a small room with only a telephone for company.

'Answer the question'.

She swallowed nervously.

'Was it a Scouse accent? You've heard it a hundred times.'

'Ah ...'

'Or Mancunian?'

'I don't—'

'Think very hard, Mildred,' Drake said, getting just the exact amount of menace into his voice that he'd intended. 'You are almost certainly the only person to have spoken to the killer.' He leant forward. 'He's killed two police officers. He's capable of killing again.'

Mildred blinked and then her eyes darted around the room as she gathered her thoughts.

'It wasn't Scouse. Definite, I'd remember that.'

'Mancunian?'

She gave him a puzzled look.

'Manchester,' he said, adding, 'what did he say?'

'I can't remember every word. He just wanted the envelope delivered to Police headquarters."

The smug look on her face disappeared when Drake responded, 'That's all?'

'Yes.'

'Nothing else.'

'No.'

'What about the fare?'

'He left twenty quid on the counter.'

Drake sat back, imagining the scene in the small taxi office.

'And the accent?' he said, giving up any realistic prospect of anything substantial coming from Mildred.

'I'd guess he was local. Didn't sound English to me.'

She folded her arms, now, as though she was ready to leave.

Drake turned into the small track leading to Caren's farmhouse, and when one of the tyres found a pothole the car lurched to one side. After years of working with a sergeant who had more interest in Liverpool Football Club than policing, it had taken Drake time to find the right approach to working with Caren. She could be annoying and untidy but when he pushed a suspect too far she could be there to pull things back. A part of him didn't want to admit that he had become accustomed to her and that he was beginning to rely on her.

He pulled the car into the gravelled area by the back door and saw Alun walking down through the fields behind the house. His T-shirt had a picture of a large red tongue against a black background that had faded badly. Alun raised a hand and Drake nodded.

'She's on her way,' Alun said, as he approached Drake.

Alun was the odd half of the couple and Drake failed to see the attraction for Caren. The beard was a limp attempt, with wispy bits of red-coloured hair below his chin, and when he got closer Drake could smell sweat and manure and the rich loamy smell of animal feed. There were bits of alpaca wool on his T-shirt and for a moment Drake worried that Caren would bring some onto the car's clean leather upholstery.

'Hope you catch the killer,' Alun said, standing by Drake.

'Me too,' Drake said.

Caren appeared from the back door and crunched over the gravel. Then Drake noticed her shoes – they were scuffed and untidy and he could imagine the dirt that they might leave in his car. Perhaps it had been a bad idea to agree to collect her. Drake gave her a furtive look as she climbed into the car, flaring his nostrils, hoping there wouldn't be a smell, but relaxing when he couldn't see any alpaca wool or detect the odour of the farm.

Drake powered the Alfa down the Conwy valley, retracing their first journey to the crime scene. Caren took the opportunity to tell him how hard Alun was working with the alpacas and that she had plans to redecorate over the summer.

They reached the top of the Crimea Pass and pulled into a lay-by. In daylight, Drake could see how the road had been forced through the rugged terrain. He noticed old tracks made by slate workings scarring the side of the mountain. One side of the valley rose off the road to a narrow plateau leading away towards a summit in the distance. Drake knew all the mountains would have names. He reckoned that everywhere in Wales had a name; his grandfather had had names for all the fields on his farm.

The sun was bright but there was still a chill in the air. Drake scrambled to a vantage point, Caren struggling behind him. Drake saw the steep sides of the mountains and the smoke trails from chimneys in Blaenau Ffestiniog. Even in early summer it was barren and windswept. He built an image in his mind of the scene on Monday night. The patrol car would have stopped. A routine RTA – no problem. The killer must have been waiting for them: sitting in his car – or was he hiding by the side of the road? Drake looked down – there was nowhere to hide. The killer had walked over to them, greeted the officers, and then shot them.

'Why here?' he said.

Caren sounded breathless as she stood by his side before launching into an in-depth analysis. Drake had learnt to curb his annoyance at her enthusiasm. He turned in a complete circle trying to picture the killer. Why had the killer chosen the Crimea? What made the pass special? There had to be something and he had to find it. His eyes followed the contours of the mountains, searching for inspiration.

They returned to the car and continued towards Blaenau Ffestiniog. They were early for their appointment with the engineer who had found the bodies, so Caren suggested lunch. The massive tips of slate-waste cast a gloominess over the town, making the atmosphere feel dark and oppressive. They walked along the high street, passing shops converted into homes or boarded-up altogether, and Drake remembered the anger in his father's voice whenever their conversations turned to history or politics. 'Years of exploitation, Ian. Makes my blood boil,' he would say.

In a cold, almost empty café, Drake stared at the sandwich on his plate and at the dirty yellow liquid passing for coffee in a chipped mug. The bread was like plastic cotton wool and stuck to the roof of his mouth as he chewed. Caren was enjoying a pasty that she had covered with brown sauce. She ate mouthfuls between noisy slurps of tea.

'Anna's going back to work tomorrow,' she said.

Drake looked at the crumbs Caren had left on the plate, trying to imagine how she could have enjoyed the food.

'Isn't it a bit soon?'

'She doesn't want to sit around getting depressed.'

'Is she still staying with her mother?'

Caren slurped her tea, before stirring a third teaspoon of sugar into the mug.

'Yes. When she moved in with Mathews she gave up her flat.'

Drake nodded. 'Did she help at all?'

'She knew about his reputation. But she was single – younger than him. She has her own career. And she never made any demands of him.'

Another noisy mouthful of tea.

'No help at all then,' Drake cut across her. He moved his plate further away and tugged at the cuffs on his shirt, before checking his trousers for spills and food crumbs.

'She did say something about the children. Mathews had regular contact – once a month.'

'Really?' Drake thought about Fiona – *he couldn't be bothered*.

'So Fiona's comment doesn't add up.'

Drake had seen the hatred in Fiona Trick's eyes and guessed that time had not healed her wounds.

'And he had chlamydia.'

Drake raised his eyebrows.

Caren finished her mug of tea but Drake left half of the weak coffee, before paying their bill and leaving. The power plant was well signposted from the middle of the town, the road narrowing to a single-track road as they reached the main building. Leaving the car, Drake turned to look down towards the town, at the uniformity of the terraces and the drabness of the houses. Behind him Caren was shaking hands with a man who had emerged from the offices.

'Malcolm Naton,' the man said, holding out his hand to Drake.

'Detective Inspector Drake.'

Naton led them inside. The flickering bank of dials and computer screens was in marked contrast to the old and ageing faces that had passed the window of the café where Drake and Caren had just eaten their lunch.

Drake immediately noticed the trace of bleach in the air of Naton's office and, apart from a pile of bound reports in one corner of the desk, the office was clean and spotless.

'I was the duty manager,' Naton said, when Drake asked why he had been out in the small hours.

'What does that mean?'

'If there's an emergency then I could be called at any time. A little after midnight a problem arose with one of the generators. A telephone call couldn't resolve it.'

'Do you always turn out for a problem?'

'No, we try to resolve it on the telephone. Once the engineer couldn't solve the problem, he rang back. I knew then I'd have to turn out.'

'Describe your journey.'

'I gave most of the details to the officer on the night.'

'Well, tell it to me again. Even the merest scrap of information might be relevant, just some recollection from your journey. Take me through it step-by-step.'

Naton gave Drake an irritated glance.

'I left the house about half past one, quarter to two. I can't be certain of the time. It's a forty-minute drive from where I live. I know the route very well. When I got to the top of the Crimea it was about two-fifteen. First thing I noticed was the headlights of the car. They seemed to be on full beam. Then I noticed the passenger side door was open. At first I didn't think there was anything wrong.'

'What, a car with its passenger side door open and lights on full beam? That must have told you something was wrong.'

Naton made a non-committal reply, looking hurt, before he continued. 'I slowed down and passed the car. As I did, I saw the man in the driver's seat. I rang the emergency services.'

'Do you remember anything unusual on your journey?'

'No. Nothing.'.

Drake wanted to know everything Naton could remember. He pressed the engineer – getting him to search all his memories. 'Do you pass much traffic that time of night?'

'No, hardly any.'

'If you had noticed a car travelling towards you, it would have been unusual?'

'Yes, I suppose it would.'

'Try and remember. Did you pass another vehicle coming down the pass?'

Naton hesitated. 'I've already told the other officers.'

'Well, tell me.' Drake persisted. 'If the killer was travelling by car he's likely to have passed you.'

A frightened look crossed Naton's face. 'The only thing I can remember is near the Waterloo Bridge. I noticed this car with its full headlights on. I was slowing down for the junction onto the main road and the car turned left over the bridge. It seemed to be travelling very fast. I can't say whether it'd come off the pass.'

'What type of car was it?'

Naton hesitated. 'I can't be certain ... I think it was a Ford Mondeo.'

'And the colour?'

'Red, definitely red.'

'Did you get a look at the driver?'

'Man, I think. Don't ask me anything else about him.'

'Registration number?'

'You must be joking. It was the middle of the night.'

After finishing with Naton, they walked back to the car. Looking out over the town Drake noticed a thin plume of smoke climbing into the afternoon sunshine behind houses with pristine slate roofs and then he heard the sound of the narrow gauge engine rattling over points as it approached the town.

'Did you check Naton out?' Drake said.

'Nothing known, sir. He had a warning for possession of cannabis when he was at university.'

'That's almost an essential requirement for a CV these days.' Drake sighed. 'At least we have something.'

Approaching the car, he retrieved his mobile from his jacket pocket and dialled Winder's number.

'Gareth, suspect may have been using a red Ford Mondeo. Concentrate everything to see if you can identify a car like that on the CCTV footage.'

Chapter 9
Friday 4th June

It had to be same routine every time, move the phone a couple of millimetres, check the paperwork was in neat piles, close the blinds, ensure the bin was in its proper place and then switch off the lights. Luckily nobody ever noticed the ritual at work, but if Drake had to leave the office in a hurry he could feel the anxiety rising like a mist at dawn. Once he was finished he dragged on his jacket and stuffed his mobile into a pocket. Caren joined him and they walked down to the car park.

It took them half an hour through traffic chocked with caravans and trailers to reach the hospital mortuary. A man in a dirty white coat sat slumped before a computer screen playing patience. He gave Drake and Caren a blank stare but once Drake had flashed his warrant card the man let out a tired sigh, got up and led them into the mortuary. The smell of formaldehyde hit them. Drake looked at Lee Kings, who turned to his colleague.

'Detective Inspector Ian Drake. This is Dr Nicholas Crewe.'

Drake held out a hand; Caren did the same.

'How do you do?' Crewe was a tall man with short-cropped hair, a clipped public school accent and a brisk handshake.

The mortuary assistant wheeled the first of the bodies to the centre of the floor. Both doctors began to look excited. Drake had always thought that being a pathologist required a certain macabre approach to medicine. Rather than the job of treating the living, mending the sick, and looking after children with running noses and sticky ears, the pathologist's task was gruesome. It seemed so mechanical, without risk, cutting up a dead body, moving the bits around like a pass-the-parcel game. It often struck Drake that after years of academic training it took a particular breed of person to spend their professional careers with dead people.

Crewe started removing Mathews's clothes, then cleared his throat and began dictating his report. He held the scissors in one hand and expertly cut the shirt and laid the fabric carefully into receptacles.

Crewe peered into the bloodied mess in the middle of Mathews's chest. 'There's a bolt of some sort. Interesting.' Kings nodded slowly.

Crewe straightened and looked at Drake.

'The only weapon I know of that uses bolts like this is a crossbow.'

Crewe continued with his examination, until he leant down and carefully tugged at the projectile, eventually pulling it clear.

'The bolt entered the body at an angle. Approximately forty-five degrees, I'd say. It would suggest that he was shot while sitting in the car.'

The bolt made a dull clanking sound in the receptacle. Kings had a curious look on his face as he lowered his head and scanned the greying flesh. Crewe had moved his attention to Mathews's left shoulder and then moved his latex-covered hands further down the torso. He asked Kings for a second opinion and stood back for a moment as the junior pathologist repeated the examination.

'Interesting, don't you think?' Crewe announced.

Kings murmured in approval.

'What do you make of them?'

'Can't be certain.'

'Are you thinking the same as me?'

Kings moved away and began a more detailed examination of the clothes removed from Mathews's body.

There was an edge of sarcasm to Drake's voice when he spoke. 'Sorry to interrupt gentlemen. But do you have something to share with us?'

Crewe raised his right hand and gave a wave, inviting them towards the table.

'There are two puncture wounds on this man's body. Quite high up, just above the shoulder blade. There is a distance of approximately fifteen inches between both wounds. As you can see, the wounds are tiny. Once we have completed a more detailed examination we can tell how far these wounds penetrate the flesh.'

His manner was cold, emotionless.

'The wounds suggest a Taser weapon was used.'

'Can you be certain?' Drake asked, inching nearer the table.

'That's why Dr Kings is examining the victim's clothing,' Crewe said. 'As you know, Inspector, every Taser or, I should say, every *lawful* Taser, discharges tell-tale dots that enable the weapon to be traced.'

Kings laid out all the clothes Mathews had been wearing and was picking through each one, examining every fold and crease. The look on his face made it clear he wasn't finding anything.

'Nothing. No sign of any dots.'

Crewe continued. 'A conundrum for you, therefore, Inspector Drake. Evidence of a Taser weapon on the body but no remnants of any dots on the clothes. Did the crime scene investigators find anything in the car?'

Drake thought about the CSI report and knew there had been no suggestion of the discharge of a Taser. Drake ran through the alternatives in his mind – the dots might have been discharged outside the car, far enough away not to contaminate the officers' clothes. He dismissed any possibility of the killer having cleaned away the dots.

Before he had time to reply, Crewe continued. 'A Taser fires two projectiles that hit the body up to twenty-five inches apart. It depends, of course, on the distance between the person discharging the Taser and the target. The projectile can pierce clothing and penetrates the skin to about half an inch.'

It meant an urgent call to Foulds once they had finished,

Drake concluded. The sound of a rattling saw blade brought his attention back to the post mortem table. Drake had never been good with the sight of blood and seeing the drills and saws splattered red on the various tables made his stomach turn. Crewe continued dictating into the microphone, occasionally seeking a second opinion from Kings. Eventually Crewe finished and placed various body parts back into the gaping hole in the rib cage. Once he was done, the body was sewn up and then removed. The mortuary assistant returned, wheeling in Danny Farrell.

Crewe announced with obvious enthusiasm, 'Well, let's see if we can find some Taser dots on this gentleman.'

The look of learnt curiosity had returned to the faces of both pathologists as they removed Farrell's clothing.

'Nothing so far,' Crewe announced to no one in particular.

Irrational, perhaps, but Drake was taking a dislike to Crewe, with his lengthy vowels and condescending manner – maybe he was too English, maybe too upper-class: the accent was definitely a relic and nobody said *How do you do* any more. He glanced at Caren and noticed a strained look on her face, as though she was concentrating too hard.

'As I understand it,' Crewe continued, 'this officer was found outside the car. The bolt has entered further, suggesting the crossbow was fired at point-blank range. Death would have been instantaneous.'

'And the Taser?' asked Drake.

'Yes, of course. I'm coming to that.'

The pathologist hesitated, adjusted his footing and inspected more of Farrell's flesh.

'I can't see any evidence at present which suggests a Taser projectile.'

'So it's clear then,' Drake added. 'Both killed with a crossbow: only one shot with a Taser. Thanks, Doctor. We have a killer to catch.'

Drake found himself hurrying out of the mortuary with

Caren. He pushed open the doors and strode into the car park, where the air tasted fresh and clean. An ambulance was arriving at A&E, its lights dying as it slowed. High above, thick white clouds were floating in the summer sky. They walked quickly to the car.

'I hate post mortems,' Caren said between deep breaths.

'We'll need to talk to Mike,' Drake said, reaching for his mobile.

Back at headquarters, Drake pushed open the door to the Incident Room and saw his junior officers crowded round a computer, surfing the internet. Winder sat alongside Foulds; standing behind them was Howick, the stitches evident on his broken nose, the flesh around his eye turning dark brown. After standing in the mortuary for hours, Drake's clothes stank of reeking flesh and now he could barely conceal his annoyance.

'Haven't you got enough to do?' Drake began.

'You might like to see this, sir,' Winder said.

Foulds left his chair and motioned for Drake to sit down.

The computer screen flickered with a clip from YouTube. Winder clicked the 'play' button and the screen came to life with the scene of a man shot with a Taser, his body recoiling and then falling flat, incapacitated, as he screamed in pain.

'Yes, I know. I've seen these videos before.' Drake sounded impatient.

It had been a couple of years since a superintendent in Western Division had subjected himself to a Taser attack, as part of a publicity stunt, that ended up on YouTube.

'But you haven't seen this before, sir,' Winder added, flicking back to the Google search.

In just a couple of clicks the screen came to life again. The video title said *How To Build Your Own Taser*. Drake sat and watched the instructions played out on the screen with growing interest. It looked simple and straightforward – the presenter even said it was 'child's play'. All the parts were assembled on the table and the voice gave a running commentary on how helpful a Taser could be. They all watched in silence, guessing that the killer must have watched the same clip.

'It's about the only explanation we've got, Mike,' Drake said. 'There's no other way he could have killed Mathews in the car.'

'The killer must have used a Taser on Mathews. That would have given him enough time to reload the crossbow. Jesus, this guy was really well prepared.'

Drake's thoughts were back at the mortuary. Back watching the pathologists cutting and slicing dead bodies. He shivered.

'Thanks Mike. I'll get the pathologist's report to you as soon as. Gareth, we need to find the car and Dave, my office now for an update on Dixon.'

Howick's optimism that Dixon would provide a breakthrough had disappeared. There was a reflective matter-of-fact tone to his voice.

'The alibi checks out – at least with his wife, sir.'

'Details, please.'

'Dixon's wife was quite clear. She gave a specific account of all his movements that afternoon and early evening and through the night. He hadn't gone to the gym that afternoon – she seemed to know all about his girlfriend. Anyway, he picked up his grandchildren from school at the end of the afternoon. Took them for a milkshake. Later that night there was a family party at one of the pubs nearby.'

'And there are lots of family members who will confirm he was there.' Drake sighed, frustrated.

'That's about it, sir.'

'But get them all checked. Just in case.'

Howick looked please with himself as he turned to

Drake, 'And I've found a contact for you in the North Wales Archery Association.'

Drake and Caren followed the sat-nav directions and found themselves in an industrial estate that had old pallets and rusting second-hand cars piled into a fenced enclosure with a sign warning about dogs on the loose. Drake cursed before starting a ten-point turn.

At the main road, Drake parked and Caren darted into a local newsagent before emerging seconds later looking pleased with herself and pointing across the road at a narrow lane leading down past the side of a launderette, towards what looked like a disused railway yard. Drake noticed a dark blue Volvo, which seemed familiar, parked on the opposite side of the road as he drove down the lane. At one end was a flat-roofed building, its white paint fading badly. Drake pushed open the door and heard the sound of a radio from the far corner. A man standing by the side of the bar waved them over.

'Mr Drake? Matt Tudor,' he said, hand outstretched.

'Detective Inspector Drake and this is Detective Sergeant Waits.'

'Come in.'

Tudor took them into the small office behind the bar, stacked high with boxes. He squeezed into a chair behind the desk and motioned for Drake and Caren to sit down.

'The North Wales Archery Association,' Drake said.

'Yes. I'm the secretary.'

Howick had explained that Tudor had complained bitterly about the intrusion into his daily routine. Tudor had eyes that looked like a map of the world and a paunch that was straining the buttons of his shirt to breaking point. Drake imagined that the only competitive sport in which Tudor participated would have been the yard-of-ale.

'Do you have a list of members?'

'Yeh. Somewhere.'

'We need lists for the last three years. Did you know Paul Mathews?'

'Yeh. He was really popular. A real ladies' man.'

Tudor booted up his computer. Caren moved nearer the desk and tilted her head. 'What does the Archery Association do?'

Tudor rolled his eyes. 'Archery. Bows and arrows.'

Drake began to fidget with his hands. Caren persevered. 'Where do they meet?'

'Here, of course.'

'But they don't do the archery here?' Drake said, the irritation clear in his voice.

'Of course not. This is where they come to *socialise*.' He emphasised the last word, as though he were sharing a secret of grave importance.

'You mean …?' Drake said, not really certain what Tudor meant.

'Exactly that. Socialise, make new friends.' Tudor winked at Drake.

'So there wasn't much actual archery?' Caren asked.

'Every Monday night in the summer, down on the sports field and then everyone piles back here. Big ball every summer. Prize-giving and all that.'

Tudor began to mop his brow with a dirty handkerchief. The screen began to glow, and a couple of clicks later Tudor smiled. He stuffed a narrow data stick into the computer and clicked again. Drake was vaguely impressed with Tudor's efficiency.

'Do they shoot crossbows?'

'A few of the members have them. Maybe a dozen. The more serious members.' Another half smile.

Tudor remained in his chair and tugged at the data stick which he handed to Drake.

'You should talk to Sam Walters. He and his brother do a lot with crossbows.'

Chapter 10
Saturday 5th June

Drake found himself on the promenade at Colwyn Bay before realising that he had driven past the turning for headquarters. His thoughts had been dominated by guilt – he'd forgotten Sian's plans for the afternoon with Megan and Helen; he'd promised to see his parents and he'd been lecturing himself that he really had to change. Not even the sound of Springsteen's voice on 'Thunder Road' had distracted him. Drake parked and watched the water lapping against the edge of the concrete. Gradually, his mood improved as he thought about their impending family holiday. He powered down the window and smelt the salt in the breeze. Tomorrow, he determined, they would do something as a family: maybe the beach or the zoo.

In his office Drake fought with the catch on the window before it reluctantly gave way and fresh air streamed into his room. The weather forecast promised high temperatures and Drake saw the faintest whisper of a cloud. After ten minutes on a sudoku – labelled hard – from one of the books in his desk he knew his mind would focus more clearly.

He logged on to his computer and scrolled through his emails. He had to open every one, just to check, convincing himself that he had to read them all. There were three from the press office, all saying the same thing. The press wanted more details, asking when the next press conference was going to be, and the woman from PR wanted to know when she could tell them something. There was a pleading tone to her final email. He deleted all but one. He replied, telling her he had nothing further she could give the press. An urgent email from a CPS lawyer reminded him about an imminent court case. Drake left the email in the inbox, hoping he wouldn't forget.

Drake was pleased with the interruption when the telephone rang.

'Someone in reception for you.'
'Who?'
'Says she has information about the Mathews case.'

'I sent them death threats.'

Geraldine Evans hadn't slept for days by the look on her face. The bags were black and she had the burnt-out look common in drug addicts. Drake glanced over at Caren who was giving the woman a wary stare. There were always time-wasters in every case and Drake wondered if this was just another.

'What threats do you mean?' Drake knew the details weren't public knowledge and worried that information might have been leaked.

'The one I sent to Paul Mathews.'

'Why did you send them?'

'Because he was a bastard and he ...'

'And he what?'

'I only meant to frighten him.'

'Why?' Drake asked again.

'Because he was a bastard and—'

'Geraldine, why was Mathews a bastard?'

'He promised me everything. Said I was the one ...' She started crying and, fumbling for a handkerchief, blew her nose.

'When did you meet Paul Mathews?'

'It was at the Archery Club. You know – that *social club*. I'd just finished with my boyfriend. And we'd lost a baby and I didn't know what to do. I went with my friend. Said I should get out and meet people. I wanted to get back with my boyfriend but I met Paul and he told me I was the only woman he'd ever loved. And we had sex all the time. Even in his patrol car.'

'What happened?'

She began sobbing. 'And then I found out he'd been

with my friend.'

Caren had her brow knotted now and her arms crossed.

'Tell me about the threats?' Drake said.

Geraldine recounted how she'd torn pieces of newspaper and arranged them in a message she'd sent to the police with Mathews's name written on the envelope. She'd even been careful to buy a self-adhesive envelope. Caren was nodding as she made notes while Geraldine was talking.

Drake realised that Geraldine seemed far too sad to be the killer.

'Why come forward now?'

'He's dead and I never wanted him dead. I just wanted …'

She stopped crying when Drake formally arrested her, telling her they'd need to interview her again. He let Caren process her in the custody suite and returned to his office, already thinking about the middle square of the sudoku.

Superintendent Price had developed a stripped-down and economical approach to writing emails. No pleasantries or the customary *Hi* and *Regards* – just a simple one line.

'Con call with CC – 13.00.'

Glancing at the time, Drake saw he had over an hour to prepare. He took off his watch and propped it up on his desk. He reached for his notebook, reviewing his to-do lists. His thoughts were dominated by the need for order, precision and he turned to look at the desk. It was still chaotic. He had to cope, had to make sense of things. He needed coffee. In the kitchen he found the cafetière and alongside it a tin of ground coffee. Once the kettle had boiled, he counted a minute in his head before pouring the water. He pushed back the cuffs of his shirt – a powder-blue button-down, standard sleeve, worn with a striped tie – and set the time. The coffee had to brew for two and a half minutes. Any less and it would taste weak, any more and it would be tacky.

Comforted by his routine, he returned to the office where he turned his attention to the human resources files of Mathews and Farrell. They were heavier than the versions he had seen before.

The files read like a manual of how-to-be-a-shit-policeman and Drake felt a growing sense of resentment that they had remained in the force. It was officers like Mathews and Farrell that made his work that much harder. There were regular complaints from the public, all dismissed with the minimum of inquiry, despite assurances that a thorough investigation had taken place. Mathews had nine lives and Farrell had done everything to equal him – they must have had a guardian angel, thought Drake.

Farrell had transgressed with another officer and that made it worse. Drake read the complaint about his conduct. He guessed how the bitterness could build up as Farrell's behaviour worsened and each successive complaint was ignored. A pattern was clear: in every transgression of Farrell's, Mathews accompanied him, but Mathews needed no company for wrongdoing, until Traffic had the good sense to ensure he was always partnered. Satisfied that the files were complete, he placed them on the edge of his desk before refastening his watch and heading out to the bathroom.

Drake stood before the mirror and washed his hands, then drew a comb through his hair before checking his tie. His only concession to the informality of working on a Saturday was to wear a jacket rather than a suit. Content with his appearance, he made his way over to the senior management suite.

Drake was early, so he talked to Hannah, Price's secretary, exchanging small talk about the investigation.

'There are so many rumours going around,' she said.

Drake mumbled a reply, thinking about the rumours about her and Price. The door to Price's office opened and he greeted Drake warmly before he marched over to the video conference room.

'Did you watch that programme on TV last night?' Price asked, pausing outside the door.

'Yes, sir,' Drake, said recalling the documentary he had watched when he eventually got home. It had contained various commentators and politicians reassuring the viewers about the WPS's ability to find the killer.

'They're right of course,' Price said. 'Killing police officers strikes at the heart of our society. It'll reopen calls for the death penalty and there'll be more talk about arming the police.'

Drake nodded. The newspapers had been full of the details and he knew there would already be journalists all over North Wales digging into the story.

Inside, the large monitor was already glowing when they entered. Price fiddled with some controls and Riskin's face appeared on the screen. By the time they'd finished Drake had heard the words *political dimension* and *high profile* a dozen times. No pressure then, he concluded as he walked back through headquarters, realising he was hungry.

The canteen was quiet; a couple of civilian support staff chatted loudly before ordering a pizza and joked about all the overtime they were earning for working on a Saturday. He picked up a tired-looking tuna sandwich and a bottle of water. Once he'd paid, he scanned the room, looking for a table and saw John Moxon, who raised an eyebrow and motioned to the empty chair at his table.

'All right, Ian?'

Drake smiled at his friend and sat down. He broke open the sandwich.

'Another Saturday away from the family?'

'I know. I know,' Drake replied. 'How's life in operational support?'

'Same shit – different day. You know how it is,' Moxon said, tearing open the Cellophane of a flapjack. 'How are you coping?'

Moxon was five years older than Drake, but they had joined the force on the same day. Somehow, Drake always knew that Moxon wouldn't aspire to the promotion that he himself wanted and because of that they became friends. Moxon had been the one person that Drake had confided in when the rituals and worries became so severe that one night he had been at his desk until midnight staring at a pile of papers. Moxon had sat with him until he had finally managed to go home.

'Sian says I'm getting obsessed again.'

Drake crunched on a piece of cucumber and then swallowed a bite of tuna sandwich. 'Are you?'

Drake raised his eyebrows.

'Sian wants me to have counselling.'

'Does Price know?'

'I was in the office late one night last week when he came into the Incident Room.'

'What did he say?'

'Told me to go home.'

'Fat chance of getting the WPS to be supportive.'

Drake shrugged, recalling the incident when Moxon had talked to a man perched on a ledge of the Britannia Bridge for an hour before he threw himself to his death. The man's final words – *I don't know how you'll live with yourself* – had haunted Moxon for months until the pain seemed to subside. Drake had persuaded Moxon to ask for counselling but the chairman of the police authority rejected the request on the grounds of costs-saving. Eventually Moxon got shunted into operational support, pushing paper around, his prospects of promotion extinguished.

A flattened piece of white bread had as usual stuck limpet-like to the top of Drake's mouth. He raised a hand to his lips and stuck a finger into the middle of the sticky mass.

'Family well?' Moxon continued.

'Yes. Busy. Sian complained like hell last week when I didn't get home until after midnight two nights running.'

'She knows what it's like.'

'I couldn't remember why I was in the office. I left at eleven but I had to go back just to check the paperwork.'

Moxon nodded. Drake finished the water, dislodging the final scraps of the bread with his tongue. Moxon finished the last of his tea and they stood outside the canteen.

'Thanks for the chat,' Drake said.

It was the nearest he got to thanking Moxon properly, and as he walked back to his office he felt the burden of his worries rested, somehow, even if the darkest corner of his mind knew it might only be temporary.

Drake had spotted the blue Volvo when it turned off at the same exit as him. It might have been a coincidence but he took a different route from usual and then parked, feigning a call on his mobile and watching as the Volvo passed him. He noted down the registration number before resuming his journey.

A mixture of nostalgia and apprehension dominated his mind that afternoon as he slowed the car and then turned down into the drive to his parents' smallholding. He appreciated the views over Caernarfon Bay more now as an adult than he ever did as a boy. The sea shimmered and Drake could see small craft out in the bay enjoying the summer sunshine. The haze over the land made him think of the expressions his grandfather had about predicting the weather – passed down through the generations of farmers who had to know when it might rain or when the winds from the north would cut through the warmest clothes and chill people to the bone. And then in the spring they had to know when the temperatures would rise. The older Drake got the more he thought about his grandfather, the more he recognised the familiar affectations in his father's expressions, the more he realised how much he missed his grandfather.

He parked outside the front door and watched his mother walk out to greet him. The sound of vulnerability in her voice on the phone had told him something wasn't right.

His mother was tall with short, grey hair and a round, warm face. She looked heavier than Drake remembered, but then she always complained about her weight.

'It's lovely to see you, Ian.'

He kissed her and gave her a hug.

She made tea and fussed about, offering him sandwiches and cakes.

'Just tea, Mam, thanks.'

'I'm really worried about your father. He doesn't seem to want to do anything,' she began. 'It's not like him: I know something is wrong. He's made an effort today to mend the fences, knowing you were coming.'

Drake listened as his mother told him her worries. His father had been losing weight, and she was trying to get him to eat, but nothing seemed to work. Drake could imagine how his father would get restless and introverted by his wife's attention.

'And he is so short-tempered,' she added.

And you can be quite awkward, Drake thought. Perhaps his father was just irritated by retirement, angry at the unfamiliarity of domestic routine. He considered suggesting a cruise, but thought better of it.

After finishing his tea, he pulled on a pair of old wellington boots and made his way to the bottom field where his father was busy mending fences. He was wearing a one-piece overall and underneath Drake noticed a crescent-shaped band of perspiration on the T-shirt.

'Not overdoing it, Dad?'

'Take that jacket off and give me a hand.'

'Another time maybe.'

They stood and talked – about the fences, about how his father was going to improve the drainage in the fields, about the hedgerows and the grants available to stop farmers being farmers. It wasn't like the farming his father remembered as a boy. They stood in the warm June sunshine, passing the time of day.

Drake could sense his father knew why he had called and was making an effort, being too talkative. 'Mam's worried about you,' he said eventually.

His father bowed his head slightly and said nothing. Now, Drake knew something was wrong.

'I've got something to tell you,' he said.

Chapter 11
Monday 7th June

Caren could hear Drake's muffled voice through the door but it was difficult to make out exactly what he was saying. It reminded her how difficult it had been to fathom out Drake when she started working with him. One of her friends had curled up her nose when she'd heard that Caren was going to work with Drake. Rather you than me, she'd said, adding something about him being a bit odd.

Caren had been thinking about the interview with Paula Farrell, pondering how Drake might have handled it better, how he might have been more sympathetic. She had often found herself softening the edges of interviews that he conducted with witnesses and grieving families. The interview with Laura Mott would need sensitive handling and she'd been considering the alternatives as she drove into work that morning, trying to decide on how best to mention it. After all, Drake was her superior, but it was an interview with a former police officer who'd made a complaint of sexual harassment, and it seemed only fair to her that it be handled in a certain way.

It had been difficult finding Laura Mott. The address provided by human resources proved a blank and she wasn't listed in the telephone directory. Eventually, Caren found a serving police officer who knew where she lived. After a long period of silence from Drake's room, she tilted her head forwards trying to decide if he'd finished. She walked to his door and he waved her in.

'Just finished,' Drake said, adjusting the telephone on his desk and tidying the papers into square piles. Caren noticed two long columns of Post-it notes set out on the desk, neatly arranged by colour.

'I was wondering, sir. Laura Mott.'

'Yes. We ready to go?'

Drake stood up. Caren took the initiative.

'I think it might be better if I were to take the lead in the interview with her. She might be more cooperative with me. Might see you as a threat.'

Drake narrowed his eyes slightly and rearranged the rest of the papers on his desk. 'Yes. Might do, I suppose.'

Caren could see him working on the alternatives in his mind.

'And we do want to get the most out of her. She might be crucial for the case.'

Drake walked round the desk, reached for his jacket from the wooden hanger, and draped it over one arm. He cast his eyes over his desk and around the room. Caren followed his eyes – everything was in its rightful position, no empty coffee mug or scrap of paper out of place. A newspaper had been folded carefully and she noticed the half-finished sudoku with pencil marks in the margin.

'Okay. You do the interview but I'll interrupt when and if.'

She turned to leave, pleased with her small victory.

After a few minutes' driving they'd left Colwyn Bay and were heading down narrow country lanes. Caren had her window open, and the wind ruffled her hair, blowing it across her face untidily. They found the house easily; a clean white painted sign at the bottom of a long drive made it difficult to miss. The driveway was immaculate, lined with new fencing and clean pebbles in the borders.

Laura didn't appear surprised when she found them standing outside her front door. She was five-foot-six with shoulder-length blonde hair and perfect make-up.

'I've been expecting you,' she said, turning on her heels.

They stepped into the hall – fresh flowers in a tall vase sat on a dust-free table – and followed her into the lounge. Laura waved vaguely at the sofas, and Caren and Drake sat down. Before Caren said anything, Laura spoke.

'He was a slimy piece of shit.'

Good start – it can only get better, thought Caren.

'I was expecting you to contact me,' she continued, sounding disinterested.

'It took a bit of time to find you.' Caren explained about the former address.

'I haven't lived there for years – before I was married. And my married name is Harrod.'

Caren nodded – that would explain the wild-goose chase.

The room was like a photograph from one of the magazines you might flick through in the dentist's waiting room. A large seascape dominated one wall above an immaculately polished sideboard made of some exotic wood. Laura sat across from Caren on the edge of another matching sofa, and Caren noticed the expensive jeans and the still more expensive perfume that hung in the air. Drake sat by her side, notebook in hand.

'How long did you work with Danny Farrell?' Caren asked.

'Far too long.' She emphasised every word.

'I know you made various complaints about him—'

Before she could finish Laura interrupted. 'And each complaint was ignored. I don't really want to think about it. But he's dead now. At the time, I believed the complaints procedure might have worked. I followed all the right protocols. But it was no good.'

'Can you tell me a bit more about the complaints?'

'Haven't you read the file?'

'Yes ... but I was hoping you could ... sort of fill in the blanks.'

Caren noticed the perfect eye shadow above the unblinking eye contact – she could never spend the time such make-up needed every morning.

'He was a slimy piece of shit.'

Caren got the picture – the woman *really* didn't like him.

'What exactly happened?'

'It began with the groping in the car. Couldn't keep his hands to himself. It just got worse after that.'

'When did you make the first complaint?'

'God, I can't remember. It'll be in the file.'

'What did the investigating officer tell you to do?'

'Follow the standard bullying procedure,' she said. 'And all that meant was seeing if I could resolve it myself. Fat lot of good that did. He just got worse. Always made innuendos about having sex. And at the start, I'd just got married, so he must have thought it was a big joke.'

Caren flicked through the file on her lap. 'You asked to be moved.'

'Twice. Two formal requests not to work with him.'

'And?'

'Nothing happened, surprise, surprise. Then I applied for a transfer – that took ages. I even applied to do the sergeant's course. Then I made a formal complaint about him. Eventually that got some results – one of the officers in Traffic spoke to me about *my career.*'

'Who was that?' Drake interrupted.

'Inspector Prewer.'

'What happened?'

She gave Drake a look that said *what do you think?*

'Prewer suggested that if I wanted to move ahead with my sergeant's exams it would be best if I reconsidered. By then I was getting stressed. It was affecting my work. I couldn't sleep and Jim was furious. I thought about giving up quite often.'

Caren sat back in the sofa and allowed her body to fold into the soft leather. Her eye caught the books of photographs of Snowdonia and back issues of *Cheshire Life* neatly arranged on the coffee table. They were all perfectly square, not a millimetre out of place – exactly as Drake would have had them. The eye contact disappeared when Caren asked about her husband. James Harrod was into property, refurbishments and commercial development. She wondered why Laura had needed the aggravation of police work if her husband was a successful property developer.

'What did Jim think of Danny Farrell?' Caren asked.

'How would your husband react?' She looked Caren straight in the eye.

Caren blinked and thought about how Alun might react – storm down to headquarters and make a fool of himself probably.

'Where were you on the night of the murders, Laura?' Caren asked.

'I was out with some girlfriends. Stayed over. I'll give you their names. And James was in the Manor Court Hotel in Chester – business dinner.' She sounded defiant.

Caren scribbled down the details. The interview came to an end and Caren thanked her and stood up.

'You have a lovely home, Laura,' Caren said.

'Thank you.' For the first time Laura seemed to relax.

'Lived here long?' Caren continued.

'Couple of years – we've been doing it up. Jim's business is doing really well. I don't need to work now.'

As they left Caren caught Drake casting his eyes around the room, absorbing the details. Outside the gravel crunched under their feet as they made their way over to the car. Caren swung the door open and allowed the temperature in the car to cool as Drake took off his jacket before folding it neatly onto the back seat.

'What did you make of her?' Drake asked.

'The house didn't look lived in at all.'

'Everything was new, as though she'd gone to a shop and bought the whole showroom.'

'She's an obnoxious cow with the perfect motive,' Caren said, powering the window open.

Drake kept darting glances into the rear-view mirror and on an impulse turned down into a narrow country lane. Caren gave a surprised look. He slowed the car, powered down the window and felt the fresh summer air on his skin. He glanced again into the rear-view mirror but the blue Volvo wasn't there and for a moment he thought he might be too paranoid. But he had the registration, and a couple of telephone calls would find the identity of the driver.

'Where are we going exactly, sir?'

'When I was travelling to see my parents last night I was convinced I was being followed. The same blue Volvo was parked near the Archery Association on Friday. I'm certain that I've seen the car before.'

'There are lots of blue Volvos around. My dad's got one.'

'Maybe it was when we were in Blaenau Ffestiniog.'

'I didn't notice anything.'

'It could have been behind me when I was driving to the area custody suite,' Drake said.

He slowed the car as a tractor approached, followed by a Volvo, but it was red and an estate car, but Drake still stared at the driver, fixing the image of his face in his mind.

'So I thought we'd take the scenic route to see Sam Walters.'

Caren propped an arm on the open window and looked out over the countryside as Drake negotiated various twists and turns. Eventually they pulled into an industrial estate alongside the main A55. When Drake got out he paused, but no blue Volvo was following them.

Walters Bros had their livery adorning the side of a dozen large articulated lorries and smaller vans in the yard. The sign above the door had the company logo and the girl on reception wore a polo shirt with the corporate image stretched over her ample bosom.

'We've got a meeting with Mr Sam Walters,' Drake

said, looking the girl in the eye.

When he appeared through a side door Sam Walters was wearing a white shirt with button-down collars and the Walters Bros image sewn into the fabric. He led them through into a small office that had a window open without any appreciable effect on the temperature inside.

'Tudor at the Archery Association tells me you do a lot with crossbows,' Drake said, passing an evidence pouch over the desk. 'Can you confirm this is a bolt from a crossbow?'

Sam picked up the bag and gave it a quick cursory examination, turning it in his hands.

'Yes. Looks like a very common projectile. Is this what killed …?'

Drake nodded. Sam placed the bag carefully down on the desk.

'Are there groups that use crossbows?'

'The UK has no regulations about owning crossbows. Unlike some European countries where they're classed as weapons.' Sam sat back. 'There's a group of us in the Archery Association. We meet and socialise, have a bit of fun after work – that sort of thing. There's nothing illegal in owning a crossbow. You can buy them on the internet. I know loads of people have done that. Then they give up and sell them on eBay.'

'Can you tell what type of crossbow fired the bolts?'

'They could fit a number of different types.'

'Could you give us the name of different manufacturers?'

'I could have done better than that. I could have shown you a couple of sample crossbows.'

'And?'

'I had a break-in a couple of months ago and two crossbows were stolen.'

'I'll need all the details.' Drake couldn't hide the urgency in his voice.

Once they'd finished he dialled the officer in charge of the burglary and almost shouted down the mobile, demanding for the file to be on his desk within the hour.

Winder spent the afternoon watching CCTV coverage, pretending he was an MI5 intelligence officer in a television drama. Somehow, tracking a red car through North Wales wasn't quite the same. After Drake had told him to concentrate on Betws-y-Coed he double-checked all the possible locations for CCTV coverage. Even if the car had driven through the village, the driver could have turned off before reaching a camera. He knew it was going to be a needle-in-a-haystack job.

He prioritised by trying to track the police car before the killings. He scribbled outline timings in a notepad on his desk, as he scanned the various traffic cameras. After a couple of hours he felt pleased as a timetable took shape. An earlier call to the garage where the car had stopped for petrol had secured the CCTV tapes. He flicked to the date and time recorder. He slowed the search until he found the right time. He pressed 'play' and watched Mathews using the petrol pumps, and then Danny Farrell getting out of the car.

Winder tore open a chicken sandwich and gnawed at the bread as he watched them talking. A sports car pulled up on the forecourt and an attractive woman with long legs climbed out of the car. The patrol car pulled away but he let the CCTV coverage run on and continued admiring the woman's legs as she filled her car with petrol.

Then he saw a Mondeo passing and he stopped eating.

He put down the half-eaten sandwich and checked the timings. It was three minutes after the patrol car had left when the Mondeo passed the camera. Crafty bastard, he thought. Not quite clever enough, though. He replayed the coverage and zoomed in on the car, blowing up the registration number until he was confident he had all the digits. Closing the CCTV coverage on his computer, he accessed the DVLA database and within seconds had a full description. He felt excitement rising; now he knew which car to look for.

Drake had been right: it was red – Admiral Red. He had the name and address of the owner. He fumbled through the telephone directory, but there were pages of Smiths and his impatience grew until he found the right number. He double-checked it again before making the call.

'I sold the car a few weeks ago mate,' Frank Smith replied, giving Winder the details of the garage where he had part-exchanged the vehicle.

This was never going to be an easy case, Winder thought. His heartbeat quickened as he picked up the telephone and dialled the garage's number.

'This is Detective Constable Winder of the Wales Police Service. I'm ringing about the red Ford Mondeo—'

'Oh good, have you found it?'

Winder's heart sank.

Drake had become a regular visitor to the senior management suite on the top floor of headquarters since the morning of the murders. Drake smiled at Price's secretary who motioned her head towards the door into Price's office.

'She's arrived,' Hannah said.

Price stood up and walked towards the door as Drake entered.

'Inspector Drake – this is Dr Margaret Fabrien.'

Fabrien was about five-foot-seven, had a narrow face with a pronounced chin, shoulder-length hair cut into a neat fringe and expensive clothes. Her perfume was spicy and sensuous and filled the air.

'Good afternoon, Inspector.'

He caught a French lilt to the accent. He nodded and returned the greeting.

'I want you to bring Dr Fabrien bang up to date with everything. She's to have access to all the records, all the interviews and statements – everything.'

'I have arranged a desk—' Drake began.

'I shall need privacy,' she cut in. 'It would be inappropriate otherwise. A desk in a room, somewhere quiet.'

'Of course, of course,' Price sounded suitably obliging.

Drake thought about the various rooms that might be available and who might be inconvenienced. There was a small room at the end of a corridor far away from the Incident Room, full of boxes from a previous case. Drake knew it had to be tidied but if she wanted a room, a room they would provide.

'I suggest Dr Fabrien meets the team and works in one of the conference suites for today until we organise a room.'

Price sounded enthusiastic. 'Excellent idea.'

Once the preliminaries were finished, Drake led Dr Fabrien down the main stairwell back to the Incident Room. The weather was still hot, despite the forecast for cooler temperatures, and it felt sticky and uncomfortable. As he pushed open the door, the conversations and tapping of keyboards and clicking of mice came to a sudden halt.

'This is Dr Fabrien, who's going to be working with us,' Drake said.

'Margaret, please,' she said.

There were acknowledgments around the room and snatches of greetings as Drake introduced the team.

'Dr Fabrien is going to be working in one of the conference suites, until we organise a room. So Caren, can you take Margaret—'

Dr Fabrien cut across him. 'I wonder if I may say a few words first?' Not waiting for an answer she continued. 'My role here is to support you as police officers. It's important that everyone understands that. I spoke with the Chief Constable this morning and I appreciate how important this inquiry is.'

Winder and Howick exchanged worried glances. Name-dropping the Chief Constable was clever. No pressure.

Dr Fabrien thanked them all formally and waited for Caren to collect various files and records. Drake returned to his office, picked up the telephone, and called the Incident Room manager.

'We need an office for the profiler. Can you clear the office full of the boxes from that burglary case by the morning?'

'It's very small,' the manager said.

'It'll do,' Drake replied.

He sat by his desk, glaring at the computer screen. He didn't want a profiler messing around with this case – meddling, distracting his attention – it was hard enough without any more interferences. Demanding an office and then implying that she was in charge.

He turned a biro through his fingers and then tapped it onto the desk, clicking it violently. This was his investigation. He was in charge. He ran through the options in his mind, recalling Price's comments – *I want this madman caught* – and dreading the possibility he had missed something and that more deaths would be down to his mistakes.

Chapter 12
Tuesday 8th June

Back in his office, after the funerals of Mathews and Farrell, Drake found it hard to concentrate. The service had been attended by all the senior officers of the Wales Police Service and local and national politicians who looked serious and then gave interviews to the television crews that had taken over the middle of Colwyn Bay. His mind drifted back to the dispassionate stare of Fiona Trick sitting in the congregation. The father of her children had been killed and she gave an Oscar-winning performance as a cold-hearted bitch.

'Caren,' Drake shouted. She appeared at the door of his office and he waved her in.

'Fiona Trick.'

'What about her?'

'Let's look into her some more …'

'You don't think …'

'I don't know what I think,' he said. 'But we need to check out what she said about contact for the kids. It struck me in the chapel that she sat there cold – totally cold. She was married to the man. He was the father of her children.'

'Love can turn to hate so easily.'

'Yes, I know but …'

'What do you want me to do?'

'What do we know about her?'

'Nothing much.'

'Then do all the usual stuff. Background checks, money, friends and lovers, and so on.'

Once Caren left, he loosened his tie and undid the top button of his shirt. Although the papers and notes were multiplying on his desk and his inbox littered with emails needing his attention, he would spend ten minutes on the morning's sudoku.

Geraldine Evans returned promptly for the formal interview and she looked rested. Drake concluded that the catharsis of telling someone what she had done had been beneficial – even her skin looked healthier.

She sat on a chair in the interview room while Drake and Caren fussed with the tape recorder before starting the formalities.

Drake pushed over the first of the death threats with a typed copy of the text.

'Can you confirm that you sent this death threat?'

Geraldine looked down the collection of newspaper cuttings. Then she whimpered and put a hand to her mouth before confirming that it had been her.

'Why did you send this message?'

'I couldn't sleep. And I blamed him for everything that had happened in my life. I didn't want him dead. I just wanted to frighten him.'

Geraldine barely paused for breath as she explained about the circumstances. Occasionally tears welled up in her eyes and she sobbed before pausing to take deep lungfuls of breath. It was an hour later when Drake had finished and the picture of the North Wales Archery Association as a venue for singles and couples meeting for casual sex and fun was complete. Tudor's innuendos had been replaced by names and events and lists of people connected to the club.

'For the record could you please confirm that you also sent the other threats?' Drake said, pointing to the papers on the table.

Geraldine paused, furrowed her brow and looked up at Drake.

'I had nothing to do with these,' she said.

Drake sat, nonplussed for a moment, so Caren took the initiative.

'This is very important, Geraldine. Did you send all of

these other death threats?'

'No. Definitely not.' She blew into a handkerchief. 'Only one.'

'Are you *certain*?'

'Of course.'

'Did you tell anyone that you'd sent the message?'

'No. Of course not,' she said, before adding, 'will I go to prison for a long time?'

Drake stared into her eyes and he knew that he wasn't looking at the murderer.

Caren spent the rest of the day working through the personal papers of Paul Mathews. She sorted everything into piles, postponing a decision about their relevance until she was finished. This was the part of any investigation that she liked the least.

Bank statements were placed in one neat pile, next to them details of Mathews's car loan, a stack of mail from an insurance company and all the guarantees for the television and hi-fi equipment. From the mass of papers, a pile of letters from solicitors began to accumulate, but reading them out of turn made no sense. She shuffled them into date order before starting at the beginning. A picture emerged, enabling her to blank out the noise from the room. She picked up the telephone and made three calls. When she finished she knew progress had been made. She smiled to herself – Drake had been right, again.

Drake sat looking at the lists on his desk.

There were lists of officers who had worked with Mathews and Farrell. Another list of cases where Mathews and Farrell had been together and supplementary lists of cases where they were involved with other officers. A list of the members of the public that had complained about them and now lists of members of the North Wales Archery Association, and also lists of people that Geraldine Evans knew.

It struck him that in the middle of these lists was the name of a person who wanted both officers dead. The scale of the task struck him as Winder almost fell into his office.

'The car's been found, sir.'

'Where?'

Drake was already on his feet as Winder spoke.

'Bangor, burnt out.'

Winder gave Drake a summary of how the car was discovered as he hammered along the A55 until the turning for Bangor. Drake sat silently, hoping there'd be some evidence in the car. Something the killer might have discarded, forgotten in his or her rush.

The industrial estate was a sprawling collection of builders' merchants and timber yards. Half a dozen men in hard hats and dirty high-visibility jackets stood by a burger van looking towards a car park where the remains of the car smouldered. A fire tender was parked nearby and a couple of uniformed officers guarded the entrance.

Drake hurried from the car as the Scientific Support Vehicle parked alongside the Alfa.

'When was it found?' Drake said to Winder.

'Fire brigade was called in the small hours.'

A thick smell of burning plastic hung in the air. Drake walked round the car and knelt by the driver's side. The driver had emerged from this door. Did he have the crossbow with him? What was he wearing?

He heard Foulds talking to the CSIs as they moved boxes of equipment.

'Looks like he did a good job on torching the car,' Foulds said, leaning over Drake. He pointed to the footwell.

'See where it's been burning. Most people who torch a car just throw petrol on the seats which means the footwell still has lots of evidence we can collect. But it looks like the footwell was torched here.'

'So he knew what he was doing?'

'Yes.'

Both men stood up and walked round the car. Drake stopped by the boot. The metal still had the faintest hint of red paint.

He called over to Winder.

'We'll need to know where the car had been from CCTV.'

'That could be practically—'

Drake stopped him. 'Start where the car was stolen. Identify any CCTV locally and then work up a radius. Then get all the CCTV coverage for the last two weeks. He must have filled the car with petrol somewhere.'

Winder looked stricken. It would be a marathon job.

'This could take days, sir.'

Winder would have to learn that police work meant grind, and lots of it.

'Doing anything else?' Drake said.

Foulds crowbarred the boot and they stared inside at the charred remains of a crossbow.

Chapter 13
Wednesday 9th June

He parked under the sagging branches of a tall sycamore at the far end of the car park. He peered into the rear-view mirror and adjusted the ponytail. He took off the baseball cap and adjusted the strap on the back before replacing it on his head until it fitted perfectly. He studied the view of the car park reflected in the mirror.

In the distance, by the side of a gleaming BMW, he saw him kneeling and then struggling with the long laces of his boots. A tall, thin woman with pronounced teeth was standing, arms folded, looking at the fumbling hands. He guessed that the teenagers kicking their heels behind him were the two boys he'd read about. He knew a great deal about the man adjusting his laces, the reason he was here, now, at the foot of Snowdon. He knew where the man lived, what car he owned, where they shopped as a family and the destination of their last holiday. There was a scrapbook at home full of press cuttings and comments. It wasn't that he was obsessive, he concluded – it was thoroughness.

Being prepared.

It was because of who the man was that he had to prepare. The others would be easier. Like Mathews and Farrell had been easy. Easier than he had thought. It had given him extra confidence. Not that he was weak – he had to be strong, for her. It was the right thing to do.

He watched as the family set off. The woman looked irritated and there was a flustered look on the man's face. Then he waited. Ten minutes at first, then fifteen. A bus turned into the car park and disgorged a group of tourists.

The sun was warm and the air humid when he leant down into the boot for his walking boots, neatly stored in a plastic bag alongside the rucksack. He moved to one side of the car, out of sight, and knelt to lace up his boots, as he had done a hundred times before. He checked the contents of the rucksack, pulled it over his shoulder and fastened it carefully in place. A final tug of the cap, the ponytail adjusted again and dark sunglasses thrust high onto his nose finalised his transformation. The thought that even she might not recognise him now brought a brief smile to his lips.

A glance at his watch and a mental calculation told him they had a twenty-minute head start. He could usually do the summit in two and a half hours from Llanberis but he guessed that the family in front of him would need at least three, plus a couple of stops on the way. He could have walked the paths in the dark and still have found the right boulders to stop and rest at, the sheer cliffs to avoid and the places to watch the moonlight dance off the peaks.

He strode down past the terraces leading to the mountain path, keeping his head low and his eyes straight ahead. He passed an elderly group already complaining about the temperature, and then fell in behind a group of scouts until the need to be alone became overwhelming and he strode ahead of them.

As he pushed on up the gradient of the first steep section out of the town, his calf muscles burnt. A short detour away from the main path took him onto a promontory where he removed his rucksack and, taking out a pair of binoculars, began scanning the path snaking up the mountain. They should have been in his eye line and he moved the binoculars smoothly up and then down the path, trying to suppress the growing sense that he had given them too much of a head start. He stopped and squinted up into the distance and, seeing the line of smoke from the train ascending the mountain, followed the smoke trail until he picked up the path. All he could see were couples and large groups. Had he missed them on the way? Had they actually begun the walk as had been planned?

Hurriedly he yanked on the rucksack and once back on the path he lengthened his stride. Soon a bead of sweat ran down the small of his back and a dampness spread over the fabric at the base of the rucksack. Another half an hour took him to the next section where he'd planned to stop and scan the path. Nothing again. His heartbeat increased and he contemplated the possibility of failure. He dismissed the notion. They had to be on the mountain. He had seen them prepare. Even if they were still in Llanberis, talking or doing the things important people do, there would be another time: he would make certain of it. He strode on, his pulse thumping, the anxiety at failure beating in his head.

When he saw the halfway café, he stopped in his tracks.

There they were. Playing happy families.

For a moment, he stood rigid. Realising people were walking round him, he restarted as if nothing was out of place, keeping a sure footing, head looking forward, but with his eyes fixed on the family eating bananas and chocolate bars. They looked happy, like he should have been. The boys were drinking from cans of Coke and the woman was looking at the man as he fumbled with a Smartphone.

After five minutes, he stopped and walked away from the path. He sat down, his back against a rock, the rucksack at his feet. Slowly his breathing returned to normal and the anxiety subsided, replaced by the hatred that had become his closest companion. He reached into the rucksack and pulled out a flask. The coffee was lukewarm and he opened the wrapper of a chocolate bar. He ate and drank, thinking about the summit ahead of him.

He waited until he'd seen them pass. The boys were joking that their father was struggling and he noticed the damp patches across the man's chest and the streaks of perspiration through his hair. Now he kept his distance but was always close enough to know where they were and to anticipate when they'd arrive at the summit.

The heat of the sun burnt his skin. Birds of prey swooped around the cliffs, soaring up on the hot-air currents before diving away far below him. He passed a train full of tourists heading for the summit and another descending, full of laughing, smiling faces. Near to the summit station, he watched the ramblers walk towards the peak and he scrambled down to the railway tracks and walked alongside them until he reached the platform. He ignored the sullen look from the driver of the train about to leave.

The door into the summit café opened easily as he pressed his weight against it. Standing by the entrance, he moved to his right along the wall, then stopped and scanned the inside. Nothing looked out of place. There were small queues waiting at each till for teas and sandwiches. He heard the chattering voices and faces looking out over the view. Swirling clouds passed overhead and cast warm shadows over the window. In the far corner there was a small shop doing a brisk business in maps and books about Welsh legends. It was exactly as it should be. Exactly as he remembered it and exactly as he wanted it to be.

He put the rucksack down slowly by his feet and rested his back against the wall, directly beneath the only CCTV camera. Then he waited.

They walked in sooner than he had anticipated. Maybe time had gone quicker than he'd reckoned. They sat down at a table in the middle of the floor. The woman took out some fruit and passed it over to her husband and the boys, before getting up and walking over to the counter.

He looked away, fearing that she'd notice him.

Soon she returned with steaming mugs.

He moved his hand down towards the rucksack, sensing it was time, as he watched the man take off his fleece, his paunch falling out over the belt of the trousers. His heart beat faster and the blood vessels pounded in his neck.

Suddenly, his body tensed.

The man was moving. He'd swung his legs over the side of the bench and was talking animatedly to his wife who nodded back. Then he stepped towards the door.

It was time.

He adjusted his footing and swung the rucksack up and

then smoothly onto his shoulder. Within a few steps, he was behind him. He had no idea he was there or who he was or why he was there. They left together through the doors at the opposite end of the café.

He could see the rough hair on his neck and he could smell the perspiration of a man unfit and unused to walking the hills. He edged closer and as they entered the toilets, he pushed him. Gently at first, didn't want to alarm him too soon.

They turned away from the washbasins and he stepped forcibly into the man who stumbled towards the wall. He mouthed a protest. A fumbled cry of surprise. He saw that his man had his hands by his fly, ready. He wouldn't be needing that any longer.

He made the thrust of the blade deep and deadly, feeling the body dying, until it slumped into him and he pushed it into a cubicle exactly as he'd rehearsed a dozen times in his mind. He dropped the body onto the floor and turned to leave.

Over his shoulder as he left the building, he heard a scream.

Chapter 14
Wednesday 9th June

Drake followed the same ritual with the sudoku. Always slice and dice to get the easy solutions and then pick out squares individually. The slicing and dicing had proved problematical so he had to concentrate on one square. Just looking at the numbers was comforting, but finally unravelling the puzzle would give him a real feeling of control. A half-eaten biscuit sat on a plate on his desk but the fruit that Sian wanted him to eat was sitting on the kitchen worktop at home.

He felt a ripple of annoyance when the telephone rang. He pulled the handset to his ear and kept concentrating on the puzzle.

'Roderick Jones has been killed on the top of Snowdon.'

At first it didn't register – Drake had been looking for the number four. He'd managed a couple of numbers in the middle box – always the easiest, he found.

'Sorry?' he said.

The voice louder now – Price. 'Call just came in. Found dead in the toilet of the café. It's bloody mayhem.'

Immediately Drake thought of the song lyrics and the number four. 'Is there a message?'

'Nothing. And they've been told not to touch the body.'

'How was he—?'

'Helicopter will be here any minute.'

He stood up, still holding the telephone in his hand, before shouting for Caren who appeared at his door. He grabbed his jacket and they strode briskly, then half ran out of headquarters, hearing the clatter of the Sea King helicopter as it turned to land. They saw Michael Foulds and a CSI running over, eyes peering skyward. The helicopter descended, sending clouds of dust into the air. Drake cursed as he felt the dust travelling down his collar, covering his hands and face. The noise was deafening and Drake shielded his eyes.

Once safely landed, the door swung open, a crew member waved at them, and they ran towards the helicopter. An outstretched hand helped Caren and then Drake inside. Foulds and the other CSI lifted two forensic bags into the cabin and pulled themselves in.

The winchman hauled the door closed, spoke into his microphone; the sound of the engine increased and a thundering vibration rocked the cabin as the rotor blades turned. Soon they were airborne and the helicopter rose high above Colwyn Bay. Drake noticed the name Harper stitched onto the service man's one-piece suit.

'Anybody been winched down before?' Harper said.

Foulds nodded – the rest tried to hide their nerves.

Harper sounded reassuring. 'There's nothing to be frightened of,' he said. He clipped them all into harnesses and told them that once they were on the ground the manager of the summit café would release them.

'And remember, once you're out of the cabin the wind will knock you sideways.'

He raised his thumbs and they all nodded back, terrified.

The helicopter flew directly overland and within minutes, they were hovering above the summit.

'Only way to travel,' Harper said.

Nobody had enough saliva to reply.

He wrenched the door open and it slid back with a thud against the fuselage. There was a rush of air and the roar of the blades exploded into the cabin. The winchman motioned to Foulds.

'Show them how it's done.'

With his harness securely fastened, Foulds sat on the edge of the open door before pushing himself out. Harper hung out of the door and stared down as Foulds descended to the small, narrow strip of ground behind the café. Once the second CSI was standing near to Foulds, he winched the harness back into the cabin.

Drake moved towards the door and as the harness snapped into place, he swallowed hard before swinging his feet out of the helicopter. He peered down at the face of Foulds before pushing himself out.

Immediately his body was buffeted by the downdraft of the blades and the wind swirling around the summit. Halfway down the line swayed in the air and the blood pounded in his head. Once he stood on firm ground, he waved an encouragement to Caren. Within seconds, she stood by his side, her breathing heavy. The winchman raised his arm and pulled the door closed as the helicopter climbed and then roared away.

'Are you the manager?' Drake said to the older of the two men who'd helped him from the harness.

'Frank Hughes.' He nodded.

'Where is he?'

Hughes led them down a flight of granite steps towards the southerly entrance, stammering an apology that some walkers had already left the summit. Drake grunted a dismissive reply. Teams of officers were waiting to interview everyone coming off the mountain.

Empty plastic cups and discarded crisp packets littered the entrance. After opening the door of the toilets, the manager nodded and gesticulated inside. Drake and Caren approached the body lying crumpled in a cubicle. They knelt down and looked at the familiar face they had seen countless times.

Drake turned to Hughes, who was still standing by the door.

'Is there CCTV?'

'In the café.'

'Are the tapes secure?'

Hughes nodded.

The blood had pooled on the floor under Roderick

Jones, staining his clothes a dark colour. Drake stood up and scanned the toilet. Nothing out of the ordinary – urinals and cubicles and washbasins and soap and hot-air driers. The CSI investigation might turn up something, but he had his doubts.

'Who found the body?' he said to Hughes.

'Two guys taking a piss.'

'We'll need to see them.'

'They're in the main café building. I've put his wife in the office,' Hughes added.

Drake turned to Caren. 'Let's go and see the family first.'

They followed Hughes through the café, past the tourists whose Saturday outing had pitched them into a murder inquiry. In the kitchen the smell of warm bacon and melting cheese hung in the air. The staff huddled together in one corner, staring at Hughes as he led Drake and Caren to his office.

The room was stifling, the air dank and stale. Jan Jones sat by the table, her head in her hands; two boys sat by her side, their eyes red and swollen. Her hair looked greasy and a film of perspiration covered her face.

'Mrs Jones. Detective Inspector Drake.' He held out his hand. Seconds passed before she raised her head. She had pronounced teeth that stuck out as she breathed deeply.

'I am very sorry for your loss.'

Her eyes looked distant, as though the life had been sucked out of her. She moved her lips but said nothing. Drake saw the tears in her eyes and eyeliner smeared into her crow's feet. Her world had come crashing down upon her and Drake could sense her struggling to deal with reality.

'Did you see anybody or anything out of the ordinary?'

Jan Jones replaced her head in her hands.

'It was a family day out … We haven't been walking for ages. I even bought him a new top …' Then the tears began again.

'I need to interview the men who found your husband, Mrs Jones. DS Waits will stay with you.'

She choked on a reply.

On his way to the main café area, Drake passed piles of pre-baked baguettes and humming fridges. Overhead, he heard the increasing volume of the Sea King returning with Winder and Howick.

He stared at the two men who had raised the alarm. 'I want you to tell me exactly what you found.'

The Sea King almost drowned out the older of the two men but soon Drake had an idea of what they had seen. Baseball cap and grey fleece, grey trousers and a dark beard and a ponytail with a red knot. It had to be a joke. The beard would be fake and the ponytail a distraction.

Nothing to go on. The bastard's ahead of me again.

He glanced at his mobile, half expecting Price to ring. Lots of battery, but no signal. He was noting the names and addresses of the men when Winder and Howick strode towards him.

'Boss. The superintendent wants you to call him. He can't get through.'

'No signal,' Drake said, turning the mobile in his hand. 'I want the names and addresses of everybody.'

Then he marched over to the toilet door, forced open by a wooden wedge. Foulds was crouched over the body, doubling as a photographer; the look on his face told Drake he was going to be some time.

Back in the kitchen Drake found Hughes pursing his lips and looking frightened.

'CCTV?' Drake asked.

On the wall of another small untidy office were two plastic-coated sheets, one with staff rosters, another a holiday chart. Hughes sat in a plastic chair and replayed the tape. Drake curbed his impatience as Hughes fiddled with the computer, playing and then rewinding the tape, mumbling an apology as he did so.

'It's ages since I did this.'

The picture stopped and in the bottom left-hand corner a counter displayed the time and Drake focused, staring at the screen.

'We start the tapes at nine o'clock in the summer.'

He moved the time on to nine-thirty and then to ten o'clock. Drake saw walkers and visitors milling around the café, holding mugs of steaming drinks in their hands and carrying trays of hot food to tables full of hungry faces. He watched Roderick Jones enter the café at eleven o'clock, followed by Jan and then both boys. He saw Jones shaking hands and smiling at an older couple. Jan moved off towards the counter, her movements exaggerated and jerky. Jones removed his rucksack, dropped it to the floor before sitting down and swinging his legs over the bench and under the table. He appeared to be talking to one of the boys. Jan returned, carrying hot drinks and he watched Roderick Jones sip from his cup. *Was that his last sip of anything?* When the clock said eleven-thirty, a stream of visitors came into the café.

'Train arrived,' Hughes said.

'How many people come in on the train?'

'Fifty, usually.'

'Don't suppose there's a list?' The optimism in his voice was more from hope than expectation.

'No. But some of them might have booked with a credit card.'

It took Drake a millisecond to decide that the killer wouldn't have used a card to book his ticket. On the screen, Roderick Jones swung his legs back over the bench and stood up. He stretched his arms and, saying something over his shoulder to Jan, began to walk over towards the toilet.

Then Drake saw him.

A figure in a baseball cap and grey clothes moved into the line of the camera and followed Jones as if they were attached by an invisible cord. The ponytail seemed to wave at Drake. Taunting him.

'There he is! Stop the tape.'

The time said eleven thirty-six.

Drake stared at the figure.

'Got you. You bastard,' he said, under his breath.

Drake tapped Hughes on the shoulder and he restarted the tape. He watched as Jones left the café, the killer hard on his heels.

'Any other cameras?'

Hughes sounded nervous at the aggression in Drake's voice. 'No, we only have one.'

'What bloody use is just one CCTV camera? I want that tape kept secure, understood.'

A startled look lingered in the man's eyes. Drake closed the door behind him and made his way back into the café. He stared up at the CCTV camera. Moving towards it, he stopped and stood underneath it, exactly where baseball-cap-man would have been watching Jones. He moved his eyes along the café floor towards the door. It would take no more than a few seconds to walk from the table to the door and finally, the toilet.

To his right he saw the cliffs falling away and the early afternoon sunshine poured through the broad windows. Nervous walkers stared at him, exchanging glances, but he ignored them and looked over at the opposite wall, trying to imagine the right position for a second CCTV camera.

Caren walked over and stood by his side.

'Anything on the tape?'

'Baseball cap, grey fleece, grey trousers and a ponytail.'

'Just as the eyewitnesses described?'

'He knew exactly what he was doing. Standing under the camera watching Jones all the time; then, when Jones went to the toilet, he followed.'

Winder and Howick were moving around the visitors in the café, taking names and addresses and contact details. Drake hoped, prayed even, that there might be a better description than a baseball cap and grey clothing. He paced over to the toilet. Mike Foulds stood by the cubicle and motioned towards him. Drake walked over.

'Something here you'd better see,' Foulds whispered.

Jones's body was now lying flat, his eyes closed. The pool of blood around him seemed wider. Foulds cast one eye over his shoulder and lowered his voice.

'I found this under the body as I moved him,' Foulds said, passing Drake a plastic envelope.

Printed in bold red ink was the number three.

Chapter 15
Wednesday 9th June

Drake and Caren stared at the screen, a grim determination on their faces, both willing the killer to turn and look at the camera. Winder and Howick stood behind them. Eventually Drake paused the images.

'We've got one hundred and twenty people to interview,' he said. 'That's thirty each.'

Caren winced. 'This could take all night.'

'Let's stick to the basics. No more than ten minutes each. Get their personal details. Find out if they saw anything or anybody. Somebody must have seen him.'

Winder fiddled with a baguette as he spoke. 'Who do we interview first?'

'Anybody with a medical condition we see first – there can't be that many. Everybody else we'll see in turn. And every hour a train can leave.'

The interviews took longer than Drake expected. Some had wanted to provide detailed descriptions, and extracting information from others was a long and painful process. Will I have to give evidence? Was it a serial killer? An American tourist was astonished when he realised Drake didn't carry a gun. The smell of sweaty T-shirts and muddy boots disappeared as the café emptied, leaving the floor covered with dirt, the bins overflowing.

By early evening, a wave of tiredness hit him. A pain tugged at the back of his shoulder and, standing up, he moved his arm in a circular motion, trying, unsuccessfully, to massage it away. He'd eaten nothing since breakfast and an ache gnawed at the edges of his forehead. He took a bottle of water from the chilled counter, and drank half without stopping.

Faint wisps of cloud hung along the tops of the mountains far away in the distance, and down the valley Drake could see Llanberis and further on towards the green fields of Anglesey. He picked out the occasional tree and isolated farm building on the lower reaches of the mountain. On the final ridge at Clogwyn station, a train was stationary. He moved his head, catching his own reflection in the glass.

'Spectacular view,' Caren said.

Drake mumbled a reply.

'He must have been on the mountain when we arrived.'

'I know.'

He moved closer to the window and imagined the dozens of officers scattered over the paths and fields at the base of Snowdon, stopping everyone coming off the mountain.

Drake had hiked all of the seven paths to the top of Snowdon but he guessed that the killer would stay well clear of the tourist trails. Then he realised where part of the answer might be.

Caren followed him as he headed towards the office.

'Replay the CCTV. Now,' Drake demanded.

He became impatient when Hughes again struggled with the computer. 'Get on with it.'

Eventually the grainy pictures of Jones and his family appeared. They watched the scene unfolding. Then Jones stood up and after he had taken two steps, the killer stepped into view.

'Stop it! Stop it!' Drake said.

Frozen on the screen in front of them was the back of the killer.

'There it is,' Drake said.

Halfway down the killer's back was a small rucksack. There were two mesh pockets on either side, each holding a water bottle. A light-coloured band of material curled around the zip of the rucksack and the bulge in the material told them it was full.

'Get a description of the rucksack down the mountain, now,' he said to Caren.

He stared at the screen. He could imagine the killer

leaving the café, and in one swift movement taking off the false beard and wig and stuffing them into the rucksack. Then, walking down, away from the café, hearing the sounds of the screams diminishing, he would be away, back to safety. Without saying a word, Drake marched out of the office, through the servery and out beyond the toilets, passing the yellow flickering CSI tape. Pushing open the outer door, he stood on the granite slabs. To his left were steep steps up towards the summit and to his right, steps down towards the paths off the mountain. After four steps to his right, he was on the path, fragments of rock and loose shale underfoot. He found a vantage point and looked down towards the wide-open expanse of the lower fields. His heart sank as he realised that once the killer had been safely off the summit and the narrow ridges of Bwlch Main and Llechog he could have traversed any number of fields before finding safety. Drake retraced his steps and went up towards the summit above the café. He looked down over the sheer cliff face and noticed the last solitary hikers walking down the Gladstone path. Back at the café entrance, he hesitated, realising the killer had been at this very spot.

A small plume of smoke was rising from the chimney of the engine waiting to take their train down to Llanberis. Drake and Caren sat on one side of the small compartment, Winder and Howick squeezed in opposite them. A cool breeze blew through the carriage from the open windows and Drake looked down into Cwm Clogwyn and the glistening water on the surface of Llyn y Nadroedd. The sun descended towards the horizon; he held a hand up to his forehead to shade his eyes. He made out the route of the Snowdon Ranger path as it left the Llanberis track. It had been his grandfather's favourite route: a slow, comfortable climb. He thought about whether the killer might have used the same route. He might have stopped at the same places as his grandfather, sat on the same rocks, pushed open the same gates, stood looking at the same views.

Caren sat by his side and her head sagged as she fell asleep. Gradually, her head leant on to his shoulder. The clatter and bumping of the carriages as they crossed the rails approaching Llanberis station woke her. She straightened her head and moved in her seat, her face flushed with embarrassment as she looked at Drake.

'How long have I been sleeping?'

Winder and Howick grinned at her.

As the train slowed to a halt, Drake saw Price standing on the platform – full uniform, a wide stance and hands on hips. A guard unlocked the door and Foulds and the CSI officer were the first to leave. Drake ducked his head and stepped out onto the platform. Price walked up to him and pointed to the Jaguar idling in the car park.

'Let's go,' Price said.

They hurried past several patrol vehicles and uniformed motorcycle officers milling around the station concourse. Sirens screeched as two outriders led them out of Llanberis.

'Diabolical. We've got to do everything to catch this crazy bastard,' Price said.

'Did Uniform pick up anything?' Drake said.

'They stopped over three hundred people.'

Drake whistled in surprise.

'Somebody should have seen something,' Price said. 'From your description we should be able to build a better photofit and then make a public appeal. The description matches the man in the taxi office.'

'A disguise, of course,' Drake said.

Price nodded slowly.

'We'll get a photo fit for a man without a wig or a beard.'

Drake knew how difficult that would be. The killer must have known that people notice ponytails and thick beards, before a person's height or hair colour or cheekbones. Soon they joined the A55 and the driver accelerated eastward.

With the outriders clearing the traffic, it took them

twenty minutes to reach headquarters. In Price's office, Drake fell into one of the chairs by the conference table, the tiredness burning his eyes.

'There's something you should see, sir,' Drake began, before turning to Foulds.

From his bag Foulds took out a plastic folder with the A4 paper slotted inside. He pushed it over the desk. Price picked up the folder and clenched his jaw so hard his ears changed shape.

'Who knows about this?'

'The three of us, so far,' Drake said.

Price placed the folder back on the table and stared at the red number three, shimmering beneath the plastic.

Chapter 16
Thursday 10th June

Drake's request to see the reports from the teams of uniformed officers who had interviewed walkers descending the mountain had produced a pile of paperwork. The Llanberis path had been the busiest and he scanned through dozens of reports. He knew he could have got Winder or Howick to do this mundane exercise, but something told him he had to do it himself.

A second team had stopped walkers coming down the Pyg and Miners track. The reports recorded names, addresses and contact details. There was a group from France, a couple from Spain and two Americans, but nobody had seen a man with a ponytail and baseball cap and beard.

He moved a half-finished coffee to one side and opened a map of Snowdonia, unfolding the various parts until it covered his desk. He could see the green dotted lines of the paths towards the summit and the close contour lines of the deep sides of the Cwms. He scanned the area surrounding Snowdon and realised how easy it would have been for a killer to make good his escape. He refolded the map and read the reports for the Rhyd Ddu path, his determination heightened, his focus more acute, believing that the killer had taken this route off the mountain. He read each report more carefully but the results were the same – nothing. He finished the last dregs of his coffee and turned to the reports from the Snowdon Ranger path. Not even the caffeine was going to help, as he realised the reports were drawing a blank.

At least they had the names and addresses of three hundred possible witnesses. He sat and thought about everything. He heard the office partitions creak and the muffled sound of a footfall somewhere in the building. Before long, the sound of the first officers arriving broke the silence.

Drake yanked open the door from his office into the Incident Room and, suppressing a yawn, stretched his back and arms before walking over to Caren's desk. She looked surprised.

'You're in early, sir.' It was a combination of statement and question.

'Couldn't sleep.'

'Have you seen the papers?'

Then Drake saw the pile of newspapers on Howick's desk. *Cop killer strikes again* and *Serial Killer Murders Prominent Politician* were two of the headlines. He flicked through the various papers and scanned the reports, groaning with annoyance. The investigation wasn't out of control. The press had no right to suggest a serial killer was on the loose. He was still reading when Lisa, the public relations officer, stalked into the room.

'It's a nightmare, Ian. An absolute nightmare,' she began.

'I've just started reading the papers.'

'That's not the half of it.'

He raised his eyebrows.

'The TV companies are having a collective orgasm. Best story they've had in years. And all they want to do is put the blame on us.'

Drake, trying to read the papers, was deep in thought and not listening.

Lisa continued. 'And the press have booked all the best hotel rooms from here to Chester. There are literally hundreds of them hunting for the story. Cardiff want to organise a press conference tomorrow. The head of corporate relations has been on the phone – he got me out of bed at seven-thirty. Then the TV journalists rang. How they fuck they got my home number I. Do. Not. Know.'

He turned the pages of the newspaper absently, as he thought about the CCTV images on the screen from the summit.

'Ian?' She raised her voice.

He turned to her slowly.

'You're not listening.'

He ignored her and carried on reading. His fingertips were black – he would have to wash them as soon as he was finished. There were awkward glances around the room and Lisa let out an impatient groan and left. Once he'd finished, he walked to the kitchen and washed his hands, watching the dirty water flushing down the sink. Back in his office, he found a copy of the paper with the number left on the body of Roderick Jones, strode out into the Incident Room, and pinned it to the board with a flourish. He sensed the eyes of the team on his back.

'This was the message left on Roderick Jones's body.'

There was a squeaking sound as Winder straightened his chair and Caren cleared her throat. Nobody else moved and Drake could sense the tension in the room.

'What does it mean?' Winder asked.

'He's off his fucking head,' Howick snorted.

'We don't know what it means,' Drake said. 'We'll assume the worst: that there are going to be two more killings.'

'How does it fit in with Farrell and Mathews? After all, there were two of them and only one number.' Caren asked the question Drake had been posing to himself all morning.

Drake looked up at the board, folded his arms, and then turned to Winder.

'See if you can find the rucksack,'

'Sir?'

'The one the killer was wearing.'

Winder looked as though a heavy weight had been dropped on his shoulders. Drake was certain there was something in the investigation that would tell them who the killer was. They had to catch him before he killed again.

It was going to be another long day.

Drake nodded to the waitress and she came over to the table with the menu. Dr Fabrien gave the girl the briefest of smiles and read the daily lunch specials pinned to the folded plastic menu. The Queen's Head was quiet; a retired couple sat by the door and a man in a bold pinstripe with a broad smile sat in a corner opposite a thin blond girl half his age.

'What do you recommend, Ian?' Dr Fabrien said.

Drake scanned the menu. 'Smokies are good.'

Dr Fabrien turned up her nose.

'Scottish recipe,' she added, as though it were contagious.

The waitress appeared by their table, 'Good morning, Mr Drake,' she said before giving Dr Fabrien a curious look. Drake ordered a fish and chips – he liked the beer batter – and Dr Fabrien chose a salad, checking that she could get fresh bread rolls.

'I miss French bread,' she sighed.

'Of course,' Drake agreed.

'Your bread tastes of nothing. Just plastic.'

Drake nodded. Dr Fabrien sipped on a glass of lime juice with sparkling water: no ice – she had been very insistent.

'Do you come from a family of policemen?'

It was an odd thing to ask, thought Drake – nobody had ever asked him that before. He could remember the look of disappointment on his father's face when he'd announced his intention to join the WPS. A look that said the police service wasn't quite the right career path. His mother had looked flustered. But his grandfather would have understood.

'I've met so many policemen who come from families of police officers. Like doctors and lawyers. It can run in the family. You seem to be dedicated to your job.' She opened her eyes wide and Drake noticed, for the first time, their clear blue colour.

Drake didn't want to talk about himself with Dr Fabrien

and he became alarmed at the prospect of the lunch turning into a counselling session. The arrival of their meals gave him the opportunity to move on politely. Dr Fabrien looked around the table as though she had lost something; when the waitress returned with the bread, she looked relieved.

'Some olive oil and balsamic,' she said.

Drake diverted the conversation by asking about her hotel, which was apparently quite comfortable even though the water was only lukewarm in the morning. Her complaints to the Polish staff on duty had been met with blank stares. Eventually he ran out of small talk and returned to the case.

'So what do you make of everything?'

'There is a lot of unhelpful publicity.'

'Two policemen and a politician are dead,' Drake shrugged.

Dr Fabrien scooped up a mouthful of red salad leaves and a piece of shredded radish. 'For sure. It is very bad.'

'What do make of the song lyrics?' She looked on in disgust as Drake dusted the chips on his plate with salt and then added tomato ketchup.

'It is too early to say. I have a lot of work to do. I shall have to listen to the songs. Perhaps there's a message.'

'What could the killer be trying to tell us?'

'He certainly likes rock music,' she said, without a trace of sarcasm in her voice.

Drake pierced the batter, and then dragged a piece of the flesh to one side of the plate as the steam escaped.

'Did you recognise the song?' she continued.

Drake mumbled an acknowledgment through a mouthful of cod. The look of revulsion on Dr Fabrien's face had persuaded him to leave the dollop of tomato sauce on the edge of his plate untouched.

'I'm more worried about the numbers,' Drake said.

'Ah. Yes, the numbers. Maybe he has an obsession. What do you think?'

Drake hesitated and the possibility that she knew about him flashed through his mind, only to be dismissed as an impossibility. She'd only just arrived. How could she know about his rituals?

'Are there going to be two more?'

'It is impossible to say. I shall need more time.'

How much time do you need?

Dr Fabrien pushed her food around the plate, before stabbing her fork into a piece of tomato and some thinly sliced fennel. Drake hid a spasm of irritation by spearing two chips and then prodding them into the tomato sauce.

'We've got very little at the moment. We've interviewed a woman police officer who was harassed by Farrell and she …'

Dr Fabrien shook her head.

'I don't think you're looking for a woman.'

'Why not?'

'Too brutal. Too macabre.'

Drake wanted to tell her about a case where a woman had tied a man to a bed and watched as he was gang raped and then left him to bleed to death.

'Women can be brutal too,' he suggested.

'It has the hallmarks of a man.'

She added more balsamic vinegar to her salad and watched Drake eating a couple of mouthfuls of fish.

'Then we have the widow of Mathews. She hated the ground he walked on. Made no attempt to hide that.' Drake tried to sound defiant.

Another shaking of the head, this time slower, as if she was exasperated.

'Revenge. The oldest emotion. But why would she kill another officer and Jones? No motive. There is always a motive, Ian.'

It occurred to him to remind her that he was the Detective Inspector, but the circumstances persuaded him not to overreact. They spent the rest of the lunch discussing the possible profile of the killer – age, family, education and personality – and by the end Drake wasn't certain if it had helped.

Dr Fabrien drew the final remains of her bread roll carefully round the salad plate, picking up the rest of the diced spring onion and the final traces of balsamic vinegar and olive oil.

'Killing two police officers was bad enough but then killing Jones raised the stakes. It's difficult to imagine a more direct attack on society and democracy,' Drake said, pleased that he'd found the right words.

She gave him a look that suggested she was going to impart a wisdom and knowledge only a profiler with her vast experience could have acquired.

'Politicians are probably the most unpopular class of person in the country. Maybe in the world.'

She was right of course, but the prospect of having to work through all of Roderick Jones's papers filled him with dread. It was going to take days, maybe weeks and it was time they did not have. The press would be writing stories that wouldn't help and Price would breathe down his neck, demanding results. And now he had Dr Fabrien to contend with. For a moment he thought about the comfort that working on a sudoku puzzle would give him – at least he was in control when he was slicing and dicing the riddle.

It was a relief when his mobile hummed and he read the text from Caren telling him Jan Jones had arrived at headquarters.

His annoyance at Dr Fabrien's attitude began to dominate his mind as he drove back, and he worried that the investigation itself would soon be out of his hands. He felt damp patches gathering in his armpits, soiling the clean shirt. Inside headquarters, he headed straight for the nearest toilet, locked a cubicle door and unravelled lengths of toilet tissue, which he rubbed into his armpits and pressed onto the shirt, trying to dry the perspiration.

There was an expectant look on Caren's face as he entered the Incident Room. She called out to him.

'The train driver has just left.'

'Who?' Drake said, before he remembered the statement from the driver on the summit of Snowdon. 'Helpful?'

'He noticed the ponytail.'

'Age?'

'Couldn't help. But the description about the man's height and weight was better than Mildred's.'

'Let's hope Jan Jones will be more helpful. She's our only real eyewitness to date.'

He nodded an acknowledgment with a weak smile.

Standing by his desk, he tried to compose his thoughts. What did he need for the interview with Jan Jones? Notebook – CCTV footage – but his mind wandered. Dr Fabrien was looking over his shoulder – somebody else to cock up the inquiry. Then Caren stood by the desk.

'Jan Jones is in the VIP suite, sir,' she said.

Drake picked up his papers and they headed downstairs. He knew Caren was talking to him and he heard what she was saying about the questions she wanted to ask Jan Jones but he wasn't listening.

Jan Jones sat upright in one of the stiff conference chairs, her face gaunt, dark bags under her eyes.

'We need to ask you about yesterday,' he said, sitting down opposite her.

Jan Jones waited for him to continue.

'Did you notice a man with a baseball cap and a ponytail at any point during the morning?'

Caren began taking notes.

'No, I can't say I did, Inspector.'

'But he was standing right behind you.'

'I didn't see him.'

Caren put her biro down and interrupted. 'Why don't we play the CCTV coverage?'

She opened the laptop on the table and clicked until the screen filled with images from the summit. Jan Jones blinked several times and chewed her lips as they watched Roderick Jones move away from the table, the killer behind him, walking in his shadow, preparing to strike.

'He must have been standing right by you,' Drake continued.

'I didn't notice him.'

'Nothing about his facial features? You must have seen his face.'

Caren interrupted, her voice soft and calming. 'It must have been difficult with so many people in the café.'.

Drake ignored her and carried on.

'We believe this man has killed two police officers and your description of his face could be crucial.'

'I wasn't paying attention to the faces of the other visitors.'

'But there can't have been many with ponytails, a beard and a baseball cap. Nobody wears a baseball cap on the top of Snowdon.' Drake didn't hide his exasperation.

Caren interrupted again. 'What was it like walking up Snowdon? Did you notice anything odd as you walked up?'

Jan raised her eyebrows, as if she didn't know what to say.

'It had been a lovely day. We enjoyed the walk. I wanted to be with Michael. I didn't notice anybody else. I wasn't looking for anybody *suspicious*. A couple of times, he met somebody he knew. We heard a French couple and there were some Americans. But—'

Drake snapped his notebook shut and asked her again. 'Can you give me a description or not?'

'No, I cannot. As I've told you several times. And I don't like your manner, Inspector. My husband is dead. How is this helping to find his murderer?'

Jan picked up her coat and pushed her chair away from the table. She glared at Drake and left.

'She was doing her best,' Caren said.

'She must have seen something.'

Caren sat in a chair across from Drake, a coffee mug nestling in her hand. 'You pressed her too hard, sir. If she had seen something, surely she would have said so already?'

Drake crumpled his lips. 'We've got to find him.'

'And I can't make sense of the death threats, sir. Geraldine must have sent them. Or she told someone. A friend or anyone, really.'

Drake ran his tongue over the top part of his gums, trying to dislodge a piece of potato or batter from lunch that had stuck between his teeth.

Caren continued, 'Or it was someone who had seen them.'

He tried sloshing tea around in his mouth, hoping it would help; and he was going to ask Caren if she had a toothpick when the door was thrown open and Price entered the room.

'Look at this,' he said, as he threw a piece of paper across Drake's desk.

Drake's mouth went dry and he could feel Price's eyes burning into his face as he read the latest song lyric from the killer. Words formed in his mouth, but they stuck on his lips until eventually he drew his tongue between his lips and pushed the question out.

'When did this arrive?'

'Just now. Marked 'Superintendent Price and Detective Inspector Drake'. What kind of sick fucking psycho are we dealing with?'

'It's ... it's a song by Queen.' Drake sounded hesitant.

'"Crazy Little Thing Called Love" – it's well known.'

Chapter 17
Friday 11th June

Drake stared at the sudoku and blocked out the sound of the domestic arrangements swirling around him. The breakfast table was a mess of plates and mugs and pots of easy-to-spread margarine and marmalade. He was slicing and dicing the squares and was confident that he could finish the puzzle.

'Has your father called Susan?' Sian said, as she stood by the sink.

'He wanted to wait until after the results.'

Sian threw a dishcloth onto the drainer. 'Then he's foolish. He should have told her immediately.'

Drake seldom called his sister and the less he spoke to her, the higher the barriers became. Susan lived in Cardiff and had married an accountant from Pembrokeshire, who made clear his intense aversion to anything Welsh by openly showing his displeasure at family gatherings when the language was spoken.

'I'll speak to Anthony West today,' Sian said.

'Who?'

'The oncologist. See if he can give your dad an early appointment.'

Drake nodded but his mind returned to thinking about what he could say to his sister. He stared at the crockery on the table, thinking of his parents. Sian was right: his father needed to call Susan and tell her. Drake imagined the recriminations that would surface in the conversation when she realised that she was the last to know. Drake looked again at the sudoku in the morning newspaper while Sian got on with clearing the crockery, the sound of dishwasher-stacking filling the kitchen. He might do some more of the puzzle mid-morning with his coffee and then some more at lunchtime.

'And have you organised the holiday insurance?'

Drake looked up from the sudoku. 'I'll do it today.'

He finished the dregs of the coffee and left the kitchen. In the hall he glanced in the mirror, adjusted the collar of the white shirt – Egyptian cotton and double cuffs – before straightening his tie. Outside he bleeped the Alfa and put his jacket carefully in the back. He pushed a U2 CD into the player. Bono still hadn't found what he was looking for and Drake knew how he felt.

In his office Drake looked over his desk and knew that Sian was right. He would call his parents and tell them they had to call Susan. But first he had to reorder the desk from the night before. He hung his jacket coat, wondering why he bothered to bring it with him to work on hot summer days.

The telephone had to be moved into its correct place before the photographs of the girls were adjusted and then the papers tidied. He hadn't finished when Price appeared at the office door. The superintendent narrowed his eyes slightly as he gazed at Drake.

'Good morning,' Price said

'Sir,' Drake replied, moving the pile of papers on the corner of his desk.

Price sat down in one of the plastic visitor chairs and cleared his throat. 'Jan Jones,' he said. 'She spoke to me on the phone.'

Drake said nothing.

'I think you should have been more temperate when you spoke to her.'

'She's our only eyewitness. She must have seen something.'

'For Christ's sake, Ian. She's just lost her husband.'

'Is she going to complain?'

Price folded his arms. 'Not this time. But—'

'We've got a murderer to catch.'

'And pissing off Jan Jones isn't going to help.'

Price stared at Drake.

Maybe Drake had been too hard, but the killer had been standing right next to them in the café.

For another half an hour Drake brought Price up to date with the latest developments, knowing they had to prepare for the press conference later that afternoon, timed to catch all the early evening news programmes. Occasionally Drake pointed at the pile of statements and evidence that had been gathered and Price nodded his understanding. But the reality was that they were no further forward and Drake began to contemplate that this was going to be a long and exhausting inquiry: the sort that would sap the mental reserves of all his team.

Once Price had left, Drake felt compelled to have coffee and he fussed in the kitchen until he had the right consistency to his cafetière. Back in his office the desk was tidy enough for him to start work but he reached for the sudoku and completed one square, which meant that he could properly turn his attention to the investigation.

It had worried him that only a fragment of the Queen song had been sent. And the tune kept playing over in his mind. In the middle of the night he had woken, convinced that a radio was playing the song very loudly somewhere on the road where he lived. He had walked downstairs and through the house before he had realised that everything was quiet. He checked all his emails and read the press release that Lisa had attached to her message before replying that he thought the wording was right. It struck him how resourceful the PR department could be in finding different ways of saying the same thing.

He had barely settled down to work when the telephone rang and he heard his mother's voice.

'Mam. How's Dad? I was going to call you,' he said, feeling rather guilty for his silence.

'Your father's the same,' she said, but Drake could tell there was something on her mind.

'I think you should tell Susan as soon as possible.'

'Sorry?'

'That's why I was going to call. You should tell Susan before the results of the tests.'

'We've had something odd in the post this morning.'

Drake hesitated. 'What do you mean?'

'We've had this photograph.'

Drake sensed the anxiety in her voice.

'It's a photograph of that poor man, Roderick Jones. A Polaroid.'

Drake was on his feet now.

'What? I mean— where? How did it arrive?'

'I'm worried, Ian. Why has it been sent here?'

Drake drew a finger along his drying lips. 'Is there anyone else in the photograph?' Drake thought frantically about the possibilities.

'It looks like his family.'

Drake muffled the handset and shouted Caren's name.

'Can you tell where it was taken?' Drake asked, as Caren appeared at the door.

'It looks like a café.'

'Did you tell her to be careful with the photograph?' Caren said.

Drake squeezed the steering wheel hard as the car raced along in the outside lane of the A55. He'd already flashed a dozen cars and some had blasted their horns without realising who they were.

'Of course I bloody did.'

Caren leant an arm on the window.

'Did your mother say anything else?'

Drake had left Northern Division Headquarters so fast he hadn't gone into the details with his mother.

'It could be a prankster,' Caren said, without sounding convincing.

'And how the hell would that work?'

The car raced up towards a caravan and Drake blasted his horn and swore profusely. Eventually the caravan pulled in and they passed the driver who raised the middle finger of his right hand as he mouthed an obscenity.

Caren didn't reply. Once Drake was off the A55 he had to slow down, but they reached the farm quicker than he'd ever driven there before. He accelerated down the gravel track to the farmhouse before he braked hard, the car skidding to a halt.

His mother sat by the table in the kitchen, a confused look on her face. She gave Drake a wan smile.

Caren stretched out her hand. 'Caren Waits.'

His mother shook her hand limply.

Drake saw the photograph on the table. He picked it up with a handkerchief and the dryness in his mouth returned as he looked at the images. He had stood where the photograph had been taken. Exactly where the killer had been, looking at Roderick Jones and Jan and the two boys enjoying the views from the summit café.

It meant the killer knew where his parents lived.

It meant he wanted to frighten them.

He could feel the tension gripping his chest.

Something made him turn the photograph over. He swallowed and it hit him hard that now the investigation was personal. He read the missing verses of the Queen song that had been playing through his mind the night before.

Chapter 18
Friday 11th June

It took three calls to reach the area sergeant from Caernarfon and by then Drake wanted to swear, really badly, but with his mother sitting by his side, he decided against it.

'In the post?'

'Yes,' Drake almost hissed.

'To your parents?'

The accent was Liverpool or Birkenhead and when the sergeant repeated the address, he fumbled over the pronunciation.

'I want you get a regular patrol calling at the farm,' Drake said.

'Well … I don't …'

'Is that going to be a *problem,* Sergeant?'

Drake could hear him draw breath.

'We're short at the moment.'

'Shall I get Superintendent Price to call you?'

The sergeant paused.

'I'll do what I can.'

Drake killed the call and smiled at his mother but she didn't smile back. Caren reached over and touched her arm.

'It'll be all right.'

His mother nodded. 'Why did he send us this photograph?'

'It's a really sick individual,' Drake said.

Caren added. 'And he wants to upset you, of course. But it's a way to get at Ian more than anything.'

Drake understood that his parents were involved because of him.

Robert Stone chewed on a piece of gum, hoping for inspiration. He longed for another opportunity to ask an awkward question at a WPS press conference. But now he had to consult with the editor if he received another call. And he wasn't to ask any more questions in any press conference without clearance.

He'd written two hundred words of a thousand-word piece about an award-winning dog kennels. The owners had been delighted to talk to the press and greeted Robert like a long-lost son. An overpowering smell and the layers of dog hair in the kitchen persuaded him to decline the offer of coffee.

After three years at university, being a journalist had come down to this – interviewing two fat, boring dog owners about their fat dogs and then finding something interesting to say.

He stared at the computer screen trying to decide how serious the flirting with Sarah had actually been. That morning she was wearing high heels and a short skirt. She'd given him a smile when he arrived that had preoccupied him every moment since. He sat by his desk hoping no one would notice his erection.

The telephone rang. The call was short and quickly dispelled his lust.

Drake had to prioritise. The photograph proved nothing and he guessed that the forensic results would find nothing conclusive. So he sat at his desk, hoping he could suppress the feeling of being powerless to prevent his mother and father having become involved.

An hour digging into James Harrod's background helped to dispel the anger in his mind. He reckoned the house must have been worth three quarters of a million on a bad day. He had noticed the personalised number plate on Laura's silver Mercedes. And Harrod's probably got a Range Rover, Drake had thought.

When he looked for details, they were everywhere. The Harrod group of companies sponsored a local football team, providing youngsters with kit and new boots. The smiling face of James Harrod adorned the local newspaper, making announcements about new projects, taking on new apprentices and shaking hands with local dignitaries. Checking the electoral register told Drake only what he knew already – the full address and postcode of the property James Harrod shared with the smooth-talking Mrs Harrod. The entries on the register went back for five years and Drake input different parameters, hoping Harrod's name would appear somewhere else, but he drew a blank.

Drake knew that accounts for any limited company could be downloaded but protocol demanded that it had to be the Economic Crime Department that accessed Companies House website, so he scrolled through the directory of contact names until he found the number for Ryan Kent.

'Never heard of him. Should I?' Kent sounded interested.

'He's on the radar.'

Kent was surprised. 'What, for the Mathews and Farrell killing?'

'It's a long story.'

'So's *Lord of the Rings,* but in the end the good guys win.'

It was the sort of remark that reminded Drake how much of a geek Kent was. He could sense the interest he had generated as Kent began a detailed explanation of what could be done to investigate Harrod. It could take months, he said.

Drake gave him a reality check. 'This is a murder investigation, Ryan.'

After twenty minutes Drake extracted a commitment from Kent to review the accounts of the Harrod Group.

The discovery that brought a smile to his face was the result of the police national computer check. Hull City Magistrates – six months, actual bodily harm. He leant back in his chair and smiled to himself. The man rubbing shoulders with the local politicians and dignitaries had done time. He thought about whether Laura Harrod knew about her husband's record – it had been before they were married. After four phone calls he tracked down the sergeant in the Humberside Police who had dealt with Harrod's case.

'So he's in Wales.'

He made it sound like the other side of the world. 'We were lucky to catch him. Without the CCTV coverage, we'd never have got a conviction. Made a no-comment interview, until we showed him the tapes. That fucked him up, so he coughed.'

'What's the background?' Drake asked. He scribbled notes as the sergeant ran through a summary of the case. Harrod had been running an extended drug-dealing network, although it had been small-scale enough to avoid attracting serious attention from the drug squad.

'Cannabis, and cocaine – the recreational drug of choice these days,' the sergeant added casually, the frustration evident in his voice. 'At least we got him off the streets for six months. Is it nice in Wales?'

Drake realised there was rather more to James Harrod than the public persona.

Drake walked through into the Incident Room, meaning to add this new information about Harrod to the board. The atmosphere was stifling – none of the air-conditioned luxury of the CSI programmes in Northern Division Headquarters. The closest they got to air conditioning was an open window and an electric fan. Winder wasn't wearing a tie and Howick had the top two buttons of his shirt undone. Drake noticed the shine on Howick's black eye beginning to fade.

Drake looked at the song lyrics printed in large font on three pieces of A4 paper pinned prominently on the board. The frustration at not making any headway in understanding the lyrics riled him. What had 'Brass in Pocket' got to do with anything? And why choose a song from 1979? He sat down at a desk, looking at the board.

'What's so special about 1979?' Drake said.

Winder looked up. 'Who was the prime minister?'

'Wilson, no Thatcher – or was it Major?' Howick said.

Drake listened but didn't correct him.

'And who was the American president?' Winder asked.

Howick sat back, folding his arms behind his head. 'Nixon, definitely.'

'The song keeps playing in my head,' Drake said, to no one in particular.

Howick and Winder glanced at each other.

'The Pretenders are still touring, sir,' Howick tried to sound informative.

Drake ignored him and stared at the lyrics, waiting for some inspiration.

'I'm sure I heard the song on the radio the other day,' he said.

At the other end of the board was the number four and, by its side, the red-coloured three, both screaming for attention. Drake knew he couldn't ignore the question they posed.

'Where's Caren?' he said, looking round the Incident Room.

'Said she had to go out,' Howick said. Drake stifled his exasperation; Caren knew she was supposed to clear things with him first.

'Sir?' It was Winder. 'Are we dealing with a serial killer?'

Drake started a reply when the door banged against the wall as Caren walked into the room carrying two large files under her arm. She dumped them on her desk, making certain they didn't fly all over the floor.

'Fiona Trick lied to us about Mathews seeing the children. He had regular contact every couple of weeks. I found a shed-load of letters from solicitors to Mathews about the problems he was having with contact.'

Howick piped up, 'But that doesn't give her a motive to kill him.'

Caren continued. 'Recently, she'd been trying to limit the contact, being really aggressive. Making life awkward for him and telling him that the children didn't want to see him and that he was a bad influence on them.'

'I thought that was pretty usual for estranged couples,' Winder added.

'Then I spoke to Mr Mathews senior and his wife. They went to see the solicitors about getting an order for them to see the children.'

Drake could see where this was going. 'And that only made matters worse?'

'Sure thing – she stopped contact altogether and then told Mathews that Anna wasn't to be present when he saw the kids. The granddad, Donald Mathews, is ex-services – spent twenty years in the Royal Welch – so he didn't take things lying down. He started a court case himself to see the kids. She went ballistic. Told Paul she would move away and that he would never see the kids again.'

Drake began to feel that Caren was wasting time. 'Look, that may be, but we're investigating a murder.'

'It is odd though, sir. You'd agree.'

He waved a hand in agreement. She continued. 'Amongst Mathews's papers were letters from an insurance company. Mathews had a policy worth £300,000.' Caren slowed her voice when she said the figures.

Immediately all the faces turned towards her – mouths open, eyes alive to the possibility that money was the greatest motivator of all.

Drake responded. 'Who is the beneficiary?'

Caren stood perfectly still and looked around the other officers. 'The beneficiary is Fiona Trick.'

'Better add her to the board,' Drake announced. Winder whistled quietly and Howick crumpled his face into a serious expression as he stared at Caren.

'And we need to add James Harrod too,' Drake announced. 'He's got a conviction for violence and he was furious when Farrell assaulted Laura. Evidence: let's go after the evidence. There has to be something in the songs and the numbers that we're missing.'

He paused before continuing. 'The numbers could mean anything. They could be part of a house number or a street number.' He wasn't convincing himself and it wasn't convincing the team. 'But it could be a signal from the killer. That there are four victims or that Mathews or Farrell were the fourth together or apart.'

'Or that one of them was,' Caren added. 'Whichever one was the intended victim, the other could have been collateral damage.'

Drake baulked at the word 'collateral damage' – it sounded too American for his taste, too cold-blooded. He knew that serial killers were rare in the UK, even if American television was full of them.

Howick followed Drake back to his office, a pleased look on his face.

'Found the details of that blue Volvo for you.'

'And?'

'Hire car. Took me a bit of time to track down the details but it's been hired to a journalist who works for one of the tabloids.'

Drake stared at the name, relishing the opportunity to meet the journalist and hoping the reporter would be at the press conference later.

Drake recognised some familiar faces in the press conference but the reporter he really wanted to see was absent. His gaze settled on Robert Stone, who was uncomfortable in his chair as he looked nervously around the room. On the board behind Drake was an enlarged image of the photofit as well as the image of the face, without the disguise. It would probably fit a dozen faces in the audience that afternoon.

Price's voice was loud as he explained about the description available and how the WPS depended on the public being able to help. It wasn't long until Price struggled to vary his answer to the same question asked a dozen different ways. The WPS had no idea who was responsible.

Do you have any meaningful lines of inquiry?

Is there any DNA?

Will we have an announcement soon about progress?

Price cleared his throat and then stood up. It silenced the voices in the room.

'This is the most serious triple murder investigation the WPS has ever undertaken. We are using all our resources to apprehend this killer.'

Drake watched the blinking, the swallowing, the quiet fidgeting, and the humming of the cameras but nobody said anything. Then Stone raised his hand.

'Is it true that you've received the lyrics of a Queen song and that it's connected to the investigation?'

Drake sat in his office, his mind racing. He thought about his mother, then his father. He tried to comprehend why the murderer would want to send them the photograph. And now Stone was getting his information from somewhere. It had to be from inside the WPS but there was nothing he could do. He eliminated Caren, then Winder and Howick as culprits.

Could it be Dr Fabrien? Could it be one of the support staff with a petty grudge?

He flicked through the emails, and reading the results from the forensics test on the crossbow made him even more sullen. Nothing in the car: nothing from the crossbow.

He kept thinking about the song so he turned to the computer screen and clicked on the Wikipedia icon, searching against 1979. Howick was miles out with Nixon as the American president and double-clicking on the name of Jimmy Carter brought up a separate page about the peanut farmer who became a one-term president. Drake knew from his studies at university that 1979 had been an important year in Welsh politics, with the failure of the devolution referendum followed by seventeen years of Conservative government. All of the commentators Drake had studied believed Mrs Thatcher's policies contributed to the subsequent success of the devolution debate. Perhaps the killer was pointing them towards the year, towards some event that made the year relevant. Drake had been seven and he remembered the family holidays in a caravan and silly arguments with his sister. Now, he rarely spoke to Susan. And if he had to speak to her husband, things got worse.

Outside he could hear the roar of the chainsaws echoing around the open space of the parkland – the tree surgeons were working late. He remembered the film of fine sawdust all over the car after their last visit. He had been convinced there was sawdust inside the car, which required a thorough cleaning. Sian's reaction had been typically impatient, telling him the inside of the car was perfectly clean and that his obsessiveness was going to drive her mad.

He made his way through to the Incident Room and dragged an office chair before the board. He stared at the photographs, the names, the numbers, and the song lyrics. 1979 must be important. The office was tranquil and he let his mind concentrate on everything they knew. He blocked out the muffled sound of a text message bleeping on his mobile and minutes later felt a pang of irritation when the telephone in his room broke the silence he was enjoying.

He had missed something: of that he was sure. And what if they couldn't stop the killer before the next death? It would be down to him. There would be recriminations. An investigation and a review – lessons to be learnt.

Drake read and reread the song lyrics. Then he studied

the statements and reports until his eyes hurt. He blanked out the noise from the late-night cleaning staff. He turned back his shirtsleeve, caught sight of his watch and realised the time. He jumped out of the chair and it fell back onto the floor.

It was after midnight. He was hungry and thirsty. He knew he ought to leave but first he had to tidy his desk.

Chapter 19
Sunday 13th June

Drake stood by the open patio door, letting in the fresh morning air. The house was quiet. A sense of disappointment briefly clouded his mind once he had realised there were no messages on his mobile, so he checked again. Then an unfinished sudoku puzzle nagged at his mind but he tried to resist it. He thought about his mother and the look of disbelief on her face when he'd explained about the photograph of Roderick Jones. There was still no sign of an appointment with the specialist and the thought of their family lunch today put him on edge.

He heard movement upstairs and then the sound of footsteps on the staircase. Sian yawned as she walked into the kitchen.

'Been up long?'

'Not long.'

She sat by the table. 'Ian.' Her voice was heavy. 'You've been late home from work every night this week.'

He sat down, sensing her mood was serious.

'I know, but …'

'The girls complain they don't see you.'

'But I can't just leave when we're in the middle of a murder investigation.'

'Didn't you get my text on Friday? And why didn't you answer the phone? Reception didn't know where you were.'

'I was in the Incident Room. I've told you. I might miss something. Something might happen. It's hectic.'

'Too hectic to be home at a reasonable hour at least one night in the week?'

He got up and flicked the kettle into life. Once the water had boiled he waited: the water had to be off the boil for coffee. Then he filled the cafetière and pressed the timer on his watch. Sian rummaged through a cupboard for cereal and filled a bowl. He stood by the worktop and when the timer sounded, he plunged the coffee.

'Do you always have to do that every time? How long is it?'

'Two and half minutes,' he said.

'Would it be the end of the world if it was a minute and a half? This is beginning to control your life and ours.'

Sian sat down and began eating her breakfast. 'I think you should get counselling before the obsessions get the better of you.'

He wanted to talk about the rituals but there was something holding him back, tugging at his mind. He could talk to Moxon; that was how things worked. Talking to Sian was different. He had to think in boxes, compartmentalise everything. When he talked to Moxon, it was just that and nothing else.

'I don't know,' he said.

He definitely wanted to stop the discussion going any further. He wanted to divert the conversation and his thoughts returned to the investigation. The numbers came back to his mind. The number four, and then three, as though they were unresolved clues in one of his sudoku puzzles. He looked over at the fridge and saw the number-shaped magnets clinging to the door. There was a four there too, and two threes. Numbers were everywhere, when he looked.

'And another thing,' Sian said. 'We haven't made love for three weeks.'

Megan and Helen were sitting in the back seat of the car, firmly plugged into their iPods, the white cords dangling down around their T-shirts. Drake wanted to say something to Sian, something meaningful, something that might tell her he was in charge of his rituals, of the obsessions that could dominate his mind, enough for her to know that his behaviour could improve.

He struggled, and the space between them seemed to

amplify the silence and ramp up the tension when he couldn't find the words. He thought about his possible promotion, but he made an effort to bury his ambition in a corner of his mind. After all, Sian earned more than him and she only worked part time.

He had the window open a few centimetres and the cooling breeze blew against his face. After negotiating the tunnels near Penmaenmawr, he glanced in the rear-view mirror, and caught sight of the blue Volvo. He accelerated on towards Llanfairfechan and Bangor. To his right dinghies raced on the waters of the Menai Strait.

Sian broke the silence. 'We should suggest your father go private.'

He knew from what Sian had said that paying for a private appointment would be the only way to avoid the waiting list.

'I don't know that he'd agree.'

'If he wants an early appointment it's the best thing to do. With all the NHS cutbacks these days …'

'How long would he have to wait?'

Sian sounded positive, 'Only a few days. I could talk to the clinic.'

He turned off the main road and slowed, eyeing the Volvo behind him. He took a detour and Sian looked at him anxiously.

'Something I need to do.'

Reaching for his mobile, he pressed a speed-dial number, eventually getting through to the patrol car he'd passed minutes earlier. He reached a long, straight section of road, and for a moment thought the Volvo had gone but it reappeared and he sensed the anger building as he gripped the steering wheel hard.

Moments later he heard the officers' voices confirming they were right behind the Volvo. Drake slowed the car to a stop as the patrol car flashed its lights and sounded its horn at the Volvo, forcing it to stop behind Drake's car.

Drake strode over to the Volvo; the window powered down slowly. The driver stared straight ahead chewing hard on some gum. Drake knelt, hoping he could control the urge to reach in and throttle the journalist.

'If you ever follow me or my family again, I'll arrest you. Is that clear?' Drake said through clenched teeth.

The driver still stared straight ahead. There was a camera with a telephoto lens on the passenger seat and various notebooks and pencils.

'This officer has some questions for you.'

Drake left the reporter to an interrogation from the Traffic cop and restarted his journey.

'What was that all about?' Sian said.

'It won't happen again.'

He drove through the villages that he had passed through a hundred times before, almost on autopilot – as if the car knew its own way to his parents' home. At the top of the drive, he stopped the car. Sian turned towards him, an uncertain look in her eyes.

'What's wrong?'

'Isn't that a wonderful view?' Drake said, looking out over Caernarfon Bay.

Sian gazed out through the windscreen. An air sea rescue helicopter hovered over Llanddwyn Island in the distance, the white render of the lighthouse shimmering in the summer heat.

'You've seen this view a thousand times before, Ian.'

'You don't appreciate things when you're younger, do you?'

'Your mother's expecting us.'

They bumped down the track and pulled up outside the house. His mother was on the drive as soon as he switched off the ignition and the girls had opened the rear doors and jumped out, calling to their *Nain* as they did so.

His mother had a tired look in her eyes and she squeezed his arm as he kissed her.

'A young policeman called twice yesterday. Elwyn Thomas's son from the village.'

Drake looked blank.

'You know, his father delivered eggs. He had a bad stammer.'

Drake nodded and looked round for his father. 'Where's Dad?'

'He's gone to chapel.' She made it sound routine even though his father was not a regular worshipper. Drake opened his mouth but the words faltered. He wondered at first why she had not gone with him – they did everything else together. He gave his mother a serious look and could see the don't-ask-any-more expression on her face. His father had been a member of the congregation all his life but Drake couldn't remember when his father had last attended a service. Until the teenage years of rebellion Drake had gone to Sunday School, usually with his grandfather and grandmother, who would collect him in their battered old car that coughed and spluttered its way down into the village.

Before he could think of anything to say Sian had slammed closed all the car doors and was standing by his side.

'Hello Mair.' Sian kissed her mother-in-law on the cheek. 'Where's Tom?'

'Let's have some tea,' Mair Drake said.

Sian gave Drake a bewildered look, raising her shoulders slightly in a gesture that asked what she was missing. He smiled back weakly.

The house was cool and a welcome change from the sultry temperatures outside. By the time the tea had brewed and a plate of biscuits had been set on the table Drake heard the sound of his father's car crunching against the gravel of the drive. He looked well, tanned, and walked with confidence, but there was a sadness in his eyes.

'Looking well, Dad,' Drake began.

'He spends all his time in the fields. Feels at home when

he's outdoors,' his mother said, her voice laced with regret.

'Weather's been hot recently,' his father said.

She poured the tea and Drake and Sian sat at the table in the kitchen crunching biscuits, waiting for the tea to cool. His father changed into a rough white polo shirt, crumpled and yellowing with age. He took a long draught from a full mug of tea.

'Need to check down the bottom fields. Coming, Ian?'

His mother gave an impatient look that his father didn't notice. Drake found a pair of old boots, the leather scratched and torn and they both left the house. Drake squinted at first against the sunshine; it felt hotter now and he could feel the first tinge of perspiration on his forehead. They strode down through various gates towards the bottom paddock where his father kept the pigs.

'Your Aunt Minnie was in chapel this morning. Asked about you.'

The recollection of a stick-thin fierce-looking woman with a blue rinse came to Drake's mind. 'How is she?'

'Complaining about her hips. Waiting for an operation.'

'Why didn't Mam go with you?'

'She didn't want to face people, knowing … you know.'

'I didn't know you'd started going back to chapel.'

'With everything at the moment … Well, it was the right thing to do.'

Drake wanted to ask why and whether his father had found the solace he was after. He played with various questions in his mind, dismissing each in turn. Talking about religion or emotions had never been easy in the Drake family and, now more than ever, he felt tongue-tied and embarrassed.

His father stopped by a gate and leant heavily on the top metal rail. He turned to Drake and looked him directly in the eyes.

'If anything … I mean … When … You'll look after your mother won't you?'

Drake felt his mouth dry, lips cracked.

'That business with the photograph hit her hard. Do you know who sent it?'

Drake wanted more than anything to say that they knew exactly who was responsible but all he could do was shake his head.

They walked round the fields and his father pointed to the troublesome gates and poor pastures that needed attention every year. There were lengths of fencing that he wanted to change and he complained about the cost of the contractors that had given him a quote to complete the work.

'I've had the results of the blood tests,' his father said, wrenching open a stiff gate.

'When?'

'Yesterday. Saw Dr Parry in the surgery.' He bowed his head. 'Not good. He was worried.'

'What else did he say?' Drake wondered what else his father wasn't telling him.

'He's going to refer me to a specialist.'

They kept up a good pace walking back to the farmhouse, Drake kicking at the tufts of long grass, his father looking out over the distance and commenting on the weather and predicting when the rain that was needed would arrive.

In the house Drake found Sian sitting alone reading a newspaper and told her about the test results. She made a resigned face as her eyes softened.

Lunch was roast lamb with all the trimmings; Megan and Helen argued over who was going to eat the last of the roast parsnips. Sian tried to encourage Drake to talk to his father with the occasional glance and grimace that he failed to comprehend.

'We think that you should arrange to see the specialist privately,' Sian said eventually, once the table had been cleared.

He nodded slowly. 'GP said there'd be a long wait.'

'Always the same,' his mother said, a frightened look on her face.

'I can talk to the clinic,' Sian said.

Tom nodded.

'How long would the wait be then?' his mother asked.

'A few days maybe,' Sian replied. She looked at Drake. 'Ian, will you go with him?'

Drake looked across the table at his father, expecting him to reject any offer of help. It scared him to see his father nodding slowly.

Chapter 20
Monday 14th June

Caren decided that the space between the BMW and the Ford Fiesta was just large enough to park her car. She pushed the gear stick into reverse with a loud crunching noise. She peered over her shoulder and manoeuvred the car backwards until the nose jutted out into the road. She finally parked neatly after the third attempt and switched off the engine.

She picked up the notebook lying on the passenger seat and had her hand poised on the door handle when she noticed a tall man with thick-rimmed spectacles emerging from Fiona's house. He carried his jacket casually over his shoulder, lowered his head and gave Fiona, standing on the doorstep, a lingering kiss. Caren watched the picture of domesticity unfolding before her. They exchanged a final word and, pulling the small gate of the front garden behind him, the man walked towards a Land Rover Discovery. It bleeped as his remote opened the vehicle.

Caren had a biro in her hand as the four-by-four turned out of its parking slot. She had plenty of time to write down the registration number. She reached for her mobile.

It took her a few seconds to get through to the right person.

'Can you run these plates for me?'

She reckoned by the time she was back at headquarters she'd have the name of Fiona's boyfriend. She could just ask her, of course. But Caren was paid to be suspicious, so she waited in the car until Fiona had returned inside.

Fiona wore a thin silk dressing gown that looked expensive – too expensive for Caren's pocket – and a look of mild panic when she opened the front door and saw Caren. She hesitated before inviting Caren in. There was an empty bottle of champagne and two soiled glasses on a large square table in the centre of the sitting room. Fiona picked up a box of luxurious chocolates, making room for Caren to sit down.

'Celebrating something?'

'A friend came round ... she's ... been promoted – bit of a celebration.'

How the lie slips effortlessly from the lips, thought Caren. And then she wondered, why? Caren had seen the kiss and it looked like a regular domestic routine. She opened her notebook and glanced down the list of questions, knowing that what she really wanted to ask would have to wait.

'I just wanted to clarify the position regarding Paul's private life and about contact with the kids.' Caren was trying hard to sound non-confrontational. 'You told us that Paul wasn't seeing the children very much.'

Drawing Fiona into confirming her original statements was a good place to start.

'He never made an effort. The kids hated going to see him.'

'Anna has told me a different story.'

'Well, she would, wouldn't she?'

Fiona avoided eye contact, her arms folded and her body language defensive. Paul Mathews's solicitor had been quite clear when he described Fiona. *Very difficult. Very uncooperative. One of the worst I've seen.*

'I've spoken with Paul's parents.'

'The kids hated them too.' Fiona narrowed her eyes.

Caren persisted. 'They wanted contact with their grandchildren.'

'The kids wouldn't go.'

'But you were aware they were thinking about court proceedings.'

'My solicitors dealt with all that. And anyway, what does this have to do with Paul's death?'

Caren paused; Fiona gave her a sideways glance and turned away. There was a shallow thud as letters fell on the floor in the hall, then the clanking of the gate closing behind the postman.

'I need to ask you some personal questions about Paul.'

Fiona turned to look at Caren.

'Were you aware that he had suffered from chlamydia?'

The question hung in the air like a bad smell but the look on Fiona's face spoke volumes. Fiona turned to look out of the window. It was going to be another warm summer's day and the sitting room was hot already.

'No I didn't. But it doesn't surprise me,' Fiona said eventually.

Another whopper, thought Caren.

'Is that all?' Fiona asked, when Caren thanked her for her time.

The early morning clouds had disappeared and the sky was clear blue. As she walked towards her car she caught a glimpse of Fiona's silk dressing gown in the window of the sitting room. After she opened the car door and started the engine, a text message reached her mobile.

It gave her the name of the boyfriend.

Drake was about to suggest that someone open a window when the CPS solicitor got up and fiddled with the catch of the metal frame. It gave way with a squeaking sound, allowing fresh air to flood into the room. Phil Myers sat down heavily in his chair and drew a hand round his shirt collar, then wiped away a bead of perspiration from his forehead.

'You know what Judge Machin is like,' he said. 'If all the paperwork isn't pristine he'll go for the jugular. My jugular in particular. So I want to go through everything again.'

Drake made his impatience obvious by doodling in the margin of the morning's newspaper, folded open at the sudoku puzzle he had already started. A couple of months previously he had been the Duty Inspector when a distraught woman rang emergency services. He had a woman police constable and a couple of uniforms in the team and they found Audrey Embers, a crumpled mess sobbing in her kitchen, naked from the waist down, a pair of jeans discarded in one corner and blood all over her face and T-shirt. She told them, between large gasping breaths, that her husband was at his mate's house playing on the computer.

On the other side of the council estate, they had to force their way past a woman standing at the open door, who screamed that they needed a warrant and that she'd sue. Eventually it had taken three of them to restrain him – Drake reckoned that a mixture of cocaine and lager had given him some added strength. Sat on by two police officers and then cuffed, he was bundled into the back of the car. The sight of domestic violence had always sickened Drake and he never shared the view of some senior officers that these incidents had to take a low priority. An assault was always just that.

Phil Myers had been talking uninterrupted, reviewing the events, occasionally pausing and raising his eyes, looking for confirmation. But Drake was thinking about crossbows and song lyrics and numbers – always the number four. And the photograph of Roderick Jones lying on his mother's kitchen table came back to his mind. Then he recalled the bewildered look on her face and it reminded him to chase forensics about the photograph and the envelope.

This was wasting his time, he decided. He had to say something; he could feel his impatience rising.

'This guy is a grade-one smack-head. Look, do you …'

Howick appeared at the door. 'Traffic have found a crossbow, sir.'

Howick drove and Drake sat, playing with the air-conditioning control of the unmarked car and thinking about the possibilities of what finding the second crossbow might mean. Soon he gave up trying to get the dials to work and he opened the window. Howick was in the outside lane and the traffic was light. A coach, full of tourists on a *Castles Tour*, passed on the opposite carriageway.

Howick slowed for the junction and then parked behind the Scientific Support Vehicle. Behind the flickering yellow crime scene tape Drake saw two large vans by the side of the road. Their bumpers were faded, the paintwork was scratched and rust streaked along the bodywork. Piled all over the kerbside were wooden crates and cardboard boxes. Two men wearing jeans and faded T-shirts stood to one side.

A tall Traffic officer with a serious frown on his face walked up to Drake as he made his way under the tape.

'We had an anonymous tip-off that these vehicles were illegal and that there might be drugs bound for Rhyl.'

Drake nodded as they walked over, recalling the regular memos about the organised drugs trade in the nearby town. The officer continued.

'When we opened the back of the second van and began a search we found the crossbow. That's when we called you.'

Drake stood by the rear door of the nearest van and looked down at the crossbow. It looked well cared for and clean. Maybe even recently used, thought Drake. Foulds appeared by his side and snapped on a pair of latex gloves.

'Think this could be the one?'

Drake shrugged, his mind turning to the two men standing by the kerb. The taller of them had his arms crossed and the second man was shorter but leaner, a defiant grin on his face. What struck Drake immediately was the second man's ponytail and beard.

'This is police harassment,' the first man said.

'I'm Detective Inspector Ian Drake, and you are …?'

'Tex. It's fucking harassment. I could sue for this. We've done nothing wrong.'

Second man now: 'This has ruined our day in the car-boot. This is the best time of the year for us. We've lost hundreds because of you.'

Drake curbed a desire to shout at both men and settled for simply telling them what was going to happen.

'Two policemen have been killed with a crossbow. The officers have found a crossbow hidden in your vehicle. We are going to complete a full investigation of your vehicles and if there's evidence to link you to their deaths then we'll charge you with both murders. That always carries a life sentence and it means years in a high-security prison with few visits and fewer privileges and shit food. Do I make myself clear?'

Neither man said anything. Behind Drake, Foulds and the CSI team were working on the vehicles.

Drake lifted the top slice of the toasted sandwich and looked at the dirty-yellow-coloured mass oozing over the edges. He prodded the cheese and uncovered a slice of greying ham. He looked into the mug of coffee but it was so weak he could almost see the bottom. He took a spoon and stirred, as though it might turn into a double espresso. He was regretting agreeing to Moxon's invitation for lunch.

'How's Sian?' Moxon asked him.

'Fine.'

'And the girls?'

Drake was looking at the white specks of sugar on the front of his trousers.

'Fine, fine ... you know, busy. Rushing around. Like being a taxi driver.'

'Must be great watching them grow up.'

'Of course.'

'I always wanted kids.'

Drake glanced over at the waitress, thinking that he might suggest a rescue attempt on his coffee – perhaps adding a spoonful of instant might help. The local radio played the lunchtime talk show in the background.

'We've had another song lyric.'

'Really?'

'A song by Queen this time – 'Crazy Little Thing Called Love.' The bastard sent some of the lyrics to my parents.'

'You're probably looking for some failed rock star.'

'My mother's really frightened.'

'She must be. Do you think there's a connection to the lyrics?'

'They're songs everybody knows,' Drake said. 'You hear them on the radio all the time.'

'Rather you than me. What does Price think?'

'That he's leading us a merry dance.'

Drake poked the pile of crisps on his plate and decided against them.

'How's the profiler?' Moxon stuffed his crisp wrapper into his empty mug.

'Working hard, I suppose.'

'I reckon this profiling stuff is all crap. Smoke and mirrors. You could figure out most of it yourself.'

'I'm inclined to agree'. Drake glanced at his watch, knowing he had to be back at headquarters.

'We'll have to go out for a drink sometime,' Moxon said, as they paid.

Since Beverley Moxon's death from cancer, Drake had seen less and less of his friend. As he mumbled his agreement, a pang of guilt hung in his mind – that he should have supported his friend better, but he dismissed it; his mind already returning to the investigation.

Drake had seen Caren add two – or was it three? – spoonfuls of sugar to her tea before adding a dribble of milk and then squeezing out the teabag. There were spots of tea on the worktop and on the floor leading to the bin. Now he could imagine the mug spilling all over his desk. He reached for a coaster and pushed it towards her. He relaxed once she put the mug down.

'What's happening with house-to-house?' he said.

'Nothing. All the teams have drawn a blank.'

Caren fumbled with a large-scale plan, the towns and villages highlighted in yellow, before launching into a detailed explanation. Drake became nervous at the prospect of the carefully ordered papers on his desk falling all over the floor, so he stopped her in mid-flow, suggesting she pin the map on the board in the Incident Room.

Drake used one hand to hold a corner of the map in place as Caren pinned the other to the board. Once Caren had finished they stood back and paused, looking at the towns highlighted in yellow, and the red circles showing the perimeters of varying distances from the Crimea Pass.

'We've done Llanrwst.' She pointed to the town. 'And Blaenau Ffestiniog.'

Drake moved closer to the board.

'What do we know so far? He was in a red car. From the Crimea, he drove down towards Betws-y-Coed.'

Caren interrupted. 'We know he was following them earlier.'

Drake stroked his chin, and then pulled at his lips before interrupting her.

'The car was found burnt out on an industrial estate outside Bangor,' and with two quick strokes of a blue marker, he underlined the location of the industrial estate. 'So we know he travelled from Blaenau Ffestiniog to Bangor.'

'Where did he go in between?'

Drake started by pointing to Anglesey. 'He could have gone on to the island or down the peninsula or back over to Llandudno.'

He dragged one of the chairs near to the board, sat down, and stared at the map and the circles around the towns. Nobody had seen the red Mondeo – the citizens of

North Wales were safely tucked up in bed.

Except one.

Howick waited for the right opportunity. 'I found the details about the second song, sir.'

'What do you make of the lyrics?'

'It's not the lyrics that are important. It's the year it was recorded.'

Caren joined Drake staring at Howick.

'1979.'

'There was something special about that year. Has to be,' Caren said.

'Could be something else,' Drake said. 'A serial number, identification or a code.'

He ran out of options, the frustration building in his mind. They were all numbers and his world revolved around numbers and rituals and now the killer was sending them numbers. He thought again about his parents and the photograph, knowing that the killer knew where they lived. It was as though the killer wanted to torment him.

Winder's entrance into the Incident Room, still talking into his mobile, broke Drake's concentration enough for him to be annoyed. Winder dropped on the desk a bag of pastries that filled the air with a warm, sweet smell.

'Good news, sir,' he began, ending his call. 'Just got back from Chester. Spoke to the receptionist at the hotel where Harrod stayed.'

Winder tore open the bag and thrust it towards them. Caren looked hungrily at the pastries.

'And?' Drake asked.

'Harrod's a lying toe-rag. He left early in the evening.'

'Really?'

Winder nodded enthusiastically and then took a mouthful of pastry.

'The receptionist saw Harrod's car leave. It's got personal plates – JH – same as hers.'

'Well that and his pre-cons does make for an interesting

picture. Tick. VG.'

Winder was still munching a Danish but managed to give Caren a confused look. She made a movement with her forefinger in the shape of the Nike brand and mouthed *very good* just as Drake got up and walked back to his office. Winder rolled his eyes in understanding and looked into the bag for another pastry.

Drake sat down and drew his chair hard against the desk before looking at Caren, who had followed him.

'So Harrod's become more interesting, hasn't he?'

Caren nodded as she pushed the last of the pastry into her mouth. 'Fiona Trick has a boyfriend – Aled Walters.'

'Worth a look?'

'Something's not right there.'

'Okay, but be careful. Grieving widow, etc.'

Drake glanced at the pile of files on the corner of his desk. He noticed Caren's tea – which must have been cold – was still unfinished. She lifted the mug to her mouth and hesitated.

'How's your mother?'

'Frightened.'

It reminded Drake that he still hadn't heard from Foulds so he punched a text on his mobile, hoping the killer might have got sloppy.

'I just can't get the numbers out of my mind,' Caren said.

Neither could Drake. An edge of despair crept into his mind, gnawing away – there was nothing he could do – he didn't know where to begin to look for two other potential victims. Options, there must be other options, he said to himself.

Caren took a final noisy slurp of her tea and after putting the empty mug on the coaster, continued. 'Are there going to be more deaths? Are they revenge killings? How does Roderick Jones fit into all of this?'

His mobile bleeped – *Nothing. Clean* – the message

adding to his frustration. He heard raised voices and furniture being moved in the Incident Room. He guessed that Dr Fabrien had arrived. He got up from his desk, stretched his arms behind his back, straightened his tie and nodded to Caren who followed him.

'Margaret,' he said, giving her a weak smile.

She remained seated and gave him a cool smile back. He noticed flecks of pastry on the floor and the remains of the torn bag in one of the bins – the cleaners would have to work a little harder tonight. He restrained the urge to kneel down and pick up the mess himself. He turned his back to the board and saw the concentration on everyone's faces.

'We need to discuss the numbers.'

Howick straightened in his chair, Winder fastened his collar, adjusted his tie and opened his notebook. Caren sat with one leg folded over another, her gaze focused on him.

'There has to be a connection between all the murders.' He scanned the assembled officers, making eye contact with them all. They waited for him to continue. 'We may not catch him until he's killed again.'

It was as though Drake had read their minds and then said aloud what they were thinking.

'We have to assume he had a motive for killing Mathews and Farrell and Jones. That's why we have to keep digging. Margaret?'

Dr Fabrien got up and moved to stand alongside Drake but as she did so peered at the board.

'You're looking for a man. He plans carefully and meticulously. There's something about the numbers that has significance for him. The easiest explanation is that there are two more deaths. But only one of the deaths on the Crimea Pass had a motive—'

'So one of the deaths had no motive at all,' Caren interrupted and ignored the sharp glare Dr Fabrien gave her. 'It was entirely random.'

'There can be no other explanation for the single

number.'

Howick cleared his throat and asked, 'So all we have to do is find whether Mathews or Farrell was the intended victim?'

Winder groaned loudly, 'That's a needle-in-a-haystack job.'

'Yes. That will be most important,' Dr Fabrien ignored him before moving quickly to explain her theory about the song lyrics. She moved to the end of the board where the words were prominently displayed. She moved her hands over the pages as though the meaning would appear. 'The lyrics mean something to him. They have a special significance in his life. First love. Celebration or birthday and family event.'

'What if it's a code? Maybe we should be looking at the numbers backwards,' Howick said.

There was a silence before Winder spoke. 'Don't be an idiot, Dave.'

Howick was the first to break the silence. 'I've gone back four years. Drawn a blank. After all, they were Traffic cops.'

Drake glanced at Dr Fabrien before speaking to Howick, 'Then look at them individually. If that doesn't work then go back another four years.'

'The crossbow,' Dr Fabrien announced.

'Sorry?' Drake said.

'Have you looked at the crossbow connection? There will be something. A link, for sure,' Fabrien added, almost under her breath.

Drake said, 'And what about the photograph sent to my parents – why me?'

'Don't think he has an interest in you, Inspector. He's got another agenda.'

Drake knew that if he told Dr Fabrien how little he thought she was helping it would be a guarantee for a reprimand from Price.

'Why the horrific injury to the eyes?' he asked, crossing his arms.

She didn't respond at first but chewed her lips slowly. 'If it was a ritual it would have been done to Jones as well. They might have known the killer. Nothing more than simple hatred. A strong emotion, Ian.'

As she finished, a woman civilian support officer came into the room with an envelope.

'Special Delivery,' she announced, handing the envelope to Drake.

It was a plain envelope with a printed label: *Strictly Private And Confidential Detective Inspector Ian Drake*.

He tore open the envelope and unfolded the letter inside.

As the blood drained from his face, a silence descended on the room.

'Call CSI,' he said.

Chapter 21
Monday 14th June

Drake looked over at the Indian takeaway, wanting to believe it had been sensible to call the Armed Response Unit. Caren sat by his side in the unmarked car, drinking from a plastic water bottle. Price had insisted, telling them that he wasn't going to take any risks. Even when Drake had radioed in that the return address on the letter was a curry house, Price was adamant.

The Armed Response Unit team leader was a short man with a military twitch to his jaw who had made clear he was in charge at the scene and that all his officers were correctly trained. Watching a man leaving the restaurant with a plastic bag full of takeaway food containers only made Drake more worried.

He didn't have time to dwell on things as the ARU vehicle screamed to a halt and the officers streamed out. Two officers entered the main restaurant and another three pushed open a side door, taking with them the battering pole that hadn't been needed.

From the car, Drake could hear the screams and shouts.

'Armed police,' and then, after a delay, 'Stop! Armed police. You're under arrest.'

A crowd gathered on the opposite side of the road.

Drake got out and drew on his stab jacket. He walked over towards the restaurant, Caren by his side and a uniformed officer behind him, as a BMW with blacked-out windows pulled up. The driver's door opened and a tall man wearing various gold necklaces jumped out. Drake arrived at the restaurant door at the same time as the man from the car.

'What the fuck is going on here?' he said, pushing past Drake.

'This is a police raid,' Drake said. 'You can't go in.'

'But I own this place. It's my fucking place. You've got no fucking right. I'm going in.'

Drake nodded to the uniformed officer beside him, who stepped in front of the man.

'I'll have to ask you to stay outside. If you don't, then this officer will arrest you.'

'This is fucking unbelievable. I'm going to call my solicitor.'

The man scurried back to the BMW, a Smartphone pinned to his ear. Drake took the stairs to the first floor, Caren following behind him. The property was a warren of small bedrooms with three beds to each room and dirty clothes piled everywhere. Drake and Caren walked up to the second floor without saying much; occasionally they heard the raised voices of the ARU officers demanding identification and the unintelligible responses.

'This place stinks,' Caren said, as they peered into another small room, filthy bed linen piled in a corner. 'It's not fit for anyone to live here.'

Drake nodded.

He heard the ARU team leader call his name from the first floor. Drake shouted an acknowledgment and made his way downstairs.

'Fifteen altogether, Ian,' he said, a pleased tone to his voice. 'None of them can speak a word of English. There must be some illegals amongst them.'

Drake wondered if the killer was outside looking on and enjoying the whole fiasco that was taking place.

'We'll need all their personal details,' he said.

'They're all in the kitchen downstairs. No sign of any firearms and definitely no hazardous substances, unless you count the curry.'

Drake ignored the attempt at humour. An hour passed, before Drake and Caren had finished gathering all the details they needed. There was still a crowd on the pavement when they left but there was no sign of the owner.

'Covered in prints, of course,' Mike Foulds began.

Drake stared at the remains of the envelope on the table of the CSI lab. Price stood by Caren's side with arms folded, a severe look on his face. Dr Fabrien maintained an aloof pose.

'There are four sets of complete fingerprints on the envelope and at least that many partials. I expect one to be Ian's and the other from the civilian support staff who delivered the envelope.'

Drake nodded as Foulds continued.

'Then there will be postal workers. No real way of telling how many people might have handled the envelope.'

Price let out a long frustrated groan. He turned to Foulds. 'And the letter?'

'Guess what, only one complete set of prints. If I'm a betting man, they'll be Ian's.'

They all knew that was a certainty – no one would offer them odds on any other outcome. Foulds dropped the envelope and letter into a clear plastic evidence wallet. Once they had finished, the envelope would be subjected to the full range of forensic analysis. There might be minute particles of skin or hair inside the envelope, attached to the letter, saliva on the stamp – they had ruled out the envelope – it was a self-sealing variety.

Foulds passed round photocopies of the letter.

'So what do we make of it?' Price said, to no one in particular.

'It's another song lyric,' Drake said.

'What is it with this guy and songs? What the fuck is he trying to say?'

Drake continued. 'It's a Pink Floyd song – 'Another Brick In The Wall'. It was a hit. Can't remember when.'

And then Drake realised he knew.

'1979,' he said.

'What?'

'The year, sir. I'm sure it'll be 1979.'

Foulds hummed the tune. 'I'll dream about *that* song now,' he added.

Another song to repeat itself, Drake thought. Another beat for his fingers to drum on the steering wheel. Price unfolded his arms, stuck his hands into his pockets and walked round the table. 'And there is no number on this letter. So what do we make of that?' He added in an exasperated tone, 'If anything.'

'You seem to have caught his attention, Ian.' Price faced Drake. 'The letter's personally addressed – he must have a thing for you.'

Drake tried a half-hearted smile but the muscles waned. He clenched his jaw as he thought of his parents with the CSIs on the morning the Polaroid had arrived and how they'd have felt having their fingerprints taken. But he had to stop the anger getting in his way.

'Anything from the forensics on the photograph?' Drake said.

Foulds shook his head.

Drake's name on the envelope had to mean something: he'd been on television, his name was in the newspapers and the killer had posted a letter to his parents. And since then, it had become personal.

Drake noticed Caren tapping her mobile until eventually she looked up.

'You were right, sir. 1979.'

'Margaret, what do make of these lyrics?' Price said.

'I shall have to read them, carefully,' the profiler said, 'and I shall have to read them with the other lyrics. It is all very troubling.'

Drake and Caren left the lab for the Incident Room after picking up copies of the envelope and letter. As Caren pinned up a photocopy of the song lyrics, Winder walked in.

'I hope you've got some good news for me,' Drake said to him.

The sub-postmistress of the post office from where the

letter had been sent had enjoyed every minute of her discussion with Winder. Her favourite television programme was *The Bill*, after *Coronation Street*.

'It was like being on one of the soaps for her,' Winder said. 'She knew all the jargon.'

'Well, is there a description?' Drake said.

'Yes,' Winder began. 'Dark glasses, heavy beard, baseball cap and a deep voice.'

Howick spluttered into a coffee. 'Fuck me, I thought you were going to say he had a red nose and big ears.'

'Very funny.'

'Any CCTV?' asked Drake.

'None. It was a small sub-post office.'

'Thought they'd closed all of those,' Caren added.

'Well, she's still going strong. She's sixty-five next week and could talk for Wales.'

It was after midnight when Drake sat in the Alfa and began his journey home. He pressed play on the CD player and the car filled with the sound of Bono's voice. He had drunk two glasses of tepid water in the past three hours and was starving, although the chances of getting anything to eat at home were now slim.

The house looked quiet when he turned into the drive, the downstairs rooms in darkness and the curtains to the bedrooms closed. In the kitchen, he opened the fridge and extracted a bottle of Peroni. He found a sudoku and sat, drinking the cold beer, trying to solve the fiendish puzzle, until his mind was a complete blur.

Chapter 22
Monday 14th June

He poured two sachets of white sugar into his cappuccino and stirred carefully. He took his first sip of the hot coffee before unfolding the newspaper.

There were two photofit impressions in the middle pages but it was the one without the disguise that made his pulse quicken. It wasn't anything like him of course. Nobody had seen his face. The fat woman in the taxi company hadn't even looked up. He'd put the envelope on the counter with enough money to cover the fare and then walked out without saying more than a few words. And there was an odd smell in the place, like piss and sweat and old clothes.

He wondered whether she'd be able to recognise his accent. But what if she could? It wasn't going to tell them where to look. It wasn't going to help them find him, but as he'd got so much to do he couldn't afford for that to happen. He knew it was only a matter of time but it had to be at a time that he decided.

Then he thought about the CCTV cameras on the summit of Snowdon. Nobody would have paid him any attention. It had been full of tourists having coffee and tea. He could remember his excitement as he watched Jones walking in, sweaty, well fed. Jones didn't notice him. Just like Jones didn't notice her. She was just another statistic, a case, a file. He didn't speak to anybody that day, not even nod of the head. So nobody could tell them about his accent. Impossible.

There was a photograph of Detective Inspector Drake in the newspaper; he had an intense look on his face, and a quotation alongside the article. He was wearing one of those expensive shirts and he'd spent hours getting the tie fastened correctly. He imagined what Drake would make of the disguise. Beard, ponytail and baseball cap would make it difficult, very difficult, for someone to describe his face.

Drake was going to spend hours going round in circles. He was going to make sure of that. He didn't care. She was gone.

He looked again at the second image and a worry fluttered through his mind. He had to be careful. He wasn't going to take any chances.

It had been a risk standing in that crowd by the Indian restaurant, watching the debacle. He realised then that it was all going to be worthwhile. He wanted to laugh out loud. Those officers from the Armed Response Unit must have been waiting for some action. Sitting on their backside all day and then nothing – just a bungled raid on a takeaway restaurant.

He hadn't paid any attention to the music playing in the background until a cover version of 'Crazy Little Thing Called Love' began playing. He had to stop and putting the newspaper on his lap for a moment listened to the words. He replayed in his mind the initial conversation with the snivelling journalist. The team at Northern Division Headquarters wouldn't understand a thing. They wouldn't have a clue.

He hummed the words under his breath and then caught himself changing to 'Brass In Pocket' and then the baseline from the Pink Floyd song crashed into his head. He would miss these songs.

But the last couple of days had been enjoyable.
Really fucking enjoyable.

Chapter 23
Tuesday 15th June

Drake drew his forefinger over the dust on the computer screen, cursing the cleaning staff who should have dusted the night before. He reached for a box of tissues and wiped his finger, before discarding the crumpled remains. He pulled the chair towards the desk and sat down. He sensed the belt around his waist straining and, running his fingers along his waistband, tried to loosen his trousers.

'We both need to do some exercise,' Sian had said when she explained that they were both joining a Pilates class in a tone that implied disagreement was ill-advised. In a vague way, he was looking forward to the class the following day.

The fiasco surrounding the Indian restaurant had only made the frustration creeping into the inquiry worse. He scanned down his inbox and read an email from a divisional inspector in Wrexham. Had he heard the rumour about George Tench being promoted to Detective Chief Inspector? The muscles in Drake's chest tightened and his heartbeat increased. Tench was in the Economic Crime Department and universally disliked, but if the rumour was true, he had made DCI before Drake, even though he was a year younger.

He scanned through his emails, part of his mind thinking about Tench, and stopped when he saw one headed *Important message from Superintendent Price*. But every message Price sent had the same heading and it soon lost its impact. Drake deleted a dozen circular emails before returning to Price's message.

He picked up the phone.

'I've been expecting you to call,' Hannah said. 'Have you seen the papers this morning?'

'No.'

'Better get a copy and then come over – he wants to see you.'

Drake replaced the handset and he noticed more dust on

the telephone. He would have to talk to the office manager. He typed the name of the local newspaper into a Google search and then clicked on the result. On the first page was a picture of the owner of the Indian restaurant – angry stare, arms folded. The strapline read: *Restaurant Raid Fiasco.*

He clicked on the link but nothing happened, and he grimaced with irritation. He picked up the phone and dialled reception only to be told they hadn't got a copy of the newspaper.

'Don't we get a copy?' He raised his voice. 'Can you—'

The line went dead.

Drake's annoyance was rising and he could feel his mood darkening. The press was having a field day about the Indian takeaway. He would have to find out about Tench. There was dust all over his computer and telephone. Reception didn't have a copy of the newspaper. And the receptionist had cut him off mid-sentence.

The telephone rang as soon as he put it down.

'Seen the paper this morning, Ian?'

It took him a moment to recognise Lisa's voice.

'Why don't we get a copy in reception?' His voice was terse.

'Go on the website,' she replied.

'I want to see the paper in my hand.'

'I've got a copy of the full article.'

'Aren't they supposed to contact us in advance or something?'

'The editor rang me yesterday – fishing for a quote. Told me they'd been to interview the owner.'

Drake remembered about his meeting with Price. 'Look, the super wants to see me.'

'Me too. I'll see you up there.'

Drake stepped out into the Incident Room and Winder called

out, 'I found that bag, sir.' He pointed to the computer screen on his desk.

Drake watched as a colour picture of a rucksack filled the monitor. It looked exactly the same size and shape as the bag he had seen on the back of the killer.

'I want this checked with everyone interviewed last Wednesday.'

'But that could—'

'Just do it, Gareth.'

Ten minutes later, Drake sat alongside Lisa in Price's office. A copy of the newspaper was open on his desk and Lisa had her copy folded on her knees.

Price immediately started on Lisa. What were the press playing at? Had they spoken to the PR department? Why wasn't he being kept informed? Does the press know something they're not telling us?

'Is there no way we can control what the press reports?'

Drake noticed Lisa raising her eyebrows in astonishment. He guessed what she was thinking – press freedom, civil liberties and human rights.

'My understanding, superintendent,' her voice was calm, 'is that the Armed Response Unit overreacted and broke their own standard operational procedures.'

An exasperated look passed over his face. She continued. 'And we wouldn't want that reported in the press, would we, sir?'

Price glared at her and Lisa blinked, before playing with the folded newspaper on her lap. Price turned to Drake, wanting to know if there were positive developments that might interest the press. Drake mumbled a non-committal reply.

'I think we're done,' Price said.

The morning forecast had been right to predict changeable weather, as a light drizzle had begun to fall on the windows of his office. It matched the mood of the meeting. Drake decided to ask about the promotion of

Inspector Tench and waited for Lisa to leave.

'Is it true about George Tench?'

'What?'

'The promotion?'

'Yes, the board made a final decision last night. Good man. How well do you know him? Fight your corner, Ian. Do a good job with this ... and ... well ... you might be next.'

Price gave him a disarming smile. Drake screwed his eyes and gave Price a bewildered look. He worried about his promotion – he'd had better results than Tench. Once he left the senior management suite, he became more bad-tempered. The bad start to the day was getting worse.

Caren had left headquarters earlier than usual the night before. When she'd arrived home, Alun had pointed to the two pairs of walking boots by the back door and told her the summer evening was too good to waste. She changed into a pair of shorts and pulled on her boots before joining him outside.

At the top of the field, they clambered over a narrow stile and found the wide bridleway that led up the valley. The path was clear and well trodden and the trees on either side were full of colour. They walked until they were out in the open countryside with the warmth of the sunshine on their faces. After an hour, Caren felt hungry.

'There's steak in the fridge,' he said, reading her mind.

'Wine?'

'Best Chilean, opened already.'

She kissed him on the cheek and held his hand as they walked back. Caren rummaged through the fridge assembling a salad from tomatoes and the remains of a lettuce. They sat outside, warmed by the coals of the barbeque. When they were halfway through the second bottle of wine he leant over and kissed her, his hand warm against her leg. She ran her hands over his face and drew him closer. He pulled her out of the chair and folded his arms around the small of her back. They shuffled over towards the door, their tongues intertwined. She tripped over the threshold but he caught her before she fell and then locked the door. In the kitchen, Caren closed the curtains and, turning towards Alun, realised she was overdressed.

Sipping her second mug of sweet tea, she recalled the sight the night before, of Alun walking naked round the kitchen, and decided that she had to leave work earlier more often. Grinning, she reached for a pencil from the mug crammed with spare pens and biros and ran it along the seal of the large brown envelope lying on her desk. Out of it fell a handwritten note that used her full title, *Dear Detective Sergeant Waits* and a dozen unopened letters, all addressed to Paul Mathews. Donald Mathews went on to explain that he thought she should have the letters, rather than the solicitors dealing with Paul's affairs. She made a neat pile of all the envelopes, which she discarded in the bin by her feet. She took another sip of tea and began reading. It was like looking into someone's grave, knowing there was nothing she could do to shape events. There were two circulars from Sky inviting Mathews to upgrade his membership and a credit card with an enormous automatic limit – it included a concierge service, but Caren doubted that Mathews would have benefited.

The final piece of correspondence she unfolded from the bottom of the pile carried the emblem of the Australian consulate. She read its contents and another piece of information about the life of Fiona Trick fell into place.

She read the letter a second time.

> *As you will be aware, Miss Trick has made an application to emigrate to Australia and as part of the verification process we need to be satisfied that all the appropriate court orders and consents have been obtained. The application includes both of your*

children and as such we shall require either your consent or an appropriate court order before we can continue to process the application.

The realisation struck Caren that without Paul Mathews to object, Fiona Trick no longer needed his consent or an order from the courts. She leant back in her chair and ran through the options in her mind. Was Fiona Trick a realistic suspect in her husband's murder? And how did Fiona's boyfriend fit in?

She had called in favours long overdue to find details about Aled Walters's personal life, which included a messy divorce a couple of years before. A successful business meant he could spend his time as a county councillor and further his political ambitions with a place on the regional list for a seat in the Welsh Assembly.

It didn't strike Caren that he was likely to emigrate.

A hurried lunch of two pasties and some healthy low-fat coleslaw had only postponed the frustration building in Drake's mind as he walked to his office. He pushed open the door and noticed the intense expectant glint in the four sets of eyes converging on him. Caren was the first to stand up and attract his attention. He sat down on the corner of a desk and touched the front of his tie with the palm of his hand, sensing the beginning of indigestion.

'Caren, want to start?' he said, glancing over at her.

Caren walked up to the board and pinned up a photograph of Fiona Trick and Aled Walters.

Between mouthfuls of apple, Winder interjected. 'What's so special about her and who is this Aled Walters?'

Caren cleared her throat. 'After parking outside Fiona's house on Monday I saw Aled Walters leaving. When I was interviewing her later there was an empty bottle of champagne, two glasses and a box of those expensive Belgian chocolates in the sitting room. She gave me some excuse about a friend celebrating her promotion. Then she lied to me about knowing Mathews had chlamydia.'

'Might have been genuine,' Howick said.

Everyone in the Incident Room sniggered.

'Right, let's move on,' Drake said, the impatience clear in his voice. 'So what's new Caren? We know that Fiona Trick and Aled Walters are an item.'

'Donald Mathews dropped in Paul's letters this morning. There was one from the Australian consulate. It seems that Fiona wants to emigrate. She would have needed a court order or Paul's consent—'

'Or Paul Mathews out of the way.' Howick finished the sentence for her.

Caren pointed to the face of Aled Walters on the board behind her.

'My guess is that he doesn't know she wants to emigrate.'

'Come on Caren,' Drake said. 'We're police officers, not gypsies.'

Caren persisted.

'She lied to us about Paul's contact with the children, she withheld information about her plans to emigrate and there's a boyfriend on the scene that she doesn't admit to. And we shouldn't forget the small detail of the £300,000 insurance payout.'

Drake nodded, acknowledging that there was enough to justify their interest in Fiona Trick. 'Before we get too excited let's just think about it. How would she have killed Mathews and Farrell?'

Winder finished his apple and threw it into a nearby bin. 'Maybe Aled Walters did it.'

'Maybe they were both up on the Crimea,' Howick suggested.

'Of course, once they saw Fiona, they stayed in the car,' Winder said.

'Then Aled Walters comes out from behind the car and

bang,' Howick appeared energised the more he constructed the scenario.

Ryan Kent had been sitting quietly. 'Always think outside the box. That's what I say. Anything is possible. Do you remember that scene with Gandalf—'

Drake's patience snapped. 'Spare us the *Lord of the Rings* crap.'

Kent looked offended and a nervous, embarrassed mood fell over the meeting, broken only when Foulds pushed open the door into the Incident Room.

'I've got the results of the crossbow found in the vans on Monday.'

'Good,' Drake said. 'Anything of interest?'

'Lots of partials we can't trace.'

He handed Drake the report. 'Only one partial we can trace. It's from a guy called Aled Walters.'

'What?' Drake said.

Winder whistled under his breath and Caren took the report from Drake's hand and flicked through the pages. Foulds looked surprised until Caren explained the connection.

Drake continued. 'Before we go charging in let's do some more background checks. I want to know everything there is to know about Aled Walters – family, work, etc. – and Fiona Trick.'

Drake could feel the anger pinching at his mind. They should have found all this out already. They were supposed to be police officers. They had to be suspicious, dig up everything they could.

He stood up, hoping it would help to alleviate the heartburn.

'Was there anything else?' Drake hoped that nobody in the room had heard his stomach turning over.

'Harrod, sir.'

Howick picked up the marker pens on the top of his desk and walked over to the board.

'We know Harrod has done time,' Howick began. 'And he wasn't where his wife thought he was on the night.'

'Motive?' Drake said.

'Revenge for Farrell's behaviour towards his wife.'

Howick sounded unconvinced. Drake raised his eyebrows and pursed his lips.

'And we know Harrod was banged up on the same wing as Dixon,' Howick said; a smug, self-satisfied look passed over his face and, having dropped this piece of information into the meeting, he watched his colleagues' reaction.

Winder gave another slow whistle and crossed his arms.

Drake was the first to say anything. 'Really ...?'

'Normally, Harrod would have been sent to a nick near Hull. But for some reason he was sent to HMP Chokes Lane, near Wigan – one of those prisoner movement exercises. And a friend of mine works in admin. So I gave her a call. She sent me a list,' Howick said, visibly preening himself.

Drake turned to the board, his mood improving, even the indigestion was subsiding. 'Dixon is back in the frame. Happy days.'

Howick shuffled the markers in his hand. 'Ryan's been doing some work on the accounts, sir,' he said.

Kent launched into an explanation and his strong booming voice grew louder the more he talked – he even managed to only make two references to *Lord of the Rings*. The analysis of the Harrod group accounts became ever more technical until Drake forced his mind to concentrate. Like rabbits caught in a car's headlights, they were transfixed by Kent's voice, unable to function normally. Eventually, Kent relented.

'Harrod hasn't come onto the radar with us,' he said, rubbing his hands. 'But I've checked and we did have a sniff of a bribery complaint a couple of years ago.'

Winder had a relieved look on his face. 'Harrod was slipping backhanders?'

'Nothing came of it ... but ...', and as Kent drew

another large breath, Drake intervened.

'Well I'm sure we're all grateful to ...' His mind went blank – he thought only of Gandalf and the hobbits and Bilbo Baggins and Frodo.

'Ryan, sir, Ryan Kent,' Winder said.

'Of course, thank you.'

Before Kent could say anything further, Drake strode across the Incident Room towards his office, back to the order on his desk. He grimaced as his indigestion returned. He pondered whether he could achieve anything further that afternoon when the telephone rang.

'Drake.'

'There's another body, sir.'

Chapter 24
Tuesday 15th June

Drake kept the car in a low gear, the engine screaming, until he reached the A55. Then he accelerated hard in the outside lane, blasting the horn at frightened motorists in his path.

'Where is this beach, sir?' Caren said, fumbling with the folded sheets of a roadmap.

'It's on the southern side of the island. See that sand-coloured section,' Drake said pointing to an open part of the map on Caren's lap.

'Looks remote.'

'Very popular.'

He pulled down the visor against the sun streaming through the front windscreen, cursing himself for having left his sunglasses at home.

The call from Area Control had given him just the bare details of where the car had been found. Drake guessed that it would have taken at least half an hour for local officers to arrive at the scene. He crossed the Menai Strait but found his impatience growing as he slowed behind a caravan. He drew the Alfa hard up against the tailgate then pulled out when he thought it safe to do so and flashed the driver who suddenly braked, allowing Drake to overtake.

Drake accelerated along the narrow country lanes, cursing the drivers that slowed his journey and flashing his lights at the oncoming cars who pulled into the grass verge out of his way. It was the middle of summer and he'd driven this route many times to the beach but today there was an urgency that made the caravans and tractors an irritation. He could feel his annoyance building.

He had his mobile pushed at an angle into the cradle on the dashboard. He rounded a corner and came to a stop abruptly as a farmer stood in the middle of the road hand raised as a tractor manoeuvred out of a field. The mobile rang as the farmer finished and Drake saw Price's number.

'Sir,' Drake said.

'Have you arrived yet?'

'Caught in traffic.'

'It's a mess. Uniform are doing what they can to preserve the scene and the CSI team are ahead of you.'

'Any more details?'

'It was a young woman officer on the scene first. A member of the public saw the blood. That's about it really. Call me as soon as.'

'Any messages?'

'No.'

'Song lyrics?'

'Not yet. No.'

They passed two officers standing by a marked police car at the end of the road leading to the beach. Every speed bump slowed their progress down the road through the forest and Drake's thoughts turned to the killer. There had to be a reason for choosing the locations of his crimes. The Crimea was an isolated mountain pass and he'd killed Mathews and Farrell in the middle of the night, but Roderick Jones had been killed in broad daylight in a café full of people, and now a car with a body in the middle of a forest and a vast open beach. Maybe there was no significance at all.

There were more uniformed officers visible as he approached the car park; groups of tourists milled around cars and camper vans. The Scientific Support Vehicle was parking near a red car – another red car – and he saw Mike Foulds changing into a forensic overall.

He parked, locked the Alfa, and strode over the sand and shingle to the red car. Drake could tell from the plates that the car was ten years old – probably stolen. They reached the car just as Foulds stood up and stripped off his paper suit.

'Waste of fucking time,' he said.

'What do you mean?' Drake said.

'It's a dummy.'

'What?' Drake raised his voice

'It's a fucking dummy.'

Drake could hardly believe what Foulds was telling him. He leant down to double-check and looked into the car.

'I moved that hoodie to one side when I checked for a pulse. There's even a ponytail.'

Now they were entertainment for the killer. Drake stood up sharply and looked at the people in the car park, the realisation striking him that the killer might be there, gloating at them. There were probably fifty, maybe sixty, people all dressed in shorts and summer T-shirts. There were children with buckets and spades. He felt like shouting out for the killer to come forward.

'What's wrong, Ian?' Foulds said.

'He could be here. Now. Today. I want the details of everyone here. Addresses telephone numbers and their contact details.'

'But there are people walking in the forest,' Caren said.

Foulds added. 'And on the beach. You know the beach goes for miles here. He could be anywhere. He may have had an accomplice and they may have had a car. He could be miles away.'

Drake ignored him and said to Caren. 'Get as many uniformed officers to stop people coming off the beaches and out of the forest as you can.'

She nodded and scrolled through her mobile.

Drake leant down again to look into the car. The bullet wound in the forehead of the life-like face would have been convincing on first glance. The clothes looked clean but old, and Drake recognised the smell as upholstery cleaner. It smelt like the one he used every week on the inside of his car.

'Kept the car clean,' Foulds said. 'So it probably means he was clever about not leaving any traces.'

'Bastard,' Drake said under his breath.

He got up slowly and stood with Foulds, looking at the

life-like dummy with the fake blood and the hoodie and then realised the killer must be laughing at him, enjoying every minute. He kicked a tyre but it didn't improve his mood.

On the journey back to headquarters, Caren tuned the radio phone-in and they listened to the introduction of a programme that would address *'the profound issues raised when police officers are murdered'* and *'what significance this could have for society'* and what the announcer called *'society's perceived decline in moral values'*.

The first guest on the programme was a member of parliament with an accent that Drake knew had come from an expensive English education. The man managed a pessimistic tone as he pondered whether the Wales Police Service was up to the task of finding the killer.

'I wasn't in favour of criminal justice being devolved from Westminster,' the politician said. 'And it's at a time like this that we really need to consider whether it was the right decision. After all, we are much stronger as nations if the UK is united.'

Drake gripped the steering wheel and said aloud, 'What the hell does that have to do with the murder inquiry?'

'Politicians, sir,' Caren said. 'He doesn't want any more devolution so he's using this as an excuse to make that point.'

The interviewer then brought in a caller from Scotland, who laid into the politician, accusing the UK government of wanting to interfere in the devolved administrations of Wales and Scotland. When he described the politician as an interfering idiot, the journalist cut across him and finished the call. Another caller from Birmingham visited Wales every year on holiday and thought it was a lovely country, with wonderful scenery but, when asked for his opinion, he wanted to bring back capital punishment.

Drake and Caren listened in silence as various callers

made clear their horror at the killing and hoping the culprit would be caught.

'I never thought I might be killed as a police officer,' Caren said.

'Nobody does.'

'It only happens in the American films.'

'You know that's not true.' Drake reminded her.

Caren nodded. 'I suppose the politicians are right.'

'Of course they're right.'

'Why did you become a police officer, sir?'

'Because what we do is important. It matters and when two officers are killed then that's serious. And the press and the politicians are right to say it's about the "fabric of society" but in the end we've got a killer to catch.'

Once the programme ended, the headlines of the news were about the latest trade deficit figures. Drake switched off the radio.

Drake faced the board in the Incident Room: behind him sat the rest of his team and Dr Fabrien. A single sheet of paper with the word 'dummy' written on it had been pinned alongside the songs on the board. Caren had earlier circled the location of the murders and the beach on the map pinned to the board.

'Margaret. What do you make of the dummy?' Drake said

'I think he is playing with you.'

Nobody responded. There was a silence in the room. Drake turned round and she continued. 'He likes dramatic scenes. The deaths on the Crimea. The killing on the mountain and now the dummy on a popular beach.'

'What sort of person are we looking for?'

'He's clever and prepares thoroughly'

'I need something more constructive.' *And less obvious*, thought Drake.

'Well, at the moment there is—'

'I need something positive, Margaret. The press are going to go ballistic over this when they get wind of the story. It'll be all over the papers tomorrow.'

'It might not be the killer, of course. It could be a prankster.'

Winder made a contribution. 'That makes sense. Some saddo getting off.'

Dr Fabrien was nodding her head slowly. 'I think it is him.'

'We could always tell the press that we have nothing to link it to the killings and that it might well be a hoax or a sick prank. But that we're treating it with the usual urgency and seriousness.' It was Howick now.

Drake heard the telephone ring in his office. He strode over to his desk and, picking up the receiver, recognised the sound of his mother's voice.

'Ian, so pleased I got through to you straight away.'

'Mam, how are you?'

Drake could hear her voice shaking.

'It's your father – he's got the appointment on Friday. He's really scared, Ian, though he's trying not to show it. Promise you'll go with him?'

Drake thought of everything he still had to do, but he couldn't let his parents down. 'Of course Mam. I'll be there.' Whatever happens, he thought.

Chapter 25
Wednesday 16th June

It was a cloudless morning, the sky a clear sapphire colour. Drake heard a dull roaring sound, turned his head upwards, and managed to pick out the approaching plane on its descent into the airport. He walked towards the main building as the BAE Jetstream 31 made its final descent, its wheels squealing as it touched down on the tarmac.

A group of passengers disembarked and snaked their way towards the small terminal building that stood at the perimeter of the Royal Air Force base. Glancing around the passengers waiting to embark, he recognised two politicians busy reading the broadsheets and a television presenter who was trying to look anonymous.

Drake found a window seat and smiled at the student who sat by his side but she looked back at him blankly, an iPod thumping in her ears. Once they were airborne, Drake looked down and saw the RAF base below. There were training aircraft parked along the runway apron and he thought he recognised a couple of tornadoes. Every fast jet pilot in the RAF trained at the base and the regular passenger shuttle to Cardiff was a minor distraction to the regular training flights.

Drake drank the complimentary coffee as he watched the fields and roads of Anglesey passing underneath. As they reached the mainland, the aircraft turned southwards. He saw a narrow trail of smoke from a train taking passengers up Snowdon and the reflection of the morning sunshine on the granite and glass of the summit café. It all looked very peaceful, with no sign of the tragedy that had taken place there the previous week.

He tried to pick out his parents' farmhouse and then a cold stab of fear struck him – what if the killer really meant to hurt his parents? He knew where they lived, he must know their routine. There was tightness in his chest as anxiety gripped him and he turned his head away from the window and stared at the back of the seat in front of him. He had to stop the killer and he ran through a to-do checklist in his mind before finding the sudoku in the folded newspaper on his lap and focusing on the numbers. Eventually the claustrophobic feeling subsided, replaced by a sense of achievement as he finished four of the squares.

The journey passed quickly and soon the small aircraft began a smooth descent into Cardiff airport. The young civilian officer waiting for Drake was holding up an A4 sheet with his name on it and Drake introduced himself.

During the short drive to the headquarters of the Wales Police Service, Drake rang the area sergeant in Caernarfon but the earlier apprehension returned when he heard an automated message. He speed-dialled his mother and she answered after the third ring and he stumbled for the right words.

'We're fine,' she said.

It wasn't her usual confident voice.

'Have the local lads visited again?'

'They called yesterday. Nothing to worry about.'

But he wasn't convinced.

'I'll ring you later,' he said, as they pulled into the car park at headquarters. He strode over to the main building, making a mental note to call the area sergeant again.

The reception staff took Drake to a conference room with a large gleaming desk. The room had a clean feel. He ran his fingers over the edge of the desk – no dust, just the polish residue. A plate with fresh fruit and coffee mugs were already set out, alongside a vase of fresh flowers. Two of the morning newspapers were open on the table.

'Sorry to keep you waiting,' the Chief Constable said, offering his hand when he entered. 'Have you seen the papers?'

'No, sir.'

Riskin pushed them over towards Drake. The first was a

broadsheet – *Beach Hoax in North Wales*; the second was one of the tabloids – *Maniac Strikes Again.*

'What does Margaret make of this?'

Riskin poured some coffee and gestured for Drake to help himself.

'She thinks it's him.'

Drake picked up a mug, poured a coffee and, once satisfied with its strength, took his first mouthful.

'Any possible forensics?'

'We're still waiting, sir.'

Then the door to the conference room opened and another officer entered.

'Morning, John.'

'Sir.'

'Detective Inspector Drake this is DI John Marco. He'll be your liaison in southern division.'

Marco had three days'-worth of stubble and his hair touched the collar of his jacket, which looked way past its sell-by date. The top button of his shirt was open, and the tie, knotted clumsily, had been pulled away from his neck. He slumped in a chair and helped himself to coffee.

'I need you both to realise how important this case has become. Certain people didn't like the idea of policing being devolved from London to Cardiff. So I don't want to give our critics any more ammunition. The first minister wants to discuss the investigation with you both. Especially you, Ian.'

Drake nodded, not having expected a meeting with the first minister that morning. He took another gulp of the coffee. He glanced over at Marco who scratched his stubble and let out a long sigh. 'When do we start, sir?'

Drake was expecting a Cardiff accent but there was a colourful inflection to Marco's voice.

'You'll need to go through all of Roderick Jones's papers. I've spoken with the first minister. You'll have everyone's complete cooperation.'

Drake had a suspicion that he knew what that meant.

Cooperation, but only as far as it suited everyone. The Chief Constable drew back his shirtsleeve and Drake noticed the Rolex.

'You haven't got much time.'

The same driver took them into the Bay and as they walked over to the Welsh Assembly Government buildings, Marco pulled out a crumpled packet of cigarettes.

'Only five a day – trying to cut down.'

Drake frowned and tapped his watch.

'I'm going in or else we'll be late.'

He straightened his tie, checked his shirt and entered the building – this was his investigation and he wasn't going to let Marco's attitude reflect on his career. Drake found the office of the first minister without difficulty. The signs all around the building made it difficult to miss. He wondered how long it would be until the English language title for the first minister reflected his Welsh title – Prime Minister. Drake had been waiting for about five minutes before Marco walked in and introduced himself to the first minister's staff. He gave Drake a half smile before sitting down. He smelt the tobacco smoke on Marco's clothes and turned up his nose.

A telephone rang. One of the reception staff turned to both men.

'Mae'r prif weinidog yn barod i'ch gweld. The first minister will see you now.'

Caren looked at the to-do list that Drake had dictated to her the night before. Investigate Aled Walters; more work on Fiona Trick; double-check the analysis of the records from the archery clubs ... the list went on, but by lunchtime, she had done very little.

She decided not to tell Dr Fabrien that she would be out for most of the afternoon at the constituency office of Roderick Jones and when she explained her absence to Winder and Howick, a worried look passed over their faces.

She found the office without difficulty, a small terraced property full of old desks and peeling wallpaper. Frances Williams, Jones's constituency secretary, had a large round face and spectacles that were too small for her eyes, giving her the appearance of squinting.

'I don't know how I can help you,' Frances said.

Caren wasn't going to give up quite as easily as this woman imagined. 'I'm sure there must be lots of ways you can help.'

Frances moved her lips, trying to smile, but failing. Caren continued. 'For example, have there been any death threats?'

Frances laughed aloud. 'What, against Roderick Jones?'

'Well, have there?'

The secretary's face took on a serious look again. 'No, of course not.'

'Any difficult customers?'

'They're constituents, actually.'

'Any difficult *constituents* then?' Caren said, knowing that Drake would have raised his voice by now, unable to control his irritation.

The woman pouted and moved awkwardly on a chair. 'All we ever dealt with were the trivial problems.'

'Did anybody else work for Roderick Jones?'

'All the important ministerial work was done in Cardiff. One of the girls here went with him when he was promoted. She got to do all the interesting stuff.'

'What do you do here?'

Frances moved her head and pointed towards the filing cabinets lined up against the wall.

'Those cabinets are full of letters of complaints: people who can't get benefits, people who have lost their jobs and general whingers.'

Caren got a clear picture that Frances didn't have a great deal of job satisfaction.

'Where can I start?'

Frances got up from her chair and took Caren through to Roderick Jones's office at the rear of the building. She pointed at the computer on the desk.

'Not all the cabinets have Roderick Jones's stuff,' Frances said, beginning to relax. 'Some of the other assembly members work from this office too.'

'Show me.'

Another bored look passed over Frances's face as she walked over to the first of the cabinets. She opened a drawer and removed folders suspended against the metal sides.

'Is there a central record of all these *constituents?*' Caren said.

'Of course not.'

It was too much to expect, Caren supposed. All this chaos would get up Drake's nose. Caren turned her back on Frances and searched through her bag for her mobile. She jabbed one of the speed-dial buttons and pressed the phone to her ear.

'Gareth,' she began, 'organise a couple of lads from Uniform, and boxes, and then get down here. We've got a lot to do.'

Robert Stone was finishing a piece on the development of new flood defences after the disastrous flooding the year before. He thought about Sarah from sales and not even the prospect of a repeat of their frantic love-making in the kitchen after work lifted his spirit

The telephone rang and he cleared the papers away from the receiver.

'Stone.'

'I've got some information.'

Once he recognised the voice, he straightened in his chair and flicked to a clean page in his notebook. His mind went back to the press conferences and the look on the face of Detective Inspector Drake when he'd asked about the messages.

This was the sort of journalism he longed for.

'Who is this?'

'I'm sure your readers would be interested in the Roderick Jones killing.'

Robert's pulse beat a little faster. He could see the headlines. *Campaigning journalist exposes police ineptitude.* It was the story every journalist wanted and this would be his ticket to a national tabloid.

'Who are you?'

'Just listen.'

Drake had never before experienced the stabbing, cramp-like pain in his thighs, which he blamed on a combination of sitting in a car and Pilates. He'd hoped that after the day's travelling and the evening's exercise he'd be asleep as soon as his head hit the pillow. But after an hour he still hadn't found the right position. He listened to Sian's steady breathing by his side and hoped that he wouldn't disturb her. He turned to face the alarm clock, willing himself to sleep. Then the telephone rang and he reached for the receiver.

'Drake,' he said his mind instantly back to that first telephone call about the deaths on the Crimea.

'Ian …'

It was his mother's voice.

'There's someone in the bottom field. I've seen a light.'

Drake almost fell out of the bed.

'Have you called the local sergeant?'

'All I get is a message.'

Drake cursed under his breath.

'I'll be there as soon as I can.'

Sian was rubbing the sleep from her eyes as he hurriedly dressed, dragging on a pair of jeans and then fumbled as he laced his trainers.

'It's Mam,' he said. 'She thinks there's an intruder.'

He left the bedroom as Sian mumbled a reply.

In the kitchen, he picked up his mobile and dialled the sergeant in Caernarfon but the message clicked on after the first ring. He stared at the face of the mobile and swore. The local officers were supposed to be available; they should be there to answer her call. He found a jacket and after pulling the door closed behind him strode to the Alfa.

The night sky was clear, the streets empty, and when he reached the A55 he floored his right foot and the car hurtled into the outside lane. He pressed the speed-dial for Area Control.

'Find me the area sergeant for Caernarfon.'

'What's his name, sir?'

'I don't know or else I'd have bloody well told you.' Drake wanted to add, *he's a Scouser who can't pronounce Welsh names properly.*

Drake slowed the car through the tunnels at Penmaenmawr and Llanfairfechan but then accelerated hard. He started counting the articulated lorries passing him on the opposite carriageway, streaming from the ferry terminal at Holyhead for England and beyond. He reached one hundred and six before the turning off the A55. He left the lights of the main road and flicked his headlights to main beam.

He grabbed the mobile from the passenger seat as it hummed into life.

'Area Control, sir. I've got Sergeant Davis for you.'

There were two clicks and Drake heard the Liverpool accent thick with sleep.

'Clive Davis.'

'Why in Christ's name don't you answer your bloody phone?'

'What ... I'm ...'

'I've tried twice this morning.'

'There's must be something wrong ...'

'And my mother's been trying your number.'

'I'll have to check ...'

'I don't want fucking excuses. Get down to my parents' place. Now. I'm on my way. There's an intruder.'

At a little after one o'clock Drake drew the car to a halt by his parents' front door. A light came on and his mother stood by the open door, his father behind her. Over his shoulder he heard the sound of the patrol car as it turned down into the lane.

'It was in the bottom field,' his mother said, as she sat by the kitchen table.

'It'll be all right,' he said. 'One of these officers will check everywhere.' He looked up at Sergeant Davis and the officer with him.

His father cupped a mug of tea and stared at the table as Drake's mother gave them a detailed explanation of how she'd been woken by the sound of something outside which she'd tried to dismiss until she heard it a second time. Drake's father nodded agreement occasionally.

'It looked like a torch. And it stood still by the gate by the stream.'

Drake was looking at his father, wanting to reach over, touch his hand and tell him not to worry. He could sense the frustration building in his mind, knowing the killer wanted this to happen.

Chapter 26
Thursday 17th June

Drake stared at a girl with skin the colour of burnt chocolate, and with lifeless hair, sitting behind the reception desk at the offices of Miles and Powell, trying to guess her age.

'I've got an appointment with Mr Miles.'

'She gave him a gap-toothed smile. 'Your name?'

'Ian Drake.'

'Just a moment.'

'I've got a Mr Drake in reception,' she cooed down the telephone.

Drake sat down and immediately started to regret involving his friend, but after their Pilates the night before it had seemed like a good idea. He admired the clean modern design of the offices: the reception had a high ceiling; granite-coloured tiles covered the floor. Miles and Powell Accountants were doing well by the looks of things. He heard the echoing sound of footsteps on the tiles and then saw Robin Miles approaching, hand outstretched.

'Morning, Ian. How are you feeling today? I'm bloody suffering I can tell you. Whose grand idea was Pilates anyway?'

'I've felt better,' admitted Drake. 'Lovely offices.'

'Cost me a fortune,' Robin said and led Drake through to his office. From the window Drake could see out over a carefully landscaped water feature.

'Some financial advisor persuaded me to use my pension plan to buy this bloody place. But I'm going to be paying for it until I'm eighty.'

'James Harrod?' Drake said, impatient to move the conversation on.

'Yes.'

'This is entirely confidential.'

'Of course. This meeting never took place,' Robin managed a mysterious smile and tapped the side of his nose with his forefinger, indicating that he was in on the secret.

'I need some information.'

'What sort?'

'Anything really. Background.'

Robin was a thin man with a narrow nose and a tall forehead. Drake often thought that he didn't need to go to the Pilates group – he seemed fit enough. A pair of reading glasses was perched on his nose and he peered over them at Drake.

'Harrod's become quite a big player in a short period of time. Somehow he's been able to win contracts that have transformed his fortunes. Gossip is that he's bribing people to win the jobs. All the usual stuff – holidays in Spain, new kitchens.'

Drake nodded.

'I spoke to a colleague of mine before you arrived. Made a pretext that I was running a course and wanted to invite Harrod – possibly trying to get his business.'

Drake flashed a smile – his friend was enjoying this.

'Harrod's involved in a big leisure development along the coast that's in planning – shops, offices, bowling alley.'

Drake scribbled the details in his notepad and waited for his friend to continue.

'He's got a reputation as a vindictive bastard too. I work for a sub-contractor who crossed him.' Robin paused for effect. 'He was walking home one night when Harrod and his thugs gave him a going over. Broke some ribs and couple of fingers, and his nose will never be the same again.'

Drake pulled himself up in his chair.

'Did he complain?'

'He reckoned there was no point. Harrod made sure there were no witnesses.'

'Did he recognise the thugs?'

'No, but he thought they were Scousers.'

'Can I talk to him?'

Robin sounded uncertain. 'I'll ask him.'

Drake placed a business card on Robin's desk as he left. 'Get him to call me.'

On the journey to headquarters, Drake hummed the opening beats of 'Brass in Pocket' and then repeated a line from 'Another Brick in the Wall'. They were classic tracks and he knew they meant something. Or were they simply random messages, sent to entertain the killer and frustrate the investigation? He kept thinking about 1979 and whether the killer had been born in that year or whether he had married that year or ... the list was endless.

Ten minutes later, Drake squeezed the Alfa into a parking spot and bleeped the car. His first task when he arrived in his office was to hang the jacket of the grey lightweight summer suit on a wooden hanger before he organised a coffee. He managed one sip before the telephone rang.

'Someone wants to speak to you,' said one of the reception staff.

'Who is it?'

'They didn't say – just that they want to speak to you.'

There was a click as she transferred the call. Drake introduced himself.

'You in charge?'

'Yes.'

'Well, you'd better do something about it?'

'Sorry.'

'I'm buggered if I'm going to pay any fine.'

Drake could feel his patience wearing thin.

'Excuse me, who are you?'

'I'm John Garnett. I own the garage. You know, from where the red Mondeo was stolen. I've just had a bloody speeding ticket for the car.'

'When?'

'This morning – just now,' His voice rose.

'No, I meant the day of the speeding ticket.'

There was a silence and Drake heard Garnett fumbling with pieces of paper.

'31st May.'

'Where?' Drake held his breath.

'How the hell would I know?'

'It's on the bloody form.'

'Okay, Okay.'

More silence; Drake waited until his patience broke. 'Look, just bring the paperwork in as soon as you can.'

'But I can't leave the garage.'

Drake wanted to shout but settled on a steely tone instead. 'Stay exactly where you are. I'll get someone to collect it.'

Drake and Caren stared at the speeding ticket on the desk in front of them, as if the name of the killer was written on the back. It gave them a time and a place. It was another small part of the jigsaw. A telephone conversation to double-check confirmed that on 31st May at eleven am the red Mondeo was clocked by a speed camera for speeding.

'Type up the details,' Drake said. 'I want them up on the board. And I'll get Margaret here too.'

In the Incident Room he cast his eye over the various photographs, notes and fragments of maps on the board. He fiddled with his elasticated cufflinks and ran a finger around his collar. Through the open windows he heard the roar of the traffic on the A55 as well as the rattle of chainsaws from the tree surgeons.

Caren was pinning an A4 sheet with the details of the traffic offence to the board when Dr Fabrien arrived, fanning herself with some papers, complaining about the heat. Drake folded his arms and tried to concentrate on constructing a picture of the killer.

'Margaret. He was clocked speeding,' Drake said. 'Why

the hell take the risk of being stopped in a stolen car?'

Dr Fabrien stood by his side. 'He takes risks. Must be a man,' she said.

'I need to know about him,' Drake said.

Drake's thoughts were a mass of questions he had to answer and he wanted Dr Fabrien to answer all of them. Was the killer tall? Was he overweight? Did he have a family?

'Let's recap,' Drake continued. 'We know that red-Mondeo-man was here in Colwyn Bay on the morning of 31st May. That was four days after the car had been stolen.'

'I just don't see Harrod or Walters driving around in a stolen car,' Caren said.

'That's why we need to look at all known associates.'

Before Drake could continue, they heard the sound of a loud conversation approaching the Incident Room from along the corridor. The door opened and Winder and Howick entered. Howick draped his jacket over the rear of his chair and Winder sat, arms folded, eyes narrowed, as Drake explained the significance of the speeding ticket.

He looked over at Howick. 'Dave, I want you to look at all of Harrod's associates. We need to identify everybody who might be of interest. And do full PNC checks. Gareth, you're to do the same for Dixon.'

They both nodded and turned to their computers.

For the rest of the morning Drake read all about *The Wall* in the several pages of its Wikipedia entry. The screen on his computer filled with various open tabs, where he had clicked from one link to another, following anything that drew his attention. He had to make progress, so he called Dr Fabrien again and she sat in his office, a film of sweat covering her face.

'What do you make of the songs?' Drake said. 'I can't get them out of my mind. There's got to be something we're missing.'

'The songs could be anything. His favourite tunes or maybe—'

'But why are they all from 1979?'

'Are there any connections between the bands who recorded the songs?'

'None. But I'll get Gareth to double-check.'

'I think it is unlikely the bands are relevant. I think the year is important. You have to find something that links the victims to 1979—'

'There's nothing. Nothing,' Drake said, an edge of despair to his voice.

'Don't keep interrupting me, Ian. It's not going to help.'

He gave her a sharp look. 'But I need you to profile this guy. He's going to kill again—'

'We don't know that for certain.'

'I want to stop him before he has a chance.'

Dr Fabrien left, telling him she still had work to do and Drake sat back in his chair, feeling his eyes burning and an odd sensation in his thighs that shot up to the small of his back. No more Pilates for a while he concluded. After an hour, his mind was darting from one thing to another.

He went to the kitchen but found to his intense irritation that there was no more ground coffee. He had to settle for instant and added plenty of sugar to sweeten the bitter taste.

Caren called out to him as he left the kitchen. 'Reception after you. There's a Mitchell Fisher to see you.'

'Who?'

'Says he was to ask for you.'

Fisher was sitting on one of the sofas in the waiting area, his hard hat perched on his lap and the yellow high-visibility vest crumpled over his back.

'Robin Miles told me to speak to you,' he said.

Drake ushered Fisher into one of the small rooms near reception. Caren cleared the table of plastic cups and an old copy of the regional newspaper.

'I understand you allege Harrod was responsible for assaulting you.'

Fisher snorted. 'He kicked the shit out of me. I had a

broken nose, two broken fingers and cracked ribs to prove it.'

'How long ago was it?'

'A month ago.'

'Why didn't you make a complaint at the time?'

'Didn't think you'd be interested.'

Drake paused. He knew a delay might make a prosecution difficult.

'Let's get some background,' he said.

Drake opened a notepad, flattened the seam and clicked the top of his ballpoint.

'He's a fucking bastard. Screws all his sub-contractors to ridiculous prices knowing there is no other work around.'

'Why did you fall out?'

'I told him I wanted payment every fortnight. Told him I'd leave the job if I wasn't paid. He went fucking ape-shit. Called me all sorts.'

'And?'

'I was out with some lads one night in Rhyl. I was walking back to the car. They jumped me. Dragged me into a side alley by an old boarded-up pub.'

'Did you get a good look at the others?'

'Yes. They were all Scousers. One was an old bastard, short hair and a neck like a tree trunk. He didn't do very much but he did all the talking. He must have swallowed a fucking dictionary. *You do realise Mr Harrod has a business to run.* All that sort of crap.'

Drake exchanged an are-you-thinking-what-I'm-thinking glance with Caren. She raised her eyebrows slightly, acknowledging his thought process.

'We'll need a better description.'

'Fine by me,' Fisher said, crossing his arms.

Both men were clean-shaven; both had tattoos on their arms, which Fisher described in detail. He described the kicks and the pain of the cracked ribs and didn't hide his anger. But Drake could hear the reluctance from a CPS lawyer looking at the evidence. *It'll be his word against theirs.* He's got the bruises to prove it. *There's no corroboration. No eyewitnesses.* He'll make a good witness. *It's less than 50–50.* What about natural justice? Sometimes he knew that the criminal justice system was a lottery.

'So what do you think, sir?' Caren said once Fisher had left, a glint of excitement in her eye.

'Sounds like Dixon. And now we've got a reason to talk to Harrod.'

Chapter 27
Thursday 17th June

Aled Walters sat upright in the chair, turning his iPhone through his fingers. Before the interview Drake had put a large black plastic bag with the crossbow inside it, on the floor behind the table. He spread out the notebook in front of him and looked up at Walters who gave him a typically insincere political smile back.

Drake knew he had to be careful. A partial fingerprint didn't make a case. But it helped. And it helped that years before Walters had spent a year as a special constable, meaning his fingerprints were on the national database.

Once he'd asked some preliminaries he got onto the question he really wanted to ask.

'Do you have a crossbow?'

'Yes. As a matter of fact I do. Or did.'

Drake paused, not expecting the answer, before lifting the bag onto the table. 'Your fingerprints were found on this crossbow,' he said, removing the bag.

Walters moved forward and looked down at it. 'That's because it's mine, Inspector,' he said, an edge to his voice.

'Why was it found in the rear of a van in Rhyl?'

'It was stolen a couple of months back.'

'Did you report the theft?'

'Eventually.'

Drake sensed that Walters wanted to make this as difficult as possible. 'What do you mean?'

'There was a break-in at my home a couple of months ago. I was away for the weekend and the thieves broke into a cabinet where I usually kept three crossbows. The one I use regularly wasn't there but two antique crossbows were taken.'

'So how was this crossbow stolen?' Drake narrowed his eyes as he gave Walters a hard stare.

'It was stolen from my brother's place a week or so

later.'

'Your brother?' Drake said, as he realised who he meant.

'Yes. Sam Walters.'

Drake found himself before the board in the Incident Room, having forgotten why he had left his office. What did the song lyrics have in common? It had to be more than simply 1979. He had woken singing the songs in his sleep. The words had forced their way into his mind when he was driving. He stared at the photographs of Paul Mathews and Danny Farrell, their blank emotionless faces telling him nothing. The photofit was pinned next to an enlarged photograph of the rucksack.

'You were right, boss,' Drake hadn't noticed Winder standing by his side.

Drake turned towards him and Winder continued. 'We've had confirmation from eyewitnesses who saw a walker with a similar bag coming down the south side of Snowdon.'

It confirmed for Drake that the killer knew his way around the mountain, must have known the paths, which one would be the safest descent.

'Where did the witnesses see the man?' Drake said, with urgency in his voice.

'One couple were a bit vague. Another couple saw him passing them in a rush on his way down. He went off, away, from the main path – that's why they remember it …'

Drake was already marching back to his office as he spoke to Winder, 'Show me.'

He opened an ordnance survey sheet over his desk and Winder pinpointed the location where the eyewitnesses had seen the suspect. Drake found a pencil from one of the drawers in his desk and shaded an area south of where Winder had marked.

'Is there anything from the helicopter?' Drake almost stumbled over his words.

'I'll double-check.'

'Check this area first.' Drake pointed to the shading.

He stared at the map. He tried to think of where the killer would have gone. How did he escape? Where was his car?

Drake sat huddled with Winder as they stared at the computer screen displaying the recording from the helicopter camera. They watched as ascending walkers were turned back and the mountain emptied of activity.

The helicopter circled Cwm Tregelan before passing a stream of walkers on the Watkin Path heading towards the waterfalls of the Cwm Llan valley. The helicopter veered south and then west and headed over towards Yr Aran. Drake had scribbled a timeline that he stuck to the edge of the computer screen. He worried that the details were wrong. He shouted over at Caren who double-checked from her records of the interviews on the summit. The clock on the computer screen ticked away and he tried to guess where the killer would have been at the time flickering on the screen in front of him.

'Pause the damn thing.'

Back in his office, he went through his notes again, trawling his memory. How long would it take a man to walk down the mountain? Two hours? He sat back and noticed Winder standing by the door.

'Come in, come in.' Drake swirled his hand in the air. 'We know that Roderick Jones was killed at around eleven-thirty.'

'Yes, sir.'

'The new witnesses think they passed the suspect at about twelve-thirty.'

Winder nodded. 'But that could be out by fifteen minutes.'

Drake dragged over the ordnance survey sheet.

'He could have gone down towards the Watkin Path or down towards Rhyd Ddu or he could have cut across and down.' Drake threw the pencil onto the map. 'Of course,' he almost shouted. 'He avoided the well-known routes and walked down towards Beddgelert.'

Winder turned on his heels. 'I'll check the helicopter coverage from twelve-fifteen onwards.'

Drake sat down on his chair, his mind heavy with frustration. They were always two steps behind the killer. As soon as they got close, he pulled further away. Drake folded the ordnance survey sheet and tidied his desk. He moved the papers around into neat piles, with Post-it notes identifying what action was needed. Then he turned to the inbox on his computer. He had to have a clear, tidy mind. He adjusted the telephone and then picked up the sudoku from his desk and completed two missing squares that had troubled him all day. A mild sense of achievement filled him; at least he was in control with the puzzle.

Dr Fabrien smiled at Drake and Caren without opening her mouth as they walked into the conference room. Dr Fabrien drew breath and shuffled the papers on the desk. Drake had spent hours putting the papers together in a neat ring binder with coloured dividers and grimaced when he noticed the ring binder discarded, and the papers in no apparent order.

'Let's look at the salient features of the murders so far. The killer operates in dramatic locations. And the murders are all premeditated. The two deaths on the Crimea Pass were clearly well planned. And the same could be said for the killing of Roderick Jones on the summit of Snowdon.'

Drake played with a biro, hoping he could hide his impatience. 'But the killing of Roderick Jones was opportunistic. The killer could never be certain that he'd have the chance to kill him.'

Dr Fabrien gave him a fractious look.

'I was coming to that. It's not about certainty of opportunity. It's about planning. The baseball cap, the bag, the ponytail – they are all signs of careful planning. And he knew how to limit exposure to the CCTV camera on the summit, which suggests he knew what he was going to do, given the chance.'

Dr Fabrien moved some of the papers and Drake glanced at Caren who had leant forward, her eyes narrowed.

'As for the modus operandi, there are no similarities in respect of the weapons used. On the Crimea he used a Taser to stun the officers and then a crossbow. It is a quick and effective weapon, but old fashioned. The killer feels comfortable with the crossbow and you can assume that he has used them before. You've been working through the archery clubs. You'll probably find your killer has visited these places.'

Dr Fabrien made them sound like a sordid nightclub.

'He used a knife on Snowdon. Simple, clean and effective. In that respect it's very similar to the crossbow.'

She scanned the papers again before continuing.

'The song lyrics do intrigue me. It suggests a clever killer who wants to tell you something about himself. He wants you to know who he is. He wants you to catch him.'

Drake moved self-consciously in his chair. 'No killer wants to be caught.'

'He's taunting you,' she added. 'Telling you he's out there and what he's done. He's challenging you with the song lyrics. Find out what they mean and you'll be that much closer to finding the killer.'

'What do *you* think they mean?'

She averted her eyes and blinked uneasily.

'Well, I've read the lyrics – several times – and they don't suggest anything to me.'

Caren cleared her throat and made her first contribution. 'It's difficult to believe that a killer wants to be caught.'

'I know. I know.' Suddenly Dr Fabrien sounded

engaged again. 'But it's true. It's about power. They need to be in charge. By taunting you, he gets complete control. He knows that you're scratching around for an answer. He probably knows there's a profiler involved ...'

'Come on, Margaret, that's taking it a bit far. And why did he send those lyrics to my parents?'

'He wants to be in control.'

'He frightened them.'

Drake rubbed his eyes, fighting the tiredness, thinking about his parents and worrying how helpless he'd been feeling.

'It is bad. For sure.'

'What about the numbers?'

Her eyes hardened and she looked serious.

'Two more.'

Drake stopped fiddling with the biro and sat upright, staring at Fabrien. Caren let out a long sigh.

'Two more deaths,' she continued. 'That's the only explanation – but you didn't need me to tell you that.'

'When?' Drake said.

'You have three deaths close together. It could be any time, but he's not a classic serial killer. There's a link to these murders and he's telling you how many more to go. It will be soon.'

Drake had known this was the case, but nobody had dared say it out loud before.

Soon.

The word reverberated around the silence of the room. Drake drew his tongue over dry lips, Caren coughed; the room seemed airless. He looked towards the windows but they were open.

Dr Fabrien continued. 'The killer is probably mid-thirties to mid-forties. He has a responsible job and lives a perfectly normal life and functions satisfactorily. But the boundaries in his mind are blurred.'

'Blurred!' Drake spluttered.

Dr Fabrien lifted her head and looked at him disdainfully.

'Mid-thirties to mid-forties: that puts both of our suspects in the frame.'

'Both have normal lives and function in society,' she nodded.

'They have a motive.'

'Have you thought about other suspects? Somebody with a grudge against the officers and Roderick Jones …'

'If we can't place them at the scene of both murders then it would be down to accomplices. Do you think we have a professional assassin on our hands?'

A surprised look crossed her face. 'That's an interesting scenario. It's not one you've canvassed in the reports so far. Either man could have had an accomplice but I think we are more likely to be dealing with a lone killer.'

Before Drake could reply, the door of the conference room flew open and Lisa tumbled breathlessly into the room.

'Ian, haven't you had my emails?'

Chapter 28
Friday 18th June

The remains of the overnight rain lay in small puddles on the shimmering tarmac. Drake guessed that with the grey clouds skimming north over the sea and the sky to the east clear, it was likely to be another warm day. The forecasters had become blasé about describing the summer weather as Mediterranean.

He set the air conditioning of the Alfa to cool and checked his watch. He was early for the meeting with Price so he stopped at a newsagent and bought the local newspaper, dreading seeing the headlines that Lisa had warned him about the day before. They made depressing reading – *Police Investigation Falters*. The report recycled the information from the press conferences but it wasn't until the third paragraph that Drake caught his breath. Nobody had released details of the messages. The reporter even had details of all the song lyrics and made reference to the numbers by the bodies. Drake's heart sank – this could only make matters worse. He turned to the second page and continued reading, until he had finished the article and then read it a second time.

Fifteen minutes later he was sitting in Price's office, watching the superintendent reading the same article and uncharacteristically saying nothing. Drake was accustomed to displays of annoyance, anger even, from Price and the more measured response unsettled Drake. He noticed a hardback edition of *The Life of Pi* on the desk next to a Cross biro. Sian had been pestering him to go with her to see the film of the book recently and he'd been making one excuse after another

'You're seeing the editor later?' Price said, without raising his eyes.

'Yes, sir.'

'It must be him.'

Drake nodded. By late the previous evening Drake was so tired he could barely think straight but the team meeting had concluded that the only explanation for the press reports was that the killer was communicating with the journalist.

Price raised his head and gazed over at Drake.

'I wanted to speak to you about the investigation.'

The unsettled feeling returned.

'Sir?'

'How are you coping?'

The question hung in the air like a morning mist from which you didn't quite know what was going to emerge next.

Price continued. 'The other night when you were working late, I couldn't help but notice that you seemed distracted.'

Drake didn't know what to say or how he should respond. Price continued before he had time to reply.

'It was late and the team had left but you were on the floor of your office. *Sorting papers*. And it's not the first time you've been working long hours, is it? It hasn't gone unnoticed.'

Drake swallowed now, not wanting to reply, his mind working on the alternatives.

'I now how it must look …'

Drake knew it was a feeble reply, but it was the best he could manage. He darted a look at his watch – he thought about making an excuse about the appointment with his father – but Price cut in.

'The business with the letter to your parents must have been distressing and I can imagine how they feel. But Ian, I need to know that you're in charge.' Price leant forward slightly. 'In charge of the team and of yourself. We'll have to bring someone in to assist if you're not coping.'

'It'll be fine, sir. I've been tired, that's all,' Drake knew it sounded lame and Price gave him an unconvinced look.

'You need to relax when you're off duty. Enjoy your family. Do some reading,' Price patted the book on the desk.

'How old are your children now?'

'Seven and five.'

'They grow up so quickly. My daughter lives in Florida; she married a swimming pool engineer. I hardly see her.'

There was sadness in Price's voice Drake had never heard before.

After the meeting Drake stood in the corridor outside Price's office, wanting to smother the tension gripping his chest. The image of his parents in the small hours of the morning, terrified of possible intruders in the fields, still haunted him. He had to keep them safe, had to cope.

A sweet, almost acrid smell filled the waiting room and Drake looked for the culprit; there had to be flowers somewhere creating the odour that was clawing at the hairs in his nostrils. He could feel a sneeze gathering so he squeezed his nose tightly with his thumb and forefinger and he breathed out slowly.

He sat with his father on blue plastic chairs lined up against the wall. By his side in one corner, magazines were laid out carefully on a table, all chosen for their potentially soothing and tranquil qualities. He picked up a *Cheshire Life* and then *Good Housekeeping* and flicked through them without any obvious enthusiasm. He recalled the article in the paper and started composing the sort of comments that he might use with the editor later.

'I don't like that sergeant,' his father said, breaking the silence. 'No manners at all.'

'How's Mam?'

'She's taken to checking all the windows and doors twice every night. The young officer has promised to call by every day. He was decent enough.'

His father wore a light grey suit, fashionable thirty years ago and a new shirt, a size too small, judging from the way he kept running his finger round the collar. They had been waiting for ten minutes when the receptionist announced that Mr West was ready. Drake noticed the vase of lilies on a narrow table in the corridor and pinched his nose again.

Anthony West was a big man with a large hand that he held out to Drake's father. He nodded to Drake before sitting down. Open on the desk was a file that had his father's notes and a hand-held dictating machine.

'Let me explain the results of the blood tests,' West said. 'They do show positive for cancer.'

Drake noticed his father swallowing hard. Drake listened to West explaining the intricacies of the treatment available and the side effects and the survival rates. He hoped his father was listening.

'We will need to do some more tests in due course. But we do need to discuss treatment ...'

Drake knew there was going to be a *but* and he wondered what the treatment would mean. His father sat impassively by his side, hands clasped on his lap. West hesitated, scanned his notes again and cleared his throat. 'I want to start treatment as soon as possible.'

'When will that be?' Drake asked.

'Next week.'

'That soon.'

'I've arranged a bed for Tuesday.'

Drake and his father sat with West for another twenty minutes listening to an explanation of the various treatment alternatives. West was supportive when he explained what the treatments meant and reassuring in telling them how effective they might be. Once West had finalised the arrangements for his father's admission, they left. Drake's father offered his debit card to the secretary who gave him an ingratiating smile once he paid the bill.

The parkland around headquarters seemed greener and Drake caught a glimpse of light glistening on the water droplets on the tall grass underneath the trees. He took the steps up to the entrance two at a time. Caren sat huddled over the computer in the Incident Room. Howick looked up, an energetic look in his eyes.

'I've been through the membership lists again, sir.'

Caren raised her head anticipating some revelation from Howick.

'You'll never guess who was president of the association a couple of years ago?'

Winder leant back in his chair, a smug grin on his face, 'Robin Hood, and William Tell was the vice-president.'

Howick gave him an angry look, 'Piss off Gareth.' He turned to Drake. 'Aled Walters was the president.'

Drake curled up his mouth, uncertain whether this really was a step forward.

'I want all the club's records impounded,' Drake said. 'There might be something we've missed.'

'Ready?' he said to Caren, who was reaching for her jacket.

It was the first day for weeks that he hadn't been feeling oppressed by the hot weather and for the second time that day he found himself thinking about the family holiday. It would be hot, every morning he would collect fresh bread and pastries, and then they'd go swimming. He would build a barbecue in the evening and grill chicken and sausages. Unless they made a breakthrough soon, he could see the holiday slipping away. And now he had his father to think about.

It was a short drive to the offices of the local newspaper and Drake sat tapping his fingers on the file lying on his lap and staring out of the window. The more he had thought about the consequences of the article the angrier he became. If there were more deaths then he might be to blame. And what then? An investigation, then recriminations and he would never see the promotion he wanted. He lifted the file and banged it down on his knees.

'Damn the bloody papers.'

Caren slowed the car at traffic lights. 'We need their help.'

'It should never have been printed. They'll have to stop.'

Caren raised her eyebrows in surprise. 'We want their cooperation, sir.'

She accelerated away from the lights and overtook a stream of children on bicycles.

'Go easy, sir,' she said, not looking at him, as she turned left off the main road into an industrial estate.

The newspaper office was a small, ugly building and the young girl at reception gave them a wide-eyed, curious look, tilting her head to one side.

'I'm here to see the editor,' Drake said.

She picked up the telephone and mumbled into the receiver. She pointed in the direction of leather sofas. He snorted back at her. 'We'll stand. We won't be waiting long.'

Soon enough the receptionist led them through the corridors, past inquisitive staring eyes.

The conference room was small, with two narrow windows from floor to ceiling that looked out over a courtyard filled with planters. Both men around the table had defiant, determined looks on their faces. The older man stuck out his hand.

'Brian Johnson. Editor. This is Robert Stone,' he added, introducing the younger man.

'We want to talk to you about this,' Drake flung the newspaper across the desk.

'How can we help, Chief Inspector?'

'Inspector, actually.'

'This investigation is complex,' Drake said. 'We are dealing with a psychopath who will not stop at killing police officers. All my men are at risk from this man and you have the temerity to say the investigation is faltering.'

'Well, have you arrested anyone?' Johnson said.

The meeting hadn't started well. Drake was on the defensive and Brian Johnson had the upper hand.

'This conversation is, of course, entirely off the record. So you can stop your scribbling,' Drake said to Stone, who was busy making notes. 'We want to know how you came by some of the facts in your report. It may be hampering our inquiry.'

'You know we cannot divulge our sources,' Johnson said.

'You've printed details that were not released by us and—'

'And we are journalists. We investigate stories.'

'Even when it puts lives at risk.'

'Come off it, Inspector. You can't try that angle with me.'

'You could be assisting the killer. That could well be an offence.'

Stone rearranged the papers on the desk before looking first at the editor and then over at Drake.

'I've been working on the story since last Thursday morning. A source made contact quite early and told us about the number found on the body of Roderick Jones. The same source rang before the press conference. And we checked—'

'Did you say on Thursday morning?' Caren interrupted.

'Yes, early – before eight o'clock.'

Caren turned to Drake. 'Nobody on the investigation team knew about the number on Roderick Jones's body then.'

Suddenly the atmosphere in the room changed. A serious look passed over the face of Brian Johnson and Robert Stone looked intently at Drake.

'What are you saying?' Stone asked.

'I'm saying the killer is your source,' Caren said.

Stone cleared his throat and then began to chew on a

fingernail. Drake decided to emphasise the point, to regain the upper hand.

'He knows where you live.'

Stone sat quite still. Drake had his complete attention.

'And he knows your phone number. Smart cookie isn't he?'

Drake folded his arms. Despite the defiant look on his face, he could see the fear in the young reporter's eyes.

'How many times has he called you?'

Drake glanced over at Johnson, who sat looking at Stone waiting for an answer.

'Three times. Once before the press conference. Then on Thursday morning and finally on Wednesday.'

Drake wondered where the killer had been when he made the call. In his car, in a kiosk, at work – functioning satisfactorily, as Dr Fabrien had said. And then he wondered what she would say about this. Perhaps it was part of functioning normally that killers did this sort of thing, making regular contact with the press.

'Would you recognise the voice?' Drake asked

'Yes.'

'What exactly did he tell you?'

Stone opened his notebook and read from his shorthand notes, summarising each of the conversations as Drake scribbled his own record.

'Do you think this man will kill again?' asked Johnson, sounding sombre.

Drake placed his arms on the table. 'Yes. We do.'

Johnson flinched but Drake could see he understood. The body language told him that the edgy defiance had gone. The killer had seen to that.

'Don't answer the telephone at home until we've put a trace on it,' Drake ordered. 'If he calls back, this might be our best chance to catch him.'

For a few moments, the room went quiet, and then Stone nodded, slowly.

Chapter 29
Monday 21st June

'Why the bloody hell didn't we know about this?' Drake asked.

Caren had an inscrutable look on her face.

'But why isn't there an election?' he said.

He noticed the time, knowing he had to leave for court within the hour.

'And have you seen Dave's memo about the Archery Club? Walters was a member at the same time as Mathews.'

Caren nodded.

The newspaper open on Drake's desk had the news of Roderick Jones's successor filling the second page. He read the comments made by Aled Walters, paying tribute to Roderick Jones and pledging himself to work hard as his successor.

Thorsen, sitting by Caren's side, cleared his throat. 'Because Roderick Jones was elected from the regional list, there doesn't have to be an election. His seat automatically goes to the person after him on the same party list.'

Drake stared at the lawyer and, out of frustration, asked. 'Even when that person is a possible suspect in three murders?'

Neither Thorsen nor Caren bothered to reply.

'And now we've got the death of Jones,' Drake continued.

'Surely you don't think that Walters is involved?' Thorsen raised his voice.

'He has a perfect motive,' Caren said, in a matter-of-fact tone. 'With Roderick Jones out of the way, he inherits a seat in the Welsh Assembly – quite a step up from being a county councillor. We know he's ambitious.'

'And he owns a crossbow. Possibly the one that killed Mathews and Farrell.'

Thorsen flicked through his papers reviewing his

scribbled comments. 'I thought you were looking for the same suspect for the murders of Jones and the two police officers.'

'Same description,' Drake corrected.

Thorsen wet his forefinger and ran through various pages in his notebook. 'You mean the ponytail ...' he said, after finding the relevant section.

'And the baseball cap and beard,' Caren added.

'So how do we proceed, Andy?' Drake said.

'Carefully. I'll want to review all the evidence against Walters. He's already made a call to Price asking about the Jones inquiry.'

Drake screwed up his eyes and stared at Thorsen in disbelief. 'You've got to be joking.'

Thorsen's expression told him he wasn't.

Drake broke all the speed limits to get to the Crown court on time. He ran from the car park and entered the courtroom, breathless, his face flushed. The prosecuting barrister nodded an acknowledgment, broke off from his discussions, and straightened his wig as he walked over to Drake.

'Our star witness hasn't appeared,' he said.

Drake gaped. No witness. No case.

The logic was simple and the defendant knew that as well as anyone. And when the witness had been in love with the defendant, a love that was blind to the beatings and kickings she received, it made the case all the more difficult. Drake could see her huddled on the floor of the house, shaking in fear, the blood running down her face. He had promised her then that he would do everything to see that justice was done and now she had lost her nerve. Myers, the Crown prosecutor, joined the discussion, turning off his mobile as he did so.

'Tried her mobile and the landline. No luck.'

The barrister folded his arms. 'The judge won't be

happy.'

'You handle the judge,' Drake said. 'I'll go and find her. But just make sure you crucify this bastard afterwards.'

For a second time that morning he broke the speed limit as he raced towards Rhyl and the home of Audrey Embers. He knew time was short and if he could find her and get her back to court, the judge might let the case proceed. He had no intention of letting the defendant walk free.

He passed a deserted fun park as he entered Rhyl and immediately turned left towards the part of town squeezed between the sea and the railway line. It was an area the police knew well – a squalid collection of bed-sits, amusement arcades, pubs and more drug dealers than the police could catch.

He followed the streets towards the narrow terrace huddled behind the rear of an old hotel, where Audrey lived. The torn net curtains were streaked a dark, dirty colour. He banged on the door and stepped back into the street. A curtain moved in the upstairs bedroom, the one where Drake had found the burnt silver foil remnants of her boyfriend's heroin habit.

He called out, 'Audrey.'

Nothing moved. He banged on the door again. The house sounded empty. A fragment of memory came back to him and he jogged, then ran, towards the end terrace and banged on the door. No answer. He spotted the side gate and pushed it hard with his shoulder and when it gave way, he almost fell onto the concrete path.

The rear door of Audrey's house was half-open and inside he saw a familiar face. The head was bobbing to an iPod playing in the man's ears and his eyes were closed as he drew on a joint. Drake tugged the iPod leads and a rap beat broke the silence of the room. The man opened his eyes suddenly.

'Where's Audrey?'

'Fuck knows.'

Drake pushed him to the floor, knocking his head against the fridge door.

He squirmed around the dirty lino floor, 'You can't fucking do that,' he cried, dabbing a finger against the blood on his forehead.

Drake swung his right foot at the man's thigh. He let out another sharp cry of pain.

'What would your probation officer say if he knew you were back on the smack?'

'It's only a joint, man.'

'You'd be sent back to jail faster than you could say smack-head. How do you fancy that?'

The man shouted an address at Drake. 'Now, piss off.'

Drake duly obliged and once he was back on the street he ran for his car, after glancing at his watch. He'd been an hour already – at least nobody had called from the court.

He fired the engine into life and hammered down the side street. He screeched to a halt and glanced at the street name – it looked familiar. Where had he seen it before? He parked on a double-yellow line and noticed the CCTV camera perched high on one end. He worked out where the house might be and ran down the street, only to find himself running against the flow of house numbers. He stopped and looked down the street. It had a Chinese takeaway at one end, next to a public house with chipboard screwed to the windows, flyposted with adverts for the circus visiting the town. Across from him was a narrow passageway and then he recalled the statement from Fisher about Harrod and Dixon – what had he said? Dark passageway – no witnesses and no traffic. *Boarded-up pub.* As he stepped across the carriageway, he saw a door open and Audrey stepped out, the look of astonishment clear on her face when she saw him.

'Audrey. Audrey!' he shouted.

She stood motionless. He ran over to her.

'I can't go through with it.'

He saw the tears welling up in her eyes.

'We'll put the bastard away.'

'His brother was here ... threatened the kids. Told me I'd never see them again.'

'We'll put him away, too.'

Drake took her by the arm into the house until the tears had gone and she'd agreed that giving evidence was the only way to stand up to Jason. He called the barrister, who sounded relieved, telling Drake they had until the afternoon to produce her in court – after that, Jason walked.

Stepping out onto the street, he looked around and held her arm tightly. As they walked towards his car, he noticed again the CCTV camera. Once they reached the car, he snapped the door closed and reached for his mobile.

He pressed a speed-dial number and thrust the handset to his ear – it was a one-way conversation, his instructions clear and precise.

Detective Inspector John Marco hated only one thing more than paperwork and that was doing someone else's paperwork. The pile of folders on the table in front of him made him crave another cigarette and his rule of no more than five a day was in danger of being broken.

Marco glanced over at the two young officers sitting across the table who were busy working on the files. They looked keen, excited even. And it wasn't even his case. He sensed the packet of cigarettes in the pocket of his coat draped over the chair next to him, and longed to feel the smoke filling his lungs.

His mind drifted to the meeting he had with Drake and the first minister. The politician was shorter than he appeared on television. And fatter. And the DI from Northern Division was just as he'd expected – buttoned up, formal; but then everybody from the north was like that.

Marco spent the rest of the day trawling through the

files and papers exercising just enough patience with the two young DCs to make sure they stayed focused. By the time Marco was standing outside, drawing on his fourth cigarette of the day, the headquarters building had emptied of staff and he had at least another two hours' work ahead of him.

It was after eight o'clock when a name leapt out at him and he did an immediate retake, hardly believing what he was reading. He closed the folder and read the title again and then reopening the file, he pressed on, scanning the pages, blanking out the groans from across the table.

Once he'd finished he picked up his mobile.

The minute timer on Drake's Tissot bleeped and he stretched out a hand to the small cafetière on the desk and pushed the filter downwards. He poured the coffee, allowing the oil to gather on the surface, feeling pleased that he had delivered a key witness to the Crown court, earning the thanks of Judge Machin for his efforts. He had seen the angry faces of Jason's relatives staring at him and made certain they noticed him pointing them out to the burly sergeant on duty that morning. The officer gave them a long hard look as Drake spoke to him. He reckoned Jason would get a four-year stretch – maybe five – but with good behaviour and parole, he would be out in three. Time enough for Audrey to move on and rebuild her life.

Winder stood at the door to Drake's office.

'Ready boss?' There was an eager look on Winder's face.

Drake's instructions earlier in the day had pinpointed the CCTV camera and Winder had little trouble finding the tapes. The computer screen had a frozen image, various codes and numbers displayed, until Winder clicked the mouse, and the images sprung to life.

'This is from the camera nearest to where Fisher said the assault took place,' Winder said.

Drake leant over Winder's right shoulder and Caren squinted at the screen over the other. Drake looked at the time elapsing on the clock at the bottom of the screen.

'Slow it down. Slow it down,' Drake barked.

'Can you see Fisher, sir? He's the one in the dark shirt.'

'Okay, good.'

'Now comes the interesting bit.'

A Range Rover drew into the screen and three men dropped out of the vehicle. Then Winder zoomed in and froze the computer screen with a clear image of Dixon's face.

'You bastard,' Drake said.

'It gets better,' Winder said, restarting the tape, then zooming back out and waiting until all three men stepped away from the Range Rover. The tall man who left the passenger side straightened his jacket as Winder zoomed in. The face of James Harrod was unmistakable, despite the blurred image.

Chapter 30
Wednesday 23rd June

After the file of papers had arrived from Cardiff the day before, carefully tied with a thick plastic band and accompanied by a scrawled note from Marco, Drake had taken the rest of the day to read them carefully. Once he had finished, he knew the Crown prosecutor would have to be involved and he'd arranged to see Thorsen that morning.

As Drake entered the room Thorsen gave him a stern look.

'Well. What do you think?' asked Drake.

The label on the file was clearly marked '*James Harrod Planning.*'

'We'll need to get an expert to explain everything. I've spoken to a colleague and he's going to have a look at the file later.'

'It gives Harrod a connection to Roderick Jones,' Drake said. 'The planning application was recommended for approval by the officials in the department.'

Thorsen raised his eyebrows, opened the folder and tugged at a yellow Post-it note that marked a section.

'It seems that Jones was minded to refuse the application and made his views very clear indeed. It's unusual for a minister to go against the advice of officials,' he said eventually in the matter-of-fact condescending manner that annoyed Drake so much.

'Can he do that?' Drake said.

'Yes, but it could be challenged in the courts.'

'So, Jones takes the risk.'

'Politicians, what else do you expect?' Thorsen said, trying to sound world-weary.

Once they were finished, Thorsen promised to keep him informed and Drake returned to his office. He wondered what his father was doing that morning. He wanted to be able to think that his father was working in the fields every morning, now that he was retired and that he would go on forever. He often thought that he didn't want things to change. He slumped onto the chair, hoping the latest development with James Harrod was the breakthrough he needed. It occurred to him he might tell Price but decided to wait, hoping for more news, something to reassure the super he was still in charge. He thought about the telephone conversation with his father the night before, after he'd returned from the first day of treatment. He had to reassure himself so he picked up the telephone and rang his mother.

'Your father's still asleep.'

'I'll call later.'

By mid-morning it felt like grit was swimming around in his eyes and, deciding that coffee would be the only suitable medication, made his way to the kitchen. Howick came in as Drake was halfway through the carefully timed routine and gave him a puzzled look. Then Drake worried what Howick might think.

Howick was waiting for him as he returned to his office. Drake sat listening to Howick telling him about the results of the photofit images released to the press. Three sightings matched the approximate date and times of the CCTV images of the red car, and Howick's enthusiasm for the task impressed Drake. It was what police work was all about – grind and more grind, until the hard work produced a nugget of intelligence.

He had a brief respite after finishing with Howick, before Caren appeared at his door.

'We've found Mrs Walters,' she said. 'And we've had a breakthrough with Dixon.'

He waved her into his room.

'She lives in Alnwick.'

'Where?'

'Alnwick, Northumberland. Where they filmed *Harry Potter*.'

Drake mumbled a reply.

'She works for the National Trust – some sort of manager. Moved there after her marriage broke down. No kids, lives on her own. I'm going to interview her tomorrow.'

'And Dixon?' he said.

'CID in Birkenhead were checking his alibi. Somebody saw him leave the party early.'

For a moment, Drake thought they were making progress. 'Better check the pre-cons: you know what these Scousers are like.'

He looked up at Caren.

'Does Mrs Walters like rock music?'

Caren gave him a strange look. They were going round in circles again. 'We're still working on her family and friends,' she said.

Drake finished the dregs of the coffee and returned to the reports with little enthusiasm.

'Good. How're Alun and the alpacas?' he asked.

She gave him a half smile, trying to make out if he was serious.

'Alun's fine. The alpacas are better. We had quite a scare with them a couple of weeks ago. He's building a new enclosure and he's helping a neighbour with his smallholding.'

Drake looked out of the window at the trees by the road. Caren stopped for a moment.

'Would Megan and Helen like to come and see the alpacas?'

Drake heard the names of his daughters.

'Sorry?'

'Megan and Helen – would they like to come and see the animals?'

He smiled. 'Yes, that would be lovely. I'm sure they would enjoy it.'

Caren cleared her throat, but before she could say anything, Drake continued.

'We're not making any progress.'

Caren nodded slowly.

'I know we need to talk to Mrs Walters, but I get the feeling we're going further and further away from the killer,' Drake said.

'Walters and Harrod are the only suspects we've got.'

'I know, but we've got all those lists. Members of the Archery Club. Officers who worked with Mathews and Farrell. And their cases. All of Roderick Jones's constituents.'

'Walters and Harrod have both got motives.'

'I know, I know,' Drake said. 'But where are we going with it?'

He stood up and adjusted the waistband of his trousers – the shirt was sitting uncomfortably and he smoothed his tie.

'Look, let's go back to the beginning.' He walked out into the Incident Room and looked at the board. Another dark cloud descended in his mind, as he peered towards the faces. Roderick Jones was the strident politician, simultaneously smiling and looking important. The faces of Paul Mathews and Danny Farrell were humourless and blank – standard personnel photographs. The song lyrics were still pinned alongside each other and along the top of the board were two plain pieces of paper with the numbers four and three, printed in large fonts.

'What have we got?' Drake forced out the words. 'Two police officers on the Crimea. It was staged. Killer uses a Taser and then a crossbow to kill them.'

The images of both men in the car came back to his mind. He shuddered. 'The guy stalked them all night. He was behind them. There all the time, waiting. He must have known where they were going. He'd been planning this for weeks.'

Caren moved from one foot to another before adding.

'And the song lyrics. Does he know you like rock music?'

'Don't be insane. Lots of people like rock music.'

'But why send them as messages if they don't mean anything? So there must be a meaning to the lyrics.'

'Yes. I suppose.'

'What, then?'

Drake stared at the lyrics of each song. The opening chords of 'Brass in Pocket' played in his head and then images from the Pink Floyd and Queen videos appeared. His eyes moved across the board to the faces of Harrod and Walters. Someone had moved the image of Stevie Dixon to the bottom of the board. He had to stop and think, but with more deaths coming, they had to stop the killer before he struck again.

'Maybe 1979 was special to this guy. Maybe we should try and find out if that year had any significance for Harrod or Walters,' Drake said.

'And the numbers, sir?'

Drake let his shoulders sag. 'That's what makes it depressing. We know there's going to be two more deaths and unless we find this guy, there's nothing we can do.'

Drake spent a miserable lunch break eating a tired ham salad in the canteen, while Caren talked incessantly about alpacas. He filled a glass from the plastic bottle of sparkling water and tried to look interested in Caren's conversation. She explained how valuable alpaca wool had become and he tried to concentrate on what she was saying, failing to block out the sound of Chrissie Hynde's voice and then the chorus from 'Another Brick in the Wall' playing over in his mind.

Chapter 31
Thursday 24th June

He watched as the tall man in a designer suit walked over to the silver Mercedes. It was an expensive model and it had all the usual extras. He'd checked the Mercedes website and read all about the E Class and the various versions available. They had leather seats and air conditioning. He knew that the car would have been ordered with all the upgrades for the sound system, and the headlights and the satellite navigation would be the best, too.

The man took off his jacket and folded it neatly before resting it on the back seat. He had to be ready, so he turned the ignition and fired up the engine. The Mercedes drove away and he pressed the accelerator and followed the car away from the hospital and down towards the A55. A simple call that afternoon had confirmed everything he needed to know.

At the clinic he saw the Mercedes parked in its reserved slot and he smiled to himself. He parked under the trees and waited. Occasionally, he sipped a bottle of water. Soon his patience would be rewarded. A plastic picnic container full of sandwiches wrapped in silver foil sat on the passenger seat. She had taught him that the bread for sandwiches had to be thinly sliced and the ham cut fine, and the mustard had to be English. She always used butter – never margarine – softened in the microwave.

He had all the time in the world and now it was time to see things right. Reset the balance. He watched the patients arrive for their appointments and then leave, some with worried despondent faces, others relieved. Inside this private clinic was the man who had taken her away from him.

In the car park, he sat and ate the sandwiches. Next time, he would add mayonnaise. She didn't like mayo – watching her weight, she had said. Until it was too late.

They had no idea. They simply had no idea: he was

convinced of it. It was so funny watching them scratching around. That press conference had been the funniest thing he had seen in years.

He thought about leaving for a couple of hours, but then he worried how his plans might be affected if he missed him. He decided to wait. He turned his head to one side whenever someone looked towards the car and he moved its position twice. There wasn't any security – he had checked. Definitely no CCTV cameras.

Ideal.

He felt the pressure on his bladder. He reached for an empty bottle and removing the cap relieved himself. He could leave nothing to chance. His buttocks ached as the afternoon dragged and he repeatedly adjusted his legs, trying to find a comfortable position.

When he saw him leaving, he straightened, then immediately clipped the seat belt into place. The aching disappeared replaced by his escalating pulse and the buzz of expectation. He followed him to the golf club.

Then, he waited.

Chapter 32
Friday 25th June

Drake arrived at headquarters early having slept badly but found it difficult to focus as he kept thinking about his parents. He opened the folder with the results of the forensic tests – on the photograph posted to the farmhouse – hoping that he'd missed something. The cold technical language of the report just confirmed what he knew – the killer didn't make mistakes: no prints, no traces, nothing to help him. The image of the area sergeant tramping off into the darkness of the empty fields at his parents' farm came to his mind. Drake doubted that the killer had been there but the effect on his mother made him want to scream.

The area sergeant had sounded bored when he'd reported back to Drake. He'd sent a couple of young officers back in daylight and they'd walked the fields for a couple of hours but turned up nothing of value. Drake had spoken to his mother the night before and the relief in her voice was clear as she repeated the assurances the officers had given her about regular patrols calling past the house.

Progress. He had to have progress before the pressures from Price meant that the case would be out of his hands. He could imagine the meeting. *Operational imperatives. Public anxiety.* It was only a matter of time before Price brought in another officer to review the case – pick holes in his work, point the finger of blame. And then he'd be invited to another meeting when the case would be formally reassigned.

He was still ruminating when, at a little after eight, the telephone rang.

The message was short and simple and he found his grip tightening. His lips dried and his pulse quickened before he got the message repeated. He was standing by the time the call finished and then strode towards the door and out through the Incident Room, calling to Caren as he left.

He had hammered the Alfa along the A55 towards the private clinic, driving too quickly into the private car park and braking hard, just missing a brand-new Audi. He nodded to a young uniformed officer standing by the front door who lifted the yellow crime scene tape. He hesitated – it was exactly a week since his visit with his father. He could still smell the lilies but there was a pile of unopened mail strewn on the desk in reception, and the sound of activity from the room where they'd seen Dr West. He walked past the table that had the same magazines neatly set out and turned towards the oncologist's room.

West's body was slumped over the desk, his head on one side and his arms lying neatly on each side. The room was hot and stuffy. The smell of a body beginning its slow process of decay hung in the air. The pathologist was already at work.

'Time of death?' Drake stared at the body as he spoke to Dr Kings. The pathologist removed a pair of latex gloves and snapped closed his bag.

'Hard to say. A few hours at least. I'll know more once I've done the post mortem.'

'Did you know him?'

'Yes. Very well.'

Kings sounded unnervingly matter-of-fact. Drake sensed no emotion in his voice.

The CSIs straightened the body against the chair and then Drake saw the thin plastic needle protruding at an angle from the doctor's neck.

Then he saw the message.

A small luggage tag had been tied to the knitting needle with thin green string. It hung limply and one of the CSI officers reached over and closed a hand around it before turning it to show Drake. He peered down and saw clearly what was written.

No 2.

Last but one.

Drake scanned the office of Anthony West. The walls, papered in a light pink pattern, were covered in prints of famous golf courses. It was odd that he hadn't noticed them the previous week. He flicked through various files and papers but nothing caught his eye. He went through to talk to Vera Frost, West's secretary, who had deep red furrows running down her cheeks and her eyes burnt into her face.

'What time did you find the body?'

She began to sob before reaching for a lace-edged handkerchief from a bag by her feet.

'What time did you arrive at work?'

'About eight.'

Vera was in her mid-fifties, with greying hair and a pronounced double chin. The carefully applied make-up and the clothes matched the image of the private consulting rooms.

'Was Dr West here last night?'

'Mr West,' she corrected him. 'He was a surgeon.'

'Last night?' Drake asked again.

'He had private patients all afternoon until five o'clock and then he went to play golf.'

'When did you leave?'

Vera breathed heavily again before blowing her nose.

'Do you know of anyone who might want to kill him?'

'No,' she snorted, offended by the mere suggestion.

'Can we have a list of all his patients in the last three years?'

Vera nodded.

Drake left the CSIs hard at work and walked outside with Caren. The car park was full of Audis and Mercedes, all under a year old, most with concertina-designed sunshades inside the windows, and in one of the reserved parking spaces two investigators were working on West's E Class.

'We need to find this maniac. And soon.'

He stood for a moment, feeling the sun on his face.

'This means one more,' Caren said.

He managed a cold wintry look and nodded slowly.

Drake had spent a fruitless afternoon working through the papers, reporting the events to Price (in a fractious meeting attended by Thorsen, who still managed to say little of any value), and avoiding Lisa, who wanted to organise yet another press conference. By the time Winder and Howick were standing by his desk his patience was paper thin, and massaging his forehead wasn't having any effect on the developing headache.

'Well?' Drake glared at them.

Winder started, 'Yes, sir. The pathologist said death was caused by the knitting needle piercing the brain. Not exactly unexpected.'

'Get forensics in here.'

Winder trooped off to find Foulds, and Drake returned to the board.

'What about the golf club?' he asked, remembering where Howick had been.

'It's taken me three hours to track down West's playing partner. West had a good round. Not a care in the world. When you can afford a Mercedes like that you shouldn't have, I guess.'

'We're missing something.' Drake ignored Howick and looked back at the board. 'Numbers. I keep thinking about numbers all the bloody time.'

'It's the year, sir. 1979.'

'Numbers – one thousand nine hundred and seventy-nine.'

Caren came into the Incident Room and threw her bag onto her desk. 'I've just spent all afternoon with a load of completely clueless CSIs. West has one of those luxury flats overlooking Llandudno. Concierge looked like a boxer.'

'And, anything?' Drake squeezed his eyes closed against his incipient headache.

'Great view,' she shrugged, as she slumped into the chair before continuing. 'But Mrs Walters was more helpful.'

Drake stopped and looked over at her having forgotten her trip to Northumberland the day before. Caren continued.

'She knew Mathews. They met in the Archery Club and guess what? They had an affair. Then Aled Walters found out and—'

'Did she contract …?'

'Yes.'

Winder was the first to break the silence. 'Mathews is one serious player.'

Drake's mind was already drafting his first questions for Aled Walters. If Drake noticed the harassed look on Foulds's face when the CSI manager entered, he paid it no attention.

Drake's voice was raised a decibel louder than normal, 'Tell me you have something?'

'The lads haven't finished yet.'

'Preliminary, then.'

'He wasn't killed in the office. My guess is he was killed in his car. There were signs of a struggle.'

'So he moved the body into the office.'

'And he must have used a wheelchair. We picked up scratches on some of the furniture that match a wheelchair we found in the foyer of the clinic.'

Drake saw the prospect of evidence. 'Any prints?'

'Lots, but …'

Drake knew the answer.

'I'll have a full report tomorrow morning,' Foulds said.

Drake went into his office and sank into the chair. There was little further he could achieve until the morning. Clearer thinking was needed, he concluded, and more focus. He glanced at his watch. He wasn't going to be late home. Then he straightened the telephone on the desk, adjusted the papers, lined up his Post-it notes, took the coffee mug to the kitchen and then double-checked everything again.

Vera Frost knew that any other employer would have sent her home. It had been terrible seeing him like that. His body slumped on the desk. And that inspector had been abrupt, almost rude. What did they teach them these days?

She had laboured at preparing the list all day and by late afternoon it was finalised. She formatted the information into nice, neat columns and headings. It was most comprehensive, even if she thought so herself.

But she'd had enough upset for one day.

It was the weekend tomorrow, it could wait until Monday.

The sofa was comfortable and, as Drake sat watching television, he started to relax. He thought about West and recalled his father sitting in the consulting room, talking to the surgeon, discussing the treatment for cancer and the survival rates and the side effects of the treatment. What emotions had gone through his father's mind? What questions did he have unanswered? Had his father liked the doctor?

Megan and Helen were staying with their *Nain* and *Taid* and when Sian returned from her parents' home she'd reminded Drake that he didn't have much time before they left for the dinner party with Robin and Jennifer. He nodded.

Sian had the radio playing upstairs. Drake heard the voices of the broadcasters but couldn't make out the words. It was like the investigation. He had the lyrics pinned to the board but couldn't understand the messages they sent.

The telephone rang and he picked up the cordless handset by his side.

'It's Robert Stone …'

He heard fear in the journalist's voice.

'I've had another message.'

'When?'

'Few minutes ago.'

'What did he say?'

There was a pause and he heard Stone's voice falter.

'He said for me to ask about a knitting needle. What does that mean?'

Drake saw the scene at the clinic in his mind but said nothing.

Stone continued. 'Then he said I had to watch the numbers. What does he mean …?'

Drake hesitated. 'I don't know,' he said. 'I really don't know.'

Chapter 33
Saturday 26th June

Drake reached out an arm under the duvet and searched for the warm sensation of Sian's body, but his hand reached out through cool bedding. He glanced at the alarm clock. His mouth was dry and chalky. He picked up his watch, lying on the floor next to the empty condom packet, which he scooped up and returned to the half-opened drawer.

Robin and Jennifer's dinner invitation had come at the end of a long week when Drake had felt further than ever from the killer, and more frustrated with the song lyrics and numbers that had come to dominate the inquiry. The initial hope surrounding the killer's calls to Stone had faded after it became clear that each call had been made from a different unregistered pay-as-you-go mobile, used once, then discarded. Yet another dead end.

By the end of the evening Robin had opened several bottles of expensive wine that stood in the middle of the table with the bottles of San Pellegrino. Robin talked incessantly about his time-share and his plans to buy more weeks. It would be an upgrade and he insisted on showing Drake and Sian the brochures, with the glossy photographs of swimming pools and unnaturally tidy apartments.

Later he ushered Drake into the study and slurred badly.

'Have you heard about Harrod's planning application?' Robin said. 'Word has it that Roderick Jones took a personal interest in the case.'

Drake knew most of this already but sensed his friend had more to tell.

'He's got every last penny riding on it. Mortgaged up to the eyeballs. If he was turned down he would have been completely fucked.'

He heard the sound of movement on the stairs and wondered how he'd explain to Sian that he might have to work, when he had promised it would be a family weekend?

Sian wore a purple three-quarter dressing gown and Drake smiled as he gazed at her legs.

'You drank too much last night,' she said, putting a glass of orange juice down by the clock.

He ran his hand up her leg and felt the warmth of her thigh.

'And it's time for you to get up. My mother will be here soon,' She tugged his hand away from her knee and left the bedroom.

He stretched out on the bed – it had been the first Saturday since the investigation began that he hadn't been preparing to go to work. It was going to be a day with the girls. Harrod and Walters and Dixon could wait until Monday.

He thought about breakfast, strong coffee and toast. He dragged on a pair of faded denims, thrust his arms through an old T-shirt and slipped his feet into a pair of slippers. In the kitchen Drake pulled out a grinder from the bowels of a cupboard, filled the bowl with beans and pressed the 'on' button. The high-pitched crushing noise filled the kitchen and then a strong velvety odour drifted through the air.

The doorbell rang and he put down his coffee and walked through to the hall where Megan and Helen were standing with Sian and her mother. Drake nodded at his mother-in-law who gave him a weak smile before she fussed over the children and left.

'The children want to go the zoo,' Sian said.

'That's a great idea,' he said.

Megan ran towards the stairs followed by Helen. Drake returned to the kitchen. He listened to the sounds of the children upstairs while watching the news on the television, wondering how Sian would react if her told he had to work that afternoon. He blanked out the words from Stone the night before and the troubling news about Harrod that Robin had shared with him.

A few minutes passed before Megan came into the

kitchen holding a glass milk bottle, a piece of white paper protruding from its neck.

'Mam, what's this?' she said, hand outstretched.

'Where did you get this? Sian said.

'It was in my cupboard. I've never seen it.'

Sian put the milk bottle on the worktop and pulled out the tube of paper. She unfurled it, paused to read the contents.

'Jesus. Ian … It's …'

She let her hands fall but the back of her wrist clipped the bottle, sending it crashing onto the floor. It shattered into tiny pieces that scattered all over the tiles. Megan screamed, Drake jumped up from the table and strode over to Sian.

'It's a message,' Sian said, thrusting the paper towards him.

Then he noticed Helen standing by the kitchen door.

'Stay where you are girls. There's glass all over the floor.'

Sian stammered. 'The paper. It's him.'

Drake took her by the arm and tried to move her.

'Listen to me, Ian. Look at the damn thing!' she shouted.

Then she drew in deep lungfuls of breath.

Megan started to cry.

He picked up the paper and he read the seven lines of text. He knew the words, had heard then sung a hundred times. But now they screamed at him, tormented him and threatened everything he valued most in the world.

Then Drake saw that Helen had a bottle in her hand, a roll of paper protruding from its neck. Now Helen began to cry and he strode towards her, kicking the glass to one side, taking Megan by the hand as he did so until they stood by Helen. Ignoring every instinct to protect the forensic evidence on the bottle he took it from her hand and read the four lines of text on the message. He knew his heart was beating faster than it ever had and his anger was building.

The words were more than a threat. The killer had been into the house, around the bedrooms and into their belongings.

He took the girls into the sitting room and they slumped onto a sofa. He marched through into the kitchen and found Sian sitting by the table, ashen-faced. He kicked the glass aside from under his feet and dialled headquarters on the landline.

'I don't think Mike Foulds is working, sir,' the operator said.

'Put me through to his mobile.'

'I don't know—'

'Just bloody well do it this instant. It's an emergency.'

There was clicking sound.

'Foulds.'

'Mike. I'm at home. I want you here now,' Drake said. 'We've had another song lyric.'

He rang off and kicked more glass aside with his slippers. He dismissed the needs of the Crime Scene Investigators – his family was more important. Drake knew that his kitchen was a crime scene and that he had to preserve the evidence, protect the fragments of glass. They had to leave the kitchen.

'Let's go into the sitting room,' Drake said to Sian

Sian nodded. Megan and Helen were curled up on the sofa, a bewildered look in their eyes. Sian sat by their side and told them everything was all right. Megan moved closer to her mother. Drake knelt on the floor by the sofa.

'Megan, where did you find the bottle?'

She curled her mouth and made an unconvincing shrug. 'It was in the cupboard.'

'And mine too,' Helen said.

'You'll have to show me,' he said.

In her bedroom, Helen pointed to the spot where she'd found the bottle. Someone had moved toys to one side, creating a neat space. Drake cursed to himself and walked with the girls into Megan's room. She pointed to the gap between the clothes where the milk bottle had stood. The muscles in his jaw tightened.

Tyres screeched on the drive outside. He took Megan and Helen downstairs before opening the door to the familiar face of Foulds.

'What's happened?' Foulds asked, as he followed Drake through into the kitchen, his face taut.

He stood and read the message.

'Megan found it in her bedroom.'

Foulds let out a shallow whistle.

'What kind of sick bastard are we dealing with?'

He looked at the glass littering the floor. 'Looks like an old-fashioned milk bottle.'

Drake nodded. It made no difference – it could have been a plastic bottle, a beer bottle, or a water bottle. Foulds began the task of recording the crime scene and collecting the evidence. Through the open front door he heard voices and saw Caren, breathless, as she strode into the house.

'I've just heard,' she said, her eyes narrow. 'How's Sian?'

He nodded to the sitting room.

'We'll need a statement,' she said.

Drake stared at her.

It hadn't occurred to him that his wife would now be a witness. Her name would appear in the list of witnesses for the prosecution. He cursed the man who brought his sad mind to threaten his family. Then he realised how parched his mouth was and that the dull thumping pain in his head was turning into a proper hangover. He found some painkillers in the kitchen and swallowed a glassful of water. Back in the hallway, family liaison officers were standing by the door.

'Where are the children?' one of them asked.

Drake mumbled something about the sitting room. It was hard to comprehend they were talking about *his* children. He was accustomed to talking about other people's children in a crime scene – not Megan or Helen. He thought about the children of Audrey Embers who had seen more violence at home than any child should see. How would they be affected? And what sort of human beings would they turn out to be? He wanted to envelop Megan and Helen and protect them from the world, from everything, and especially from the killer.

He stood in the hallway, unable to decide where he should be or what he should do. Drake sensed things were out of control, he wanted to shout at the world – I want this to stop. They had to find the killer, this song-master, this relic of the 1970s who was taunting him.

'There are formalities, sir,' Caren said.

Drake heard her but wasn't listening. He kept thinking about the investigation and trying to block out of his mind the events of the morning. It hadn't really happened. None of this – it was all a dream. He thought about all the previous songs and about the numbers. The song lyrics had come with the murders and then later independently. There was no logic to it. If the lyrics had a link to the deaths then why send them separately?

'We'll need a statement,' she continued.

'Yes of course,' he replied, looking at the front door step.

'And fingerprints.'

He stared at her – fingerprints.

'So we can eliminate Megan and Helen and Sian.'

Fingerprints. It meant his daughters giving prints.

Caren continued. 'Mike can do it now. Get it out of the way.'

Drake knew she was right. His mind focused. There might be some prints on the bottle, although a massive doubt appeared in his mind as he thought about it. Once they had finished, Sian sat down by the kitchen table, looking older and more tired than ever.

'The girls will be fine,' Caren said. 'They'll think it was

a big adventure.'

Sian raised her eyes, unconvinced by Caren's reassurance.

Drake went to the door when he heard a car parking on the drive. Price strode into the house in full uniform – the hair on his scalp a golden colour.

'Just heard, Ian. Awful. Awful. Haven't got long. Came as soon as I heard. I've got a presentation to a group of councillors this morning. All these cutbacks – effect on crime rate. That sort of thing.'

Foulds passed him the messages. Price held the plastic evidence pouch between his fingers, as though it had some dreadful disease. He read the contents – Drake and Caren waiting.

'It's more gobbledegook,' he said.

'It's a song lyric,' Drake said, rubbing his temples, hoping the painkillers would begin to work.

'I suppose you recognise them?'

Drake nodded. 'The Police'

Price gave him an exasperated look. 'What do you mean?'

'Song by a band called The Police.'

'You're joking of course. What sort of sick fucking world are we living in?'

'"Message in a Bottle".'

'I know that.' Price sounded irritated.

'That's the name of the song.'

Price's eyes opened in astonishment as Drake spoke.

'What's more important, sir,' said Caren. 'Is the year – 1979.'

Chapter 34
Saturday 26th June

'Ian, get up here. Now.'

Drake heard Foulds's voice and he took the stairs two at a time. Foulds was in Megan's bedroom and when Drake entered, he pointed into one of the open drawers of a chest.

'You better see this.'

Drake stepped towards Foulds and then saw the plastic bottle lying on its side amongst Helen's clothes. For a moment he stared at the bottle, not wanting to believe the killer had been in his daughters' rooms. It had to be a mistake; the bottle was for a popular soft drink. Helen must have put it there, he thought to himself. It was then that he noticed a piece of paper protruding from the neck and he stepped over and grabbed the bottle.

'Be careful, it's evidence ...'

'Fuck that.'

In the top left-hand corner a number five was printed and below it were four lines of verse. He read them a second time and then a third time until the words screamed at him, and then he stared at the number and he realised there must be more bottles. He wanted to open his lips and say something but the saliva caught around the edge of his mouth. The killer had been in the house last night. While he had been drinking Robin's wine, someone had calmly walked round his house and left bottles with verses from the song by The Police.

'There are more,' Drake said.

'Sorry?'

'Bottles. We've got to find them.'

Drake started with the unopened drawers of the chest.

'For fuck's sake, Ian, wear these,' Foulds passed him a pair of latex gloves.

Once he'd put them on he joined Foulds, who was flicking through Megan's clothes in the wardrobe. Just as the killer had done the night before. Drake knew that he had to ignore his anger or else he couldn't think straight. He clenched his jaw and wanted to tell Foulds that *he* would search through Megan's clothes. He didn't want anyone else looking through his family's possessions. Not now. Not ever.

'How many are they going to be?' Foulds asked.

'Six or seven, maybe eight.'

'How'd you know?'

'They're the verses from the song.'

Drake marched into the main bedroom and stood for a moment.

'What song you talking about?'

''Message in a Bottle' by The Police. You must have heard it.'

Foulds nodded.

'The bastard has printed verses from the song and pushed them into the bottles.'

'That's really sick.'

'We found three so far. So there's more in this room as well.'

'How many verses are there?'

Drake knelt by a cupboard, opening each of the drawers in turn, his pulse rate increasing. He yanked open the bottom drawer and saw an empty San Pellegrino bottle with a shard of paper protruding from its neck.

'You bastard.'

He picked up the bottle at the same time that Foulds found another in the bottom of the wardrobe.

'That's five,' Foulds said. 'Any more?'

Drake said nothing.

'It's a crime scene,' Foulds said.

Drake chewed on his bottom lip as he sat in the kitchen. Caren leant against the frame of the door and Price stared at him over the table. Drake kept thinking about Robin Miles pouring San Pellegrino at the dinner party the night before. He knew something had been said but his mind wanted to blank out the bottles the killer had left.

'Ian, the house is a crime scene,' Foulds said again.

Crime scene. He wished he could turn back the clock, that none of this had happened, that his family wasn't involved. He wanted to scream but instead managed to blow out a lungful of air.

'We'll need a full CSI team,' Price said.

Foulds nodded.

'Sian and the girls will have to leave,' Caren added.

Drake started to focus when he heard Sian's name.

'What?' Drake said.

Caren replied, 'Mike and the CSI team will have to go through everything.'

'What do you …?'

Foulds came to stand by the table.

'All the rooms could have traces of the killer. He's been into the bedrooms, so it's likely he was in every room.'

Every room.

Drawing his hand over their furniture, fingering the clothes in their cupboards, admiring their possessions. Now Drake knew what it was like to be the victim of burglary. But nothing had been taken: just five plastic bottles placed carefully, with messages they couldn't decipher.

Drake nodded. 'I'll talk to Sian.'

Foulds was finishing a call requesting a full CSI team when Drake returned to the kitchen having watched Sian, Megan and Helen leave for her mother's house. He slumped down onto one of the chairs and rubbed both temples with his forefingers, regretting how much wine he had drunk last night and worrying that his breath must reek.

'We'll have to get Dr Fabrien back,' Price said.

He had an intense look on his face and the muscles below his ear lobe were twitching as he clenched his jaw. He had a half-finished mug of tea on the table.

'We have to do everything to stop this maniac.'

The last person Drake wanted to think about was Margaret Fabrien. He gave Price a troubled look. He half listened to Price, but his thoughts turned to Fabrien's voice telling him about the killer.

She had scoffed when he suggested a personal link. *Don't think he has an interest in you inspector. He's got another agenda.* Well, she had been wrong and now the killer was right into his life. He had walked through the house.

Message in a bottle.

He had placed the bottles in the cupboards and drawers. Then he had left. Perhaps he had turned his head to look at the house, smiling to himself, and imagined what would happen once the bottles had been found. Drake suppressed an urge to run outside – perhaps the killer was sitting in his car, revelling in all the attention, but he dismissed the notion. Where was he now? He thought about Fabrien again: *he has a responsible job and lives a perfectly normal life and functions satisfactorily.* Drake pictured him in a park with his children playing on swings, kicking a football and buying ice cream. How normal could he be and still kill people? He would make a mistake and they would find him.

'Margaret?'

Drake heard Price's voice and looked over.

'There's been another message. We'll need you back.'

Price was holding his mobile between his thumb and forefinger and Drake sat up a little straighter on his chair.

'I'll arrange a car to collect you.'

Price rang off and turned to Drake.

'She'll be on the first train from London on Monday. And she's finalised a report.'

Drake remembered the conversations from the night before and his mind turned to James Harrod. It had to be him. The bastard.

'James Harrod,' he said.

Price looked interested. Drake continued. 'Apparently he's got everything riding on the planning application that was being dealt with by Roderick Jones.'

Price raised his eyebrows. 'That would give him a huge motive for killing Jones, but why kill Mathews and Farrell, and West?'

Drake's head sagged – it was the part of the jigsaw that didn't fit. All the evidence was pointing at the same killer committing all the murders.

Price looked at his watch.

'We'll discuss this again later, once we've had some forensics done,' he announced before getting up.

Drake walked with Price to the front door and out into the warm morning sunshine. He thought he saw anxious faces in windows along the estate and he caught the movement of net curtains in a bedroom. He wondered what his neighbours would feel when it became common knowledge that the killer had been in their house. He could see the headlines.

Serial killer on the loose.

He watched Price holding his mobile close to his ear as he sat in the car, before the Jaguar powered away.

Drake sat in the Alfa and Chrissie Hynde's voice came into his mind, singing the chorus from 'Brass in Pocket'. He turned the key in the ignition and revved the engine hard until the song disappeared and he drove down towards the A55. He swung the car into the entrance of headquarters and cursed as the words of the other songs over and over in his head.

On his way to the Incident Room, he detoured into one

of the toilets. He stared into the mirror, pulled at the bags under his eyes and ran his fingers over the patch of grey stubble he'd missed when shaving. He filled a bowl with hot water and washed his face again, rubbing his hands over his cheeks. He thought about the message printed on the paper he'd held that morning. He had to clean away any trace of the killer so he scrubbed harder until another officer came into the toilets, and, noticing the odd expression on the other man's face, Drake finished and left.

Caren looked up from her desk and gave him a reassuring warm smile. Howick stood up straight, a sharp look on his face.

'I've just heard, sir,' Howick said. 'It's terrible.'

Drake sat down and looked at the papers on his desk. Caren was standing by the door and behind her, he saw Winder arrive – bag of cakes in his hand – looking flustered.

'Is it true about the bottles?' he heard Winder ask Howick.

Caren gave Drake a half smile.

Drake stood up and walked past Caren until he was standing in front of the board. He scanned the details of the information displayed. His eyes moved from one photograph to another: he read the opening lines of each song lyric.

'Family all right, sir?' Howick was the first to break the silence.

'They're pretty shaken up,' Drake replied.

He turned to look at the team.

'Did he choose the songs first?' Drake asked.

Caren screwed her face up. 'Sorry. What do you mean?'

'Are we looking for significance in the songs where none exists? Or is there some relevance to the individual bands? Or is it 1979?'

Winder put down a jam doughnut and announced through a mouthful lined with icing sugar, 'If there is no significance to the songs, why choose them?'

'Because he's a dick,' Howick said.

Caren nodded. 'He's probably getting off somewhere merely thinking that we're looking for significance in these songs.'

Drake paced up and down. 'So we're agreed there is no significance in the songs. Let's assume I agree. Is there any significance about the individual bands? Why send the messages if there's no reason? All the bands so far are well known. Only The Pretenders are still playing but that's because of Chrissie Hynde. Pink Floyd have broken up, Queen are not the same without Freddie Mercury and The Police split up acrimoniously.'

Winder had finished eating the doughnut. 'None of them wanted to say anything particular with the songs – except Pink Floyd, I guess.'

'Okay, okay,' Drake said, arms crossed tightly. 'Pink Floyd may have been trying to say something but where does that take us? We could read any significance into these lyrics. They could fit any scenario. Then I keep hearing Freddie Mercury. I'm looking for some meaning in the words. But there isn't any.'

'It's a love song,' Howick said. 'Maybe he's telling us that he's in love.'

'Or was,' Drake continued. 'Maybe she's dead.'

'Or maybe he's just a nutter.'

Winder licked his fingers before adding. 'Gets my vote – pulling our chain. Getting a hard-on from the excitement it gives him, knowing he's sending us these messages.'

'I don't know that it's that simple,' Drake said. 'Our profiler believed there was significance to the tunes. It must be the year. 1979 must have been special for this guy. Something happened. A death, a marriage, or a celebration. Or something.'

'What about the number? Is there some significance to the number? One thousand nine hundred and seventy-nine.' Caren emphasised each word.

Drake cleared his throat and pulled himself up,

straightening his posture. They needed to stop going round in circles.

'Gareth, Dave. We want to know everything about James Harrod – revenue, customs, special branch, bank accounts, etc. Get Kent to help. Any problems, let me know. This has priority over everything. If it means buggering up the weekend, so be it. Any problems, I want to be told.'

By the end of the afternoon Drake's eyes were burning. The songs kept returning to his mind, destroying any lateral thinking he was capable of maintaining. He started a mind map, trying to make sense of the messages, the songs and the bands. He thought they had to be missing something. It was there for them. They just couldn't see it. He tried doodling with a red biro. He set about tidying his room, rearranging the papers, stacking folders, emptying the bin.

He realised that he had achieved nothing throughout the afternoon. He nodded to Caren as he left the Incident Room. She gave him a worried look. Neither Winder nor Howick looked up from their computers.

When he pulled into the drive at the home of his parents-in-law he couldn't remember the journey. Had it been raining? Was the traffic heavy? Did he go through a red light? He pushed the doorbell and heard the approaching footsteps. Then his mother-in-law opened the door, forcing a narrow smile.

'Sian's in the small sitting room.'

Sian looked tired; he could hear the sound of the girls laughing as they watched television in the living room. She raised her head and smiled.

'How are you feeling?' he asked

The smile waned.

'I'm taking the girls to stay with my sister for a couple of days.'

Chapter 35
Sunday 26th June

Drake felt something tugging at his shoulder and woke in a panic.

He was lying diagonally across the bed, the duvet wrapped round his neck and as he moved, it pulled against his shoulder. He wriggled free and ran a hand over the perspiration on his skin. The atmosphere in the bedroom was musty and stale.

Then he heard a banging on the front door and the chimes from the bell. He made his way downstairs, opened the front door and squinted at the face of Moxon, who looked worried.

'Ian, is everything all right? I heard what happened.'

'Ah, yes …' Drake had forgotten his invitation to his friend.

'Yes, sorry. Come in.' Drake closed the door after Moxon.

'It must have been stressful yesterday.'

'Coffee?' Drake asked, before walking through into the kitchen and flicking on the kettle.

'I tried your mobile,' Moxon continued. 'How's Sian?'

'Had the stuffing knocked out of her.'

Drake found two mugs in the cupboard and heaped instant into both.

'And Megan and Helen?'

'They think it's a bit of an adventure.' He filled the mugs and pushed one over the worktop at Moxon. 'Profiler's coming back tomorrow.'

'I suppose you need all the help you can get.'

Drake cradled his coffee mug in both hands. They walked through into the sitting room and Drake stood by the window as Moxon sat back on the sofa. Drake thought about Megan and Helen as he noticed some children playing in the road.

'Do you remember the case of that undertaker years ago where they got a profiler in? Waste of time,' Moxon continued.

Drake still stared out of the window, half listening to what his friend was saying. 'The answer must be simple,' Drake said, turning back to look at his friend.

'How are your parents?'

'My father started treatment for his cancer this week. He's still very weak.'

Before Moxon could reply, the telephone rang and Drake looked for the handset. He lost his temper and swore under his breath as he moved scatter cushions, searching for the muffled ring tone. The caller rang off as soon as he found it. He looked at the screen and read his sister's number. He raised an eyebrow in surprise; she rarely called.

'My sister,' Drake said.

Moxon finished the last of his coffee.

'You should call her,' Moxon said as he left. 'You take care.'

Drake sat by the kitchen table contemplating a conversation with his sister. He tried to remember when he had last spoken to her. Their conversations always felt stilted, as though she wanted to lash out at him verbally. He knew he ought to call her more frequently, get on the offensive and take the initiative. Then he thought about his mother and how she must have felt, knowing that brother and sister rarely spoke. He glanced at his watch and wondered if he should return her call. Perhaps it was lunchtime and she would be busy. He put his reservations to one side and pressed Susan's number.

'Mam told me what happened.' Susan sounded concerned. 'How's Sian?'

'She's gone to stay with her sister for a couple of days. Back on Tuesday – ready for work on Wednesday.'

'Mam is very worried about Dad.'

'What did she say?'

'Not much. But I can tell.'

Drake felt like asking how she could tell when she barely saw her mother.

'How often do you go to see them, Ian?'

Drake heard the implied criticism in her voice. *More often than you.* He sensed the barriers rising in his mind and tried to deflect the conversation. He asked about David. He was very busy – lots of new projects at work. The children were doing well at school and they were off to Italy in three weeks time.

'Are you going to see Mam and Dad over the summer holiday?' he asked.

She hesitated. 'Things are very busy. When we get back, David has got so much work on and the children have their commitments. It's going to be very difficult.'

When the call ended, Drake was pleased that the conversation had finished, but irritated with his sister. She had a cheek to chastise him about their mother when he was the one that visited.

'How the hell did he get all this credit?'

'Friends in high places?' Drake suggested.

'The borrowing secured on these assets is phenomenal,' Kent continued. 'It's not loan-to-value ratio but value-to-loan ratio.' He smiled and leant back in his chair.

Drake was sitting with Kent in front of a computer screen filled with bank statements and tax returns. Kent folded his arms behind his head. 'There is a technical name for this.'

'And?'

'He's fucked.'

'Very funny.'

'No, seriously. There is nothing to suggest that Harrod could survive if the planning application was turned down.'

Drake turned his attention away from the bank statements and tax returns and thought about the outline of an interview with Harrod.

'Anything else we need?'

Kent looked amused. 'The man's companies are debt laden and it doesn't seem he has the cash flow needed to fight his way out of it. He'd need a miracle to survive.'

'How would the planning permission help?' Caren asked.

Kent sounded serious. 'The value of the land goes up ten fold. He options the property to one of the major developers and, hey presto, he goes cap in hand to the bank with a property worth vastly more than the debt. Harrod happy – bank happy. Easy.'

Drake returned to his office; the tiredness of the day before had left him and he was concentrating again. They had notes to assemble, strategies to consider. He drew a notepad from a drawer and made a list of the questions for Harrod. Caren sat down opposite.

'We need to coordinate an arrest of Dixon at the same time,' Caren said.

Drake doodled on the pad and grunted an acknowledgment.

'I think we should establish his whereabouts first,' she continued.

Drake nodded.

'Do we need to discuss the case with Thorsen?'

Drake stopped the doodling and looked up, considering her question. He didn't want to. He wanted to get on with it – they had enough for an interview.

'I'll run it past him,' he said

'And what about West?'

Drake buried his head in his hands and then looked at Caren.

'We've got nothing to link Harrod to West. No motive. Nothing. That will have to wait until we've been through West's life. We can't afford to wait. We've got to prevent the final death.'

There was something obvious they were missing and must find it. He cast a surreptitious glance at the sudoku in the newspaper folded on his desk. Later, he decided, knowing that slicing and dicing the puzzle would help him focus.

'We were never going to stop West being killed,' he said eventually, a sad tone to his voice.

Caren looked baffled.

'I can see it now,' Drake continued. 'The crossbows in the car and the van they all pointed to Walters. Someone wanted to throw enough suspicion onto Walters to distract us. And the killer must have known that Walters would be elevated to the Welsh Assembly when Jones died. And that bogged us down for hours and days. How many man hours have we spent on Walters's background.'

'I know that Finance are having a fit over the overtime.'

'Exactly,' Drake said as he developed his train of thought. 'I've already had a memo telling me we're over budget on the investigation. And then the Indian restaurant fiasco and the dummy in the car.'

Drake could feel the anger building as the scenario developed in his mind. He brought the palm of his hand down sharply onto the desk and stood up.

'We've been running around to his tune all this time.'

Drake stood by the window, closed his eyes and then tilted his head towards the sky, letting the sun warm his face.

'So this business with the bottles at my house is another wild-goose chase and we'll spend hours achieving nothing.'

Caren moved in her seat.

'There must be something about the songs and the lyrics and the numbers: One. Nine. Seven. Nine.'

It sounded different somehow when Caren said each

number in this way.

He looked at his Tag Heuer and decided he should eat. Being a creature of habit, he felt disjointed not having had breakfast and lunch at the correct times. The sandwich he bought in the servery was stale – when were they actually fresh? – and after he had eaten it, without any enjoyment, he chomped his way through an apple. It was Sunday, so he had a chocolate bar as well.

Back in the Incident Room he made coffee, set off the timer on his mobile and waited for the coffee to brew properly. Once he had poured the dark liquid and the first sips had passed his lips he knew that he was back in control, of himself and the investigation.

No more lazy mornings and disorganized patterns to his working day.

Drake sat opposite Price who stared at Foulds.

'We've been through every room – and nothing.'

Drake ran a finger round his collar, hoping he would feel more comfortable despite the heat in the room.

'How did he get in?' Drake asked.

'Must have opened the lock somehow. This guy knows what he's doing.'

Drake sensed the tension in his chest again. He thought of Sian and then Megan and Helen and the anger welled up again and he hoped he could still think straight.

'So he must have been wearing gloves,' Price added. 'And he must have planned this really carefully. How did he know you were out?'

Drake blinked furiously wondering whether he had told anyone that they'd be out. But the thoughts were a blur. And maybe the killer didn't know and maybe he would have left the bottles on the doorstep if they'd been home.

Drake didn't reply. Foulds had more to report, 'Fingerprints all over the papers. Only one set we can't identify. Wait-and-see.' He sounded less than hopeful.

'And the bottles?' Drake said.

'Traces of liquids. Water, nothing else of any significance.'

'No saliva?'

'No.'

'No fabric or traces in the house?'

'Where do we start, Ian?' Foulds spread out his hands. 'There's no sign of forced entry.'

'But there must be *something*.' Drake raised his voice more than he'd intended.

'Ian,' Price cut in. 'Once your family is back I want an armed officer to stay with you overnight until we catch this bastard.'

Drake stared at Price. He had no idea what to say.

Chapter 36
Monday 28th June

Drake stared at Howick and Foulds. He wanted to dispel the miserable mood invading his mind but the forensic reports on his desk hadn't helped. It was shaping up to be a bad start to the week.

'There's no evidence in either van of anything linking these two men to the murders.'

'That's right, Ian. Just boxes of books and second-hand DVDs and CDs. Hundreds of them. All neatly stored.'

Drake flicked through the report. 'And the crossbow only had one set of prints.'

'Yes. Aled Walters.'

'Can we tell if it was the weapon used to kill Mathews and Farrell?'

'Impossible.'

Howick moved in his chair and cleared his throat. 'Anyway, we've interviewed both men and their families and they've both got cast-iron alibis. They were a hundred miles away watching a snooker competition in Sheffield. Didn't come back until Wednesday afternoon after the killings.'

'So how do they explain the crossbow?'

Neither Foulds nor Howick nor Drake had an answer.

The flickering images on the screen told Drake that the train from London was running late. A chilly breeze funnelled under the canopy and he noticed the goose pimples on his forearms. He walked to the end of the platform where he felt the warmth of the sunshine on his face. If only it could be as easy to change the mood of the investigation, he thought.

He gazed out over the bay and on the horizon saw the turning blades of the wind farms. In the distance, he saw the approaching train and turned back down the platform as the carriages passed him.

Dr Fabrien stepped off the train, reached for a small overnight case and dragged it behind her. Drake walked up to her and smiled. Charm offensive – had to work.

'Margaret, good journey?'

'Why are the trains so full these days?'

He heard the French accent but she was complaining like a proper Briton. They headed out of the station. The uniformed Traffic officer jumped out of the car when he saw them and the boot lid flew open. The car was stuffy and Drake powered down the rear window as the driver inched his way through heavy traffic.

'Busy this morning,' Dr Fabrien said.

'There's a market in the main street,' he replied. 'Not like the markets of France, of course.' He decided to ask about her accent. 'Are you from France?'

'Normandy. My father is English. He met my mother when he was teaching English in Paris. They run a hotel near Caen.'

'Do you go back very often?'

'Not as often as I'd like.'

'We're going to France for our holiday.'

Drake had avoided thinking about having to cancel. He knew what Sian might say – *can't someone else deal with it?* Even if someone could, he'd be thinking about the case every minute, worrying who would be in charge.

Dr Fabrien tilted her head and gave him an intense look, 'And how are your family now?' she asked. 'It must have been traumatic for your children.'

'It was terrible.'

'It must be awful for you.'

'I want to catch this bastard more than ever.'

The journey was brief and soon they walked into the Incident Room and Dr Fabrien looked at the board. Three pairs of eyes watched her as she scanned the words from the latest song lyric. Before she could make any comment,

Winder arrived, fumbling to switch off his iPod when he saw Drake and Dr Fabrien.

'Been with forensics to Stone's place.'

Drake nodded.

'And his office too. The guy is really spooked. Told me he can't sleep. Told me he's got a baseball bat under his bed.'

When nobody laughed, Winder sat down and Caren gave him an exasperated look – *how could you be so insensitive?* He looked back. *What have I done wrong?*

Drake heard the telephone in his office ring and he hurried over to his desk. He picked up the handset and looked out of the window at the line of trees full of green foliage.

'Detective Inspector Drake.' The voice used his full title.

He paused and listened.

'When?'

Once he had finished, he walked back into the Incident Room.

'Fiona Trick's disappeared.'

Aled Walters fiddled with a signet ring on his left hand before adjusting his tie for the third time in as many minutes. His eyes flashed around the room as Drake rearranged the papers on the table, revelling in the politician's obvious discomfort. Perhaps he should wait until Caren returned from Fiona's house before having the interview, but it wasn't under caution and he had to make progress.

'What exactly is the nature of your relationship with Fiona Trick?' Drake sat back and stared at Walters.

He cleared his throat and swallowed.

'We've been seeing each other for some time.'

'What do mean, *seeing* each other?'

'We had – have – a relationship …'

Drake said nothing; he stared at Walters and waited.

'We were close … very close …'

'How long have you been *close*?'

Walters moved his eyes around the room again.

'A few months …'

It was the first lie and Drake guessed there were more to come.

'Where did you meet?'

Walters was regaining his composure. The politician's instincts were kicking in, the need to survive paramount. Walters drew one hand over another and placed them on the table.

'I was attending some function and she was present.'

'Where was that?'

He hesitated. 'In Colwyn Bay, last year some time.'

Second lie. Drake could see them coming.

'Did you stay overnight every weekend?'

Walters opened his mouth and then stopped himself and Drake could see him gathering his thoughts.

'We … tried to be discreet … for the children. No, not every weekend.'

'I understand the children liked having contact with their father?' Drake asked as he glanced at the original statement from Fiona Trick – *the children hate their father*.

'They enjoyed their time with him. He had contact regularly. When his work commitments allowed. I'm sure you know what it's like, Inspector.' Walters was getting into his stride.

'How did you get on with the children?'

'Fine. We had a good relationship.'

'Were you planning to get married?'

Drake saw the flash of uncertainty pass over his face. Hadn't thought about that one, had he?

'We hadn't discussed it.'

'You've been married before?' Drake tried to sound conversational.

'Yes. I was divorced several years ago. Look Inspector, I don't see what this has to do with Fiona's disappearance.'

Drake thumbed through more of the papers, gathering his thoughts.

'Background, that's all,' he said. 'Did you and your former wife meet Paul and Fiona at the Archery Club?'

Drake looked him straight in the eye and Walters paused. He blinked and moved his jaw until he must have calculated that Drake knew it all and there was no point denying the connection.

'What are you trying to suggest, Inspector?' He spat out Drake's title. 'That I had something to do with Mathews's murder? If you are, that's absurd.'

Drake knew he was in charge now.

'I wasn't suggesting that at all, Mr Walters. I was asking you whether you met Paul and Fiona in the Archery Club. After all, you were the president when they were members.'

'Yes, we met there, but nothing happened … We met again last year.'

'That's not true is it?'

'What do you mean? This is preposterous. I've come here to report Fiona missing and you're asking me about the murder of her husband.'

'Your wife had an affair with Paul Mathews.'

Walters sat back in the plastic chair, a defiant look on his face. Drake continued. 'And she contracted chlamydia from him. Did she pass it on to you, Mr Walters?'

Drake saw the embarrassment in the politician's face. Drake read the thought process that threatened his world. The headlines in the press and the awkward glances from colleagues would be the start, until a quiet word suggesting it would be in the interest of the 'party' if he stood down.

'My personal life is none of your business.'

Defiance – the only mechanism Walters had left.

Drake shuffled the papers again. But he knew what the

next question was going to be and he hoped he knew the answer. He tried to read the body language from Walters. He feigned an interest in the paperwork until he'd dragged out enough time. He glared at Walters and asked slowly.

'Were you going to emigrate to Australia with Fiona?'

As he read the report Price scratched the top of his head with his fingernails. It made a dull rasping sound and Drake wondered how he would look if he shaved his head. Dr Fabrien paid little attention to the male grooming and was busy scribbling notes on a piece of yellow paper.

Drake had read the profiling report several times, underlining various sections with a highlighter. He cleared his throat and glanced at his watch. He adjusted his tie and checked the shirt that he'd ironed that morning as he listened to the *Today* programme. The weather was still warm and he had chosen a short-sleeved white shirt with a blue-and-red striped tie.

'Let's get on,' Price announced.

Drake straightened in his chair.

'We've all read the report, Margaret,' Price continued. 'But what do you make of the latest message?'

'Intriguing.'

Intriguing. The word flicked a switch in Drake's mind. He could feel the anger building. He counted to ten. And then he counted to ten a second time. He was running an investigation into three murders and she found it intriguing.

'I've looked again at all the songs. They obviously have a considerable significance for this man. The first song draws attention to himself. He's demanding your attention. Telling you, he is special. Then the second song is a cry for help. It's about the oppression of children and freeing the mind.'

Drake glanced over at Price and saw the pained look on his face.

'One could be tempted to overemphasise the third song. On the first reading, it is a simple love song. The words don't convey anything in themselves. But when you listen to Freddie Mercury ...'

Drake tapped the fingers of his right hand on his left hand, clenched tightly.

'He has such a powerful voice,' she continued. 'However, I think the killer is trying to tell us something far deeper about himself. Perhaps he has had difficulty maintaining a true, loving relationship. Possibly, he could be single, having only experienced love from a distance.'

'And the final message?' asked Price.

'Ah yes. Intriguing.'

That word again. Drake clenched his jaw. He thought about the bottles on the kitchen floor and Megan crying.

'It's a song of hope.' She paused and looked up. Drake and Price caught her gaze before she continued. 'The song is about loneliness and how love can both break and mend the spirit.'

Drake thought of something constructive to say. He wanted to shout at her. He wanted to ask her whether she had anything helpful to say.

'But then the song turns to hope. I think the profile of this killer suggests he has suffered loneliness and loss. And that his cries for help went unheeded.'

Drake interrupted before she could continue, forming the words carefully. 'And what about my involvement and how it's affected my family?'

'He's targeting you because you are in charge of the investigation. Nothing more.'

Drake was convinced the killer was saying more with the bottles. Then he realised Dr Fabrien hadn't said anything about 1979.

'And the year?' Drake asked.

'Yes, I know. It's either deliberate or pure coincidence.'

Drake flattened his hands on the desk with a thump.

'Pure coincidence – how could it be? I just don't see that?' His voice raised.

Dr Fabrien blinked and avoided Drake's eye contact.

'I believe the songs and their lyrics are important to this killer,' she said.

'Then why choose them all from the same year?'

'They could be his favourite songs.'

'That's exactly what I mean, Margaret. That would make the year significant.'

'Not as significant as the song lyrics. You mustn't lose track of that. It's the lyrics that are telling us about the man.'

'If 1979 is important, why would that be?'

Dr Fabrien pushed her papers around the table and rolled her eyes.

'It could be that something significant happened to him in that year or to somebody he loves or loved. Or there could be a connection from 1979 to each of the three deaths – have you looked at that?'

Drake gave her a pinched look and decided he wasn't going to respond.

'Did anything interesting happen in 1979?' Price asked, trying to deflect the tension.

'Margaret Thatcher became prime minister. There was a referendum on Welsh devolution. Wales didn't win the rugby grand slam,' Drake said, without pausing for breath.

'Nothing much then,' Price said.

Drake tidied his papers, closing the open report and making moves to get back to the investigation. He knew that had Price not been there he would certainly have lost his temper.

'And you shouldn't dismiss the choice of the last song. It was very theatrical. Leaving a message in numerous bottles, and of course the words of 'Message in a Bottle.' And also the name of the band.'

Drake moved his chair back and glanced self-consciously at the clock on the wall and then at his watch.

'What do you make of the death threats to Mathews and Farrell?' Drake said.

She gave one of her customary shrugs, the sort that suggested the question didn't deserve an answer.

'They are all the same and their wording is no different from the first to the last.'

'If Evans was only responsible for the first, then who sent the rest and how did he or she know about the wording?'

'Have you thought about the possibility that the killer might be a police officer or a retired police officer?'

Drake could see an expletive forming in Price's mouth before he snorted. 'Don't be absolutely absurd.'

Drake thought about replying but his mobile, sitting on the pile of papers, bleeped twice. He picked up the phone and read the text message before rushing for the door.

'I need to leave.'

Chapter 37
Monday 28th June

'It's midnight in Perth.'

Howick looked pleased with himself. He handed details of the flight confirmation to Drake; someone had already written *Down Under* on the board.

'Do we have an address?' Drake asked.

'We're waiting for the details from the Australian consulate,' Howick replied.

Drake nodded. The young officer had been busy.

'What did Walters say?' Caren was dunking a biscuit into a mug of tea.

'He lied all through our discussion,' Drake said.

Winder grunted. 'Bloody politicians.'

'He lied about when and where he met Fiona.'

'Did he know she was going to emigrate?' Caren asked, through a mouthful of sodden digestive.

'He lied about that too.'

Winder laughed quietly. 'Poor bastard. He probably didn't know anything about her plans.'

Caren finished the last of the tea. 'The house had been cleaned and tidied. An estate agent arrived to take photographs as we left.'

'So where does this take us, boss?' Howick asked.

Drake felt like saying *not very far*. A possible suspect had done a runner to Australia and her boyfriend, another suspect, knew nothing about it. Drake remembered the look in Walters's face as he tried to find an answer to Drake's last question. He had no idea she was leaving. He had seen the vulnerability in Walters's face and the pain of a loss he couldn't explain.

Drake couldn't explain this as the killer's attempts to distract their attention. But he couldn't take the risk that Walters and Fiona weren't involved. Instinctively he knew that he had to resolve the investigation into Walters before he could move on. There was a motive, but no evidence, and without a physical connection to the deaths, the case against Walters and Fiona was drying up. He tried to discount her lies, but had there been some Faustian pact to kill Mathews and then Jones? Solving her problem and advancing his career. And then there was the death of West, but there was nothing to connect them to his death. Drake didn't have the answer and Fiona leaving for Australia hadn't helped.

Drake returned to his office and spent an hour reading the statements and reviewing the evidence and his notes from Dr Fabrien. He thought about ringing Sian but decided to try later. Instead he called his mother.

'I'm so glad you called,' she said. 'Are Sian and the girls back yet?'

'Tomorrow.'

'It must have been terrible.'

Drake glanced at the sudoku in the newspaper on his desk and asked, without enthusiasm, his mind on the puzzle, 'How are you?'

'Better now. There haven't been any more disturbances and your father's sleeping better.'

Drake immediately felt guilty that he'd not been to see his parents since his mother called in the middle of the night.

'You should call to see him.'

That made Drake feel worse. They exchanged small talk and after a few minutes he rang off.

He wiped the grease off his skin and then walked through to the bathroom. The water was hot as he immersed his hands in the basin and then, pressing soap from a dispenser, lathered his hands and face. Once he'd finished, he returned to the Incident Room. Howick was busy on the telephone demanding cooperation from some unfortunate administrator. In the kitchen he began the process of making coffee before staring at the grounds falling in the cafetière.

Then he felt hungry and remembered that Sian had told him hunger was a sign of dehydration. Perhaps the coffee would help.

Back in his office, he stared out of the window as he drank the coffee. The weather was still warm, but knots of white cloud were gathering to the south. An old man was exercising his dog on the grass and a group of cyclists passed on the main road, their heads down, legs pumping. Turning away from the window, he looked at the chaos on his desk, stifling an impulse to sweep everything onto the floor. He couldn't think straight in the middle of chaos. He set about reorganising the papers. The reports were stacked to one side, then all the memos were read and urgent calls added to a to-do list.

He moved his attention to the computer and scanned through the latest emails, noticing the details about a course, later that week, on interviewing techniques for interrogating sex offenders. He typed a message to Caren, asking her to attend and clicked *Forward*. A knock on his door brought his attention back to the investigation and he waved Caren into the room.

'We need to plan the arrests,' he said.

'Of course.' Caren sounded matter-of-fact.

'First, let's talk about Stevie Dixon.'

The image of the gloating face of Dixon came to his mind and he decided that nothing would go wrong the second time. He wrote the word *Timetable* on the top line of piece of A4 paper and underneath he jotted a time for Dixon's arrest.

'I don't want Gareth involved,' he said.

'No, of course.'

'You make the arrest with Dave. Liaise with the police in Birkenhead. Get two Uniform officers to go with you.'

'Yes, sir.'

'Don't say anything to him. Just caution him. He can call his brief when he's at the station.'

After an hour Drake had a list of questions in blue ink, some of which he had underlined in red, others circled and then he did the same exercise for Harrod. The arrests would have to be coordinated in advance. There could be no risk of either man talking to each other or anybody else.

'It'll take you an hour to get to Dixon's place. Is he still there?'

'I had a call half an hour ago confirming that he hasn't moved all day.'

'Not with the girlfriend?'

'Not today, sir.'

'Call me when you're outside Dixon's house. I'll be waiting outside Harrod's.'

'Going shopping, sir?'

'Very funny.'

After Caren left, Drake read the prison reports about Harrod's time on the same wing as Stevie Dixon. He could feel the strength of the sun waning through the windows and he heard the sound of cars leaving headquarters at the end of the normal working day. As he read the paperwork, he scribbled notes; later he would put them together for the interview.

He decided to call Sian but as he picked up the telephone, a text message arrived from Caren telling him she would arrive at Dixon's house shortly. He replaced the handset; the call would have to wait.

A team of officers were waiting in the car park and he gave them last-minute instructions. He checked that he had his warrant card and then folded his jacket before placing it on the rear passenger seat of the Alfa. Winder sat in the front and Drake fired the engine into life.

'They say you're not a driver unless you've owned an Alfa Romeo,' Winder said, looking around the clean interior of the car.

Drake ignored him, negotiated his way out to the main road, and then down to the A55, followed by two unmarked police cars. Another unmarked car was parked near Harrod's property and its regular messages confirmed that he was still at home. Drake accelerated hard, earning some complimentary remarks from Winder about the performance of the car. Drake pushed the 'on' button of the radio and from the multi-function steering wheel switched to the CD player and then through the tracks until he found Thunder Road. The opening chords of the mouth organ gave him a welcome moment of relaxation.

Winder's mobile hummed.

'Where are you?' Winder said.

He paused.

'We'll be there in five.'

Drake drew up behind the unmarked police car and called the officer who confirmed Harrod was still inside. They sent a text to Caren and the convoy turned into the drive, lined with freshly painted fencing. The chippings under the wheels made a soft crunching noise and, approaching the house, Drake saw the Range Rover Sport parked next to a Mercedes coupé. He left the car with Winder and approached the front of the house, two other officers covering the rear.

Drake stood by the door, Winder by his side, two uniformed officers – broad shouldered with intense stares – stood behind him. The door opened. It was Harrod.

'James Harrod.'

'What do you want? Who are you?'

Drake flashed his warrant card. 'I'm arresting you on suspicion of the murders of Paul Mathews and Danny Farrell.'

Drake drove back to headquarters playing 'Born to Run' more loudly than usual. The evening temperature was cooling and he gathered his thoughts for the interviews. He still had all his notes to finalise, which meant working late.

Drake took off his jacket and placed it on a wooden hanger. Standing over the desk, he felt his warrant card in his shirt pocket. Usually he kept it in his jacket but after arresting Harrod he had slipped it into the pocket without realising. He pulled it out and read the details before looking at the photograph. He looked younger, with less grey hair and fewer wrinkles. He placed it to one corner of the desk.

He sat down and cleared his mind for the work in hand. Caren arrived, carrying takeaway fish and chips and the smell drifted through from the Incident Room.

'Take that into the kitchen and close the door,' he shouted.

He arranged the papers and started preparing an interview plan. Barely any time had passed, when Caren stood by the door, one corner of her mouth smeared with tomato ketchup.

Drake cursed when he saw the time – his watch said 11.00 pm – and realised that he hadn't called Sian. He had promised himself to call but work had taken over again. He picked up his mobile and sent her a text. He sat, looking at the handset, urging it to bleep. He fell into a despondent mood as he drove home, disappointed with himself, knowing he should have called Sian earlier.

The house felt cold and he sat in the kitchen drinking water, trying to decide if he should eat anything. After some cheese and the remains of a dried-up bottle of chutney, he went to bed, but sleep eluded him and he tossed and turned. Realising he was under-sudokued, after a day so busy even his rituals had been overlooked, he found a fiendish puzzle and a newly sharpened pencil. An hour later he tried sleeping again.

He dreamt about the journey to the Crimea and he saw the two officers as they parked on the top of the pass. He watched from the vantage point as they walked over to the motorist – but it didn't happen that way – and he heard someone asking them for their warrant cards.

Then he woke.

The sweat was pouring off him and the duvet was on the floor.

Chapter 38
Tuesday 29th June

Drake pulled into the car park a few minutes before seven and yanked up the handbrake on the Alfa. He looked over towards the building in front of him. One of the men inside was responsible for the bottles. Had been into his house, opening cupboards, touching their clothes. The memory of Megan and Helen carrying the bottles only made his determination stronger, despite the anger building in his mind.

Leaning over to the passenger seat he searched through the inside pockets of his jacket and found his mobile. He thumbed another message to Sian – how difficult can it be to apologise in a text? But the words didn't come and he pressed the clear button and started again. The handset bleeped once he'd finished. Then he left the car and strode over to the entrance door and stood by the security panel. He thought about the numbers: it was always the same – numbers everywhere, but why in this case? The messages from the killer were pinned to the board of the Incident Room and, for a moment, he forgot the code for the security door. Was it 4231 or was it 1324? Had he got the numbers totally confused? And, if he couldn't remember the code, how could he get access to the custody suite? His mind froze and he stood there staring at the panel with the black plastic buttons arranged in neat rows. A part of him wanted to go back to his office, get a clear order on his thoughts and then find the newspaper and do the morning's sudoku – it would help. Had to. Slowly his concentration focused again – it was 3421, so he punched the numbers into the panel.

Nothing.

For some reason he saw his fingers punching 1979 and then he waited for the buzzing to allow him access.

Nothing.

His mind went to the song lyrics pinned on the board alongside the messages and he hummed 'Brass in Pocket'.

Let's see who the special one is, he thought. If there were going to be more, it had to stop now. No more. A moment of doubt crept into his mind. He tried not to think about it. He stood back and forced his mind to think. Security number. He stepped forward and dialled the number into the panel and the door clicked open.

The custody sergeant was a tall man with a clean-shaven head and a faint smell of aftershave.

'How are they?' Drake said.

'Both asleep when I looked.'

Drake spent an hour in one of the windowless interview rooms reviewing and annotating the notes he had prepared the night before. He yawned several times and sipped a plastic mug of coffee but the taste was disgusting and he pushed it to one side, unfinished.

He saw the light on the mobile before it buzzed into life.

'I got your messages,' Sian said, once he answered.

'How are you?'

'Better. I'll be back by four. Work tomorrow.' She sounded matter-of-fact.

'I'll see you later. I don't know when I'll be home.'

'Where are you?'

'Area custody suite.'

'This early?'

'It's a long story.'

He rang off and outside heard the movement of bodies through the corridors and voices in conversation. He guessed the solicitors had arrived. The sound of Caren's voice was clear above the chatter and activity. The door opened and she walked into the room, clutching a file of papers and a pack of coloured biros. She wore tight fitting trousers, a black blouse, and her hair drawn back severely – power dressing for a power interview.

'Ready?' he asked.

Caren nodded

'Let's get started.'

Dixon glared at Drake. The solicitor had placed his suit jacket on the back of his chair. The shirt was short sleeved and the tie a mass of blue and white dots. He had an expensive-looking silver biro in one hand and balanced a notepad on his knee.

Drake spent more time than he needed setting out the papers in front of him.

'Do you know why you're here?'

Dixon groaned. 'Yes, I do know why I'm here. Get on with it.'

'Can you account for your movements on the night of the 31st May, early hours 1st June?'

'We've been through this already.'

'Tell me again.'

'I was at home and then I went to a family party.'

'What time?' Drake looked down and scanned a sheet from the pile of papers.

'I've told you this before.'

'Try me again,' Drake said.

Dixon repeated the details. Drake waited until Dixon had finished, knowing the next question he was going to ask.

'We've got an eyewitness that says you left the party at eight o'clock.'

'They're lying,' Dixon replied automatically.

Drake glanced over at the solicitor; the self-satisfied appearance had disappeared.

Drake read the eyewitness's statement and after two sentences stopped, lifted his head up and saw contempt in Dixon's face. Contempt for him, for the system and for the witness. Dixon sat back in the chair and pouted. Then he crossed his arms and leant back on the rear legs of the chair. Drake thought about the training sessions on reading body language and tried to decipher Dixon.

He decided he was a toe-rag.

Dixon said nothing and, at each pause, Drake asked him to comment. Sometimes, he opened his mouth slightly, then he pursed his lips but he didn't say anything. The solicitor glanced over at him but Dixon ignored him and stared at Drake. Drake came to the end of the statement and looked again at the notes for the interview.

'When did you first meet James Harrod?' Drake asked, looking directly at Dixon, waiting to read the response in his face.

'Who?'

Stupid, really stupid, thought Drake. 'James Harrod,' he repeated.

Dixon flapped his hands – his eyes darting around the room.

'You were on the same wing as him in HMP Chokes Lane,' Drake feigned a need to check the details in his papers, before repeating the periods Dixon had spent in jail.

'Now do you remember him?'

'Yeh, of course.'

'Were you good mates?'

'No, hardly knew him.'

'Hardly knew him,' Drake repeated.

Dixon nodded.

'That's not what several witnesses say.' Drake laid his hand on the folder in front of him. 'You shared a cell with him for four weeks.'

'Maybe.'

'What did you talk about, Stevie? Paul Mathews? Danny Farrell?'

'No comment.'

'We'll come back to that.'

Drake shuffled the papers again, bringing to the front the grainy photograph from the CCTV coverage.

'When did you last see Harrod?'

'Can't remember,'

'Try. Last week? Last month?'

Dixon shrugged.

'Try four weeks ago in Rhyl.'

Dixon pushed himself back down level with the table and put his elbows squarely on the surface. From the file of papers Drake pushed a photograph towards Dixon.

Dixon stared at it.

'That looks like you,' Drake said. 'And that's James Harrod as well,' he continued, raising his voice. 'Can you confirm that the man with you in the photograph is James Harrod?'

Drake could see the colour begin to drain from Dixon's cheeks. Dixon nodded.

'We have a statement from Mitchell Fisher. He says you assaulted him that night. Quite a vicious attack. The medical report is clear.'

'He's lying.'

'This is how I see it,' Drake announced. 'You've got two previous convictions for serious offences of assault. You did two years for grievous bodily harm with intent and then eighteen months for actual bodily harm. Now we come to the time in Rhyl when you assaulted Fisher, and you've got a connection to Harrod. Fisher had crossed Harrod, so he gave you a call and you popped down and assaulted Fisher. Suitably rewarded no doubt.'

He paused and looked at Dixon. He thought he saw a bead of worry in his eyes.

'A third conviction for assault and you're facing an indeterminate sentence.'

Now the colour had completely disappeared from Dixon's face.

'You might be out in five years. Might be eight. Could be twenty. Who knows? We'd make representations of course, when the time came, about any cooperation during this inquiry.'

The solicitor stood up abruptly. 'I need some time with my client.'

Drake and Caren waited, killing time, drinking water from small plastic cups and watching the custody sergeant processing a drug dealer, anxiously wanting to leave the station for his next fix, after admitting to a string of low-level thefts.

When the interview door opened, they turned to look at Dixon's solicitor. He stepped over to the counter and looked directly at Drake.

'We can restart.'

Dixon was sitting in the chair, his face buried deep in his hands, his skin ashen white. The solicitor turned to Drake.

'My client would like to cooperate.'

Chapter 39
Tuesday 29ᵗʰ June

'What did you make of that?' Caren asked.

Drake had succumbed to the coffee from the canteen and he was stirring three sugars into a blue mug and listening at the same time. Good coffee could wait – now he needed sugar and he needed to think.

'At least he coughed to the assault.'

They finished the last of the coffee and returned to the custody suite.

Don Hart was the local solicitor who specialised in criminal cases and he'd been waiting most of the morning, just as Drake had planned. Hart carried his weight badly and his paunch hung over the belt of his trousers. The shirt was two inches too big and his face was a lather of sweat.

'It's hot in here,' he said, pulling a handkerchief from a pocket.

'You're looking well, Don,' Drake said.

'Piss off.'

Drake signed for the tapes, found an empty interview room and waved them to the chairs.

'You've kept us waiting all morning, Ian,' Hart began. The jowls under his chin shook when he spoke. Drake mumbled a reply about operational reasons.

'You're accustomed to this procedure,' Drake said to Harrod as he loaded the tapes. He saw the contempt in Harrod's face. Drake was pleased with himself – good mind games, off-tape and Hart couldn't complain. He clicked the machine on. Once he dealt with the preliminaries, Drake looked at Harrod. This was the man. He had the motive, the opportunity and all the connections to kill four men.

'Do you know why you're here?'

Harrod sat back and gave Drake a blank stare.

He repeated the question.

No reply.

Block out the emotions, Drake said to himself.

'For the purposes of the tape, the prisoner makes no reply.' He raised his voice as he said *prisoner*. Hart sat impassively.

'Can you account for your movements on the night of the 31st May, early hours 1st June?'

Harrod turned his head towards Hart who nodded.

'I was at a dinner in Chester. Expensive do.'

'What time did you arrive?'

'Five-ish.'

'And what time did you leave?'

'The following morning.'

'What did you do all night?'

'It was at a dinner. What do you think? I had a meal and got pissed.'

'What time did you leave in the morning?'

'Nine. After breakfast.'

'Did you check out in the morning?'

'No. I settled the account the night before.'

From the files Drake found the statement he needed. He read it aloud and afterwards sat back watching the nervous twitch under Harrod's right eye.

'The witness from the hotel says you left early. What do you say to that?'

'He's lying.'

'The witness arrives at eight, and you're leaving.'

'It's a mistake.' Harrod tried to hide a nervous swallow and Drake kept eye contact.

'You're lying, James,' Drake said. 'You left the hotel early. Where did you go?'

Harrod leant back, folded his arms and clenched his jaw.

'How well do you know Stevie Dixon?'

Harrod tightened the fold of his arms and pushed them into his chest.

Drake persevered. 'Do you know Stevie Dixon?' He

paused and looked at Harrod, who had defiance and contempt burning in his eyes.

'The records from HMP Chokes Lane state that you were on the same wing as him for three months.'

Again, he looked at Harrod but there was no reply.

Drake tried to sound informative, 'Did you share a cell with him for a month?'

Harrod narrowed his eyes and stared at Drake.

'You see, the information I have is that you did. That would have given you a lot of time to get to know him well.'

There was still no reply from Harrod, and Drake ran through the previous convictions on his record. Hart moved awkwardly – the solicitor's bulk clearly made the narrow plastic chair uncomfortable.

'Stevie Dixon and you go back a long way.'

Harrod grunted and drew a hand over his head and then pummelled his eyes with both hands.

'That's a load of bollocks and you know it,' he said, spitting out the words.

'Tell me about Stevie Dixon.'

'Not much to say. I shared a cell with him. He told me about his girlfriends and grandkids. Who stitched him up. That he wasn't guilty and that his case was a miscarriage.'

All the usual crap, thought Drake. He knew from dozens of interviews that every murderer believed they should have been convicted of manslaughter and every manslaughter charge should have been grievous bodily harm. He had no time for the world of self-delusion that criminals chose to construct.

'When did you see him last?'

'Can't remember.'

At least he was answering the questions. Drake sensed the confidence building in Harrod. Drake looked at his notes again. It was a list of when both men had met: dates, times and places. Once Dixon had realised that an indeterminate sentence meant just that, he had coughed every detail of the assault on Fisher. Drake knew that the murders of Mathews and Farrell would come.

Only a matter of time.

Drake asked about the night of the assault. Harrod blanked him. He opened an envelope and pulled out a photograph of the Range Rover, which he pushed across the table.

'Perhaps this will help. That is you I take it?' he asked.

Silence.

'And the person with you is Stevie Dixon. Would you like to see a photograph of him getting out of your car?'

Hart was writing furiously – the tie discarded, jowls swaying, mopping his brow from the heat.

'Are you going to answer any questions?'

Harrod turned his head to one side. Drake drummed his fingers on the table. He paused as his temper rose. He read again his interview notes.

'The man you assaulted. You do remember his name, don't you.' It wasn't a question, so Drake continued. 'Attended hospital with three broken ribs, a broken nose ,a dislocated shoulder and severe bruising.'

'Don't know anything about it,' Harrod said, leaning forward over the table to within inches of Drake. He could smell Harrod's breath; see the mole on his neck and the chip on a front tooth. Drake saw Harrod standing in Megan's bedroom with the bottle.

'Let's come back to that,' Drake said abruptly. Caren cast an eye over the interview notes and shot him a glance. He stared at Harrod.

He turned to the events on the Crimea.

'Did you know Police Constable Paul Mathews?'

'No,'

'And what about Danny Farrell?'

'Only by reputation.'

'And what reputation was that?

'As a crooked cop and wife-beater. Otherwise he was an

all-round great guy.'

Drake's chest tightened and the fingers of his hand involuntarily formed a fist. Harrod blanked the next dozen questions as Drake asked about Farrell and Mathews. He smirked and snorted until Drake could almost hear his pulse beating in his neck.

'How well do you know Roderick Jones?'

Harrod leered at Drake, defying him to ask any more questions.

'I want to go through your financial affairs.'

Harrod guffawed. 'What next. Have you got nothing else?'

Drake counted to ten, twice. Then he picked up the interview notes, gripped them tightly and looked at Caren. He looked through the worried expression on her face and started asking Harrod about his company.

'What can you tell me about the beachfront development?'

Harrod pulled himself up in the chair.

'You don't know jack shit, Inspector Drake.'

'Is it true that your company has invested in the development?'

'Everyone knows that.'

'And your company has massive loans on the back of the project?'

Harrod hummed a non-committal answer and swayed his head.

'Would it be true to say that if the development doesn't go ahead the company would be bankrupt?'

Harrod gave Drake a tired disinterested look and then glanced at his watch. Drake blinked away another stab of anger. He carried on, his voice rising; he had given up on expecting a reply.

'In fact, if you don't get the planning consent, your company is finished – you're ruined. That would give you a strong motive to kill Roderick Jones.'

Harrod let out a long breath.

'Where were you on Wednesday 9th June?'

'On the top of Snowdon murdering Roderick Jones of course – in front of hundreds of people. What do you bloody think?'

Drake's fingers tightened around the papers. For a split second, he thought he was listening to a confession. There had to be a confession. The murders had to stop. He wanted to ask who the next victim was going to be.

Suddenly the face of Megan came flooding into his mind and he was back in the kitchen defending his family, comforting Sian and picking up the remains of the glass. He felt Harrod's gaze on his face – that self-satisfied grin. He jerked his head up and looked at Harrod.

'Where were you on the morning of Thursday 26th June?'

Harrod screwed up his face and shrugged. 'Who fucking cares?'

Drake stood up, pushed the table towards Harrod and shouted.

'I care, you bastard, and when I prove it was you …'

Drake sat on Megan's bed and leant back against the wall. She sat alongside him and smiled at him when he opened the book and read. He turned the pages without thinking, stopping occasionally when she corrected him.

'You've missed a bit,' she said.

He repeated the section, before finding the flow of the narrative again. He put an arm round her and balanced the book in the other hand. She looked up and he continued.

It seemed like a lifetime since Saturday morning when he saw the shattered glass on the floor of the kitchen. He had wanted to hold his family close, until nobody could threaten them.

That afternoon a grain of doubt had entered his mind

about Dixon. He was a thug and he deserved to be punished for the Fisher assault, but the doubts were beginning to dominate his thoughts.

'Dad,' Megan said, pushing him with her elbow.

'What?' he said.

'You've stopped.'

'Have I ...? Sorry.'

He cleared his mind and restarted.

Once he had finished with Megan, it was Helen's turn. Her bed was pushed into a corner so Drake sat on the edge.

'What did you read to Megan?'

Drake told her and she nodded knowingly.

'What do you want me to read to you?'

There were three books on her bed and she hesitated before deciding. Helen complained that he was reading too slowly. Then it struck him how infrequently he had read to her and how he had forgotten the simple pleasure it gave him. After he finished he kissed her and went downstairs.

He slumped on a chair in the kitchen and looked down at the floor, recalling the shards of glass – it had been Harrod's work; he was convinced of it. Proving it was going to be another matter. For now, he was out of harm's way. Tomorrow would mean a meeting with Price and Thorsen. He could hear their comments – irregular interview techniques, inappropriate language and embarrassing consequences – but he had enough to charge Harrod for the Fisher assault.

Since Saturday, time had passed in a blur of activity, but the absence of his family had been painful, reinforcing a helpless feeling that he'd been unable to protect them. The images of the red car through the tunnels and the baseball cap and ponytail on Snowdon came flickering into his thoughts like the images from a bad movie. Every time he got close to the killer, he had pulled away.

He punished himself by thinking that if he had spent less time at headquarters and more time with the family he might have thought more clearly. Work-life balance, Sian would say.

Sian still had the long blond hair that he had found so attractive when he first met her. She wore an expensive turtleneck sweater that clung to her figure and emphasised the roundness of her breasts. She caught his gaze and puckered her eyes as he half smiled at her.

Sian reached into the fridge and pulled out the ingredients for a salad. He opened a bottle of wine and drank a large mouthful.

'The armed officer will be here soon,' he said.

'Do we have to have this person in the house?'

'Super insists.'

'For how long?'

Drake shrugged and yawned at the same time.

Once they'd eaten, they watched television until Drake could feel his eyes closing. He tried not to think of the morning and his meetings.

Chapter 40
Wednesday 30th June

Drake sipped the first mug of coffee of the day, finding things to distract his mind from dwelling on the interviews from the day before.

'Moxie came round on Saturday,' Drake said.

'How is he?' Sian said.

'Woke me up.'

'Shame about him and Beverley.' Sian was clearing the dishes away onto the worktop near the sink. 'He was never the same. They should have had marriage guidance after she had that affair. Never thought going to that club suited them.'

The doorbell rang and Megan and Helen shouted that their lift had arrived. The girls hurried into the kitchen, kissed Drake and left. Drake helped Sian stack the dishwasher but his mind kept darting from worrying about his parents to the scene with the bottles in the bedrooms and then to the face of Price asking if he was coping. Drake wanted to solve the case more that anything but he could see the investigation slipping out of his hands unless he made a breakthrough. Maybe Sian was right and he should get counselling: it might help, but solving the sudoku puzzle helped, as all his rituals did.

In the hall mirror he checked his tie before leaning forward, his skin looked pale and there were even more grey hairs than he remembered. He stepped outside into the summer sunshine. A warm haze gathered over the town as he drove past the charity shops and cafés. A middle-aged man riding a bicycle reminded him of his father and his thoughts returned to his father's treatment. He had sounded weak when he spoke to him the previous night. The treatment left him with little appetite and Sian had warned him that he would look ill for a long time.

He switched on the CD player and flicked through the

multi-changer before deciding to listen to the radio. He ignored a telephone phone-in where the audience members were complaining about the latest fuel price increases and settled on Radio Two. He smiled as the DJ introduced 'Won't get fooled again' by The Who and, knowing it was the theme tune for CSI Miami, saw the image of Horatio Caine, standing – hands on hips, badge displayed, gun protruding – against the sultry warm background of the Florida skyline.

He had been fooled by the killer: he knew it. Caren had to be right about the numbers. They sounded different when she'd said each one in turn. Not like the year at all. Like a number, an ordinary number.

His office was muggy so he pushed open one of the windows and felt a cooling draught on his face. Scrolling through his inbox, he stopped at a message from Price. It was formal, started *Dear Ian* and asked him to attend later that afternoon for a meeting with the superintendent and Thorsen. It meant one thing. He was off the case. It annoyed him so much to realise that Harrod would have the better of him. Until then it was his case and he tried to put to one side the disciplinary problems he was facing.

Reading an email from Thorsen quoting an obscure protocol about officers with an emotional interest in a case only made him feel worse. Finally, he read the email from Vera Frost. After downloading the attachment and storing it into the appropriate folder, he started reading the list of patients. When he saw his father's name, he stopped and drew breath. Looking at the simple details – surname, Christian name, address, referring GP – reminded him that his father was gravely ill. He stared out of the window and thought about his mother. How would she cope? He could remember the time when he realised for the first time that he would not live forever. He supposed that his parents would have discussed such things. His mother would deal with the loss, resolve her grief and move on with her life. Perhaps she would come and visit more often. She might sell the smallholding.

The names were listed alphabetically, by surname. By the end of the 'O's he knew he'd missed something: a name he had skimmed over – they'd become a blur.

He went back and restarted from the 'K's. He stopped at the name Beverley Moxon. He knew that she had been ill, but he tried to dispel the uneasy feeling gathering in his stomach. She had died of cancer. Moxon had been distraught after her death. His spirit had been crushed and Drake had seen it in his face, as though the will to live had ebbed away. He rationalised his thoughts, dismissing the notion of Moxon's involvement.

Suddenly, from a dark corner a jagged edge of memory came into his mind.

He walked over to the coat stand, retrieved his warrant card before firmly closing the door. He sat and stared at his police service number.

... that the killer might be a police officer or a retired police officer ...

He had to check.

He found the statements and read them again, hoping for the one piece of information he lacked.

... have you thought about the number ...

An hour passed as he read the various bundles of paperwork. Occasionally, he saw the movement of the officers in the Incident Room and sometimes a face appeared at the door, but he paid no attention. The information he needed was absent. He drummed his biro on the desk and wondered if this was another of his obsessions. What if he was wrong? He had to find the number. An idea formed and he cleared the papers into a neat pile.

Despite the warmth, he pulled on his jacket, fastened one button and checked his tie. It would look more formal that way. He walked over to human resources and talked to one of the civilians.

'I wonder if you can help,' he said, concealing the tension raging through his mind.

She smiled and seemed responsive to the polite request.

Drake gave her the sheet of paper he had prepared. 'We're missing some information. Records for expenses and all that.'

'Can I email you the details? It's just that I'm a bit busy right now.'

Drake wanted to say that it was a matter of life and death – that it involved four murders, a fifth possibly to come. He ran his tongue over the inside of his lips and hoped she wouldn't notice.

'Any idea how long?'

'Next half an hour.'

Drake returned to his office, chewing his lower lip and tearing at the fingernails on his right hand. He glanced at his watch every five minutes, waiting and hoping the information would materialise. The door to his office remained closed.

He leant back in his chair and closed his eyes. He was back round the table in the kitchen that morning, listening to Sian and the children and the news on the radio and drinking coffee and waiting for breakfast. Then he remembered Sian's comments about Moxon and he quickly straightened and reached for the telephone.

The receptionist's voice was prim. 'Dr Drake is busy.'

'Does she have a patient?'

'No, but ...'

'Put me through. Now.'

'What's wrong, Ian?'

'This morning you mentioned Moxie and Beverley going to a club. What did you mean?'

'What's this about?'

'Please Sian – might be important.'

'Don't you remember they went to some archery club?'

Drake put one hand to his forehead and pulled the

handset close to his ear.

'Who did Beverley have an affair with?'

He dreaded hearing her answer and he breathed out slowly.

'Beverley never told me. But I think it was another police officer.'

He swallowed hard and the saliva in his mouth evaporated, causing his lips to stick together.

'Ian. What's going on?'

'Nothing. It's all right. I'll call you later.'

He stood up and pushed the chair back against the wall of his office so hard it crashed noisily. In the Incident Room he asked Howick to bring the impounded box from the Archery Association into his room. He kept the conversation concise and to the point – no explanations needed: he was in charge. Howick left the box on Drake's desk and, after giving him a puzzled look, left the room. Drake riffled through the box, moving folders and files to one side until he came across photograph albums marked Summer Ball. Slowly he flicked through the pictures of smiling faces with hands holding glasses raised in a silent toast. At the end of the second album, he stopped and sat down heavily drawing the album onto the desk. He let out a long gasp.

Then he heard the ping of an email arriving in his inbox and he double-clicked the mouse until the screen momentarily froze. He cursed and glanced through the window of the door, hoping he wouldn't be disturbed. When he finally opened the email, he scanned down to the name of John Moxon.

He read the number.

Caren pressed the top of the carafe and the hot tea poured in a dribble into her cup. She emptied a plastic container of milk into her drink before adding three sachets of sugar. From the plate of biscuits on the table, she took two digestives, broke the first in two and dunked one half in the tea, before lowering her mouth to catch the sodden remains. Drake would be disgusted, she knew.

'Bloody boring, isn't?' the voice was one she vaguely recognised.

She turned and saw Simon Brooks from western area. A serious, intense man about the same age as Caren, he was holding a cup of black coffee and had three biscuits balanced on the saucer. He had the cheeks of a marathon runner, hollowed out by the wind, and greasy hair combed back over his head.

Caren mumbled a reply through the digestive, trying not to splutter and send bits flying over Brooks.

'I wasn't supposed to be here,' she said.

Brooks sipped on the coffee and then crunched his way into the first of his biscuits and nodded back at her.

'DI Drake was supposed to attend but I drew the short straw.'

'Tell me about it,' he said, rolling his eyes. 'Is he still on the Mathews case?'

'Yes.'

'Only I'd heard there was an incident in his house.'

Caren nodded. 'He's still in charge.'

Brooks raised his eyes in surprise and started his second biscuit.

'How's it going?'

'So, so,' she replied.

'Lucky I was off duty on the day of Roderick Jones's killing. I was shopping in Beddgelert.'

Caren cast a surreptitious eye to her watch. Soon it would be time to return for the rest of the afternoon session and she could escape from Brooks.

'I was surprised that you had some of the non-operational officers on the mountain.'

'What do you mean?'

Before Brooks had finished, Caren was heading for the

door.

Drake was holding his head in his hands when Caren barged into his office. She closed the door and sat down. He saw the troubled look on her face as she leant forward against the desk, a hushed, quiet tone to her voice.

'I've just spoken to Simon Brooks.'

'Who?'

'A DC from western area. He was in Beddgelert on the day Roderick Jones was killed.'

Drake put his hands down onto the desk and turned a biro through his fingers.

'He asked me why we had non-operational officers on the mountain the day Roderick Jones was killed.'

Drake blinked, drew a hand through his hair and stared at Caren.

'Moxon, isn't it?'

She opened her mouth in amazement.

'How …?'

'1979.'

He sounded relieved, as though sharing the knowledge was a catharsis.

'That's Moxon's number.'

Caren slumped back in the chair.

'When did you …?'

'It's been there in the back of my mind. Numbers. Staring us in the face. Shouting at us. We've been running around like headless chickens trying to work out the meaning of the song lyrics and it was the number after all.'

'What … I mean, the motive. Why?' Caren was still deep in her thoughts. 'Why would he want to kill Mathews? They were fellow officers … And then Jones … or West?' She sounded exasperated.

'Let's start at the beginning. We've missed something.'

Drake thought of his last meeting with Moxon. He

scanned his memory for any snippet. He looked past Caren and saw the face of Winder at the window of his door but he gave him a severe look and Winder turned away.

'But it doesn't make sense,' Caren said, sounding positive. 'What could be his possible motive?'

Drake shrugged, a tired, frustrated look on his face.

'We'll need to go through all of Jones's papers again. You'd better contact Southern Division. Get all of the files couriered today.'

Caren nodded. 'What do I tell the others?'

He raised his head and looked at Caren, a realisation striking him, 'We'll need Beverley Moxon's medical records,' he said.

He reached for the printed report where he had left it. He read down the list until he found Beverley Moxon's name and read along the row until the name of the referring surgery appeared.

He read the name twice.

Dr Sian Drake had referred her.

He drew his hand over his mouth and silently cursed. Without saying a word, he thrust the paper over at Caren as the telephone rang.

'Inspector Drake. We've found something you ought to see.'

The voice of Jan Jones was cold and impersonal, as though she were discussing a report on the justification of the Iraq war, but by the time she'd finished Drake was already on his feet and reaching for his car keys.

Chapter 41
Wednesday 30th June

Drake peered out of the windscreen, scanning the car park for Moxon's Renault – or was it an old Vauxhall? This was madness: it couldn't be happening, and he thumped the steering wheel hard with the palm of his hand until it shuddered. He just could not believe that he was even contemplating that Moxon was involved. It had to be either Harrod or Walters – just had to be. He fired the engine and powered the car westwards along the route he had taken many times before. For the first time in the investigation, he thought about the journey to Moxon's home. It was a journey he had taken frequently over the years when he and Moxon had been young officers, but when he was promoted and Moxon's career languished, their friendship seemed to fizzle out. The occasional drink after work never seemed the same and Drake often regretted that he hadn't tried harder, especially after Beverley was diagnosed with cancer. He banged the palms of his hand on the wheel again and cursed aloud.

He should have seen this – it was his fault. Maybe West might be alive if he'd been more attentive, more careful. It was all about the numbers. And Moxon knew all about his rituals. The knowledge that he had confided in him turned Drake's stomach.

An Audi dawdled in front of him, so he flashed his headlights and shouted aloud, hoping in some way that the driver might hear him. He yanked the sun visor down as he made his way towards the Lleyn Peninsula. Another hour passed until he was threading his way through the streets of Pwllheli.

Jan Jones's house had a tired look; the windows needed painting and the pebbledash was old and grey. Even the doorbell was decrepit and when Drake pushed it, nothing happened. He pushed it a second time and then there was a faint buzzing sound as though two wires were trying to connect. There was a shout from the bowels of the house that he couldn't make out and then the sound of footsteps on a wooden floor. The door opened and Jan Jones stood on the threshold.

She had a world-weary look on her face. Drake looked into her eyes and saw a defeated spirit trying to cope. It would be difficult for her, he knew. A small community would want to share her grief, be part of it all, and everywhere she went there would be sympathetic faces, murmured words of regret and *how are you?* asked in a tone that implied she wasn't coping.

He stepped into the house and immediately felt the same mournful atmosphere clawing at his own spirit. He had to get his business done and then leave.

'I've got Rod's mobile on the kitchen table,' she said.

She flopped down on a chair by the table, her shoulders sagging. There was the sound of a radio upstairs, the creak of floorboards and then the flushing of a toilet.

'How are the children?' Drake asked.

Jan hesitated. Then she sighed, 'They hide it well, I suppose.'

'Must be hard.'

She turned her face away and brushed a loose hair from her eyes.

'I wanted you to see this.' Jan pushed an iPhone towards him. 'It was Rod's. It was new. He had only had it a couple of days.'

Drake picked up the mobile and looked at the time and date on the screen.

'I didn't pay it any attention until Stefan opened it up today and looked at the damn thing.'

'And?'

'There are some photographs …'

'Of what?'

'I think it was a mistake. I don't think Rod knew how to

use the thing properly. It was the staff in the office that persuaded him to get one.'

Jan lost interest in explaining the purchase of the iPhone. Drake slid his finger over the screen and the mobile came to life.

'What are the photographs?' Drake asked again, as he navigated through the menu.

'Rod was on the mountain.'

A small bead of perspiration gathered on his forehead. Jan continued.

'He must have taken some photographs without knowing it.'

Drake had reached the folder where the images were stored.

'Stefan says he took about twenty.'

Drake's pulse bounded as he found the first photograph.

'Do you want a coffee or something?' Jan asked.

Drake didn't reply – he had reached the tenth photograph. There were images of walkers with backpacks and poles, and families with children all badly framed and out of line. He let out a slow breath and hoped. Hoped for a breakthrough.

At the nineteenth photograph, he stopped and stared at the image on the screen. Diagonally from one corner to another was the image of a man.

A man he knew well.

'Where's Inspector Drake?'

Caren was convinced the pulse in her neck was thumping loudly enough for Price and Thorsen to hear it. Both men had given her steely dark stares when she came into Price's office. She stood; there hadn't been an invitation to sit down.

'He was called out on an urgent matter.'

How could she tell them it might be the breakthrough

they needed? Perhaps it wasn't. If Drake was wrong then she could be in big trouble.

'Did he tell you when he'd be back?'

'He said he wouldn't be long.'

'We have an important meeting with him.'

'Yes, sir.'

'And we haven't been able to reach him on his mobile.'

Thorsen looked at his watch before adding, without emotion, 'It'll have to wait till the morning now.'

Caren hurried back to the Incident Room, texting Drake on the way.

'Where's Inspector Drake?'

Winder spoke, but Howick was standing with him in front of the board in the Incident Room, both men staring Caren straight in the eye. She knew that they guessed something unusual was happening and on any other day Caren would have answered without thinking. But her pulse was still beating at an alarming rate. She heard Drake's voice insisting they had to keep this part of the investigation between themselves. It occurred to her that perhaps Drake wanted to protect his own reputation. After all, Moxon was a friend.

'Gareth, when can we expect the report from the pathologist?'

He gave her a sharp glance as if to say that he knew what she was doing. Howick exchanged an informative glance with Winder.

Caren continued, 'Dave, when can I expect a full summary of Dr West's movements?'

'Ah ...'

'We do have an investigation ongoing. And we'll need to piece together his life. Girlfriends, family, money, you know – everything that might help. We need to establish a motive. Somebody out there wanted him dead.'

Caren returned to Drake's office, closed the door firmly and knew that she had overdone the senior officer routine. She returned to the research and flicked through various tabs on a Google search. She had ten hours' work to do in five.

It all made perfect sense once Drake reflected on the evidence.

The volume of the CD player was set low and the curves and corners of the road through the Lleyn Peninsula focused his mind on the scene at the top of the Crimea. Now it seemed so obvious. Mathews and Farrell must have recognised Moxon and not perceiving a threat, Mathews stayed in the car, oblivious to what was going to happen. Moxon would have known how the car would park and he would have been ready.

Now he had more pieces of the jigsaw that he hoped would persuade Price to allow him to finish the investigation. Drake knew that missing the meeting with Thorsen and Price had been a bad move but the photographs in Roderick Jones's iPhone would surely justify his visit to Jan Jones.

Drake flashed his headlights at caravans that wouldn't pull in to let him pass. He cursed when the police lights in the unmarked car failed to work. The mobile sitting in the cradle rang, flashing up a familiar number, and he clicked the Bluetooth device in his ear.

'Mike, what have you got?'

Foulds gave a detailed analysis of the crime scene at the private patients' clinic. There were no fingerprints: only paint scraped off door casings, suggesting the killer had struggled with the wheelchair as he manoeuvred the body into the office.

'And the car?'

'We've taken some samples from the rear of the car. Soil, dirt. Could be anything. I've sent them to the lab for an urgent analysis. It'll be at least a few days, maybe a week.'

'A week! We haven't got a week,' Drake replied.

'I'll see what I can do.'

Drake finished the call and accelerated hard, knowing he was breaking the speed limit.

Caren despaired as she read the guidelines.

The release of the medical records of a deceased person needed the next of kin's consent, but Moxon was hardly likely to agree. She searched for a detailed analysis of the law, hitting various websites, including a firm of solicitors who specialised in suing doctors.

Her shoulders felt heavy. She stretched her arms until the muscles pulled, then she yawned and rubbed her eyes – it had been a long day.

The Incident Room was empty when she returned from the kitchen with a strong coffee. She glanced over the board and thought that Moxon's details should be at the top. Nobody had considered that he might be the killer. In any event, he had no motive for the death of Roderick Jones. Now he should be in the middle of the board, subject to the harsh light of the investigation.

Eventually she found the information she needed. She smiled and pulled herself closer to the screen, as she copied and pasted the information into a file.

She spent the next hour sorting the notes into a logical and presentable order. Drake would want to see clarity and, if it was going where she thought it might, then he needed to assemble every argument. She decided to ring Alun, but hesitated, knowing she had to be non-committal.

The telephone rang out until she heard the answerphone click on and the pre-recorded message played. She hated speaking into answer machines and hung up. Maybe he was out in the fields with the alpacas or maybe he had his headphones on and the stereo blasting heavy metal into his eardrums.

She clicked on the modern anglepoise lamp that Drake kept on his desk alongside the pictures of Megan and Helen, all neatly arranged and dusted spotlessly clean. The telephone rang, and for a moment, she hoped it would be Alun, but the voice of the receptionist sounded lifeless and dull.

'Uniform from Cardiff in reception. Says he has to see you in person,' she emphasised the last word, before putting the phone down.

The taller of the two uniformed officers stopped talking to the receptionist when he saw Caren.

'Sergeant Waits?' The Valleys accent sounded unfamiliar.

'Are these the documents from Inspector Marco?' Caren looked down at the boxes on the reception floor.

'Sure are. We're supposed to make sure it gets to you and nobody else. That's what he said. There's another five in the car.'

It took both officers and Caren fifteen minutes to carry all the boxes to Drake's room. Then she sat down, feeling sweaty and uncomfortable, tugging at her blouse in a vain attempt to cool down.

She pulled out the list of the files and read the details. She heard a noise in the Incident Room and through the glass in the door saw a shape cross the room. She knew Winder and Howick had left and the cleaners didn't arrive until the early hours. Who could be in the office? Perhaps it was Price or somebody from public relations. She got up from the desk and opened the door slowly.

Moxon turned to look at her.

He curled up the edges of his mouth.

Her throat froze, the muscles tightened around her vocal chord.

She watched as he turned to look at the board.

'How's it going?' he asked.

She moved two steps towards him and sat down on the edge of a desk, gathering her confidence. She cleared her throat and swallowed, hoping, praying that he wouldn't sense her discomfort. Act normal, she thought.

'Good. James Harrod has been arrested as well as Stevie Dixon.'

'So I heard. Have they coughed?'

'We're doing a second interview tomorrow.'

Moxon lifted his eyebrows. 'Really?'

Act normal. What was normal? It was late in the day and a non-operational officer was alone with her in the Incident Room. Then she remembered the files in Drake's office. She had left the door open; they were in clear view.

'Did you want to see DI Drake?' She swallowed again.

'Yes … We go back a long time …'

Caren said nothing.

'Do you think Harrod did it?'

'He had motive. Been inside as well.' A fragment of gossip might answer the question.

Moxon scanned the activity on the board. Caren frantically thought of how she was going to handle the situation.

'Where is Ian?' Moxon paced slowly in front of the board, his hands in his pockets.

'He's due back any time,' she said, turning her wrist in an exaggerated gesture to look at her watch.

Slowly he moved towards the end of the board and then walked towards the door. As he pulled the door open, he turned to Caren.

'Give Ian my warmest regards.'

Caren let out a long breath and felt a bead of sweat running down her neck.

Drake sat opposite Caren and listened as she told him about Moxon, his face darkening.

'He knows,' Caren said.

'No, he was fishing. Probably heard about the boxes from Cardiff.'

'He sounded tense. And he said *Give Ian my warmest regards.*'

There were unfinished sandwiches and empty crisp packets on the desk.

'We'll have to work through the files tonight,' he said eventually, nodding at the boxes on the floor.

'Super was after you earlier. Something about a meeting.'

Caren put a bottle of Coke to her lips and gulped.

Drake nodded. He had noticed the missed calls on the mobile, but was putting off the time when he'd have to explain himself. He thought about what to say to Price. At that moment, he had an incomplete picture but if he didn't speak to the superintendent it would only make matters worse. He picked up the telephone, his heart beating a little faster.

The call was short. Drake listened and mumbled confirmation of the time for the rearranged meeting. He hoped that before then he'd have progress to report. Otherwise, he'd face Price and Thorsen knowing that he'd be off the case.

Drake pulled out a power drink from his desk drawer. Sian would never approve, but he needed a good energy boost. Caren passed him the memo on access to medical records and he underlined phrases and highlighted sections with a red biro. Caren returned to her desk to finish reading the list of files that Roderick Jones had been dealing with.

By eleven Drake had read Caren's report.

'So there's a good argument?'

'Will the surgery agree?' Caren said.

Drake put his hands behind his head and leant back in the chair. He puffed out a lungful of air.

'I'll set up a meeting with Price and Thorsen in the

morning.'

He turned to the list Caren had been reading.

'Anything in this list?'

'Where do we start?' she asked.

Caren had used various coloured highlighters to differentiate the North Wales files from the rest. He started reading.

The first columns had the personal details and then the name of the property and a column with various numbers; he could see that one of the columns was headed 'planning application number'. His eyes stopped at the name of James Harrod. He read across the row and scanned the details of Harrod's file.

He read down again and saw names from all the counties of North Wales.

He noticed the names of the occasional high-profile planning application that had been on the television. Anything that promised more jobs always attracted lots of press coverage.

Then he read the name Beverley Owen and moved down to the next name.

He stopped and read the name again.

'Let's find the file of Beverley Owen,' he said.

Caren eventually found the papers in one of the boxes and passed it over to Drake.

Beverley Owen – planning consent for conversion of outbuilding – refusal.

He opened the file, put his head in his hands and groaned.

Beverley Owen was Moxon's late wife.

Chapter 42
Thursday 1st July

Sian didn't stir when Drake slipped into bed in the early hours.

He stared at the ceiling, fearing that sleep would elude him again. Shadows from the night sky shimmered past the curtains and his thoughts turned to the journey on the morning it had all started. The breakneck speed. The automatic weapons of the armed officers. The Traffic car and the two bloodied bodies.

He glanced over at the clock, the face lit up as he adjusted the time of the alarm. In the morning he would leave before any explanations became necessary. Someone had told him that counting in thousands helped them get to sleep, but by the time he reached fifty thousand, he was more awake than ever and abandoned the idea.

Eventually he fell asleep, but not before the images of Harrod's interview and the sight of a sobbing Jan Jones in the manager's room on the top of Snowdon came crowding back into his mind.

When the alarm sounded, Drake felt that he had only just fallen asleep. Sian murmured something by his side before turning over and going back to sleep. He hoped she wouldn't wake. He couldn't tell her anything: dared not tell her.

In the hallway, he picked up his locked briefcase and checked that the file of Beverley Owen was still safely inside. He pulled on the jacket of his suit and, looking in the mirror, ran a finger over the brown bags under his eyes and brushed back the flecks of grey hair above his ears. Outside, the temperature was still cool but the sky a clear blue, the tops of the trees moving slowly with the morning breeze. It was going to be another bright, clear day.

He put the briefcase safely on the passenger seat and pulled the car out of the drive.

Caren was waiting for him in the car park, empty apart from the occasional patrol car.

The smell of disinfectant and cleaning fluid permeated the air as they threaded their way through headquarters, taking the stairs to the Incident Room two at a time. He unlocked the door to his office and checked that everything was undisturbed. They had to review the evidence and notes. They had to prevent a fifth death.

'I keep thinking something's missing,' Caren said.

Drake shared her unease, as though a burglar had been rifling through the paperwork, leaving empty handed.

'I don't want Gareth or Dave in the loop at the moment.'

Caren nodded. It was going to be difficult.

'What are you going to do about Moxon?'

Drake had been trying to answer the same question since leaving the house. He put a biro on the file of papers in front of him and knew he had to find an answer. He glanced at the clock on the computer screen. The operational support department wouldn't start for another hour.

'I want you to ring one of the other officers in operational support and ask if Moxon is there. At least we can find out if he's on duty today. After that ... well ... it depends.'

He could barely believe what he was thinking. Arresting Moxon would be high profile. He couldn't afford to take any risks now. They read through the folder once more until they were satisfied it covered everything. Drake suppressed the dark mood dominating his mind.

A baffled look crossed Hannah's face when Drake explained that his meeting with Price and Thorsen had been organised late the night before.

'Just routine,' he added.

Before she could say anything further, Thorsen walked in, complaining about his schedule for the day.

'Where were you yesterday, Ian? I thought our meeting had been rearranged for later this afternoon.'

'There have been developments.'

'That's what Wyndham said on the telephone last night. This had better be good.'

Drake hesitated, knowing that if he was wrong then the investigation was out of his hands and that maybe his career was over too.

Then Price breezed in and Hannah asked about the unscheduled meeting.

'Won't take long, Hannah. I know I've got a busy diary. Coffee for everyone, thank you.'

Drake and Caren exchanged a furtive glance as Price led them into his room. They sat next to each other across the polished table. Drake cleared his throat.

'We have reason to believe that there are good grounds for suspecting PC Moxon is our killer.'

Price looked stunned, his mouth opening in disbelief. Drake couldn't read the expression on Thorsen's face, as always he appeared inscrutable. Drake didn't wait for a response from either.

'We established yesterday that Moxon was on Snowdon on the day of Roderick Jones's murder.'

'How?' Thorsen asked.

'An off duty officer saw him in Beddgelert, coming down from one of the paths.'

Thorsen resumed the inscrutable pose. The only sign of his unease was a muscle twitching below his left eyelid.

'And yesterday Jan called me about Roderick Jones's iPhone.'

Price clenched his jaw.

'There were photographs of Moxon wearing a ponytail and baseball cap going past Roderick Jones on Snowdon.'

'But ... the motive ... Why ...?' Price stammered.

'In Roderick Jones's files we found a planning application submitted by Beverley Moxon. He turned it down for no reason – against advice. And the property was at the foot of the Crimea Pass.'

'Bit of a tenuous link for killing them on the mountain pass,' Price said.

Drake shrugged.

'But why kill two fellow officers?' Thorsen asked.

'Mathews had an affair with Beverley Moxon some years ago and the likelihood is that she contracted chlamydia from him. Our guess is that's why she couldn't have children.'

'Guesswork. We'll need more than guesswork,' Price snorted.

Drake paused and added slowly. 'Moxon was a friend of mine. I knew him well. He always wanted children and one of the side effects of chlamydia is infertility.'

For a moment, Price and Thorsen looked at Drake without saying anything.

'And West?' Price asked, shaking his head.

'Beverley was a patient of his. We've prepared a memo,' Drake said, pushing two copies of the notes over the table.

Both men read the paper, pens raised ready. Thorsen preferred to underline, sometimes three times, and Price scratched asterisks in the margin and circled sections. Drake and Caren waited. Price snapped the top back onto his brightly coloured fountain pen and looked at Drake, a serious look in his eyes – his earlier briskness had evaporated.

'So the missing link is evidence for the motives against West and Mathews?'

Drake nodded. Thorsen let out a faint cough. 'Who knows about this?'

'Only the four of us. It's been kept from the rest of the team.'

'Good,' Thorsen said.

Milk was poured into the coffees and sugar stirred into the mugs, as they discussed how to proceed. It would be difficult. Should Drake be excluded? Would it not be better if Price was involved? When Thorsen's mobile rang, he fumbled for it in the jacket draped over the back of his chair and switched it off. Drake continued until the telephone on Price's desk rang, and he told Hannah not to interrupt again. Thorsen wanted to be cautious but Price had no time for conventions.

'If this bastard is responsible we need to close him down now, today. Before he kills again.'

'But ...' Thorsen began.

'But nothing,' Price said, waving his hand, dismissing any dissent. He turned to Drake. 'Better get on with it.'

Drake sat by a woman whose child had a cough that sounded like a rattle from an old car engine. A man opposite looked deathly pale and two obese women were discussing how they were cutting down on their intake of chips – three nights a week instead of four

Eventually, the receptionist waved them through and the practice manager took them to a conference room. Drake felt he already knew the room somehow, having heard Sian tell him many times about their practice meetings and training days.

'I need you to get the partners in here as soon as possible.'

'But it's the middle of surgery. You've seen how busy it is.'

Barbara Mills was a woman in her fifties with an intense fussy manner. She had a lanyard round her neck with a biro hanging from the bottom.

'I don't have time to discuss it, Barbara. I need to speak to Sian and Dr Walker.'

'What are we going to do about the patients?'

'Can you get both partners? Now.'

Drake paced around the room, unable to sit down. Caren sat at one end of the conference table, her hands folded on top of two copies of her carefully prepared notes. He glanced at his watch. 'How long does it take?' he spluttered to no one in particular.

Dr Rhys Walker was the first to arrive, the annoyance clear on his face.

'Ian, what the hell is going on?'

Moments later, Barbara Mills returned, followed by Sian.

'Ian, is everything all right?' she said, looking at Drake, worry etched on her face. She smiled weakly at Caren.

'This is something I need to discuss with the partners,' he said to Barbara Mills, who pouted and left the room, the biro swinging in front of her.

He got straight to the point.

'We believe John Moxon may be responsible for the deaths of Mathews, Farrell, Roderick Jones and West. We need access to his wife's medical records.'

A silence descended on the room.

'She was a patient,' Walker began. 'I cannot possibly disclose the records without the consent of the next of kin.'

Drake suppressed an urge to correct him, sensing that he had more to say.

'We have very strict guidelines about confidentiality, Ian. As I'm sure you know. We cannot possibly disclose the records without consent. We'd be struck off.'

Sian sat quietly by the side of her senior partner.

Drake cleared his throat; he had only one chance to persuade the doctor.

'During the investigation we've had a series of messages. They have all been song lyrics from 1979. This number happens to be John Moxon's police number. With each body has been a number. Mathews and Farrell had the number four. Roderick Jones had three and Anthony West, two. This can only mean one thing, that there is one more murder. We want to stop that happening.'

'We know that Moxon took the death of his wife badly. She was a patient of Anthony West. He must have blamed him for some medical reason we believe the records will disclose. And Mathews had chlamydia and I know that Beverley couldn't have children. We need to have access to the records to establish if the infection made her infertile.'

Walker moved in his chair and jutted his jaw out. 'Well, you'll just have to get a court order.'

Sian gave the papers in front of Caren a fleeting look. 'You didn't mention Roderick Jones. Why would Moxon want him dead?'

'He turned down a planning application that Beverley had for the conversion of outbuildings to a studio and holiday homes. It was something she had set her heart on and the file has dozens of pleading letters, imploring Jones to grant the application.'

Caren pushed the copies of the memorandum towards Drake.

'We've looked at the procedures governing the release of patients' records. You can release them if it's in the public interest to do so. We believe that a crime could be prevented by their disclosure.'

'But we'd still need to notify John Moxon,' Walker said.

'No. If you look at the GMC guidelines ...' Drake shuffled the papers over the desk. Walker picked up one copy. Sian furrowed her brow and they both began reading.

Drake continued. 'You can release without notifying the patient's family.'

'This is highly irregular.'

So is murder, thought Drake. Four murders and maybe a fifth.

'We haven't got much time. We need your decision.'

Walker stood up abruptly. 'We'll have to call the BMA,' he announced and left the room, Sian trailing in his slipstream, giving Drake a backward glance over her shoulder.

'Bollocks,' Drake said. He picked up the papers and found that the words on the page blurred as he tried to read. Suddenly he remembered about Moxon.

'Caren, give Moxon's office a ring. Find out if he's there.'

Caren dialled the number of main reception and waited. Part of Drake still didn't believe it was Moxon and he wanted his friend to pick up the telephone and reassure him that nothing was wrong. Of course, his number was 1979 but it could be a coincidence. And as for Roderick Jones – so what if Moxon had been on the mountain, walking. He always did on fine summer days when he wasn't working. Drake shook his head. He wasn't even convincing himself.

'Is John Moxon in please?'

Drake stared at Caren.

'Really … No, no message.'

She turned to Drake, but he already knew. 'He was due in today, but hasn't shown up.'

Drake stood up straight, clenching his fists and thumped the desk. He pushed the chair back until it toppled over and crashed against the bookcase behind him. He walked over to the window and shoved it open, breathing the fresh air into his lungs. Drake's mind turned to his parents and he wondered if it had been Moxon that night at his parents' farm, or simply a false alarm.

Precious minutes passed until Walker and Sian came back into the room.

'You're asking us to take a grave risk with our professional careers in doing this. If you're wrong and John Moxon is innocent, he could complain to the General Medical Council.' Walker glanced at Sian. 'But Sian and I have discussed it, and we're going to allow you access to

Beverley Moxon's records.'

'Thank you,' he said formally, hiding his relief.

Walker sat by a computer and almost immediately the records of Beverley Moxon flickered on the screen. He hit the print key and the printer whirled into life, spewing out the notes.

Walker sat with Drake and Caren as they read the printouts, explaining the technical definitions. The strain of chlamydia had been a virulent and Beverley Moxon had been left infertile when it was left untreated, and she had become seriously depressed. And then the cervical cancer hadn't been caught in time – the cancer that West had missed.

Now Drake had the complete picture. Moxon's life had come to this – Beverley's desire for children destroyed by Mathews, her hopes dashed by Roderick Jones and her health ruined by West. Moxon had taken his revenge. But who had he planned next?

Chapter 43
Thursday 1st July

He parked right outside, knowing that the van wouldn't attract attention. It would seem natural, even normal. He didn't look round; *just look confident* he had said to himself that morning. Nobody would notice. He wasn't going to be long and once he'd finished – well, that was the end. It would be over.

He lifted the latch on the gate to the rear of the house and walked into the back garden. There were trees and well-maintained flowerbeds that had bold coloured plants and flowers well tended by a woman's touch. In the middle of the lawn were children's toys and a large trampoline with a safety net surrounding it.

Recent grass clippings lay over the patio and the decking. The chairs around the hardwood table were all set out neatly, all in their correct place. In fact, everything seemed to be neat and tidy.

Within five minutes, he was in the house and finding his way into the kitchen.

He stopped and looked around. She would have liked the granite worktops and the island in the middle of the floor. It looked lived in and warm. Then he dawdled around the lounge, drawing his hand over the pictures of the children and fingering the expensive ornaments and paintings that hung on the wall. He saw a figure passing the window and drew back into the shadows. A handful of letters fell onto the floor and he heard the post office van drive away. He paused in the study and stared at the computer and the polished IKEA desk. It was here that he worked, completed his reports and read documents. The sort of documents that made a difference to people's lives. Now it was his turn to make a difference.

He felt odd invading someone else's space again but the feeling soon dispelled as he thought about his own life and what might have been if things had been different: if she hadn't met him, if only the doctors had got it right, if only she'd had her chance with the farm. He choked back the emotion. He hadn't cried for years and when he did it had been on his own, away from people, away from prying eyes.

He sat down on the leather sofa and relaxed amongst the scatter cushions, knowing that his work was almost complete. The sense of retribution he had felt when he pulled the trigger and shot Mathews with the crossbow had reinforced his conviction that what he had to do was right. He cursed the memory of the Archery Association that had plagued his mind every day as he imagined Mathews with her, holding her, kissing her and inside her.

'Crossbow. Just desserts,' he said out loud.

He had laughed when he heard about Walters and Harrod. People talked about innocent bystanders but only he knew the real meaning of that word, how much it hurt, how the pain could cut deep until he couldn't stand straight. A politician and a crooked businessman were never innocent bystanders in his book.

He finished his work quickly, once he got down to it. He stood back and allowed himself a brief smile. It was bound to work. He had thought of all the alternatives – nothing could go wrong.

He closed the back door behind him and then jammed the rear gate closed, making certain the family would have to use the front door. It would only work that way. He had to have certainty. There had to be closure.

He paced confidently to the van and drove away as if nothing was out of place.

He didn't look back. He wouldn't be going back there again.

Chapter 44
Thursday 1st July

'Superintendent Price has asked me to read Moxon's personnel file.'

Dr Fabrien's voice had a serious edge, as though she were now dealing with certainties rather than supposition. An empty coffee mug stood on the desk by the telephone. A lightweight fleece had been thrown over the back of her chair.

'He was a friend of yours, wasn't he?'

'Yes. I mean, I thought I knew him. Now I'm not so sure.'

Drake sat down, even though he felt like pacing round the room. Caren opened the notebook and read the notes she had hurriedly scribbled down with Dr Walker.

'Beverley Moxon had a virulent strain of chlamydia that made her infertile,' Caren said.

'And she and Moxon wanted children badly,' Dr Fabrien said.

Drake replied, 'He always said how much he wanted kids.'

'So we can assume that revenge was his motive for killing Mathews. He perceived Farrell's death as a necessary evil. Part of what he had to do.'

Caren looked up from her notepad, 'Part of what he had to do?' she said with incredulity in her voice. Dr Fabrien ignored her and carried on.

'And Jones was killed because he destroyed her dream.'

Caren still had her eyes staring at her notes, 'The letters on the files pleaded with Jones. Talked about her hopes for the future.'

Drake pulled his chair nearer the desk.

'The referral to Dr West was to test for cancer. He failed to spot it and it developed so quickly that she had only a few months to live. There was some correspondence between the surgery and West about the diagnosis,' Caren was checking her notes and speaking at the same time.

'He's taking revenge on anyone he perceives as being to blame for his wife's condition.'

Drake stood up abruptly and walked round the room, alternating between stuffing his hands into his pockets and running them over his face. If only he'd seen the numbers sooner. If only ... It was his mistake and West was dead. There was another death to come and he had to stop that happening.

'So who's next, Margaret?' Drake said.

'There must be something in his past. You're his friend. Can you remember anything else about Beverley that might give him a grudge?'

Drake stepped over to the window and stared out at the rear of headquarters. There were police cars and vans and scientific support vehicles parked at random and a delivery van was offloading pallets of vegetables and supplies for the kitchen. His mind was forcing itself to think about the conversations he'd had with Moxon, the small snippets of conversations in the canteen or in the pub, but his thoughts flashed from one thing to another, in no real order. He could feel the anxiety and stress rising.

'I can't think of anything. But then I didn't think that he could ever do this.'

'There must be something about Beverley Moxon,' Dr Fabrien continued.

'What if it's not about her?' Caren said.

Dr Fabrien and Drake turned to look at her, eyebrows raised.

'There could have been a trigger in his own life,' Dr Fabrien replied, warming to the suggestion. 'Something that drove him over the edge ...'

'Something that would make him want to kill?' Drake said.

'Please Ian. You know him well. Is there anything you

can remember?'

Drake paced around the room again.

'Anything. He's going to kill again.'

'Is he here?' Drake asked.

'No, I checked again,' Caren said.

Fabrien now. 'Only one event is needed, Ian. A single trigger.'

That word again – trigger. Then he saw the face of Moxon walking off the Britannia Bridge after talking quietly to a man standing on the railings, hoping that he wouldn't jump. And Moxon had to stand and watch as the man threw himself into the waters below. That had to be it. That was the trigger – enough to send anyone mad.

Drake sat down abruptly.

'It must be the incident on the bridge. He was talking to a jumper for over an hour and then just before the guy jumped, he turned to Moxon and said – *I don't know how you can live with yourself.*'

Dr Fabrien fumbled in the personnel file in front of her. 'Of course. I think I read the details earlier. There's reference to Moxon losing work with depression and anxiety for a while.'

Drake had his hands behind his head, a miserable look in his eyes, 'He was never the same. Complained about not getting support from the force. It hit him badly.'

'Who did he blame?' Fabrien asked, intensity clear in her voice.

Drake pushed forward over the desk.

'I remember one night we'd had a couple of drinks and he complained like hell about the chairman of the police authority who turned down his request for help.'

'Who was he?'

'Brian Johnson.'

'Not ...' Caren began.

Drake nodded. 'The newspaper editor. He was a county councillor at the time and it was his first year as chairman of the authority.'

There was a moment's silence.

'You'd better contact him,' Dr Fabrien said, as Drake reached for his mobile.

He put the handset to his ear after dialling the number. Dr Fabrien and Caren watched him intently.

Drake stood up as the telephone was answered, his grip tightening on the shiny black mobile in his fingers. 'This is Detective Inspector Drake. Can I speak to Mr Johnson?'

There was a click and the voice told Drake to wait a moment. Soothing music filled his ears and he tilted the phone, letting the sound invade the silence of the room, but the music seemed unreal. Another click.

'He's not in.'

'Can I talk to his secretary? It is urgent.'

More soothing music – this time a slowed-down version of a seventies ballad.

'Mr Johnson had to go out,' she said impatiently.

'When?'

'He just had a call. He had to go home urgently.'

'What's his home address and mobile number?' Drake said, not hiding the rising urgency in his voice. 'And what sort of car does he drive?'

'I don't …'

'His life is at risk. Now, please.'

He scribbled the details on the back of a sheet of paper, and then made for the door, Caren following him. They ran down to the car park and he fired the Alfa into life.

'Get an Armed Response Unit down to Johnson's address,' he said, throwing the piece of paper towards Caren.

Along the main road he accelerated hard towards Johnson's home. The secretary had sounded frightened by the time Drake had finished on the telephone but she had been able to tell him that Johnson had only just left. It was no more than a few miles to the editor's home. Drake knew the road well and he flashed at cars and sounded the horn repeatedly as he cleared a route through the traffic. Caren had finished on her mobile when they stopped at the red lights of a junction but Drake edged the car forward and looked for traffic coming in the opposite direction, before firing the car across the road.

'Call Johnson,' Drake said.

Caren dialled and pushed the mobile to her ear.

'Why the bloody hell doesn't he answer?'

'There he is. I'm sure of it,' Drake said, as he raced to overtake a red Mercedes.

He forced the car to stop and jumped out. The window of the car was being lowered as Drake ran over and the driver looked terrified.

'What the hell are you doing? I'm going to call the police. You're an absolute madman.'

Drake bent down and stared in at the driver, before realising that it wasn't Johnson. He flashed his warrant card at the startled man and sprinted back to the Alfa.

'Wrong man,' he said. 'How many red Mercedes can there be? Try his mobile again.'

Caren gave him a troubled look. 'It's ringing out.'

'Bloody hell.'

Within another couple of minutes they were getting nearer the address. Drake could feel the anxiety gripping his chest. What if they were too late, and Johnson was already lying in the road with a crossbow bolt through his heart? He reached a junction and turned sharply, right in front of a car that screeched to a halt, its horn blasting loudly, the driver gesticulating wildly.

In the distance, they saw a Mercedes pulling into a parking slot in front of a cottage set back from the road. Drake watched as Johnson stepped out of the car and the lights bleeped as he pressed the remote. Drake found the light controls and flashed the headlights, but the editor didn't notice and he strode towards the front door. Drake braked hard and ran over towards the porch lined with purple clematis.

He watched as Johnson pushed the key into the latch and as he twisted it, he turned his head to look at Drake, a surprised look on his face. He made a movement with his mouth, as though he wanted to say something: the door was a couple of centimetres ajar. Drake felt breathless and for a fraction of a second was relieved that Johnson wasn't lying on the ground as he'd feared. Then he noticed the smell tugging at his nostrils – it was damp and acid-like, and in an instant Drake grabbed Johnson and pulled him away from the door. They turned their backs to the porch just as the rush of the explosion shattered the windows and the glass exploded out into the road in a thousand pieces. Drake felt the rush of the explosion around his body as he was hurled to the ground, Johnson lying by his side. The blast buckled the front door and the flames leapt through the cottage high into the sky. Drake grabbed Johnson and scrambled past the Mercedes, its roof and body covered in shards of glass. They fell onto the tarmac behind the Alfa just as the Armed Response Vehicle arrived.

Chapter 45
Thursday 1st July

Drake's mobile buzzed as they raced back to headquarters and Caren picked up the call.

'There's been another message,' she said, turning to Drake.

Drake slammed his hands against the steering wheel of the car.

'What the …' But he couldn't find the words.

He went through more red lights, flashed a dozen cars with his headlights and sounded his horn so often Caren become concerned for her safety. The brakes screeched as he pulled into headquarters and they ran towards the main entrance.

Drake stood before the table in Price's room. There was a long scuffmark down the right leg of his trousers and his shirt had torn as he'd fallen on the tarmac. At first he hadn't noticed the scratch on his forehead that was fast developing into a lump, nor the bruise on his cheek, until Caren had looked at his face with a concerned expression.

Price handed Drake the message.

It had been four weeks since he first read a message from the killer. Then, he had recognised the song lyric. Now the few words on the page posed a question he couldn't answer. He couldn't sit down: he had to think, and he didn't bother asking how the message came. He moved back a couple of steps and squeezed the paper in his right hand.

What lies on the whispering wind?

'Well?' There was an optimistic tone to Price's voice.

'What lies on the whispering wind?' Drake said slowly.

He saw the uncertainty on Dr Fabrien's face and then the fear in her eyes. A buff-coloured folder sat on the table in front of her.

'Margaret?' Price said.

She made eye contact, but then averted her eyes,

picking a spot on the desk to fix her gaze.

'He's ... clever ...'

Price straightened himself in his chair. 'I think we know that.'

'Moxon's personnel file makes unhappy reading,' Dr Fabrien added, patting her hand gently on the file in front of her

Caren added. 'Took a lot of anti-depressants.'

Price looked desperate. 'Jesus. And it affected Moxon's mental condition ...' He waved a hand in the air to complete his understanding. He let out an exasperated groan.

Drake was still holding the paper in his hand and trying to make sense of the words. He walked over to the window and looked out towards the trees and the lush grassland, towards the suburbs of the town. The trees were full of foliage and the sun warm on his face through the glass. He felt tired even though he knew that an end was in sight. An end he didn't want to face.

Then as he watched a bird swooping through the trees, the meaning struck him.

'Stairway to heaven.'

'What?' Price looked puzzled.

'Lies on the whispering wind,' Drake murmured. 'It's Moxie.'

Around the table the atmosphere changed from exasperation to expectation and they moved imperceptibly in their chairs.

Drake looked winded. He put his head in his hands.

'It's Moxie,' he repeated.

Glances were exchanged around the table.

'The bastard ... he's a ... ' he faltered. 'The fucking bastard. It's Moxie. Led Zeppelin is his favourite band,' he explained. 'Stairway to Heaven' is his all-time favourite track. He plays it everyday. I always remember him telling me that years ago. And that phrase – the whispering wind – is in the lyrics.'

With two quick steps Drake returned to the table. He looked down at Price, knowing they had no time to spare. 'We need to find Moxon. Now.'

Caren was already out of her chair. Price picked up the telephone, asked for the Traffic Department and barked an order.

'I've got two officers travelling west. Get a patrol car and two outriders to clear traffic. Now. And I want an ARV deployed.'

He threw the handset down onto its cradle. Drake pushed open the doors from Price's office. They raced down the stairs into reception, passing the astonished stares of the reception staff. Outside, they saw two outriders and a patrol car – lights flashing, siren blaring – leaving headquarters. Drake and Caren hurried towards the Armed Response Vehicle and, once inside, they heard the sound of Area Control clearing a frequency direct to Price's office.

Drake yanked the safety belt from behind his shoulder and thrust the clip tight until it fastened securely. He glanced over at Caren as she fumbled with the safety belt, the car already in motion.

The driver swung the car down towards the A55 and gathered speed – cars and lorries had been swept to the inside lane and hard shoulder like pebbles in the face of an advancing tide, some with hazard lights blinking.

The comment made by Dr Fabrien as they left Price's office came flashing back to his mind. *If he had a grudge against everyone he's killed ...*

If Moxon had a grudge against West, it was possible, just possible, he had a grudge against Walker and Sian. He called Price.

Then he pushed the speed-dial for Sian's surgery. The receptionist told him she was busy.

'Put me through. Now!' he screamed.

'What's wrong?' Sian asked.

'It's Moxie. Definitely. You and Rhys might be at risk.

Lock the surgery doors. I've already sent two armed officers. They will be with you in minutes.'

He heard her gasp. 'What about the girls?'

'There are two armed officers on their way to the school now.'

'Ian, I'm scared.'

'Don't worry, it'll be okay.'

They reached the tunnels at Conwy faster than Drake had ever thought possible. The road was clear; the traffic dawdled in the inside lane. The Armed Response Vehicle changed down through the gears and as it emerged on the opposite side of the estuary, the driver hurtled the car to over one hundred and twenty miles an hour until he had to slow for the tunnels through the mountains.

After the second mountain tunnel the ARV drove straight over a mini roundabout, throwing Drake and Caren around in the back seat. Then the car had a clear run, and far in the distance, Drake thought he caught sight of the motorcycle outriders.

Patrol cars sat waiting for the ARV as it negotiated the off-ramp and circled a roundabout, tyres screeching. Within minutes, they'd arrived at Moxon's house. The motorcyclists had already established a perimeter. Drake and Caren dragged on bulletproof vests and jumped out of the car, following the two Armed Response Vehicle officers – weapons in hand – as they ran to the front door.

Bile gathered in Drake's throat, beads of sweat formed on his forehead, and his collar seemed to tighten around his neck.

'Open the door,' he yelled. 'Break the fucking thing down.'

Both officers took turns to kick at the door, the casing splitting under the pressure before the door flew open. The ARV officers streamed into the house, shouting warnings as Drake and Caren followed. Drake stood in the lounge, where there was a musty, stale smell, as though nobody had cleaned for months. He saw a film of dust on the top of the television, pictures of Beverley along the mantelpiece and, in pride of place, the stereo system. The two armed officers returned to the lounge, leaving Caren to rummage through the empty bedrooms.

'Place is deserted, sir.'

Before he could reply, his mobile rang. He frowned when he didn't recognise the number.

'Drake.'

'What lies on the whispering wind?'

His lips went dry, his throat tightened. 'Moxie.'

'Where are you?'

'Your place.'

'You won't be long then.'

The line went dead and for several seconds Drake stared at the mobile in his right hand. Caren walked into the room and stood behind him. She waited until he regained some composure.

'Well, what did he say?'

'What lies on the whispering wind?'

'We know that. Man talks in riddles.'

Drake ran his finger along the racks of CDs that stood alongside the hi-fi system. There was a complete collection of Led Zeppelin CDs, Pink Floyd, The Pretenders and Queen. He pressed the 'on' button on the CD player and the LCD display lit up. He leant down, pushed the open button and a small tray appeared. He placed his forefinger through the hole in the centre and picked up the CD. Led Zeppelin 2.

Moxon's voice replayed in his mind. And then he knew that Moxon wasn't far. He was on the bridge.

Drake rushed out of the house, yelling instructions to the armed officers.

'Britannia Bridge. Now.'

The outriders roared off and they retraced their steps to the A55. The road was silent as the car accelerated towards the Britannia Bridge. Drake leant forward, urging the vehicle on, as the car sped down the outside lane, passing scores of cars lined up on the hard shoulder. The radio crackled into life, telling them about an incident on the bridge.

The ARV jolted to a halt. Drake jumped out, crossed over the central reservation and walked down towards the bridge. He watched as Moxon moved towards the handrail and then Drake broke into a steady jog. Moxon placed his stab jacket over a Samaritans call box and threw his tie on the tarmac. He clambered up onto the handrail overlooking the sea three hundred feet below. Drake was running now, his heart pumping, tearing deep into his chest. He got closer and closer. Then Moxon turned towards him.

'Moxie!' he screamed.

Drake's lungs wanted to explode.

'Moxie!' Louder this time.

He stopped within a few of metres of Moxon and bent double, his chest heaving.

'You've taken your time,' Moxon said.

'What …' Drake gasped.

Moxon turned towards him and gave a sneer, then his eyes closed and he seemed to relax. His legs were leaning against the rail. It was one small step upwards to the top of the crash rail or a small step down to the pavement below. Drake tried to calculate if he could grab Moxon but quickly dismissed the idea.

'You have no idea,' Moxon said.

'Come down from there and we'll talk,' Drake said, between deep breaths.

Another sneer.

'What it was like waking up in the middle of the night. Screaming. Hearing his voice over and over and over in my mind.'

'Bev wouldn't want this.'

'I forgave her of course. Now he's paid.'

Drake's breathing slowed. He moved a step closer.

'No further,' Moxon said.

'We can talk about this.'

'Like we could talk about everything, Ian. Your obsessions and rituals and Sian and the children.'

The resentment dripped out of Moxon.

'Why the bottles?' Drake asked, wanting to shout at Moxon. Scream at him that he had no right to involve Megan and Helen.

'Your perfect life. Wife a doctor and a BMW and the sports car.'

'Beverley …' Drake said before Moxon shouted at him.

'Don't you fucking mention her name.'

'Come down from there.'

'As if you know. Living in your bright shiny world.'

Drake moved another step nearer. Moxon raised a hand and then pointed his finger at Drake and narrowed his eyes.

'No fucking closer.'

Drake's breathing was returning to normal and he saw two officers approaching from the other end of the bridge, unseen by Moxon. The high-visibility jacket on the telephone box fluttered in the breeze.

'We can get you help,' Drake said.

'Like the help I got from that bastard Johnson.'

'That was in the past.'

'Nobody's going to help me.'

'Come down. We can talk.'

'Nobody helped Bev either. Called himself a doctor – that West should be ashamed. Let her die.' Moxon's voice broke up and he adjusted his footing.

The officers walking along the pavement had neared.

'Moxie.'

Moxon turned his head. Drake looked deep into Moxon's eyes but there was nothing there except blackness, an emptiness he had never seen before. An officer approaching mis-timed his step over the kerb edge and Moxon turned abruptly to see both officers approaching. He turned to look at Drake, the hatred evident in his face.

He took one step upwards and perched on the top rail before looking down at Drake.

'I don't know how you can fucking live with yourself.'

He stretched out his arms above his head and pushed his body gently forwards. For a fraction of a second, the body hung motionless in the air before he disappeared from view.

Epilogue
Friday 25th August

Drake sat at his desk, stacked high with papers, a sudoku half-finished from the morning newspaper, trying to concentrate on work. He glanced over at the photograph of Sian and Megan and Helen taken on their holiday in the south of France that now seemed a distant memory. He smiled to himself as he recalled the moment he took the photograph, after the girls had emerged from the swimming pool, the high temperatures evident from the bright sunshine.

He fiddled with a biro before rearranging some of the files into neat bundles. He found his mind wandering so he got up and adjusted the open window behind him. The sky was a clear blue and the temperatures hot and balmy, just as the forecast had predicted. The previous evening, when Drake told Sian he'd booked a half day off and then suggested a trip to the beach, she had given him a curious look that turned into a warm smile. He sat down heavily and, as he pulled the chair towards the desk, Caren knocked on his door. He motioned her to sit down, pleased at the interruption. Caren held up a newspaper.

'Have you seen the headlines?' she asked.

Drake shook his head and she handed him the paper. There had been rumours about Harrod, of course, but now it seemed official.

Local Building Construction Company Collapses – 230 jobs lost.

He read the article and spluttered in astonishment at the quote attributed to James Harrod who blamed 'market forces' and a 'downturn in the economy' for the demise of his empire.

'There's nothing here about the pending court case,' Drake said.

'The CPS told me yesterday that Dixon is likely to offer a guilty plea to the assault charge,' Caren said.

Drake put the newspaper down and smiled broadly.

'That's brilliant. It makes it awkward for Harrod to deny any involvement. That sounds like a result to me. Harrod's business collapses and he's going down for assault.'

Before Caren could reply Price was standing behind her in the doorway. The visit was unplanned and immediately Drake worried that something unforeseen had cropped up that would ruin his plans for the day. Caren left, and Price pushed the door closed and sat down.

'Family well?' Price said.

'Very well, thank you, sir,' Drake said. 'I've booked a half day off today. I wanted to take the girls to the beach before the end of the summer.'

Drake could see from the averted eye contact and Price's twitching that he had something on his mind.

'How was your holiday?'

'The weather was hot, as you'd expect,' Drake said, darting another glance at the photograph.

'Going walking next month in the Pyrenees. Try and work off some of this flab,' Price said, patting his paunch.

Drake fell silent and waited, wondering what Price had on his mind.

'Ian. I know this business with Moxon was tough for you. You'd been friends for years.'

'Yes, sir.'

'It can't have been easy. And I want you to understand that we want to be supportive.'

Drake moved in his chair. He had no idea what Price was getting at. Price cleared his throat and looked Drake in the eye.

'The powers that be think it best if you have some counselling. You know, to help you over the Moxon business. Help you deal with the whole sad affair. It might be for the best.'

Drake sank back into his chair, relieved it wasn't

something more serious.

'Why … I mean, when is it supposed to start?'

Price visibly relaxed, obviously pleased that Drake had agreed.

'Some time next month. Good. That's settled then. I'm pleased we've had this chat. Did I tell you about Laura Harrod?'

Drake shook his head.

'She's reapplied to join the service.'

Drake raised his eyebrows.

'Straight into the shredder of course.'

And with that he got up to leave. At the door he turned back to look at Drake.

'Where are you going today?'

'Llanddwyn beach.'

'Better get going then.'

Drake drove home with all the windows down and let the warm air fill the car. After hurriedly changing and finding all the buckets and spades, they left the house. The memories of his recent journeys along the coast were still fresh in his mind. Drake knew that Moxon would have covered this route, returning home to his empty house every day while all the time allowing the hatred to build in his mind until the poison had done its worst. He approached the bridge, on impulse drew into a lay-by, and parked next to an articulated lorry with Polish plates, its curtains drawn.

'Something I need to do,' he said to Sian, who looked puzzled.

He strode over the grass verge onto the bridge and walked to where Moxon had stood by the crash barrier. Cars and lorries hurtled past him over the bridge. He stood and stared at the ground and then, moving closer to the edge of the bridge, looked out and down into the waters below. He felt the salty breeze on his face and watched as seagulls floated on the wind. Everything about the investigation came crowding back into his mind – the numbers and the songs and his own rituals. And, if he had been a better friend to Moxon, could things have been different? There had been four deaths and perhaps, just possibly, he could have prevented West's death. And maybe Price was right about the counselling, but the prospect was daunting. Standing alone on the bridge, he realised how Moxon must have felt once Beverley had died. Moxon had lost the one thing he cherished more than anything.

He turned and walked back to the car, saw Sian standing by her open door, peering in his direction, the worry etched on her face. He ignored her questions about why they were there. Instead, he leant over, held her face in his hands and then kissed her on the lips.

Printed in Great Britain
by Amazon